The Pandora Project

The Pandora Project

David Ward

THOMAS NELSON PUBLISHERS
Nashville • Atlanta • London • Vancouver

Published in Nashville, Tennessee, by Thomas Nelson, Inc., Publishers, and distributed in Canada by Word Communications, Ltd., Richmond, British Columbia.

The Bible version used in this publication is THE NEW KING JAMES VERSION. Copyright © 1979, 1980, 1982, Thomas Nelson, Inc., Publishers. The Scripture quotation on page 135 is from the HOLY BIBLE: NEW INTERNATIONAL VERSION®, copyright © 1973, 1978, 1984 by the International Bible Society. Used by permission of Zondervan Publishing House. All rights reserved.

Library of Congress Cataloging-in-Publication Data

Ward, David, 1961–
    The Pandora Project / David Ward.
      p. cm.
    ISBN 0-7852-7625-4 (pb)
    I. Title.
PS3573.A722P36   1997
813'.54—dc20

96–31226
CIP

Printed in the United States of America.
1 2 3 4 5 6 — 02 01 00 99 98 97

Acknowledgments

As regards this work, I would like to thank my Lord for His inspiration; my lovely wife for her unfailing love, support, and encouragement; my parents for their editorial expertise and encouragement; Jacque, Andre, Sebastien, and Jacqueline for their help with all things French; and Victor for believing in me.

Prologue

September 16 turned out to be a lousy day to be running. The rain pounded the city streets mercilessly, causing countless putrid rivulets to form in the alley and flow steadily down Hurley Street toward Sixteenth Avenue. Despite the best attempts by the forces of wind and rain, this part of town remained filthy, and it didn't seem to matter who was in office, more funds were cut from the municipal maintenance budget every year.

At 9:48 A.M., from Seventeenth Avenue there came a terrible screeching of brakes followed by the unmistakable crunch of twisted metal on metal. Somewhere an alarm went off, then gunfire and shouts, and a lone figure lurched into the alley. The man was overweight and clearly had no business running, as was quickly demonstrated by his falling headlong into one of the many piles of trash lining the alley at irregular intervals. His hat flew off, and he dropped the satchel he was carrying because he needed both hands to keep his face from hitting the pavement.

Cursing and moaning, he scrambled to his feet, picked up the satchel, and hurried down the street as fast as his legs would carry him, leaving the hat behind. His breathing was labored, coming in long, wheezing gasps, and the length of his overcoat, coupled with the lab coat underneath, was slowing his pace. The end of the alley was about forty feet away when two men in tailored suits burst through the knot of people that had formed at the other end to watch. Their quarry had a lead of maybe two hundred feet, and they knew if he made it to Sixteenth Street, they might lose him.

The taller of the two men stood up straight and took aim with his pistol. A shot rang out in the stone confines of the alley, and the man in the overcoat pitched forward on his face. It was unclear whether the man had been hit or not, for in the next instant he was on his feet again and out the end of the alley. Both pursuers broke into a sprint.

Limping on a wrenched ankle, and in shock from the bullet wound in his back, the man in the overcoat loped between two parked cars and tried to cross the street. Brakes screeched again, and he turned in horror to see a taxi bearing down on him. The front of the car hit him, just hard enough to throw him on the hood. He pushed himself off and rounded the passenger side, letting himself in the backseat before the driver had time to recover from the incident.

"Drive!"

In his agitated state, the driver stomped on the accelerator, and the taxi roared down the street and was quickly lost in traffic. The two men in suits pounded out the end of the alley and came to a stop. After scanning the street in both directions, the taller man put his gun back in his shoulder holster, then pulled out a radio to report in.

"This is Reif. The weasel has landed. Drop the net on a four-block radius from Sixteenth and Hurley. Secure the airport and bus station."

Several blocks away, the taxi driver finally got his nerves under control and brought his speed down a bit. In the back, collapsed on the seat, the man he had nearly run over was having trouble breathing.

"Hey, mister? Are you all right?" The man vomited. "Oh, man! What'd you do that for?" In the rearview mirror, the man in back looked pasty white. *If he dies in my cab, they'll nail me for vehicular homicide for sure.* "I'm taking you to the hospital."

"No! No hospital."

"Well, you can't just die in my cab! Where do you want to go?"

The man tried to think of an escape route, but all he could think was, *I'm shot . . . I'm shot . . .* The wound was whistling, which meant a punctured lung, and he knew if he didn't get help soon, he was dead. But not here, not now. He had to get out of town, and he knew the airport and bus station would be locked down tight.

Desperate to get rid of his passenger, the cabby was grasping at straws. "You got family in town? You want to go to the airport?"

"No. Take me to United Air Freight."

The driver nudged the speed up a little. He didn't even care if the guy paid him or not. *Just get him out of my cab before he dies, please. No one ever has to know he was here.*

Chapter One

The dog was something of a mascot on campus. A beagle, white with brown patches, he was often seen with his master walking across the commons. Every evening at 10:00—you could set your watch by it—he emerged from a tidy brownstone at the end of his master's leash for their nightly walk. The weather, while a nuisance, was inconsequential, for nothing short of a volcanic eruption would change the departure time one millisecond.

Professor Emeritus of Philosophy Tighe Couleah—or "Cool Tie" as some of the more impertinent students dared to call him—had been walking the same route every night for the past twelve years, since Barnaby was a puppy. His wife had displayed egregious judgment by bringing the nascent pup home from the shelter mere months before passing away. The net result of the chain of events was a complete inability on the professor's part to dispose of the poorly behaved ball of fur. And now they were inseparable.

Professor Couleah was in his early sixties and portly, with a decided predilection for cardigan sweaters and canvas slacks. He hadn't worn a tie since 1973, drank a single shot of brandy every afternoon at 4:00, staunchly denounced anyone who graded on a curve, and made a point of having few acquaintances, Barnaby not included, of course. The rumor on campus was that the departure of his wife had made him morose, but the one faculty member who knew him said Tighe had been a "sullen mule" since the dawn of time. Everything about his life was ordered precisely, some said right down to the arrangement of the paper clips on his desk, and deviations from his divine schedule were not tolerated.

The intolerance for unscheduled interruptions extended to Barnaby, so when the dog stopped suddenly in the middle of the street to explore the inner depths of a candy bar wrapper, the professor nearly tripped over him.

"Barnaby! What do you think you're doing?" The professor pulled on the leash, but Barnaby only turned and bared his teeth in a feral warning. His master loosened his grip and thrust his hands in his pockets, muttering something about the "cantankerous canine" under his breath. The walk was a ritual, but only a fool stood out in the rain, and the professor decided he had had enough.

He reached down to scoop up the "miscreant mongrel" and was startled nearly to death by the peculiar, intermittent squeal of tires on maple leaves and wet pavement. The street was adorned with a respectable carpet of autumnal fallout, and the leaves were nearly as bad as ice when water was added. A pair of headlights bore down on the curmudgeon and his hapless pup.

Thanks to the countless stops and starts during the day of cars nearing the intersection, that area of the street had been worn clear of leaves, and the advancing tires found the traction the driver was desperately hoping for. The car lurched to a stop, and the driver rolled down his window.

"Tighe! Are you crazy? Get out of the street!"

Professor Couleah stood up and thrust his nose in the air. "I might expect the students to drive like delinquents, Professor Teller, but I am most disappointed to find you behind the wheel of the car that nearly ran me down."

I can still arrange it, Lee Teller thought. "Why don't you get Barnaby out of the road before one of us 'delinquents' uses him as a hood ornament?"

Professor Couleah sniffed and huffed to the far side of the street with Barnaby, quite literally, in tow. The candy bar wrapper would endure unmolested, but the determined animal's nail prints would at the very least enshrine the effort. Lee rolled his window up, ran a shaky hand through his sandy-brown hair, and eased the car forward through the intersection.

For the past six years, Lee had been driving the same car—a yellow 1985 Toyota wagon with brown trim and soiled tweed upholstery. It was entirely appropriate for a professor of physics at Dartmouth, but he had been thinking of sports cars in the past year or two, and not because of the passing of his fortieth birthday, he was quick to point out. Lately, he had taken to referring to the car as "that crummy yellow-and-brown piece of junk," and the appellation was becoming more accurate than he intended. There were bits and pieces of fast-food papers on the floor of the passenger side, and the obligatory soda can was stuffed under the front of the seat. But it was his car, and if he wanted to use the floor as a wastebasket, that was his business.

Going out on a night like this would not have been his first choice. In fact, he was already in bed when the call came through. The last thing he expected to hear on the phone was the voice of Miles Orsen. They had never been friends exactly, but there had been a time when they had enjoyed each other's company, and in the halls of academia that was enough. As far as Lee knew, no one in town had heard from Miles in twelve years, not since he left Dartmouth rather abruptly all those years ago.

A strange memory, that. Miles stopped him on his way to class, on a drizzly fall day much like this one, and dragged him off beside the building. Miles hated the rain, so Lee knew immediately that whatever he had to say was of utmost importance. With water running down his forehead and collecting in his eyebrows, Miles explained that he and his wife were leaving immediately because his mother-in-law was ill and they needed to take care of her.

Lee knew Miles, knew that he hated his mother-in-law with near homicidal passion. The woman had nearly broken up Miles's wedding, and failing that, she had set out in earnest to destroy the marriage, all because he wasn't good enough for her daughter. The thought of him caring for the carping crone was inconceivable, unless he was planning on using the opportunity to deep-six her. Nah. Miles was too chicken-hearted to be a killer.

As soon as Miles finished his canned speech, Lee called him a liar to his face. Normally such a blunt confrontation would have him cowed immediately, and he would have mumbled an apology followed by the unadulterated truth, but this time he got angry. Miles the mouse allowed himself an instant of unfettered fury and used words Lee was quite certain had not come out of his mouth since the day they met.

Cursing and wiping water from his eyebrows, Miles told Lee the truth all right: it was none of his lousy business! With his friend's rebuke still hanging in the heavy moisture of the air, Lee watched him stomp away, never to be heard from again.

Until tonight. The call had come through just before 10:00 P.M., and Lee—in flannel pajamas and curled up under a puffy goose down comforter—was reluctant to answer it. It took an observation from the comforter on the far side of the bed, from his girlfriend, Sharon, to make him answer the phone. She said it might be his son calling from college.

The caller had not been his son, and what was worse, the call precipitated this accursed excursion into the clammy dampness of the night. The voice on the other end had been vaguely familiar, but Lee couldn't place it until it said, "Meet me at the Cumulus Cafe," and then the line went dead. There was only one other person in the whole world who knew about the Cumulus Cafe. Miles Orsen.

On the south side of the administration building, in a copse of birch trees, there was a single wooden park bench. That side of the building saw little foot traffic, which made the bench an excellent place to get away from the rush of college life for a while. Miles and Lee used to take lunch there one afternoon a week to talk and watch the clouds roll by. In a rare flash of creative frivolity, Miles christened the bench the "Cumulus Cafe."

And now, twelve years later, he wanted to meet Lee on that same bench, late at night, in the rain. Perfect. *This had better be good, Miles.*

Lee pulled into the parking lot for the administration building and parked in one of the visitors' spaces. He pulled his hunting jacket off the backseat, stepped out of the car, and put the jacket on, pulling the hood up over his head. Usually, he would have been thinking about how silly the hood looked, but at the moment all he could think was how nice it would be to lie down just about anyplace that was warm and dry.

He walked purposefully down the paved path around the side of the stone edifice of the administration building, which stood monolithic and foreboding in the murky half-light cast from the lamps at the edge of the parking lot. The birch trees seemed threatening somehow this particular evening, and Lee wondered about it. This place carried nothing but pleasant memories for him. It was ridiculous to feel apprehensive, like a frightened little boy walking home alone at night.

Lee resisted the impulse to whistle against the dark. As he entered the heart of the birch grove, he paused for a moment to let his eyes adjust to the dim light streaming anemically through the leprous white trunks of the trees. The bench should be nearby. There. And someone was lying on it.

"Miles!"

No answer. Hard to believe he'd fall asleep in the rain. Lee walked cautiously toward the bench, his eyesight seeming to improve with each step. It was Miles, all right. Twelve years older, sure, but unmistakable. Still overweight, eyes a little too close together, nose a little too wide, upper lip turned up like that of a flute player. His overcoat was scrunched up and hanging open, as was the lab coat underneath. Then in a dim shaft of lamplight, Lee saw the bandages.

Where the bench met the body, partially hidden by a bloodstained shirt, a makeshift bandage of duct tape and cloth, clearly applied by no physician, sat askew. Lee reached out instinctively to try and help the man, but recoiled in fear and revulsion when he touched him. The skin was cold, and Miles did not appear to be breathing.

Lee steeled himself and pushed two fingers against the neck. No pulse. He stood up and looked around furtively, suddenly afraid of being observed, but there was no one. He stared helplessly back up the path, mouth hanging open, water dripping off his exposed chin. *What do I do now? The police, I suppose.* His train of thought was interrupted a moment later when a clammy hand grabbed his own. Lee jumped and whirled around.

"Miles!"

The injured man coughed and spat up blood and mucus. "Lee . . . you made it." The voice was weak, and the eyes glistened with horror as consciousness reclaimed the mind.

Lee got down on one knee. "Let me take you to a hospital."

"No! No hospitals. If they find me, they'll find you, and you're a dead man."

"Who's after you?"

Miles only coughed again and shook his head. Lee had never seen a man more terrified. "No time . . . hurry . . . take this . . ."

Miles handed Lee a tiny parcel—a crumpled piece of paper with something wrapped inside—which fit in the palm of his hand. "What is it, Miles?"

The dying man shook his head weakly and motioned for Lee to come closer. Lee reached inside his jacket and stuffed the small parcel into his shirt pocket. He bent low over the tortured face. To Lee's surprise, Miles grabbed the lapels of his hunting jacket and pulled himself up off the bench until they were nearly nose to nose. Lee pulled back a little and steadied himself with both arms, while Miles stared with haunted, fading eyes.

"Don't let them bury it!"

His eyes rolled back in his head, and he slumped back on the bench, his mouth wide, and a gurgling sound came from his throat. Lee wondered if that was what a death rattle sounded like, but in the next moment, Miles took one last, wheezing gasp. His lips began moving as if to speak, and Lee moved his ear close to the man's mouth, mostly because he'd seen it done in the movies.

The choked voice was barely audible, and Lee really could hear a rattling in the throat. ". . . rain . . ." A tiny trickle of blood came out the corner of his mouth with the end of the breath, and Miles did not draw another.

Lee stood up, numb with shock. His legs twitched. He wanted to run, but his intellect was still nominally in control, and he intended to keep it that way. If taking Miles to a hospital would have gotten Lee killed, certainly leaving him here to be found would have the same result.

Indecision paralyzed his mind, which was a new and utterly unpleasant experience for a normally confident and even-tempered physics professor. Who would want to kill Miles? The Mob? Certainly not the police. A jealous lover? The idea was inconceivable. None of it made any sense, and Lee sat down at Miles's feet to try and collect his thoughts. Maybe the tiny parcel in his pocket held the answer.

A car horn sounded several blocks away, but the noise was enough to shatter his concentration and send him leaping to his feet. He had to do something with the body, fast! But where? A funeral home maybe. No, they would have to report the bullet wound. No police, no hospital, no funeral home. A sick feeling of dread slowly tightened the muscles of his stomach as he realized he was going to have to dispose of the body so that no one would ever find it. Hesitantly reaching down to try and lift the body, he found to his great distress that Miles was thirty to forty pounds heavier than he was. Lee wasn't taking the body anywhere.

The critical nature of the impasse loosened the tenuous grip of his intellect, and panic roared upward from the depths of his bowels. Suddenly he was running. Back up the path. Fumble with the keys. Unlock the door. Jump in. Drop the keys. Not now! Where are they . . . there! Key in the ignition. The engine turns over, kicks on the first try. Bless you, you crummy yellow-and-brown beauty!

The car rolled up over the curb and started down the path. Lee could only hope the wheelbase was narrow enough. When he came abreast of the bench, he lurched out of the driver's side, slipped, and ran around to the other side. There was still no sign of anyone around.

Adrenaline coursing through his veins, Lee threw open the passenger door, thrust his arms under Miles's arms, and dragged his body to the car, pushing it down into the passenger seat. He positioned the overcoat so the soiled clothing and bandages were not visible, and he latched the seat belt and shoulder strap in place. Nearer to hysteria than he would ever admit, Lee smirked at the irony of restraining a dead man with safety straps.

He should clean the bench. What if somebody comes by? What if campus security spots him while making rounds? Lee grabbed a filthy paper towel from the floor of the car and hastily wiped off the bench. The rain would have to do the rest.

Behind the wheel once more, he retraced his path back to the parking lot, having a harder time staying on the pavement. Resisting the urge to stomp on the accelerator, Lee eased the car out of the parking lot and headed down the road toward the city limits. His mind was numb. What does one do with a corpse at 10:30 on a Tuesday evening? The longer he stayed on the road, the better the chance he would be caught with the body. He needed someplace secluded, but not far away. Like the woods next to the Dolores Farm.

Lee had gone maybe three miles when he caught sight of something in his rearview mirror that made his heart skip a beat. The flashing lights of the police car came up fast from behind, and he checked his speed. He was going fifty in a thirty-five zone. Idiot! Breaking out in a cold sweat, he slowed down and pulled over to the side of the road. Before the police car could come to a stop, Lee was out of the car and walking back.

"Can I see some identification, sir?"

Lee fished his wallet out of his pocket and handed it to the officer. "What seems to be the trouble, officer?"

"You were speeding, Mr. Teller." The officer shined his flashlight into the passenger compartment of the Toyota. "Is your friend all right?"

Lee's mind locked up in terror for a moment, but he forced his tongue to move. "He's f . . . fine. He was out drinking. I was trying to get him home before his wife knew he was missing."

The officer nodded. "Trying to save him from the old rolling pin, huh?"

"Exactly." Lee's grin was manic. "Friends don't let friends drive drunk!"

The officer gave him a strange look and handed his license back. "Right. Look, you're helping out a friend, so I'll make it a warning this time. Stick to the speed limit."

"I will. I promise."

The officer walked back to his car, and Lee went back to his. As the police car pulled away, Lee leaned out of the driver's door and was violently ill. It was turning into a very bad evening.

The remainder of the drive out of town was uneventful, but Lee's senses were on full alert, trying to make out the landmarks along the road. Before long, a space wide enough for his car presented itself and he was driving cautiously off the road and a couple of hundred feet into the woods, carefully threading his car through the loosely packed dogwood trees. The rain was still coming down as he came to a stop in a small clearing, pulled his tire iron out of the wheel well, and set to work digging a shallow grave.

The work was arduous, and he soon threw his coat aside, falling into a rhythm between breaking up chunks of earth with the tire iron and then scooping them aside with his bare hands. Making the hole big enough took the better part of an hour, and by the end, Lee was wishing Miles had been born a midget.

With only the dim overhead light in the passenger compartment to see by, Lee unstrapped the body, put his hands under the arms, and put everything he had into a mighty tug upward. The body came clear of the car, and Lee stumbled backward and fell, bringing it down on top of him. He thrashed at the hideous weight in horror, flailing with open palms, knees, and feet, until the body rolled soddenly into the hole.

Lee felt as if he might pass out at any moment, but he threw dirt into the hole until the body was covered, smoothed it as flat as he could, and then covered it with leaves. The leftover dirt had to be disposed of, and then he was finished. He stood up to examine his handiwork, and self-loathing washed over his emotions as he considered the implications of what he had done.

What had he done? Murder? No, someone else pulled the trigger. Obstructing justice? Maybe, under normal circumstances, but if the Mob or some government officials were involved . . .

In the end, Lee decided he could best honor the memory of Miles Orsen by staying alive long enough to find out what he died for.

Covered with sweat and muck, Lee said a brief, awkward prayer for Miles's soul to whatever powers there might be. He then grabbed his tire iron, climbed painfully back into the car, and made his way back to the highway.

When he arrived home half an hour later, Sharon met him at the door looking somewhat concerned, but as he stepped into the light, she gasped. "What happened?"

Seeing her, his only marginal source of comfort, so soon after his recent trauma was too much for him. Tears welled up out of his eyes and rolled down his cheeks, mixing with the grime and traces of blood dried there. He screwed his eyes shut, too distraught to be embarrassed.

"Miles Orsen is dead."

An hour later, much refreshed from a shower, clean clothes, and some muffins and coffee, Lee sat in the kitchen and recounted the experience to Sharon. She was almost half his age, with cream-colored skin and freckles, green eyes, and an upturned nose. She was a former student Lee met at a reunion almost a year ago while still on the rebound from his divorce from Beth. Due mostly to mutual unwillingness to work at it, over the years his marriage to Beth had become one of convenience, and when their son, Luke, left for college, Beth moved out. Lee was surprised, but he really shouldn't have been. His wife had been visibly unhappy for a long time, and he had never made the effort to notice.

What Lee hadn't admitted to himself was that his relationship with Sharon was also beginning to wear thin. Still, being with her was better than being alone, and she was a good listener. As he related the story of Miles and the events of the evening, he couldn't escape the feeling he was talking about someone else. When he finally finished, Sharon was silent for a long time before making any reply.

"Do you know what he meant by, 'Don't let them bury it'?"

"No." Lee closed his eyes, on some level hoping Miles hadn't been referring to his body.

Sharon crossed her arms, unsure how to help. "Under the circumstances, I think Miles would have wanted you to do exactly what you did."

"Yes, but was it right?"

Sharon sighed. "I'm sorry. I'm not a priest. Why don't you find out where that key belongs?"

Lee looked at her. She seemed cool, aloof, but he didn't have the energy to try and figure out what was wrong. He looked down. He had opened up the tiny parcel during the telling of his story. The crumpled paper contained a key with the number 131 etched in the side. The paper had a message scrawled on it—well, not a message really, more of a list, like a chemist's shopping list, which read,

Magnesium	.10 g
Sulfur	.04 g
Fluorine	.12 g
Oxygen	.07 g
Boron	.01 g
Tantalum	.09 g
Protactinium	.11 g
Uranium	.02 g
Nitrogen	.08 g
Sulfur	.03 g
Tantalum	.05 g
Titanium	.06 g

Lee picked up the key and scrap of paper. "Why don't you go back to bed and try to get some sleep? I'll be in the study."

PIPER GROVE MOTEL, TAMPA, FLORIDA
SEPTEMBER 16, 10:56 P.M.

Cordoned off by a yellow police line, the motel room seemed to be a very popular place. Men in civilian clothes were going over every inch of the room, collecting hairs, fibers, cigarette ashes, even flecks of dirt, and placing them carefully in plastic bags.

At the center of all the activity, looking a little out of place in gray jumpsuit and high-top tennis shoes, Agent Tyler Stills was directing traffic. Her sweeper team was one of the best in the agency, and she was determined to keep it that way. Some of her superiors thought that twenty-eight years old was too young for a team leader, especially a woman. Add to that a pair of sultry brown eyes with a slight Eurasian cast, full lips, and a body most women would kill for, and it was no surprise Tyler had spent most of her adult life trying to get men to take her seriously.

Shortly after high school, during her first year at Boston Community College, she decided all men were pigs, cut her hair short, and dyed it black, hoping she would look dangerous and hence unavailable. To her dismay, testosterone-laden gorillas in work shirts, bent on exploring bizarre mating rituals, and masochistic wimps, bent on world-class rejection, seemed to come out of the woodwork at every nightclub she visited. Unwilling to do time for murder, she spent her evenings at home for a while, spending long hours in front of a mirror, developing a look so cold and vicious she hoped it would shatter the male ego on impact.

Her roommate used to say, "All men are Neanderthals," but that didn't seem quite fair, since some men were spineless milksops, so Tyler paraphrased, "Most men are stuck in first gear, and the rest can't find the clutch." Unfortunately, the expression had garnered a fair number of blank stares over the years, and her mantra was reduced by necessity to a pure distillate of her social philosophy: "Men are jerks."

After college, with a degree in economics and $270 in her pocket, she couldn't put off the decision any longer. Something had to be done with her life, but she not only had no clue what to do, she had no older, wiser person who could offer advice. Her mother died when she was a child, and her father was long gone to some other woman, some other life. The thought of going back to the alcoholic aunt who raised her seemed about as much fun as nailing her tongue to a table and setting the room on fire.

Barred, as she saw it, by nature from being a housewife, and loath to grovel before an endless line of managers and executives in order to make it in the business world, Tyler found herself gravitating toward the armed forces. When one of her friends suggested she'd be perfect for "spy stuff," she interviewed that same week with the CIA.

In three years, she was a field operative in Europe, doing courier work mostly, trying not to get killed in the process. Over the space of eight months, twice she was assaulted; twice she was forced to kill her assailant with her bare hands. That aspect of the job did not sit well with her, and before long she was losing sleep at night. Maybe it was those two years of Catholic school before she turned twelve, but killing was clearly not her gift.

Tyler put in for a transfer, got it, and began working investigations. That was definitely more her speed. Cruising onto a scene after the bullets had been fired and trying to figure out exactly what happened with almost nothing to go on. It was safe, challenging, and she didn't have to hurt anybody.

She did her job well enough that the superiors who weren't intimidated by her promoted her. The ones who didn't usually resented her and looked for ways to make her life difficult. They gave her the jobs no one else wanted, hoping each time that she would fail, always strengthening her deep inner conviction . . . that men are jerks.

Present company excluded, of course. Her team was handpicked and, in one case, trained by her. Smart, businesslike, and efficient, they were not mere men. They were a well-oiled machine. Tyler's machine.

One of the key components of her machine, a wiry, average fellow named Nash, came through the door with a report in hand. "Preliminaries are coming up negative. The room was picked clean. He has family in New York and Albuquerque, but I'm guessing that's the last place he'd go. He spent about eight years in Hanover, New Hampshire, before signing on with the lab. We have a list of about one hundred people he may have tried to contact there."

"Get on it."

Nash hesitated at the door. "Ty, what did this guy do, anyway?"

Tyler shrugged. "He stole something sensitive from one of the labs. I don't know what. HQ is playing it pretty close to the vest."

"His MO is strictly Norman Rockwell. I can't believe the guy is a threat to national security."

"I don't care if he teaches Sunday school. He's a fugitive, he's on the most-wanted list, and we're going to nail him to the wall."

DARTMOUTH COLLEGE, HANOVER, NEW HAMPSHIRE SEPTEMBER 16, 11:34 P.M.

Alone in his study, with midnight still half an hour away, Lee had been staring at the scrap of paper so long he couldn't see straight. Several sheets of notepaper sat nearby, covered with scribbled equations, all useless. He knew chemistry well enough, but there didn't seem to be any connection, no matter how he mixed the elements.

Lee rubbed his temples. The list was wrapped around a key, so obviously the two must be related somehow. But how? These elements produced numerous different reactions when combined in the quantities given, but none of them seemed significant or even relevant.

Lee put the paper down and rubbed his eyes, just about ready to give up. When he looked at the list once more, he noticed something about the distribution of elements and numbers. He had already seen that the sulfur and tantalum repeated, but only now did he realize that the numbers did not. *Idiot! I must be blind.* Miles was never the type for cryptography. He would have kept it simple. Lose the decimal points, and the quantities were non-repeating integers from one to twelve, the same number of items in the list.

Lee tore out a clean sheet from his notepad and wrote the elements in sequential order from one to twelve, substituting their periodic table designations for the names, until the following was on the paper,

B U S S Ta Ti O N Ta Mn Pa F

then he wrote the letters again, all in capitals,

BUSSTATIONTAMNPAF

and tried speaking them out loud.

"Bus station! Tamnpaf? Tamn . . . pa . . . Tampa! Tampa, Florida!"

Lee let out a long sigh and leaned back in exhausted triumph. So the key belonged to a locker at the bus station in Tampa, Florida. It would be light in about seven hours. With a little luck he would have time to pack and still get a few hours of sleep. He looked up the twenty-four-hour 800 number for his travel agent and reached for the phone, hoping the first flight out to Tampa wasn't booked up.

CIA HEADQUARTERS, LANGLEY, VIRGINIA
SEPTEMBER 16, 11:56 P.M.

Seated behind a large oak desk in a spacious top-floor office, CIA Director Carter Ellis was perusing project status reports. He didn't mind working late. The government was paying him to know what was going on, and there just weren't enough hours in the day. That kind of dedication got him the job in the first place, but the truth was, he didn't want to go home. His wife, Saundra, might still be awake, reading a book, and if they made eye contact, even for a second, it would precipitate five minutes of agonizing small talk, before the deafening silence encroached once more, and they took to their appointed stations on each side of the bed.

Ellis didn't know exactly when his wife became a stranger to him. No, he knew. It was right after the promotion at the law firm, when he started working fifteen-hour days. She went her way, and he went his. Sometimes he missed the warmth and the caring, but what they had now was comfortable, from a certain point of view, and it was easier to stay married than to break it up.

The ringing of the secure phone cut through his morose train of thought like a knife, and he answered it. "Ellis."

"Carter, it's Bill." Bill Sidwell was chief of special projects for the agency. "We have a Code One security breach."

"Where?"

"The Thornton Annex at INEL. About 9:30 this morning."

"About 9:30 this morning! Why wasn't I notified?"

"Agent Grange tried to keep a lid on it to save his backside. I fired him."

"What happened?"

"One of the scientists got away with an S file."

The color drained from Ellis's face. "Which one?"

"Prometheus."

Ellis slammed his hand down on the desk and swore. "Did he just waltz in and use his library card to check it out?"

"He had to have help. Probably someone in Document Control."

Ellis clenched his teeth to try to control his temper. "Bill. You've got to make this go away, fast."

"We've got our best teams on it already. You can thank Grange for that much anyway."

"I want hourly reports."

Ellis terminated the connection, sweat forming on his upper lip, and punched in a number on the keypad. After one ring, a gravelly male voice answered with a distinct southern drawl.

"Joram."

"Hank, it's Carter. We have an emergency. I need to meet with the Joint Chiefs at 0600."

DARTMOUTH COLLEGE,
HANOVER, NEW HAMPSHIRE
SEPTEMBER 17, 5:20 A.M.

Lee Teller woke up to the buzz of his alarm, feeling like he hadn't slept at all, but the drive to the Boston airport was 125 miles, and all the begging in the world wouldn't convince them to hold his flight. Instinctively, he reached out beside him in the dark. Sharon wasn't on her side of the bed, which was odd, but he didn't have the energy to think about it. He still had to pack a bag and make arrangements for someone to teach his classes.

Standing in a cool shower for ten minutes helped him wake up, and he tried to organize his schedule for departure. He would have to pack light, but the weather in Florida should be warm enough that he wouldn't need a jacket. The office was something of a disaster area, with sheets of paper strewn across the desk and one or two on the floor.

It would just have to wait until he returned.

Chapter Two

Under normal circumstances, Carter Ellis enjoyed situation room briefings. Talking about critical issues of national interest with the men who held the reins of power was always a thrill, even though he could never admit it to anyone. But today's briefing was very different. The Joint Chiefs of Staff for the armed forces, the White House chief of staff, and top-level officials from the Central Intelligence Agency and the National Security Agency were gathered around the table, listening intently while Ellis explained how someone under his command had committed the biggest screwup of the current administration.

". . . As you can see, if this goes public, some very important people are going to have a lot of explaining to do." Ellis made it sound like business as usual, but his guts were churning.

White House Chief of Staff Hank Joram took off his glasses and began cleaning them with a handkerchief—a sure sign he was angry. Joram had weak vision going into his second year of law school, a problem compounded when he attended a drive-in movie that was not adequately focused. The myopia was only a nuisance at first, but then the headaches started, and he had to do something about it. He considered contacts, but when he tried on a pair of glasses, the result was nearly professorial. Over the years, the glasses had proven to be a useful prop during negotiations. Joram was a brilliant strategist, and those who worked with him knew how to read his glasses. If he cleaned one lens, he was angry. If he cleaned both lenses, he was furious. If he breathed on the glasses before cleaning them, watch out. Heads were about to roll.

Carter Ellis concluded his remarks. "As I said at the beginning, we already have our best people on this. We estimate containment within twenty-four hours. Are there any questions?"

Joram meticulously cleaned first one lens, then the other, breathed on them, repeated the process, then spoke in a classic Alabama drawl. "How did the file escape the lab secure room?"

Ellis cleared his throat. "One of the Document Control specialists did not report for her shift this morning. We suspect she was Miles Orsen's accomplice."

Joram set his glasses on the table. "She is in custody?"

"Not yet, sir."

Joram slammed his hand on the table and swore. "What kind of operation are you running over there, Carter? Have you done anything right?"

Army Chief of Staff Harmon Kelsey cut in. "What's the subject's next move? Sell the file to the highest bidder?"

Thankful for the interruption, Ellis answered the question. "Foreign security forces would terminate him as soon as they saw the file. Orsen was smart enough to plan the heist. I can't believe he wouldn't have thought of that. The truth may actually be much worse."

"What could be worse than giving the file to a hostile government?"

Ellis paused for a moment, more for effect than anything. "We believe he may be planning to go public."

If reactions of shock, outrage, and disbelief were the desired effect, Ellis was not disappointed. A chorus of barely intelligible exclamations came from around the room, and Joram pounded on the table.

"Gentlemen! Gentlemen! Please, hold your comments! Mr. Ellis, am I to understand that Miles Orsen might actually consider trying to make something like this public knowledge? If he's not stupid enough to get himself killed, surely he's smart enough to understand the implications of a decision like that?"

"We're not sure, sir. Nothing in his profile even hinted he was capable of stealing the file. He was scheduled for termination along with the rest of the Pandora team. He must have found out about it somehow. Either he was trying to save his skin, or he figured he didn't have anything to lose. If he's not doing it for the money, he may be trying to save the world."

"Save the world?"

"He's been known to support liberal causes. A cheap source of energy looks like a great solution to the world's problems if you don't think too much about the consequences."

Harmon Kelsey put his elbows on the table, and his face in his hands. "I hope he thinks about the consequences."

TAMPA INTERNATIONAL AIRPORT, TAMPA, FLORIDA
SEPTEMBER 17, 11:42 A.M.

In a wash of hazy brightness from the late-morning light, flight 1884 sat on the tarmac, awaiting permission to taxi to its assigned gate. In the tail section with a row to himself, Lee Teller was trying to wake up. Flying usually made him nervous, which accounted for his fondness for the tail section, based on survival statistics from downed aircraft. On this trip, however, after the stress of the previous evening, a very short night's sleep, a surprise departure by Sharon, and a two-and-a-half-hour drive to Logan International Airport in Boston, he had passed out from exhaustion practically the moment the wheels left the ground in Boston.

When Lee came downstairs with his overnight bag early that morning, Sharon met him at the door with her own bag packed. His first thought was that she was planning on coming with him, and he was frantically trying to think of a way to let her down gently when she told him she was leaving—for good. She explained that it was obvious he couldn't commit to anyone, not now at any rate, and she needed more from a relationship. Lee hadn't bothered to protest because he knew she was right. But Sharon's absence made him feel vulnerable, and he called Beth before he left the house.

Beth received the news of Miles's death with polite sympathy but made sure to mention she was going to visit her mother in Oregon for a couple of weeks, in case Lee was looking for more than moral support. The only point they argued about was whether or not to tell their son, Luke, a junior at Azusa Pacific College in California, about his father's trip. Lee didn't want to distract him from his studies, but Beth countered, quite reasonably, that if he needed to reach Lee and got no answer, it would be far more distracting.

They finally struck a compromise where Lee called their son from the airport in Boston and told him that he was taking a research trip to Florida, and that his mother was going to be visiting Grandma for a couple of weeks. Luke thanked him for the information and got off the phone as quickly as he could without being impolite, showing no sign of being the least bit concerned by his parents' sudden change of schedules. Lee hung up the phone looking a little disappointed, wondering if they hadn't done too good a job of shielding him from the truth. But he told himself it was all for the best, and the situation would no doubt resolve itself in a few days.

Lee stretched and rubbed the sleep from his eyes, looking forward to breathing some moist air as soon as he stepped off the plane. *This better be over in a day or two*, he thought to himself, *I have classes to teach.* The dean of faculty had been understanding enough about his sudden leave of absence, but if his substitute, Mr. Kravis, had his students for more than a week, they might as well start the semester all over again.

The last one off the plane, Lee trudged through the terminal carrying his overnight bag and jacket—which Sharon recommended that morning as a parting attempt at compassion, and which was now a nuisance—oblivious to his surroundings, involuntarily replaying the burial of Miles Orsen in his head, until he had to shake himself to clear the unwanted thoughts. Focusing on the task at hand, he picked up the keys to a rental car and a map with directions to the bus station handwritten by the attendant. To his relief, the route to the bus station was a pretty straight shot.

The airport was only three miles from downtown, so the trip to the bus station took only fifteen minutes, even though it was nearing lunch hour. Finding a parking place took nearly as long, and he finally had to park six blocks away. Lee had to mentally lie back and remind himself he was in no hurry. The attitude adjustment worked, and he felt almost cheerful as he walked down the busy sidewalk toward the bus station.

As he walked through the double doors, he reached in his pocket for the locker key, and with that simple action, the voice of Miles Orsen rang through his mind.

If they find me, they'll find you, and you're a dead man.

Terror clutched Lee's heart, and he looked around furtively to see if a squad of armed men were advancing on his position. The station sported the usual cross section of citizens, some middle class, some poverty-stricken, many in-between, and none of them sinister. Lee sat down on a bench nearby to give his heart a chance to realize he wasn't about to launch into a quarter-mile sprint for his life. Then he saw the man in the three-piece suit and the long raincoat.

The man was standing and reading a paper. His face was rugged, the eyes cold and empty. A contract killer. Had to be. As Lee sat watching, the man set his paper aside, looked in Lee's direction, and started walking toward him. Lee's breath caught in his throat, and he burst out of his seat, almost knocking two people over as he ran out the door. He was about halfway up the block when logic began to assert itself again. *Where are you going, you imbecile? You are in a strange town, and you have a job to do. Besides, the man in the suit might have only wanted to ask the time.*

Lee slowed to a stop, his chest aching, and walked—a bit sheep-ishly—back to the bus station. When he got back to his bench, the man was nowhere to be seen. The tap on his shoulder that came a moment later nearly sent him through the roof. He whirled and found himself nose to nose with the man in the suit.

"I thought you'd be back."

"Wh . . . wh . . . wh . . . ," Lee stammered.

"You dropped your wallet." The man handed Lee his wallet, moved off, and returned to his newspaper. Only then did Lee notice his bench was right next to the rest rooms. The man had simply made a visit to the men's room. Lee could have kicked himself. *Get a grip! Start acting suspicious, and some off-duty policeman might haul you in just for kicks.*

Having no idea what might be in locker 131, Lee was reluctant to open it with so many people around. He decided to wait for the crowd to thin out a little. Unfortunately, judging from the bus schedule posted behind the counter past the lockers, things wouldn't thin out until about 6:45 that evening.

POLICE LABORATORY,
ATLANTA, GEORGIA
SEPTEMBER 17, 2:44 P.M.

The police lab in Atlanta was no stranger to visits from CIA agents with little or no warning, so when Tyler's team descended on the facility early that morning to do more detailed analysis on the samples taken from the hotel in Tampa, everyone got out of the way.

Sifting through bits and pieces of evidence for the needle in the haystack was not Tyler's favorite thing to do, but like a hound on a scent, she could sense that they were close. Before long, one of the younger fellows wearing a white smock walked over to her side.

"Agent Stills, I have a match on one of the hair fibers. Looks like your boy was at that hotel."

Nash stood up from the stool where he had been waiting impatiently for a break in the monotony. "Why would he check into a hotel for such a short time?"

Tyler thought about it for a moment. "Maybe he needed time to think. Or maybe he was going to hole up there but changed his mind. Either way, it looks like we're going to Hanover."

BUS STATION, TAMPA, FLORIDA SEPTEMBER 17, 6:47 P.M.

As the flow of buses thinned out in the evening, so did the people, and Lee finally stood up and walked over to stand in front of the locker.

He looked around once more, saw no one was watching, and inserted the key in the lock. Finally, he would know what Miles thought was so important. He held his breath and opened the door. Inside the locker was a leather satchel. Lee felt the hair rise on the back of his neck and turned around suddenly, but no one was there. He reached in quickly, grabbed the satchel, and hurried out of the bus station into the night as fast as he could walk.

Back in his car, Lee threw the satchel on the passenger side and drove well within the speed limit to a beachfront park on the edge of Tampa Bay. With the lights off, he just sat there in the dark until he could see well enough to be reasonably sure there wasn't another soul around. Then he turned on the overhead light, opened the satchel, and pulled out the contents.

It was a document lockbox, forced open at the seams. On the front in all capitals was the word *PROMETHEUS*, and diagonally in red across the upper-left-hand corner was the designation *S Clearance*. Okay, so the "they" Miles warned him about was the federal government. At least it wasn't some Mafia don who was going to leave some gruesome portion of a horse's anatomy in his bed.

He pulled a sheaf of papers out of the box and picked up the top sheet:

EXECUTIVE SUMMARY

Mr. President:

As you know, the success of the PANDORA PROJECT has created the need for some unusual measures. The options discussed at our meeting of September 10 have been evaluated and prioritized in this document, with our preferred recommendation first, followed by the project technical briefing. Understanding that dissemination of the results of the PANDORA PROJECT could precipitate world-wide conflict, up to and including global thermonuclear war, we feel the only viable alternative is a complete liquidation of the project and all project personnel.

Director, CIA

Lee set the sheet down, his stomach in a knot. He didn't want to go on, but he knew he had to. He read through the recommendation in about five minutes and realized the Prometheus file was little more than a hit list, with names and profiles of the scientists who worked on the Pandora Project, with detailed descriptions of how they might be terminated. Miles's name was near the bottom of the list. Still battling disbelief, Lee put the recommendations aside and picked up the technical brief.

TECHNICAL BRIEF
PANDORA PROJECT
S CLEARANCE
***** CIC EYES ONLY *****

The prospect of an inexpensive, virtually unlimited supply of power has spawned numerous forays into the arena of cold fusion research in the past two decades.

The possibility of a cold fusion discovery in a private sector lab necessitated the creation of the Pandora Project, a two-pronged approach aimed at beating the private sector to the market with a prototype, coincidentally with exhaustive research and mitigation of potential socioeconomic liabilities.

The project has succeeded beyond anyone's expectations. We have a working prototype that can be assembled in toto using parts available through local merchants in any moderately sized community. The unit is capable of producing 100 watts of uninterrupted AC power over a six-month period, or approximately 438,000 watt hours, on a quart of seawater. Units with higher power output have not been tested at this writing.

In fact, the prototype so exceeds project objectives, we now have critical deficiencies in the socioeconomic assessment and mitigation phase. I strongly recommend you convene an emergency meeting of S-cleared personnel to develop contingency response plans.

Respectfully,
Dr. Alan Smithee
Project Leader

Lee turned back to the Prometheus file and found Dr. Smithee's name at the top of the hit list. Anger gnawed at his belly as he reread each name on the list. They developed contingency plans, all right. They decided to kill everyone associated with the project.

The skin on the back of his neck began to crawl again, followed instantly by a wave of terror, and he flipped off the overhead light. Agents from half a dozen federal agencies were out there right now searching for Miles, and if they found Lee with the file, they would kill him on the spot, no questions asked.

By the dim light afforded by the parking lot's sole lamppost, Lee stuffed the documents back into the lockbox and burst out the driver's side door. Heart pounding in his throat, he strode purposefully across the sand toward the bay. The beach was empty, but he felt as if thousands of eyes were watching him. Standing knee-deep in the soothing lull of the surf, he drew his arm back, preparing to cast the lockbox far out into the water. *Sorry, Miles. If they want to bury it, there's nothing I can do to stop them.*

Moments from casting off, Lee paused, nagged once more by that annoying voice of reason. They were going to find him. Eventually, they were going to find him. It might take a week or a year, but the name of Lee Teller would appear on someone's list, and he would be the only one who flew to Tampa on the day in question. Then, one day, Lee Teller would disappear, and his body would never be found.

Lee clutched the lockbox to his chest, blinking back tears of anger and frustration. Why him? Why now? Twenty-four hours earlier, he had been completely satisfied with his professorial existence, looking forward to an evening of down comforters, flannel pajamas, and deliciously bland reading. Now he was a fugitive, and not a very good one at that. In his ignorance, he had left an obvious trail from Hanover to Tampa, at which the bloodhounds might already be sniffing. If he wanted even a chance at survival, he would have to start thinking and try to deal with one crisis at a time.

He needed a place to think, somewhere a bit more private than knee-deep in the warm waters of Tampa Bay. Still holding the lockbox, Lee slogged across the beach to his rented car. That would be the first thing to go. Anything with his name on it could be used to trace his location.

Too numb to care much, but still pushing through, forcing himself to think, Lee made his way back toward the airport, carefully obeying the speed limit. Upon arrival, he returned the car and bought a ticket to Arizona using his credit card. To complete the deception, he boarded the plane but exited shortly before takeoff by slipping out of the loading ramp through the airport personnel door while the attendants were preparing for departure.

He hadn't walked far when a well-meaning baggage handler offered him a ride to the main terminal, and Lee gratefully accepted. The airline would have a record of him flying to Arizona, which might buy him a few days. A short cab ride, paid in cash, brought him to a nearby motel where he paid in advance, again with cash, and registered under an assumed name.

Alone at last, Lee suddenly realized how tired he was, but sleep was out of the question. The nearest place selling food was a convenience store, so he forced himself to his feet and went to pick up a sandwich and a few other items before returning to his room to start thinking about his options. The first possibility was obvious: destroy the file and go home. But he had already abandoned that course of action. The prospect of spending the rest of his abbreviated life looking over his shoulder held little appeal.

Okay, option one stinks. Option two: turn the file over to the CIA like a good citizen and try to convince the agents that he never looked at it. Somehow, it was hard to imagine they would take him at his word. Even if they believed him, they could never be sure, and they would have to kill him. Option two was right up there with option one in the stink department.

Option three: turn it in to the police anonymously and go home, but thanks to the clumsy trail he had left, this option would most likely end up like option one. A brief lifetime of watching his back, and then lights out.

There were always the newspapers. A story like this could mean a Pulitzer prize. But the management at a newspaper might cave under pressure from the government and print a retraction. Or not print it at all. Or turn him in.

Lee looked at his list of options as if it were a dead fish. No matter what he did, it looked like Miles's pronouncement would be proved true. He was a dead man.

There was one option he hadn't considered, though. Nels. Nels would know what to do. Nels Thiessan had been Professor Emeritus of Sociology at Dartmouth when Lee arrived as a brash, young associate nearly fifteen years ago. In fact, Nels introduced Lee to Professor of Chemistry Miles Orsen. On more than one occasion, Lee had gone to the sage sociology guru for advice. Nels seemed to know quite a bit about everything, which wasn't surprising, considering his field of expertise.

Unfortunately Nels retired a few years ago—to Seattle, Lee thought—and the two men lost touch. Lee picked up the phone and dialed information for the 206 area code.

"What city, please?"

"Seattle."

"Go ahead."

"I'd like the number of Nels Thiessan, T-H-I-E-S-S-A-N."

"One moment . . . that number is unlisted."

"Is there any other listing."

"No, sir."

"How about an address?"

"No address."

"Thank you."

Lee hung up the phone trying not to feel depressed. At least he knew Nels was still in Seattle. Still holding the pen, he lay back on the bed, trying to think of a way to contact his old friend. After a few seconds, the pen slipped from his fingers and soft-landed on the carpet. Lee was asleep.

DGSE NORTH ATLANTIC INTELLIGENCE POST, GREENLAND
SEPTEMBER 18, 5:24 A.M.

Set up in a lighthouse basement on the southwestern coast of Greenland, the French intelligence listening post was manned twenty-four hours a day by six officers, who traded off in teams of two for eight hours each. Most of the equipment was ten years old, but still functional, and though no one ever talked about it, they knew it was because the post was pretty far down on a priority list back at the office in Marseilles. Had the post been on the China border, they could have ordered any high-tech toy in the book.

As listening posts went, it was recognized by most as the hind end of the network. However, while agents were not assigned here as a reward for meritorious service, a tour at the lighthouse was never handed down as a reprimand. Post Commander Gerard Dinaé, for example, had a well-known fondness for the ladies, which made him an easy mark for beautiful foreign agents. His record had always been better than average, but his character flaw made him unfit for fieldwork and some of the more sensitive intelligence-gathering operations. In fact, his superiors were unfailingly complimentary about his performance, and once every other year he got word that he was being considered for a field assignment, but the transfer never came.

Commander Dinaé was a night person to his core, so he always preferred the graveyard shift from 11:00 P.M. to 7:00 A.M. Raised in a shabby apartment near the banks of the Seine River in Paris, and forced to grow up perhaps too quickly, he had been mostly happy throughout his brief childhood. He received good marks in school, and his mother dragged him across town to the cathedral every Sunday. The walk was long and often cold, but they couldn't afford a cab, and his mother was too proud to tell any of the parishioners anything about their situation.

When his father lost his job collecting linens for the laundry from the hotel down the street and began staying out late and coming home drunk, Dinaé quit going to Mass. The way he saw it, God had abandoned his family, so he would abandon God. It wasn't long before his parents were fighting all the time, and he began taking nocturnal excursions to get away from the incessant bickering. As he grew older, the walks grew longer, and he began to learn about the seamier side of life. The young man was interested to discover that something inside him found obscenity attractive, and without anyone to guide him, he began exploring those feelings. By the time he graduated from school, he had his own apartment and was frequenting nightclubs and brothels, squandering what little money he had from his day job with the municipal janitorial service.

One night, after an evening of particularly flagrant debauchery, stumbling homeward drunk, clammy, and penniless, he nearly tripped over the still form of a male prostitute lying in the rubbish. Somewhere deep in his blurred conscience, an anguished voice whispered, "Soon, this will be you." Horror vanquished his stupor, and he ran all the way home, his heart pounding wildly. After long hours of introspection about his condition, he decided boredom was his nemesis. He must find a job dangerous enough to keep his interest alive.

Impressed by his school transcripts, the Académie de Police accepted him as a candidate, and after graduating, Dinaé was hired by the Direction de la Surveillance du Territoire, or the Sûreté, the French internal security agency. The active parts of the job certainly piqued his interest if he could ignore all the paperwork that went along with it, but after ten years of loyal service, a botched internal investigation left him at the wrong end of a disciplinary committee. He was asked to resign quietly or face charges.

Bitter and disillusioned, the thirty-two-year-old Dinaé sought to become an operative for French intelligence—the Service de Documentation Extérieure et de Contre-Espionnage. He hoped the SDECE would make him a spy and, more than that, a killing machine. In his heart, Dinaé knew he could kill without remorse if they would only give him the chance. He might have gotten his wish, were it not for his failure in two critical tests. The first was simple: walk into a mock hotel room and eliminate a sleeping enemy agent. Everything about the test was meant to simulate the real thing, right down to the blood capsules in the magazine for the pistol. Dinaé walked calmly into the room, held the barrel of the gun a few inches from his victim's head, and pulled the trigger. "Blood" spattered on the pillow and the man twitched violently. A feeling of elation filled him, and Dinaé squeezed off another shot. More blood, and the body stopped twitching. A hellish grin possessed Dinaé's face, and he began squeezing the trigger convulsively, again and again, not stopping even after the clip was empty. When the test was over, the reviewer said simply that he had enjoyed it a bit too much.

The second test came on the evening of the same day. Frustrated and disappointed by his performance, Dinaé went to a bar seeking drinks and carnal companionship. Sitting alone in a booth nursing a gin and tonic, he was approached by a stunning brunette in a blue velvet dress. After some small talk, the woman invited him back to her hotel. Dinaé couldn't believe his luck. Literally. Suspicious of another test, he told the woman rather rudely to get lost. Feeling perhaps a little too pleased with himself, Dinaé scanned the bar for other opportunities. Seated not far away was an attractive woman with wavy auburn hair and a cheerful spring dress. Her features were plain enough, but sitting there reading like that, she looked both poised and sophisticated. Surely she was no spy. Dinaé ordered her a drink, and she invited him over. The conversation was lively and engaging, her voice captivating. Dinaé invited her back to his room, and she accepted. After ten minutes of libidinous thrashing, utterly devoid of warmth or caring, he rolled over and went to sleep. Once his breathing had become deep and regular, the woman slipped out of bed, tiptoed across the room to her purse, pulled out an eight-inch sign with "Dead" written in French, and a small camera. With the sign resting against Dinaé's back, she took his picture and left quietly. That time the reviewer said nothing.

Dinaé was assigned to a nonsensitive post in London where he gradually worked his way up through the ranks to commander. Not wishing to grow old anywhere near the Thames River, he wrote an impassioned letter to his supervisor, requesting an assignment in the field. The response was a transfer to the listening post on the coast of Greenland. Dinaé resented the transfer at first, but after four years of performing his duties, he gradually became resigned to the post.

During that time, the SDECE became the Direction Generale des Services Exterieurs, or DGSE, also known as La Piscine, the swimming pool. The name originated from a description of the building housing the original agency and carried on through the name change, mostly because the French public kept the association alive. As far as Dinaé was concerned, if the agency was a swimming pool, he had been relegated to one of the deck chairs or, better, the parking lot. But his disappointments over the years had taught him patience, and he kept hoping if he pressed on, his time would come.

All of his successes and failures were documented in his file at headquarters. What was not documented anywhere was the fact that, thanks to the efforts of a friend in the strategic planning department, during the last eighteen months he had been spending three hours a day in field training. He already had level-two clearance for covert operations, and in another month he would be cleared for level three. The tests revealed a man who had mellowed with age, who knew how to control his anger and his physical drives, but even though his superiors were very encouraging, because of his age he had been placed on a classified waiting list from which he would be called if the need arose.

The Teletype machine noisily churned out its 6:00 A.M. report, and Dinaé walked over to pick it up. His shift would be over soon, and it would be time for another lesson in covert operations. The whine of the printer went on rather longer than normal, and he tore the page off with some interest. Abnormally high levels of CIA activity had been monitored all up and down the eastern seaboard of the United States. Usually that kind of activity meant one of two things, defection or fugitive, but the FBI was strangely quiescent if it were either occurrence. Under normal circumstances, they would be out in force as well. Odd.

Dinaé picked up his secure phone and called his supervisor.

OCEAN BREEZE MOTEL, TAMPA, FLORIDA SEPTEMBER 18, 8:16 A.M.

Lee awoke with a start and took several seconds to remember where he was and why. Lying back with an arm over his eyes, he blearily tried to come up with a plan for the day. He knew he had to get to

Seattle without leaving a trail, but he was unaccustomed to thinking that way. After ten minutes or so mulling over the problem, he decided to make the first leg of his trip to Birmingham via charter plane, since the Tampa airport was the first place they would check. Feeling somewhat encouraged by the plan, he ordered room service, called a cab, and jumped into the shower.

Dressed and packed when breakfast arrived, he was out the door seven minutes later and found his cab waiting for him. He checked up and down the street reflexively, but found nothing out of the ordinary and climbed into the cab.

"I need to go to a bank."

"Which one?"

"Interstate One."

A ten-minute drive brought him to his destination, and Lee asked the cabdriver to wait. Using a credit card, he took out a $2,000 cash advance, hoping this would be the only trail he left, and hurried out of the bank. With a little luck, the government wouldn't find out about the withdrawal for some time, maybe never. The cab took him to the Tampa airport, where he paid his fare in cash and then strode through the terminal to the portion of the airport that serviced charter planes.

Choosing a carrier was easy—only one had a plane available immediately—and he didn't have to wait long for the pilot to file a flight plan to Birmingham, Alabama. Paying in cash once more, Lee was quickly on board, and the plane began to taxi toward the runway. He hoped his explanation of being late for an insurance seminar was exactly boring enough that no one would remember it later.

The trip northwest in a twin-engine turbo prop was noisy, but uneventful, and he landed in Birmingham just before lunchtime. Foot traffic in the terminal was light, so he had no trouble making his way to the ticket counter where he bought a one-way ticket to Seattle under an assumed name. His flight didn't leave for ninety minutes, and the terminal was warm and dry, so Lee took the opportunity to find a seat and air out his shoes, which were still slightly damp from the previous evening's detour into the waters of Tampa Bay.

Safely out of Florida, he was able to relax a little, but he couldn't stop glancing over his shoulder. Twenty minutes before takeoff, he walked to his gate and boarded the plane without incident. Good. Still no sign he was being followed, and with one stopover, he would be in Seattle in time for a late dinner.

CIA HEADQUARTERS, LANGLEY, VIRGINIA SEPTEMBER 18, 9:46 A.M.

Special Projects Director Bill Sidwell sat rigidly behind his desk, trying unsuccessfully to focus on something other than the Promethean problem. He was tall, with thinning dark hair, and completely average in his appearance. Those features had made him an excellent field agent when he was younger because he looked more like an accountant than a spy. At forty-two years old, he was already thinking about retirement. His family owned part of an island in Maine, and right now that sounded like a much better place to be.

A knock at the door snapped him back to reality, and Charles "Chip" Nicholson, the agent in charge of the manhunt for Miles Orsen, came in and sat down across from him.

"Good morning, Bill. You look like death warmed over."

"Don't we all? What have you got?"

Chip shuffled some papers before answering. "We got a positive ID on Orsen. He was definitely in the hotel room in Tampa."

"Any idea what he was doing down there?"

"Not yet. According to our files, he doesn't know anybody in Florida. We've narrowed the list of probable contacts in Hanover to twenty-two, plus four possibles. Also, the Document Control specialists from the Thornton Annex are being held for questioning."

Sidwell bridged his fingers and rested his chin on his thumbs, thinking. "Have someone in Tampa begin searching the public storage facilities and all the airport and bus station lockers. Put Tyler's team in Hanover and chase those leads down fast. I want those Document Control specialists interrogated and their statements on my desk by three-thirty this afternoon."

SEATAC AIRPORT, SEATTLE, WASHINGTON SEPTEMBER 18, 7:53 P.M.

". . . and please remain in your seats until the captain has turned off the seat belt sign."

Lee peered out his window as the plane made its final approach to the gate. The sky was overcast, lit from below by the lights of the city, the ground wet, and a fine mist was on the windows. He was thankful for his jacket. One of his first priorities was going to have to be a Laundromat, or the authorities would be able to find him just by the smell. When it was his turn, he grabbed his bags and hurried off the plane, glad for the solid floor underfoot.

The rectangular satellite terminal was utilitarian but adequate, and he thought about stopping for a more substantial dinner at the restaurant situated in the center of the building. The restaurant seemed too exposed, though, and he decided the dinner he had eaten on the plane would have to suffice. He made his way down the escalators to the underground shuttle train, which took him to the main terminal. Another escalator ride took him to the baggage level, and Lee climbed into the first available cab.

"Where's the nearest library?"

The cabdriver thought a moment. "There's one in Burien, I think."

"Take me there."

Burien was right next to the airport, so the journey to the library took only about ten minutes. The building didn't close until 9:00 P.M. Lee asked the cabby to wait, and he walked inside to the reference desk. He found what he was looking for in a phone book from two years previous. Nels and Utta Thiessan lived in the university district across town. Lee scribbled down the address, thanked the woman behind the desk, and went back out to the cab. He handed the driver the address and settled back in his seat, thankful he wouldn't have to find it himself in the dark.

Lee closed his eyes and tried to remember what Nels looked like. The older man was a little taller than Lee, and slighter of build, with pointed features and vivid blue eyes that seemed to dance whenever he spoke. His wife, Utta, was warm and wonderful, the kind of woman who made cookies for other people's children. Not having any of their own, they had the habit of adopting students from campus. Every Saturday without fail there was a "family" dinner put on by Utta with a sort of humble flair, attended by as many as six students and anyone else they cared to invite. Lee and Beth Teller joined them once and found the experience most enjoyable. It was the only time Lee ever got background on Nels, thanks to the students pumping their host with questions.

Born and raised just outside of Oslo, Norway, Nels immigrated to the U.S. with his family before his tenth birthday. He graduated from high school with honors and attended Georgetown University. After completing a doctoral program in sociology, he was hired by the governor's office in Virginia to be an attaché to Congress. From there, he spent four years as a deputy at the Department of Health, Education, and Welfare, followed by two years as chairman of the President's Science Council. He was offered the sociology position at Dartmouth and took it, ostensibly because he was tired of working for the government, but everyone knew it was because he loved to teach.

Lee was brought out of his reverie by the sight of numerous large orange cranes lining the waterfront, illuminated by bright shipyard lights and backlit by the last, minute traces of daylight, just visible above the far shore of Puget Sound. It was beautiful. With a pang of remorse, it occurred to him he had never brought his family here. Luke would have loved it. If he survived this thing, maybe they could take a vacation here.

He watched the scenery go by with great interest and began to suspect the driver was taking the scenic route, but he didn't mind. The cab left the viaduct at the wharf, up a steep hill, then backtracked some distance until they were on another highway. Over the space of twenty minutes, Lee saw the Aquarium, the Space Needle, and numerous other sights with the net result that he forgot, if only for a little while, the seriousness of his predicament. When the cab rolled onto Nels's street, the butterflies in his stomach returned with a vengeance, and he instinctively clutched the satchel to his chest.

The Thiessans' house—if indeed it still was their house—was a modest little gray-brown townhouse, wedged in between an apartment building and a larger duplex, near the middle of the university district. Lee paid the cabby and asked him to wait until he was inside before taking off. As he strolled up the front walk toward the porch, he noticed the lawn had not been cut in some time, and his hopes of finding Nels began to dwindle. His first knock produced no response, so he tried again. The door opened slowly.

"Nels!" Lee resisted an impulse to hug the older man.

Nels shuffled through the doorway to get a better look at the stranger on his porch. He looked older, his hair almost completely gray, his shoulders slightly stooped, and the eyes no longer danced. Then recognition hit, and the eyes lit up for a moment.

"It can't be . . . Lee Teller, isn't it?"

"Yes! I'm so glad you're here."

"Well, don't just stand there. Come in! Come in!"

Lee followed Nels inside and closed the door behind him. Nels led him into a sitting room to the right of the foyer and told him to sit down. Lee chose a comfortable sofa by the front window and carefully set his bags beside him. At the end of the couch was a breakfront cabinet filled with Utta's bric-a-brac, but the window on the front of the cabinet was dusty.

"Where's Utta?" Lee asked the receding figure as it shuffled into the kitchen.

"I'll get us some tea," Nels replied as if he hadn't heard.

While he waited, Lee examined the room in detail. The place reminded him of his grandmother's home on the river. Polished wood floors with oriental throw rugs were accented by ornate antique furniture, and almost every available flat space in the room had some precious trinket or picture frame resting on it. The only truly modern piece of furniture in the room was a recliner with an afghan folded over the back. Lee was willing to bet that chair was the only thing in the room Nels had picked out.

Nels shuffled out of the kitchen a few minutes later with two mugs in hand, placed them on the coffee table, and lowered himself into the Queen Anne chair next to the cabinet. "Utta passed away a year and a half ago," he said without introduction. "Congestive heart failure."

"I'm so sorry."

"Don't be. We had a wonderful life together."

"What have you been doing?" Lee asked, taking a cautious sip from his steaming mug.

"When I left Dartmouth, I came out here to head up the sociology department. After Utta died, I couldn't keep working. I decided to retire. The university gives me a small stipend in return for which I grade papers and substitute teach when there's an emergency." The way Nels spoke, it was clear his heart wasn't in it. To Lee, it seemed he was just marking time until he could join Utta. A long silence stretched between them until Nels mentally shook himself. "At least I'm keeping in shape with all the walking, which is more than I can say for you if those love handles are any indication. So, what brings you here? Why didn't you call?"

"Your number is unlisted."

"Oh. Yes. I kept getting phone solicitors calling and asking for Utta, and the constant reminders became an annoyance. But never mind that. You still haven't told me why you're here."

Lee reached out and fingered the clasp on the flap of the satchel, toying with it. "I had a visit from Miles Orsen."

A look of apprehension crossed Nels's face, quickly replaced by an affectation of benign interest. "Oh, really? How is Miles?"

Lee hesitated. "He's dead. When I found him, he was lying on a bench next to the administration building with a bullet hole in his back."

Nels blanched. "Wh . . . who would want to kill Miles?"

"You knew him better than I did. I was hoping you could tell me."

Nels didn't answer right away. "I can't."

Something about his tone didn't sit right with Lee. "Can't or won't?"

"Can't. Did he say anything to you?"

"He said, 'Don't let them bury it,' handed me a key to a bus station locker in Tampa, then died right there on the bench."

Nels was on his feet suddenly and strode to the window. Looking like a man ten years younger, he reached through the curtains and pulled down the shade. When he sat down once more, his eyes were vivid, intense. "What did you do?"

"I buried his body in the woods outside town."

"Why?"

"He told me if I took him to a hospital, 'they' would find me, and I was a dead man."

Nels put a hand to his head, clearly upset by this last piece of information. "I assume you've been to Tampa." Lee nodded, and Nels continued, "What did you find?"

"This." He reached inside the satchel and pulled out the Prometheus file. Nels took one look at the cover of the document lockbox, and the blood drained from his face.

"Lee, do you know what this is?"

"Some sort of government file."

"Have you read it?"

"Yes. Miles was working on something called the Pandora Project. Nels, they've discovered cold fusion."

A mixture of astonishment and horror seized Nels's face. "That's not possible . . ."

"They weren't ready for it, so someone decided to kill the project and everyone involved with it. The Prometheus file is essentially just a hit list of people associated with the Pandora Project."

Nels was on his feet again. "We've got to get out of here!"

That was not the reaction Lee was hoping for, and he watched in consternation as Nels disappeared up the stairs, returning moments later with a packed bag, a bulging envelope, and a gun in a shoulder holster.

"Nels! How did you . . . where did you . . . ," Lee stammered.

Nels's face was grim. "Grab your things and come with me."

"Where are we going?"

"I don't know yet."

Nels left everything as it was and waited until Lee was out the door. Then he shut it and locked it behind them. Casting furtive glances up and down the street, Nels led the way around the side of the house to a carport where a gunmetal blue Honda Civic sat illuminated by the back porch light. He handed Lee the car keys.

"You drive."

Numbed once more by events he didn't understand, Lee blindly obeyed. They were quickly under way, with Nels giving directions from the passenger seat. Once they were on Interstate 5 headed south, Nels leaned back in his seat, switched on the overhead light, and prepared to read the file.

Concerned about missing an exit, Lee interrupted him. "Do you know where we're going yet?"

"No, but this is Seattle. Almost everything is south of here."

Lee couldn't argue with the logic and kept his mouth shut. Nels finished reading the Prometheus overview a few minutes later and grunted with outrage and turned off the overhead light. When he spoke, his voice was grave. "This is very important. I want you to tell me everything you did to get here and how you paid for it."

Lee explained in detail his movements since he left Hanover, and when he finished, Nels breathed a sigh of relief. "Well, under the circumstances, it sounds like you did almost everything right."

"Almost?"

"They'll trace you to Tampa in no time, but the trail should be pretty cold from there. You've bought us a couple of days at least."

"They're that good?"

"They're that good."

Lee realized he still didn't know who the enemy was. "Who is 'they'?"

Nels was quiet, as if struggling with a difficult decision, and then answered, "Miles was right. If they find you, you're dead. And now, the same is true for me." He spoke hesitantly, choosing his next words carefully. "It's the CIA, Lee. The project was sponsored by the Central Intelligence Agency. There's an agency within the agency. No one is supposed to know about it. These are the guys who walk around with cyanide capsules in a false tooth, ready to commit suicide at a moment's notice. Even the clearance is highly classified. You've seen it already on the front of the file. This goes way beyond Top Secret. There is only one standing order for a person who sees an S file or any S-cleared operation without the necessary clearance: shoot on sight, shoot to kill."

"How do you know so much about it?"

"I've got a false tooth of my own."

Lee's eyes widened. "You're a CIA agent?"

"Inactive. But you're sort of in it for life. That's why I always have a packed bag and an envelope full of money in my closet. Since I was nineteen, my whole career was carefully orchestrated so I would be in a position to recruit the best scientific minds in the country."

Realization crashed in upon Lee. "You were the one who recommended Miles to the lab!"

"Yes. Which means I am also partially responsible for his death."

Lee thought about that for a moment and rejected it. "Miles made his own choices."

"I know, but when I recommended him, I knew he was idealistic, and I chose to ignore it because he was also brilliant."

"Why didn't you turn me in? You said you were an agent for life."

"That statement may be true in more ways than you know. There were two things the agency didn't count on when they took me off active duty: Utta and Jesus Christ."

"Utta was an agent?"

"You can't hide this kind of thing from your spouse for very long. After I completed my training, I was paired with Utta. We were given a joint history. They didn't anticipate that we would fall in love. She attended church for years as part of her cover, but something changed her a few years back. She began to really believe all the things she'd heard over the years. As a result, she actually became the sweet woman you thought you knew in Hanover."

Lee's mind was reeling. The Thiessans were agents? Nels, he could almost believe, but sweet, gentle Utta? Not in a million years. "I can't buy it, Nels. It's too far-fetched."

"Believe what you want. It is the truth."

"What does Jesus Christ have to do with it?"

The conversation was helping Nels's nervousness to subside, and he welcomed it. "For as long as I can remember, I've believed Jesus was a fabrication of some sort or another, and a good one at that. It always seemed to me that true or false, He was a pretty good idea. He preached a doctrine of universal peace and brotherhood. Throughout history, when informed people have applied this doctrine to society, the result has seemed to bring out what is best in human nature."

"What about the Spanish Inquisition?"

"I said 'informed people.' Nowhere in Scripture does it command believers to reclaim Jerusalem from the hand of the infidel or to put nonbelievers to the sword. If I may continue that thought, however, this doctrine also brings about what is worst in human nature."

"How do you explain that?"

"People engaged in willful, destructive behavior do not react well to being told their actions are wrong, evil, or even destructive. But look at the commandments. Put God first. Put others before yourself. Don't steal. Don't lie. Take a day off to remember you are not God. Don't murder. Don't take another man's wife. History shows again and again that for the person who adheres to these doctrines, the egocentrism of human nature is subjugated. A society of people caring for one another is very strong."

"I'm still not making the connection between Jesus Christ and the CIA."

"After Utta changed, she pestered me to talk to the new young pastor at church. I finally acquiesced just to get her off my back. I was irritated and a little resentful, so I went in ready to take this poor fool's belief system apart piece by piece. I had barely sat down when I launched into a preemptive strike, proving beyond a shadow of a doubt that, while the tenets of Christianity were beneficial, the account of Jesus could not be historically accurate. I went on for twenty minutes, almost without taking a breath. When I finished, he just sat there not saying a word, and I began to feel guilty. I mean, here's this inexperienced chump just trying to serve humanity the best he can, and I've utterly destroyed him. But when he did finally speak, all he did was ask me a simple question: 'Who would die for a lie?'"

"Come again?"

"If the New Testament writings are fabrications, then every one of the eleven disciples—"

"I thought there were twelve disciples," Lee interjected.

"This is after Judas killed himself. Every one of the eleven except

John faced a horrible execution for a story he knew to be a lie, when confessing the lie would have saved him. I chewed on this fact for the longest time and did a lot of reading. At the end of six months, I prayed to receive Jesus. That's why I didn't turn you in. So you see, from a certain point of view, I really am an agent for life."

Oh, great! Lee thought. *Nels has gone off the deep end, and now we might as well be joined at the hip.* On the upside, he wasn't going to turn Lee in, and things couldn't get much worse. Lee accepted his lot with benign resignation. "Well, I hope God is watching right now 'cause we're going to need all the help we can get."

Chapter Three

Carter Ellis had not been sleeping well since the beginning of this particular crisis. Between his usual late nights and early morning meetings with the Joint Chiefs, he was starting to look haggard. The JCS was turning up the heat and had made it abundantly clear that if this thing went public, the least he would lose was his job. Still stinging from the most recent rebuke, he was having trouble not taking out his anger on his special projects chief.

"The point is, Bill, it shouldn't have happened at all."

No one at headquarters had ever seen Bill Sidwell angry, but his face looked more stern than usual. "For the third time, Mr. Ellis, we have taken additional security precautions at all of our labs, and I don't have to tell you how many people we have looking for Miles Orsen."

Ellis's eyes narrowed. "Well, send more! You don't know what it's like staring down all that brass. Kelsey was so steamed, I thought he was going to shoot me. I hate this, Bill. I don't like coming in to work not knowing if I'm going to have a job at the end of the day. I'm not taking the fall alone. If I go down, you're going down with me."

"I knew that from the beginning, sir."

Neither man said a word for some time, and the tension in the room grew very thick. When Chip Nicholson walked into the room a minute later, he could feel it. "Um, I can come back later."

Ellis broke the tension with a shake of his head. "Come in. We're just having a little family spat. Have a seat. I need to know we're making some progress here, Chip."

Chip sat down and positioned his notes where he could read them. "Please bear with me. Some of this may be repetitive, but I want to be sure we're all up to date." Ellis nodded, and Chip continued, "Miles Orsen was given the Prometheus file on September 16 by Document Control Specialist Daphne Spencer. We still don't know who told Spencer about the file, but it was probably one of the other specialists. Spencer reviewed the file and told Orsen, who then came up with a plan to steal it. Orsen placed the file in a holocaust case and sent it through the incinerator. He distracted the operator until the file was past the furnace monitor, then set off a fire alarm and retrieved the file from the ash pile during the confusion. He was off the grounds before the theft was discovered, but agents pursued him downtown. Police set up roadblocks, and he finally plowed into one at Seventeenth and Hurley. Agents Reif and Morrison pursued him on foot. Reif thinks he may have hit him with a .38-caliber slug, but we can't confirm. Orsen took a cab to the air freight yard near the airport and paid one of the attendants $1,500 to load him on the first flight out, which happened to be bound for Tampa. He spent a few hours at a roadside motel, but we know nothing of his movements. Someone matching his description bought a ticket for a 3:50 flight to Boston, but we have reason to believe his final destination was Hanover, New Hampshire. Apparently he looked pretty bad, so Reif may be right about the .38 slug. The trail ends in Hanover."

Ellis's face darkened. "That's it?"

"I'm expecting an update any minute! You called me in before . . ." The portable phone in Chip's breast pocket rang, and he answered it gratefully. "Nicholson . . . hmm . . . yep . . . yep . . . take it apart." Chip returned the phone to his pocket, looking a little smug. "That was Tyler Stills in Hanover. The day after Orsen arrived, a physics professor—a man named Lee Teller—took a leave of absence and flew to Tampa. Teller is one of Orsen's old associates on the possible suspect list. He rented a car for two and a half hours, returned it, put a $2,000 advance on his credit card, bought a plane ticket to Arizona, and disappeared. The trail ends there. Agent Stills is about to take Teller's house apart."

Ellis leaned forward, an angry sneer on his face. "I want every nail in a bag."

PIONEER ROAD AT ROUTE 238, MEDFORD, OREGON SEPTEMBER 19, 4:26 A.M.

For three years, Bob Liddle had worked the swing shift at a convenience store on the other side of town, so any intrusion before 10:00 A.M. was usually unwelcome. Still two years shy of his thirtieth birthday, he lived alone in a tiny rural hovel on a shabby quarter-acre lot replete with rocks and dirt and not much else. The persistent pounding of some moron at his front door at 4:30 in the morning did little to put him in a cheerful mood. Muttering under his breath, he lurched out of bed, grabbed a shotgun, and walked down the hall, yelling at his visitor to shut up already! It was probably the paperboy groveling from mail stop to mail stop begging for money. Bob opened the door.

The man on the porch was holding a paper all right, but he looked more like somebody's grandfather. "Aren't you a little old to be collecting for the paper?"

Nels pointed to a spot in the classifieds. "It says here you have an '85 Escort in mint condition."

Bob hastily put his gun aside. "Oh! Right. Let me get the keys." He disappeared through the front door and reappeared a minute later wearing a robe, with keys in hand. He noticed a blue Civic in the driveway and someone asleep in the passenger seat, though he couldn't make out any facial features. The Escort was white, with burgundy interior, and Nels started it up with no trouble, then popped the hood and gave the engine a thorough going over. Satisfied, he closed the hood and turned to face Bob, noting that he could see his breath.

"It says here you're asking $2,750 for it. I'll give you $2,000 cash and throw in the Civic."

Bob registered surprise, since the deal looked to be about $1,500 in his favor, but who was he to argue with a potential customer? "It's a deal. I'll go get the title."

As soon as all the necessary papers and money had changed hands, and a drowsy Lee had shuffled all their things to the new car, Nels thanked Bob and climbed into the driver's seat. Bob looked at the stack of crisp $100 bills a bit suspiciously, still not quite believing his luck. "You guys didn't rob a bank or anything?"

Nels laughed. "No, nothing like that. Just a much needed vacation."

Bob watched the Escort as it pulled out of the driveway and disappeared down the road. Vacation, hmm? Maybe after the Civic sold, he could afford to take one himself.

DARTMOUTH COLLEGE, HANOVER, NEW HAMPSHIRE SEPTEMBER 19, 6:53 A.M.

Dawn broke cool and damp over the town of Hanover, but the sky was clear and the first rays of the morning sun lit the autumn trees like a fire. Tyler Stills sat in the passenger seat of a generic brown van, staring at a maple branch suspended just a few feet above the windshield. It was an interesting fact about autumn, that a few leaves on every tree refused to fall to the ground with the rest, as if clinging for dear life to the only existence they had ever known, until winter's bitter edge was set against them, and they finally succumbed. For all intents and purposes, the leaves were already dead. They just didn't know it yet.

She shifted her gaze across the street to Lee Teller's house and wondered if the same might not be true about him. Judging from his picture, he hardly seemed like the type to aid and abet a fugitive. She didn't want to admit it to herself, but somewhere beneath her tough exterior, she was hoping Teller's trip to Tampa was an unfortunate coincidence.

Just then, Nash returned from his recon of the house and sat down in the driver's seat. "We're clear. There's nobody home. The garage was used for storage, so his car would have been parked on the street, which—as we have already established—it isn't."

"Have Kyle check short-term parking out at the airport. Listen. I know Ellis has a large African bee in his shorts over this thing, but let's start with the obvious stuff. If Teller's our man, there's a good chance he didn't know what he was getting into. It'd be a shame to trash the wrong guy's house."

Nash understood. "You're the boss."

With the skilled assistance of a younger man named Rick, Nash had the police line set up in just under fifteen minutes. Defeating the locks on the front door took thirty seconds. Tyler followed him through the door and heard a voice with a smart-aleck lilt to it on her headset. It was Wally Beason back in the van.

"Ty, this is the Wall-man!"

"Go ahead."

"At 9:53 on the evening in question, someone placed a one-minute phone call to Teller from a pay phone on campus."

"Any other calls?"

"No, sir."

"Check with the police. I want to know if they have any record of contact with Teller within forty-eight hours of that call."

Tyler looked around the room. Rick and Nash were already on their way upstairs to begin their sweep. She closed her eyes and tried to picture the room the way it might have looked on the eve of Teller's departure. Okay. I walk in the door after a hard day teaching and settle in for a quiet evening at home. Orsen probably wouldn't have come to the house, so we'll assume a neutral meeting place. The phone rings, and Orsen asks me to meet him someplace, where he tells me something that causes me to book a seat on the next flight to Tampa. I want to be on the first flight out in the morning, so I walk in the door and pick up the phone . . .

Tyler opened her eyes. There was no phone in the room, so she scanned the sides. Off to one side was a study. She walked over to the cozy little room and knew immediately that Teller had left in a big hurry. Scribbled pages from a notebook were strewn across the desk, and the top page of the pad had a single phrase underlined.

"Bus station, Tampa, Florida." Tyler's heart sank a little as she realized things were not looking good for Mr. Teller. She told the others of the discovery, and Wally informed her that Teller had been pulled over for speeding that same night, though no citation was issued. Tyler swore softly and continued her examination of the study. Sometime later, Nash's voice came over the headset.

"We found a pair of penny loafers caked with mud. Some clothes were piled in the bathroom. Same condition as the shoes."

"You know the drill."

While Nash and Rick began dumping out the dresser drawers upstairs and sifting through the debris, Tyler painstakingly examined every piece of paper on the desk and a few from the garbage. She was nearly finished when Kyle's voice came on.

"Tyler, I called security at the airport. They located Teller's car in short-term parking. They said it looks like he took it off road. There are bloodstains on the passenger seat."

Rick's voice was next. "Ty, do you think he killed him?"

"No."

"Then why haven't we picked up Orsen's trail?"

"Because Orsen is already buried somewhere nearby."

"Then Teller did kill him," said Nash.

"He had no motive. He hadn't even been to the Tampa bus station yet."

"So, who killed Orsen?"

"One of our people. He carried the slug with him all the way from Idaho. Couldn't risk a hospital. By the time he reached Hanover, he was already dead. He just didn't know it yet."

Tyler looked out the window at the autumn leaves wafting gently in the morning breeze. Things were definitely not looking good for Lee Teller.

HIGHWAY 101, TWENTY MILES NORTH OF EUREKA, CALIFORNIA
SEPTEMBER 19, 10:48 A.M.

At the moment, the only thing keeping Lee going was the large mug of cool coffee held somewhat delicately between his legs. The decision to take the coast highway had spawned his first argument with Nels. Lee argued that they would make much better time staying on Interstate 5, but Nels countered that if the California Highway Patrol was looking for them, the interstate was the last place they wanted to be. Now Nels was asleep, head thrown back, snoring away in the passenger seat. Lee fought for his life navigating one of the most convoluted roads in the state—not counting a handful of brutally serpentine mountain roads in the Cascade range.

Driving hazards notwithstanding, the scenery was beautiful. Large battalions of Douglas fir trees looked as if in ages past they had marched upon the ocean, only to have their journey stopped by jutting basalt cliffs or, in some cases, the beach itself. Maybe when he took Luke to see Seattle, they could fly to Los Angeles and drive up the coast highway.

Lee drove on in silence, lost in thought, except for occasional moments when some natural wonder stole his attention. Almost an hour later, when Nels sat up suddenly and said, "Melrose!" Lee nearly drove off the road in panic.

"What? What?"

"Dr. Simon Melrose," Nels explained, rubbing the half-sleep from his eyes, "professor of physics at Stanford. I think I've been subconsciously heading there all along. I met him when I was at Dartmouth. He put in some time at a government lab."

"Are you sure you want to share this with someone who's been at a government lab?"

"Nothing else will do. You have to understand, Lee. Any scientific 'breakthrough' that is reported in the press is usually twenty years behind what's going on in the labs. We need someone with that kind of experience, and Melrose has been involved in some pretty wild projects. The last I heard, his unit was working on matter transference."

"Tch! Matter transference! That's pure science fiction, Nels, and you know it."

"I didn't say they were successful. As I recall, no matter what they sent through, all that materialized on the other end was a lump of carbon."

"People, too?"

"They're not idiots, Lee. There's a lot of paperwork when you kill a person. But I suspect the rat population may have taken a big hit."

"Why do we need Melrose?"

"We have to assemble the cold fusion device to see if it really works. I want to be in a lab when we do it. If we end up selling it to a foreign government, we have to know how it works."

Lee glanced at Nels as if he were mad. "A foreign government?"

"Our own government has given orders to its agents to shoot us on sight, so logically speaking, a foreign government is a possibility we must consider. You have to abandon old ways of thinking if you want to survive. This isn't about borders or patriotism or politics. This device could provide a cheap, inexhaustible source of energy for every person on the planet."

"Then why is our government trying to bury it?"

Nels snorted in disgust. "You read the operation summary."

"Right. A typical bureaucratic meat-cleaver approach to a problem that ought to have a solution."

Nels arched a bemused eyebrow. "And what would you recommend in all your scholarly wisdom?"

Lee was silent for several seconds, thinking. "Convene an international symposium of scientists, show them the device, and give them detailed plans for carefully regulated implementations in their respective societies."

"And what happens when the design inevitably leaks out and the devices begin flooding communities around the globe?"

"Um . . . a temporary realignment of societal infrastructure, then universal peace and happiness."

Nels laughed out loud, but there was nothing derogatory about it. "On the contrary, an uncontrolled release of the device would have catastrophic, maybe even apocalyptic, results. Oil consumption would drop sharply. Energy-related industries would collapse within the month, with others to follow. You can bet OPEC wouldn't stand for it. Almost overnight there would be a massive glut in the oil market, and prices would plummet. Literally thousands of oil dependent businesses, with no time to adjust, would be destabilized, and we would begin to see runaway inflation, massive unemployment, cascade failure of weaker economies across the globe, then rioting, martial law, police actions, and finally a third world war, which would dwarf the first two in size and scope. Assuming the war ever ended, which is debatable, the most likely candidate for restoring order would be a worldwide totalitarian regime. You'd have universal peace and harmony all right—the peace of the police state, the harmony of the iron fist."

Lee was somewhat abashed. "Oh."

Nels smiled jovially. "Don't take it too hard. That's only one of a thousand possible outcomes."

"You made it sound like a foregone conclusion."

"Just a carryover from my teaching days, I'm afraid. It's no easy task to get students to think for themselves these days. Besides, you were absolutely correct about one thing."

"What's that?"

"The problem certainly ought to have a solution."

HIGHWAY 50, FIVE MILES WEST OF FALLS CHURCH, VIRGINIA
SEPTEMBER 19, 4:06 P.M.

Having been at work past midnight the previous two days, Bill Sidwell had decided to knock off early today. Rush hour had not taken hold yet, and traffic on the highway was still moderate. The city of Arlington was still some distance ahead when the secure phone mounted under his dash began to beep. In the old days, he had to speak in code when using his car phone, but advances in encryption technology allowed him to speak freely.

"Sidwell."

"Nicholson, sir. I have a report from Hanover."

Sidwell had to slow down suddenly to avoid an accident. "Not counting the bozo changing lanes in front of me, you have my full attention."

"Tyler has confirmed that Orsen contacted Professor Teller. They tore the place apart and found no trace of the missing file. Contrary to procedure, they left the place the way it was and boarded it up. One way or another, it's unlikely the professor will ever see his house again. Airport security found his car at the airport, covered with dried mud and traces of blood on the passenger seat. We have confirmed the blood is a match for Orsen's type. Tyler thinks Orsen is already dead and buried. A sweep of the lockers at the Tampa bus station turned up negative. And you already know about Teller's plane ticket to Arizona."

Sidwell shifted in his seat to take some pressure off his lower back. "Any idea where Teller went from Arizona?"

"We think the ticket may have been a ruse, but there's no other trail to follow out of Tampa. The good news is, we ran a cross-check on Teller and Orsen and came up with a name: Nels Thiessan."

"Why is that name familiar?"

"He's one of ours. He spent a few years at Dartmouth fishing for big brains to populate the labs. Orsen was one of his recruits. Thiessan is retired and living in Seattle. Tyler and company are en route."

Sidwell was quiet for a moment before responding. "Put out an APB on Lee Teller for the murder of Miles Orsen. Do a complete work-up on Thiessan. I want it on my desk in half an hour."

Cursing his luck, Sidwell took the next exit, crossed the highway, and headed back toward the office.

CIA HEADQUARTERS, LANGLEY, VIRGINIA
SEPTEMBER 19, 10:23 P.M.

Once again, as sane people all over the city headed for bed, Carter Ellis sat behind his desk, staring blankly at the papers in front of him.

He was glad they were getting a break on the case, but keeping abreast of the updates on three hours of sleep was becoming impossible. Glassy-eyed, he forced himself to continue putting related bits of information into separate piles. When he realized a few minutes later that he needed to visit the men's room, he welcomed the opportunity to stretch his legs and get his blood moving again. Procedure demanded that he lock up any sensitive materials in his cabinet, but he had almost sweat blood in the last half hour trying to get as organized as he was, and he wasn't about to chuck it all for a two-minute trip to the john.

Ellis locked his office door behind him and walked past the secretary—a woman from the steno pool—who was working late at his request. Darlene, his usual secretary, had some unexpected family conflicts and declined the offer to earn some overtime. Polly Sutton was a capable substitute, with blonde hair and a fresh-faced American look, and she would have given his sober judgment a run for its money when he was a younger man, but he wisely kept such thoughts to himself as he passed her station.

"Back in a few."

As Ellis disappeared through the men's room door, Polly was out of her seat and moved quickly to his locked office. Reaching in her vest pocket, she produced a key, inserted it into the lock, and opened the door quietly. In her stocking feet, she padded soundlessly to the desk and pulled a miniature camera out of her other pocket. In half a minute she had photographed every exposed page on the desk, stowed the camera, and hurried out of the room, closing the door behind her.

When Ellis returned a short time later, as far as he knew she was still hard at work transcribing dictation. He was tired and hungry, and he forced his eyes front as he let himself back into his office. The urge to make a pass at her was strong, but he had not gotten that far by being grotesquely stupid. With his luck, she probably would have turned out to be a Russian spy.

DGSE NORTH ATLANTIC INTELLIGENCE POST, GREENLAND
SEPTEMBER 20, 5:44 A.M.

The cabins were austere, but comfortable, furnished more like farmhouses than military quarters. For Gerard Dinaé, after the cloying press of apartment life in the big city, it had been love at first sight.

His cabin was neat and tidy, and his comrades liked to tease him about becoming fastidious in his old age. He didn't mind. There was no woman to care for the place, nor would there ever be. He couldn't take that chance.

Snoring loudly, Dinaé lay on top of his bedspread, a towel still around his neck. A particularly arduous stint of field training had stretched long into the previous evening, through the time he would normally be sleeping, and he had come through the door exhausted, fallen on the bed in his sweat suit, and not moved since. Living alone did have its advantages.

The phone next to his bed woke him, and he took a moment to rub his eyes before answering. It was Louis, his partner on the graveyard shift. Dinaé knew Louis didn't like working alone, but Dinaé was the commander, and if he chose not to show up for work once in a while, no questions were asked.

Louis had received something important and was not one for false alarms, so Dinaé was out the door a moment later. The predawn ocean wind was frigid, so the walk across the compound proved bracing, and he was slapping his arms trying to keep warm by the time he entered the lighthouse. When he walked into the basement, Louis said nothing but handed him a stack of papers. He knew the commander had been very curious about the CIA activity on the eastern seaboard, and now it looked like they might finally have some answers.

Dinaé looked through the pages, a collection of Photostats of official CIA documents and handwritten notes. His English was a little rusty, but not bad.

"So, it is a manhunt. The man's name is Lee Teller. Let's see . . . Hanover . . . Tampa . . . Arizona . . . Seattle . . . he seems to be leading them a merry chase."

Louis raised an eyebrow. "I don't think they say that anymore."

"Merry chase? Ah. No matter. Look at the name on this file. You can just make it out. 'Theft of Fire.' What do you think it means?"

Louis smiled slightly. "Who cares? Let the stuffed shirts at headquarters figure it out."

"I don't think they say that anymore."

Louis said, "Stuffed shirts?" and broke into a grin, and Dinaé set about preparing the Photostats for transmittal to headquarters.

Chapter Four

As the university campus gradually showed signs of awakening, a municipal garbage truck rolled slowly down the street, the driver oblivious to the fact that one of the cars parked across from the science building contained two occupants. Inside a white Escort, while Lee Teller dozed in the passenger seat, Nels Thiessan sat behind the wheel watching the front doors intently. Though he would have been embarrassed to admit it, Nels was enjoying himself thoroughly. It was like the old days, on the run, risking his life for a worthy cause, with no one at home to worry about . . .

Nels closed his eyes as the bittersweet memory of his wife came to mind. The pain of loss had faded to a dull ache, but he knew that indulging the memories would only leave him depressed. He shrugged off the thoughts, as was his custom, and focused instead on the business at hand.

With a working model of the fusion device, the problem would then become choosing the proper audience for a demonstration. He could try to get it on a national news program, but assuming he could even convince the producer it was legitimate, the government could exert pressure far beyond the confines of the Constitution. The next day, the reporter would recant, be fired, and the matter would be closed. An open session of Congress might be better, but Washington, D.C., was a long drive, and they didn't dare trust the airports. Besides, what kind of fool would entrust his life to a politician?

Nels's train of thought was interrupted by the sight of a familiar figure walking across the short plaza in front of the science building. He scrambled out of the car and started across the street.

"Dr. Melrose!"

The figure stopped and turned, recognition gradually taking hold. "Nels? Nels! Of all the people I didn't expect to see. How are you?"

"As well as can be expected under the circumstances. Forgive my abruptness, Simon, but we need to discuss a matter of some urgency." Lee stumbled up onto the plaza, holding the satchel, and Nels turned to include him in the conversation. "This is my associate, Professor Lee Teller from Dartmouth. Can we speak privately in your office?"

"Of course. Come with me."

Twenty minutes later, Dr. Melrose ordered his secretary to cancel all of his classes for the rest of the day.

SPECIAL PROJECTS OFFICE, CIA HEADQUARTERS, LANGLEY, VIRGINIA
SEPTEMBER 20, 7:11 A.M.

Fresh from another torturous meeting with the Joint Chiefs, Carter Ellis stormed into Bill Sidwell's office, spluttering threats and expletives.

"I'm sick of getting chewed out over this!" he shouted by way of greeting. "Tell me you lost him, Bill! Tell me the trail's cold! Tell me you don't have a lead. Just give me a reason to kick your worthless backside out of here! I swear, by the time I'm finished with you, you'll wish you never took the job!"

Too late, Sidwell thought. To his credit, however, his expression never changed, and when he spoke, his voice was steady. "Why don't you sit down, Mr. Ellis?"

Ellis found Sidwell's demeanor infuriating. He was spoiling for a fight, but yelling at Bill Sidwell would be like whipping an obedient dog. He would sit there and take it, and Ellis would feel worse when it was over. Ellis wiped the sweat from his brow and sat down across from his special projects director.

"Sorry about that. The JCS is making me crazy. What's the latest?"

"Tyler is at Thiessan's house in Seattle. The place was abandoned in a big hurry, so he probably went willingly." Ellis swore under his breath, and Sidwell continued, "We ran his plates and got lucky. His car turned up in Medford, Oregon. The owner sold Thiessan a white Escort early yesterday morning. We put out an APB on the new vehicle."

"Any idea where they're going?"

"South or south-central, probably. I doubt they would double back at this point. We're working on a possible contact list."

Ellis nodded. "I read Thiessan's sanitized resume. What's the rest of it?"

"He was deep cover for about five years, late '50s, early '60s, mostly South America and Europe. We were going to need someone to feed the labs, and he fit the job description, so he was groomed for the position at Dartmouth. He's had a long, distinguished career."

"Yeah." Ellis sighed and looked out the window. "And now we have to kill him."

DGSE TRAINING GROUND, WEST COAST, GREENLAND SEPTEMBER 20, 3:36 P.M.

The afternoon was cool and clear, and Dinaé was the only one scheduled on the shooting range for the rest of the day. He was hoping to bring up his marks in the prone position, but the scoring official was inscrutable as always. Something was in the air today; he felt different. Maybe it was the change of seasons or biorhythms or the configuration of the planets, but when he squeezed off eight rounds in rapid succession, all hitting the center chest area of the target, he wasn't surprised. Exhilarated, but not surprised. The scoring official only nodded slightly and made some marks on his clipboard.

"Monsieur le Commandant!"

Dinaé turned. It was the mousy little fellow from the reception area, whose name he could never remember. "Oui?"

"Retournez à votre poste immédiatement! C'est la priorité majeure!"

Dinaé ran for his jeep, wondering what kind of international emergency could have precipitated such an urgent recall to his post. The drive was forty minutes, and waiting that long for an answer did nothing to dampen his curiosity. As he drove into the compound, the first thing he noticed was the blue minivan parked in front of the lighthouse. In the old days, it would have been two black BMW sedans. Somehow, the impact wasn't the same. But why would headquarters send a team unannounced? Not another spot inspection, he hoped. It had taken two days to get back into routine following the last one.

On the ground floor of the lighthouse, gathered in the office area, four men—one in a business suit, the others in casual clothes—stood waiting. The man in the suit extended a hand, Dinaé shook it, and without introduction, the man addressed him in perfect English.

"Commander, I have orders for you from headquarters, authorization code delta-three-one-cee-three-one-one-seven. Based on the Photostats you sent, we have reason to believe that someone has stolen a highly sensitive CIA file. We have monitored an increase in CIA activity on the West Coast of the United States. Your team will fly out there immediately and attempt to identify the thief and intercept. You will be posing as an American racquetball team from a private club in California, which means that as of this moment, you will speak only English. Any questions?"

Dinaé was silent for a moment, a bit taken aback by the suddenness of the new assignment. "I was not aware we were at war with the United States."

"If they are not able to control this situation, we might be. We are just going to offer a little unsolicited assistance. You know how their budget has been cut under the current administration."

"If the CIA is having no luck finding this man, what makes you think we will do any better?"

"We are French." The man smiled as he said it, but one look in the eyes told Dinaé his entire career was suddenly on the line, and he felt a flash of the old rebelliousness. The emotion never reached his face, however, and the man in the suit continued, "Your bag is already packed and loaded on the van. If you leave now, you will just have time to catch your plane."

Dinaé led the three casually dressed men to the minivan, and he was about to climb in the passenger side when he noticed the man in the suit was not with them. He turned and saw the man standing in the doorway.

"You're not coming with us?"

The man in the suit smiled a bit condescendingly. "Who knows when you'll be coming back? Someone has to mind the store while you're gone."

SECURE LABORATORY, STANFORD UNIVERSITY, STANFORD, CALIFORNIA
SEPTEMBER 20, 11:20 P.M.

The base material for the generator described in the file was ceramic, so the first order of the day had been getting a kiln set up in the lab. Using the description of the process as written in the file, they spent most of the day pulverizing and mixing elements, then firing them in the kiln. The ceramic plates were still cooling when Nels began paging through the document again. He found some papers stuffed into the plastic inside pocket of the back cover.

"Lee, these look like pages from someone's journal. Maybe Miles's."

Lee had been working on the regulator assembly at his workbench long enough. He needed a break. "Give me some of the highlights."

Nels leaned against a table and started reading:

August 18—. . . still searching for a way to facilitate the flow of electrons . . . Alan suggested superconductivity, especially high-temperature superconductivity . . . has a friend of a friend (Horace Larsen) who had an interesting theory at a time when the phenomenon wasn't generally understood by the scientific community . . . says he never developed any mechanism to test his theory (no money) . . . no grants . . . he gave it up and took a job with a chemical company . . . Alan is going to try to find Larsen, while I begin looking into superconductivity issues . . .

August 23—I have largely ignored the niobium/titanium, niobium/tin options, as those have been rigorously tested previously . . . trying to raise the temperature, had some Josephson effects $(f=2eV/h)$ . . . need to explore combinations using thallium, barium, calcium, copper, oxygen . . .

August 24—High-temperature superconductivity may be a dead end . . . unable to break the 125K temperature barrier . . . have started swapping out elements with no success . . .

August 25—Horace Larsen has been located! . . . West Coast . . . a package arrived today containing some of his research and pages from his log book . . . of particular note: "February 4, 1992—. . . encountered an anomalous, electrochemical reaction to seawater . . .

unable to reproduce the reaction . . . working with Composite Material B2 . . . Composite Material B1 shows no sign of developing superconductivity, at any temperature . . . still adjusting the ceramic matrix . . . something about Composite Material B2 in this matrix created porosity in the ceramic (like pumice, but finer)" . . . Larsen may have been close to a breakthrough . . . ran out of money . . . the table of Composite Materials tested is quite extensive . . . refer to page 3 for mixture B2 . . . developing plan to modify Larsen's B2 mixture . . . Alan has analyzed Larsen's equations . . . believes a chemical process (instead of cryogenic), which creates a superconductor, may be the key to the fusion question . . .

August 27— . . . woke up with a revelation! . . . reintroduction of thallium into the modified B2 matrix . . . (later) All tests negative . . . investigating Larsen's anomalous reaction with seawater . . . saline tests negative . . . awaiting arrival of a 50-gallon drum of seawater for testing.

August 30— . . . test sample of the modified B2/thallium matrix seems to have built up a small electrical charge in seawater . . . minuscule particles of palladium in the seawater may be acting as a catalyst . . . drying the sample appears to stop the reaction . . . firing larger samples in the kiln . . .

August 31— . . . larger sample (3″ x 2″ x 1″) exhibits a proportionally larger electrical current . . . too hot to handle . . . increased sample size by a factor of 2 . . . the seawater is boiling! . . . attached wires, voltage regulator, and DC/AC converter . . . the electric motor for the grinder is running flawlessly off the power from the sample . . . (later) Calculations indicate the quantity of energy produced from each unit of seawater approaches the absolute maximum energy available from that water if it had been consumed in a fusion reaction! . . . it is too early to dare hope we have been successful . . .

September 2—Experimenting with uniform, square plate samples . . . we have established a direct correlation between size of sample and energy output . . . Alan thinks we've done it . . . I am not so sure . . . a sample 4″ x 4″ x 0.5″ generates enough electricity to light the laboratory for 30 days, assuming the output remains constant . . . two plates could double the electrical output . . . a container large enough to accommodate 6 plates and a quart of water should generate enough current to operate a 300 horsepower electric motor under full load continuously for 18 to 24 hours . . . in much less space than an internal combustion engine, generate enough electricity to give electric automobiles more range and higher power and performance than any gasoline or diesel engine. The car makers are going to have a fit! . . . (later) Our celebration is tempered by the announcement that Horace Larsen has been killed in an auto accident . . .

September 7— . . . still unable to prove this is a genuine cold fusion reaction . . . maybe it doesn't matter . . . the results are the same . . . Alan wants to take it to the president . . . I recommended caution . . .

September 13—Alan is dead! . . . another "auto accident" . . . I asked Daphne to do a trace on his document history . . .

Nels stopped reading and noticed Lee was back to work. "Lee, are you listening?"

Lee completed a few connections. "Yes, yes. Very compelling." He locked down a couple of screws and held the device out for Melrose's inspection. "What do you think?"

"That's it?"

Dr. Simon Melrose eyed the regulator assembly suspiciously. It had taken only three hours for Lee to put it together, and the finished unit looked, well, primitive. Scattered across the work tables was an assortment of tools, cables, empty packages, and various debris. The two physicists had done most of the work, with Nels pitching in as needed.

The design was almost unbelievably simple. A single ceramic plate sat suspended inside a watertight case, attached via wires to a regulator, then a DC/AC converter, and finally a standard power outlet. Assembled, the whole device fit into a box about half the size of a car battery.

Dr. Melrose soldered the regulator into place, then the DC/AC converter, and connected wires from the converter to the power outlet. "Your assertion that this could be made with parts from a hardware store—while essentially correct—is misleading. You'd need to know exactly where to look for some of these parts and tools to adapt them."

"Not necessarily," Lee countered. "The key element is the B2/thallium mixture and the composition of the ceramic matrix. Once you have that, the variations are nearly limitless."

Dr. Melrose nodded. "Hmm. Hand me the seawater."

Lee took a large beaker full of plain seawater—taken with permission from the aquatic section of the biology lab—and handed it to Melrose.

Nels marveled at what he was witnessing and spoke to no one in particular, "I used to play in it as a child. Now we're using it to power a reactor."

Dr. Melrose uncapped a hole in the top of the watertight container and paused. "The reaction should begin immediately. It's awfully close to perpetual motion, isn't it?"

Lee agreed. "Too bad the product of the reaction isn't seawater. Then the process really would be self-perpetuating."

Nels moved around the table to get a better angle on the device. "Could this be used to make a bomb?"

"That's the beauty of it," Melrose replied. "The energy conversion coefficient of the chemical process is perfect for producing electricity, but if it really is fusion, it is nonsustaining. The reaction is too con-trolled to provide any explosive energy at all."

Melrose held the beaker over the opening. "Well, gentlemen, here goes nothing." He poured the water into the opening and closed up the hole. With the opening covered, the only visible features were two grounded power outlets. There was a faint gurgling sound, like that of a small coffee maker. "Bring me the lamp."

Lee grabbed a table lamp off a nearby workbench and plugged it into the device. Melrose turned the switch on the lamp to the on position, and the light came on. All three men stepped back and stared with awe. "Incredible . . . ," Lee intoned in a voice of near childlike wonder.

"Built by our own hands in a single day," Melrose added sotto voce. "Having done it once, we could build another in half the time."

Nels stepped forward and unplugged the lamp. "Simon, this is going to be very hard for you. No one is supposed to know about this. You must tell no one. The government is trying to archive the process before anyone finds out about it. Lee and I are trying to come up with a plan to release the technology safely."

Melrose's face clouded. "Safely?"

"Think about all the energy-related industries that would be affected by such a device, and the far-reaching implications for economies around the world."

"Oh. I hadn't really thought about it." Melrose shook his head, dismissing the thought. "Well, let me come with you. Maybe I can help . . ."

"There are people after us, Simon. You would be in great danger."

"I don't care! Don't do this to me, Nels. Don't show me the brass ring and then snatch it away."

"I'm not snatching it away, Simon. Hold on to your life here, and watch the news. Once this goes public, we will probably need your help, and the help of many others like you."

Lee picked up the device, and Nels followed him to the door, turning to face his old acquaintance one last time from the doorway. "Thank you for all your help, Simon. We'll be in touch."

Melrose watched the door for a long time after they were gone. *We'll be in touch. I wish I could believe that, Nels.* Ignoring a strong desire to lie down and rest, Melrose sat down at the work table and reached for his tools.

RIDGEWOOD MOTEL, STANFORD, CALIFORNIA SEPTEMBER 21, 7:25 A.M.

The harsh buzz of a clock radio pulled Lee out of a deep sleep, and he reached to the far side of the night table between the beds, slapped the off switch, and gave the clock an irritated, puffy-eyed look.

"Why 7:25, Nels? Why not 7:30, or 7:45? Or maybe even 9:45?"

"It gives me five minutes to get used to the idea of being awake," Nels growled from his pillow, sounding uncharacteristically peevish.

Lee swung his legs out of bed and stood up, glancing sidelong at himself in the mirror. Unshaven, unwashed, and not very well rested, he was a sorry sight. Not wishing to be alone with his thoughts at the moment, he turned on the television and headed for the shower. Ten minutes later, still dripping, wearing a towel, and halfway through shaving, he thought he heard a familiar name on the television, but shrugged it off as coincidence.

"Lee!" Nels said sharply.

Lee nearly cut himself with the razor, and he hurried out of the bathroom. The face on the screen was very familiar indeed. Dr. Simon Melrose. "As you know, humankind has long been trying to harness the energy of the sun . . ."

Nels looked at his watch and muttered under his breath. "Get to the point, you idiot. You've got a few minutes at best."

But Dr. Simon Melrose was not about to be rushed through his one moment of glory. He spent a full ten minutes describing the history and physicality of nuclear fusion before getting to the subject of the press conference. Proudly holding up a black box identical to the one they built yesterday, he gestured grandly. ". . . and this little device . . ."

Before he could finish his sentence, men in suits and sunglasses poured onto the set seemingly from all directions. One of them reached for the lens, the image jerked wildly, and the camera went to static.

Nels shook his head. "Poor fool. We have to get out of here. Now."

Lee toweled the shaving cream off his face, then both men dressed, packed, and made a dash for the car. They left the television on, and had they been still in the room, they would have noticed with interest the special bulletin that replaced the "Please Stand By" message. The announcer mentioned two escaped convicts, considered armed and dangerous, then up came a pair of unflattering pictures of Nels and Lee with "Wanted for Murder" across Lee's chest.

In the manager's apartment, as the sole occupant shuffled to the breakfast table in his underwear, he stopped and stared incredulously at the television, and the coffee mug slowly slipped from his fingers and shattered on the tile floor.

Out in the parking lot, Nels stopped with his hand on the car door handle. "They'll be looking for this. We better leave it."

"Leave it? What are we going to do, walk out of town?"

"Here's $2,500. Get to Highway 82. I'll meet you at the first exit south of town."

Nels handed Lee a stack of bills and headed off down the sidewalk at a brisk pace. Lee watched him go in consternation, then looked back at the car. The temptation to get behind the wheel was enormous, but if Nels would rather walk than drive, that would have to be good enough for him.

Holding satchel and overnight bag, he started down the block in search of a pay phone. Three blocks down was a gas station with a phone booth, which turned out to have a complete phone book, so looking up the number of a cab company was no problem. When he called the number, the receptionist put him on hold. While he waited, he leaned against the metal shelf and watched the motel.

To his astonishment, three police cars swerved onto the street from different directions, lights flashing, but no sirens, and screeched to a stop in the motel parking lot. Guns drawn, the officers were met by the manager, had a curt conversation, and ran toward the room Lee and Nels had just vacated.

When the receptionist came back on the line, Lee was barely able to speak. "Um . . . yeah . . . uh . . . I need a taxi. I'm at the gas station on the corner of . . . uh . . . Elm and Pacific."

"That'll be about ten minutes."

"Fine!" Lee slammed the phone down and hurried across the driveway to the gas station office. Sitting down behind a stack of quart-size oil cans, he smiled sheepishly at the cashier. "I'm waiting for a taxi. Do you mind?"

The cashier looked at him curiously. "Help yourself."

Lee sat nervously chewing his lip and eyeing his watch. Barely three minutes had gone by when a pair of shiny black shoes came through the front door attached to a policeman. The officer was about to address the cashier when he noticed Lee. Still holding the handles of both bags, Lee lurched to his feet, knocking over the stack of oil cans with his shoulder, and bolted out the side door. Trying to pursue, the officer stepped on one of the rolling cans and went sprawling. Cursing a blue streak, he picked his way back out the front door and ran up the street yelling for help from his fellow officers.

At a dead sprint through an alley behind the gas station, Lee emerged onto a peaceful suburban street, breathing hard. Two houses down on the right, it looked like there was someone home, and he ran for the porch. After taking a few moments to catch his breath and smooth his hair, he rang the doorbell.

The door was answered by a woman holding an infant with one hand and a cordless telephone with the other.

"Yes?"

"I'm sorry to bother you. I've got a meeting at 9:00. I didn't even have time to shave, and now my car's broken down. I was wondering if I could use your phone?"

The woman gave him a long, appraising look, said, "Angela, I'll have to call you back," and handed Lee the phone. Lee dialed directory assistance.

"What city, please?"

"I need a taxi sent to . . . ," he said and raised his eyebrows at the woman.

"It's 323 Birch Street."

". . . 323 Birch Street."

"Sir, this is directory assistance. If you need the number of a taxi company, I can . . ."

"Twenty minutes? I don't have twenty minutes!" Lee pushed the reset button and handed the phone back to its owner. He pulled two bills from his pocket. "Listen, ma'am. I've got $200 here, and I'd be happy to give it to you in exchange for a ride downtown."

The woman thought about it for a moment, then took the money. "That must be some important meeting." She opened the door wider, so he could come in, and Lee stepped thankfully into the relative obscurity of the front hall. "My life depends on it."

The woman nodded absently and yelled up the stairs, "Jason! Get your shoes, honey. We're going in the car."

Lee waited as patiently as he could, while the children were dressed and strapped into their car seats, and then they were off. *A station wagon with a mother and two kids*, Lee thought, *what a perfect cover.* Then he saw the police car headed down the street from the opposite direction. Mumbling something about needing new laces, he bent over and retied one of his shoes, only sitting up again after the vehicle was past.

The woman said nothing for the whole trip, and once they were downtown, he pointed out a four-story office building and asked her to stop. Lee climbed out, the car pulled away quickly, and he went inside in search of a bathroom to finish shaving and a phone book to arrange for transportation.

For his part, only minutes after separating from Lee, Nels found someone who looked like he could use the money and offered him $500 to take him to the first exit south of town. Looking like an old man in trouble worked to his favor, and soon they were southward bound in the man's pickup truck. Nels offered him an extra $100 to push the speed a little, and as a result, they passed the city limits before the police had finished setting up their roadblock.

OFFICE OF THE DIRECTOR, CIA HEADQUARTERS, LANGLEY, VIRGINIA
SEPTEMBER 21, 10:53 A.M.

An unusually confident Bill Sidwell walked down the hallway toward Carter Ellis's office. With a videotape in one hand, he strode past the secretary's desk, ignoring her protests, and walked boldly into the office. Ellis did not look pleased.

"I'm in a meeting here."

Sidwell held up the tape. "Cancel it."

Ellis looked apologetically at the fellow sitting across from him. "Sorry, Steve. We'll talk later."

The man got up and walked out, closing the door behind him. Sidwell inserted the tape into the player recessed in the bookcase, then turned on the TV monitor.

"This better be good, Bill. What is it?"

"A special report. Went out live on one of the major networks this morning from Stanford, California."

Sidwell had already seen the tape, and so, while Dr. Simon Melrose explained the principles of fusion power on the monitor, he watched Ellis with some relish as the director's face slowly drained of color and the mouth began to come open in horror. When the agents stormed the studio, Ellis gasped with relief and only then realized he had been holding his breath.

Regaining his composure, he glared at his special projects chief. "That was sadistic, Bill. I think you actually enjoyed showing me that. Well? Don't leave me hanging!"

"We've sealed off the city. The police got a tip on the white Escort and surrounded a motel on the south side of town. At least one of the fugitives fled the scene on foot."

Ellis clenched his fist and smiled for the first time in days. "We have 'em. What about Melrose?"

"He's in custody."

"Excellent. Hold him until we have the other two, then dispose of all three as cleanly and quietly as possible."

"Understood."

HIGHWAY 82,
STANFORD, CALIFORNIA
SEPTEMBER 21, 9:43 A.M.

Bumper-to-bumper traffic was the last thing Lee had expected, and the waiting was beginning to take a heavy toll on his nerves. Forward motion had been stop and go for almost half an hour, and when the cabdriver told him there was a police roadblock about three miles ahead, it did nothing to improve his emotional state. Lee paid the man twice what was on the meter for his trouble and climbed out of the cab.

Walking up the shoulder of the highway, he tried desperately to think of what to do. *What would Nels do? Nels is probably already at the meeting place,* Lee thought wryly. Making the rest of the trip on foot sounded awful, but it was beginning to seem like his only option. He was starting down the embankment, hoping to head cross-country, when he noticed a police helicopter patrolling the city limits about a mile away. The terrain between the highway and the nearest copse of trees was mostly open ground, and he doubted he would make it unobserved. Images of bloodhounds chasing him down in some fetid, muddy bog flooded his mind, and he recoiled at the thought. Better to be taken nice and tidy at a roadblock. But it would be far better not to be taken at all, so once again he would have to rely on the avarice of strangers.

Hiking back up to the shoulder, and continuing his stroll along the highway, Lee finally found what he was looking for—a newer model car with a woman behind the wheel, no passenger and, most important, an unlocked passenger door. Trying to comfort himself with the thought that if this didn't work, he could still make a break for it over open ground, Lee found the thought provided no comfort at all. Steeling his resolve, he pulled five bills out of his pocket, picked his way through the stopped cars, and let himself in the passenger side of the car.

"Hey! What do you think you're . . ."

Lee shouted her down. "Here's $500! I need a ride to the first exit outside of town."

"No foolin'? You'll give me $500? You got it."

Lee settled back in his seat, trying to look relaxed despite the pounding in his chest, and wondered if a heart attack might not be preferable to all this dashing about. If this were a normal day, he would be in class, calmly examining some of the finer points of physics and wondering where he would have his lunch. Hanover seemed about a million miles away.

"Car trouble?" the girl asked, shattering his reverie.

Lee snorted. "You don't know the half of it."

"I've been to your exit before. There's not much there. You meetin' somebody?"

"Yeah."

"Girlfriend?"

Why not? Lee thought. "Yeah."

"She works at the truck stop?"

Lee opened one eye and looked at his benefactor. "Are you always this nosy, or is it just me?"

"Oh, I'm sorry!" the girl replied, abashed. "It's just that I don't know anything about you, besides the fact that you're loaded, I mean, and it makes me kinda nervous, so I guess I'm sorta running off at the mouth. I'll just shut up and mind my own business."

You do that, Lee thought, returning to the business of trying to relax. His breathing grew deeper, the pounding in his chest subsided, and a mild case of post-crisis exhaustion set in. With traffic nearly at a standstill, he dozed off. When he awoke a while later, the roadblock was in sight. The officers were stopping each car, talking to the occupants, and searching the trunk and underside of every vehicle. Lee's heart started pounding again, and his mind raced.

"Miss? I may have a problem when we get to that roadblock up ahead. The truth is, the woman I'm meeting is leaving her abusive husband to be with me. He said he was going to report her kidnapped and sic the police on us. If the police catch us and return her to her husband, he'll kill her." *How incredibly lame!* Lee thought. *She'll never buy it.*

"Oooh, that's totally romantic. Are you going to run away together?"

Lee looked at the odd girl in the seat beside him as if she had just handed him a rubber chicken. "You're missing the point. I need you to pretend you're my girlfriend. The police are probably looking for a man on his own."

"Oh, yeah! I'd be happy to help you. This is the most romantic thing that's ever happened to me."

Lee had seen some vacuous students over the years, but nothing like this. "Thanks. I really appreciate it."

The time dragged on with painful slowness as first one car and then another passed through the roadblock, and by the time their car was next in line, Lee was feeling awful. His palms and upper lip were sweating, and it felt like his stomach was about to turn over. When the officer in charge saw the pretty girl behind the wheel, he smiled and walked around to the driver's side, and she put down the window.

"Sorry for the inconvenience, miss. This is just a formality."

"What's the trouble, officer?"

"We're looking for a dangerous fugitive. Escaped convict."

The girl turned toward Lee with a wide grin. "See? They're not even looking for you."

The officer looked past the girl, got a good look at Lee's face for the first time, and his smile froze. Time seemed to stand still for an instant, then the officer reached for his gun, and Lee made a desperate lunge for the wheel and stomped on the accelerator. The woman screamed as the car careened through the checkpoint, tires squealing, and fishtailed up the road. Policemen scrambled for their vehicles and laid multiple patches of rubber as they sped after the fleeing car.

Lee had almost a quarter-mile head start, but he had no illusions about his ability to stay in the lead. The girl was still screaming, but Lee was past noticing. He was finding it difficult to control the car, leaning as he was with his left foot jammed against the floor. A green road sign flashed past, marking an upcoming exit.

"Stop it! Stop it! You're going to burn up my engine!"

"Then shift!"

Lee let off the gas slightly, and the girl slammed the stick on the side of the steering column into overdrive, nearly breaking it off in the process. Over the whine of the engine, the sound of sirens could be heard from behind. Lee pushed the pedal back to the floor.

At the first exit, the car roared up the exit ramp, showing no signs of slowing. "What are you doing?" the girl yelled, but Lee didn't let up on the pedal. The car passed the stop sign at the top doing eighty, sailed over the road, and rocketed down the on ramp. Not far down the other side, a semitrailer was rolling slowly toward the highway. The girl still had a death grip on the steering wheel, so Lee yelled "Brake!" and held on for dear life. The woman reflexively stood on the brake with both feet, and Lee bounced off the steering wheel. Dazed, but flying on adrenaline, he grabbed the passenger door handle, screamed "Drive!" and plunged out the door as the car shot away, swerving onto the shoulder as it passed the truck.

The car only made it another quarter mile up the highway before the woman figured out she was speeding for no reason and pulled over, but by that time, Lee was nearly to the truck stop. As he crested the hill gasping for breath, more police cars, sirens blaring, flew under the overpass to join their comrades a short distance up the highway, and Lee knew it would be a matter of a minute or two before they doubled back to search the truck stop.

Satchel pressed against his side and swaying slightly, he was having trouble focusing. Then the world seemed to be moving, and he wondered if he was going to faint. No, the world wasn't moving. An eighteen-wheeler was bearing down on him! He lurched drunkenly to one side, and the truck stopped beside him.

"Get in!" a familiar voice said from the passenger side. Lee looked up. It was Nels. With some help from the older man, Lee climbed up into the cab, while the truck started down the on ramp, and then both men crawled back into the sleeping area. The space was tight and a bit smelly, but it beat the back of a police car, no contest.

"I was beginning to wonder if you were coming," Nels said to the shadow beside him.

"Me, too. How much is this little trip costing us?"

"Too much. I have about $3,000 left. Anybody get hurt back there? Besides you, I mean."

"I don't think so. Where are we going?"

"He's taking us as far as San Diego. From there, we're on our own."

Lee changed position a bit to try to relieve the pressure on some of his sore spots. The adrenaline rush was wearing off, and he could already tell he was in for some serious aches and pains. When he spoke, his speech was slurred.

"Do you have a plan yet?"

"I'm working on one. Your delay gave me some time to think."

"So glad I could help."

"I'm sure. We have to get out of the country. Most international ports, both air and sea, are probably covered, which means we have to go by land."

Lee's voice was sounding farther and farther away. "Which means Mexico."

"Actually, I think we should head for Central America. I know some people there. One of them may be able to help us. It will be much easier from a foreign port to book passage to Europe without being seen. From Europe, we have to get to the Middle East. I hope no one will be expecting that. But here's the really clever part. Our final destination in the Middle East is Israel. Want to know why Israel?"

There was no answer. Lee's breathing was heavy, and Nels smiled in the darkness, rolling over to see if sleep might overtake him as well, but one too many cups of coffee at the truck stop was going to make that impossible. Instead, he put his mind to work on the details of a plan that had at least a possibility of delivering them safely to their ultimate destination—New York City.

Chapter Five

The setting sun looked beautiful over the tarmac if one cared about that sort of thing, but Gerard Dinaé had little use for sunsets beyond the fact that they heralded the coming of night. He looked away from the window and took visual inventory of the men on his team. While still in Greenland, their flight had been delayed, which gave them ample time to rehearse their American identities, and Dinaé realized with an odd sense of irony that he would probably never know who these men really were.

The man on his right, possessed of a hatchet face and short brown hair, sat looking at the complimentary magazine. Jerome Sykes, age thirty-two, high school education, owns a small textile business in North Hollywood, wife, Susan, two sons, Mike and Brian. Dinaé's gaze traveled to the next seat to René, a handsome fellow with dark hair and sharp brown eyes, nursing a gin and tonic. René Stevens, age twenty-four, doesn't know what he wants to do with his life, spends a lot of time at Malibu Beach, got the racquetball membership as a gift from his estranged father, no attachments. On the far side of the aisle was the last man. Henry Moore, age thirty, owns several small car dealerships in Encino, lives in Pacific Palisades, divorced, wife is really soaking him for the alimony, gets to see his nine-year-old daughter, Patrice, one month out of the year.

Dinaé looked out the window once more. He had learned something during his brief association with the men. They were hard-bitten, well-trained operatives, consummate field agents who would fight and die at his command. On a very personal level, that fact pleased him more than was probably healthy. They were the kind of men he had wanted to be like when he signed up in the first place, and now all their training, unique skills, and abilities were under his control.

He was puzzled, though. Headquarters had never shown any inclination at all to assign him to anything except a filing cabinet. Their mission clearly had high priority, and there was no obvious reason to give it to an officer with his qualifications. Perhaps there was more to this than that smarmy—no, smarmy is British—oily creep from HQ let on in his mission summary. If there was a second purpose (one known only to one of the men, perhaps?), it could be very dangerous. It could also mean Dinaé was assigned because he was expendable. He would have to watch his back.

As the four French agents walked off the plane, carrying two bags each, they saw their first real challenge: United States customs. While one uniformed official went through their bags, another checked their passports.

"How was the tournament?" asked the second official, once he saw the reason for the trip.

Dinaé smiled ruefully. "We came in dead last."

The conversation ended, it looked as if they were going to be passed on through, but a third uniformed man came to the table. "Hold it." He reached into one of the athletic bags and pulled out a racquet.

"Whose is this?"

Jerome raised a hand. "Mine."

The official scrutinized the racquet for an excruciatingly long time, then looked Jerome in the eye. "This is pretty old. Why don't you get a new one?"

Jerome shrugged. "It's comfortable. Besides, I like the sweet spot."

Without another word, the man put the racquet back in the bag and signaled them through. As they started away from the table, one of the officers called after them, "Da svidaniya!"

It was a lame attempt, which might have fooled a very stupid Russian agent with the IQ of a croissant, and Dinaé wanted to laugh in his face. Before he could speak, however, René responded in a perfect surfer accent.

"Like, Happy New Year to you, too, dude."

Once they were out of earshot, Jerome relaxed a little. "What a jerk!"

"You know how those uniforms ride up with wear," René quipped.

All four men broke into laughter and immediately felt better for it. In front of the terminal they found a van labeled "Sunset Racquetball," and the driver stepped out to meet them.

"Welcome back, gentlemen. How was your trip?"

"Uneventful," Dinaé replied, and with proper verbal codes exchanged, they all piled on board. Dinaé noted the communications console at the rear before settling into his seat. As the van pulled away from the terminal, the driver's demeanor changed abruptly.

"The manhunt appears to be headed south. The fugitives may be headed for the border. No word of their capture as yet."

Dinaé frowned. "Well, we can't just chase them around the highways. Give me the phone."

The driver handed him a cellular phone, and he punched in a long series of numbers. After several rings, a woman's voice answered. "This is Polly."

"Hi, honey! I'm back."

"Oh, it's so good to hear your voice! How was your trip?"

"Fine. Listen, I need some more information on that Greek gentleman. You have my mobile modem number?"

Polly sounded numb. All pretense was gone from her voice. "No."

The driver took the phone and gave her the number, then handed the phone back to Dinaé. Polly spoke first.

"How soon do you need this information?"

"Immediately. The boss is most insistent. The board of directors looked at that report you sent, and they think it may be a lot more important than we thought."

"I understand."

"I'm sorry. I know this is hard for you. With a little luck, this will all be over in a few days and things will get back to normal."

"I hope so. I miss you."

"I miss you, too, dear. Good-bye."

With a grim expression Dinaé returned his phone to its perch. He had never even met the agent who went by the name Polly Sutton, but over the past few years she had been one of his best informants, and on some level he felt that he knew her. The way she said, "I miss you," it sounded as if she were really saying, "I wish I'd known you." Dinaé felt the same way. And now he had sent her on what might turn into a suicide mission.

CIA HEADQUARTERS, LANGLEY, VIRGINIA SEPTEMBER 21, 8:44 P.M.

Walking across the parking lot, Polly was thankful for the cool night air. A bad case of nerves was causing her to perspire, and she didn't want to look nervous. She told herself she would be out again in half an hour, and out of the country before anyone started looking for her.

Looking calm and collected, she walked through the front doors, handed her identification to the armed guard, and signed in. The guard checked her ID against her signature and handed the card back.

"If it weren't for the overtime, I'd quit this lousy job," Polly muttered as she fumbled with her purse.

The guard snorted. "Tell me about it."

Access to the top floor was restricted at night, but Polly had not been idle over the past months. Using wax impressions made in haste from duplicates of Ellis's office keys, on those rare days when she was called in to cover for Darlene, she now had a complete set of the director's keys. She stepped onto the elevator, waited for the doors to close, inserted a key in the activation lock for the top floor, and hesitated. If she left now, no one would ever know the difference. She could say she just wasn't able to get in, but having given in to fear, she would lose her edge, and her superiors across the Atlantic would have her reassigned to some outpost in the Ukraine.

Wiping sweat from her brow, she turned the key, and the elevator started upward. The doors opened on the top floor, and she started toward Ellis's office. Darlene was at her desk, which meant Ellis was working late. Polly had mentally prepared for the possibility and quickened her pace slightly, slipping her hand inside her purse and wrapping her fingers around a small plastic canister. Darlene looked up and frowned.

"What are you doing here?"

"Mr. Ellis asked me to come in."

"Well, he sure didn't tell me about it."

Polly pulled the canister from her purse, extended it, and pressed the button all in one smooth motion. The spray caught Darlene full in the face, and she tumbled out of her chair without a sound. The carpet cushioned the fall, which meant Darlene would awake in about six hours with only a nasty headache as a result of her ordeal. Polly stowed the canister and knocked on the door to Ellis's office, ready to give him the same treatment. To her surprise, there was no answer, so she unlocked the door and dragged Darlene inside.

With the door closed and locked, Polly dragged the body behind the desk so it would not be visible from the doorway and moved to the computer on the small table beside the desk. The external disk drive was bolted shut and there was no phone connection on the back of the computer, but Polly had honed some valuable skills at agency expense over the past several years. Putting the monitor to one side, she popped the top off the central processing unit and inserted a modem card into one of the available slots. After fifteen frustrating minutes fiddling with the AUTOEXEC.BAT and CONFIG.SYS files, she got a dial tone and dialed out using a simple communications program she brought along. Using a regular phone jack to dial out, she bypassed the normal security on the network data switch altogether.

Establishing a link with the cellular modem on Dinaé's van then became a simple matter of keying in "ATDT" and the phone number. The message "CONNECTED 9600" appeared on the screen, and she began sending data over the phone line. She had sent two entire directories of files and was starting on a third when the doorknob rattled and there was a jingling of keys outside. The sight of Polly behind his desk might be confusing at first—as Ellis tried to recall asking her to work late—but his hesitation would buy her only a few seconds at best. She grabbed the phone cables and yanked them out of the wall, severing the connection and sending several items from the desk clattering to the carpet. Polly hurried around the desk as Ellis frantically jerked the door open to see who was in his office. Polly came toward him, and he recognized her and paused. She thrust the canister toward his face and pulled the trigger. Ellis exhaled, turned, and covered his face, but even a partial hit from the gas was enough to send him reeling to the floor.

Polly broke and ran for the elevators, while Ellis writhed on the carpet, trying to clear his head enough to stand. Out of breath, a terrified Polly fumbled for her keys and finally pushed the right one in the activation lock. The elevator started down. In the shiny metal of the door she could see she was rumpled, so she hastily tidied her hair, fixed her blouse, and smoothed her skirt. Presentable once more, she walked purposefully toward the exit. The guard saw her coming.

"Leaving so soon?"

"Could you sign me out? I was looking at the wrong week in my schedule book, and I'm late for choir practice."

"Sure thing."

Polly hurried out the door and disappeared into the night. The guard had just finished signing the woman out when his phone rang.

"Front desk."

A sound of choking came over the line. "Hehhh . . . hehhh . . ."

"Who is this?"

The voice tried to swear, gagged and choked, and then a hoarse whisper. "This is . . . ," the voice collapsed once more in a fit of coughing, ". . . Ellis. Stop the woman!"

"Her car has already left the parking lot, sir."

Still rasping and sore, Ellis put out an APB and dispatched a team immediately to sweep Polly's apartment. Mobile units from the agency and the police department searched the streets, but there was no sign of anyone matching her description. When the sweeper team finished with the apartment, they came up with nothing, not even clothing fibers.

Shortly before midnight, Ellis got a printed report detailing the efforts of the agents and officers involved in the search and their utter failure to find anything useful. No, that wasn't entirely true. The phone logs showed a call from his office to a cellular phone in Los Angeles, but the number was pirated and unless another call was made to or from the same number, they had no way to triangulate on the phone's location.

The condition of the apartment was the most disturbing item in the report. Only an agent would leave the apartment like that and make such a clean getaway, which left him with two equally loathsome alternatives, internal espionage or foreign intelligence. The idea of treason made his skin crawl, but even with the stark evidence in his hands, he would be some time believing Polly was a foreign agent.

One thing was certain. Hank Joram was not going to be pleased.

GRANGE SPORTS CENTER, SAN DIEGO, CALIFORNIA SEPTEMBER 22, 8:30 A.M.

Nels walked with purpose, as always, up one aisle and down another, depositing items in his shopping cart. By the time he found Lee, the cart contained two wet suits, gloves, backpacks, trail mix, bandages, assorted first aid supplies, hats, sun block, hiking boots, a camouflage 'arp, duct tape, and about ten quart-size plastic bottles of water. As he approached, Lee was examining a fishing rod with such a wistful expression, Nels put a comforting hand on his shoulder.

"Wondering if you'll ever fish again?"

Lee sighed. "Actually, I haven't been fishing since I was a child. Life was so much simpler then."

Nels nodded sympathetically. The entire situation had been difficult for Lee, and it was only going to get worse. He paid for all the gear and wheeled it outside, and they divided it more or less evenly between the two backpacks.

"What's all the gear for?" Lee wanted to know.

Nels held a finger to his lips and waited to answer until they were alone in front of the store. "They probably have the border locked down pretty tight by now. We have to cross over on foot."

"That sounds like a lot of walking."

"I hope only twenty or thirty miles. In the outlying areas around Tijuana, there are a fair number of migrant farm workers. I'm hoping to buy some cheap transportation."

"Wait a second. We're going to be hiking through some of the most arid land on the continent, each with about forty pounds on his back. What do we need wet suits for?"

"We'll be traveling only at night. The border patrols will be using both night vision and infrared optics. The neoprene in the wet suits will hide our heat signatures. But you'll go through all five quarts of water in about six hours."

Now Lee understood why Nels had insisted on a large breakfast before they left the hotel that morning. Being inconspicuous on a city street holding a backpack was proving to be a problem, but Nels called a cab and they didn't have to wait long. The trip down the interstate passed quickly, perhaps a little too quickly for Lee, who sat silently brooding over the prospect of a death march through the desert.

At Nels's direction, the cab headed east on Highway 905, toward the San Ysidro Mountains. After a few miles, the highway turned southeast, but Nels ordered the driver to take a dirt road heading almost due east. The last sign Lee saw said, OTAY MESA ROAD, and he realized he was utterly lost. And what was worse, anytime now they were going to be going on foot. As if in response, Nels asked the driver to stop, and they got out. Lee's heart sank as the cab disappeared back the way they came. Without a word, they put on their packs and started south. Two miles and about twenty-four minutes from the highway, Nels found a shallow depression on the east side of a tiny hillock twelve feet across. After checking the area for poisonous snakes and insects, he pulled out the camouflage tarp and secured one end with two rocks. With a little guidance from Nels, they lay down in the depression and pulled the tarp over themselves and their gear. Lee felt stir crazy almost immediately and turned to face Nels.

"Why can't we travel during the day?"

"On a day like today, you're visible for almost five miles from the air. By the time you hear the engines, it's too late."

They spent all day in the lee of the hillock and only once heard the engines of passing aircraft. Beyond that, and a repast of trail mix and water, the day proceeded in a most leisurely fashion, and Lee managed to fall into a fitful sleep after lunch, only to awake suddenly when Nels started putting the tarp away at sundown. Stripped to their underwear, they put on the wet suits and hiking boots, duct taped the gloves to the wrists, and the ankles to the boots. They hadn't taken a step and Lee was already sweating. With packs on they headed south, and Lee thought in passing if he was going to get caught, he hoped it wouldn't be like this—slogging across the desert in a wet suit.

By the time the light from sunset had dwindled to nothing, a waxing moon had taken its place in the sky, lighting the terrain ahead just enough to avoid obstacles. They trudged on into the night, gradually becoming mesmerized by the cadence of their own steps, one stride merging into another, the only sounds the steady breathing and the grit of sand and pebbles beneath their boots.

EXIT 221, HIGHWAY 82, NEAR STANFORD, CALIFORNIA SEPTEMBER 22, 10:38 P.M.

The borrowed CIA van in the restaurant parking lot had been in the same spot for the last eighteen hours. Tyler's team finished their sweep of the building almost three hours earlier and were now awaiting some word from the search teams combing the surrounding area.

Tyler stepped out of the restaurant by herself and stood for a moment watching the dozens of flashlights dotting the moonlit countryside. Somewhere a bloodhound howled, and she looked sharply in that direction, but there was no answering howl, no sounds of a chase, no gunshots. The night air was at the bottom end of her comfort zone, so she decided it was time to make that phone call she had been dreading. Chip Nicholson had always been a reasonable boss, and she hated bringing him bad news.

"Chip, it's Tyler."

"Please tell me you have them in custody."

"Sorry. We have thirty search teams out there right now. Night vision, bloodhounds, the works. If they were still in the area, we'd have them by now."

Nicholson groaned. "Ellis is going to have a stroke. Any idea where they went?"

"South or east. They could be in New Mexico by now. Wally's got the station's gas receipts for the day, and he's trying to chase down the people who were here when Teller pulled his little stunt. You know, for an average citizen, he's one greasy little pig. After the trail he left to Tampa, I figured bringing him in would be a walk in the park."

"Yeah, me, too. Listen, since you brought it up . . . I've been holding off on . . . I know how you feel about . . ."

"Spit it out, Chip. I can take it."

"I've got a change in your orders, Tyler. Ellis and Sidwell don't want them brought in. When you find them, you will terminate them with extreme prejudice."

"Chip, that's crazy! They're a couple of college professors!"

"They crossed the line, Tyler. They've got something no one was supposed to see."

"What is it? Why can't you tell me?"

"Because then I'd have to kill you."

Tyler laughed nervously. It had to be a joke, but there was a deadly seriousness to Nicholson's voice. *This stinks*, Tyler thought. *This really stinks.* "Well, I'll have to catch them first."

"I know. Good luck, and I'm sorry."

Tyler terminated the connection and walked back inside with a dangerous look on her face. Nash read her emotional state immediately and held up a hand to stop the conversation, and Tyler spoke brusquely. "Time to move out. When we get to the van, please arm yourselves. Our orders have changed. Bringing them in is no longer the objective."

Nash looked surprised. "I thought these guys were civilians."

"They are. No one's immune, right?"

After telling the local officer in charge of the search to call it off and send everyone home, Tyler joined her team at the van. While the others waited patiently for her to give the order to move out, she sat in the passenger seat, brooding.

"Bringing them in was never the objective, was it?" Nash asked quietly.

"I don't think so. If you were Nels Thiessan, which direction would you go from here?"

Nash blurted out the first thing that came to mind. "South."

"Why?"

"Dr. Melrose turned the heat way up with his press conference, and now my face is plastered all over the news. I'd want to get out of the country, and south is the quickest way to do it."

Tyler sighed, already weary of the chase. "San Francisco, here we come."

"Actually, you mean San Diego. San Francisco is north of here."

Tyler glared at her friend. "Just drive south, you insubordinate little hack."

Laughter rippled through the van, and Nash headed for the freeway entrance.

OFFICE OF THE DIRECTOR, CIA HEADQUARTERS, LANGLEY, VIRGINIA
SEPTEMBER 23, 1:27 A.M.

"Sorry to bring you in like this."

Bill Sidwell nodded to his boss and waved a hand, indicating he knew it came with the job. He pulled out a notepad to help him focus and took detailed notes while Ellis filled him in on the evening's events.

"So," Ellis finished, "as you can see, it is now more important than ever that we apprehend the fugitives."

Ellis looked like he was on the verge of losing it, and Bill Sidwell cleared his throat nervously. "Tyler thinks they may be headed south.

As I told you in my report, Thiessan has five possible contacts in Argentina and one in Belize City."

"The Interpol agent. Right. Do we have an office in Belize?"

"The Belize office was closed last year due to budget cuts. Our nearest office is in Panama, but they are heavily dedicated to a covert project. We can't pull them off."

"That's your call. Get an alert to every argent . . . every *agent* in Argentina, and send Tyler's team to Belize City."

SOUTH OF HIGHWAY 905, SAN YSIDRO MOUNTAINS, CALIFORNIA SEPTEMBER 23, 2:11 A.M.

Lee had never sweat so much in his life. They stopped every other hour to drink a quart of water, and the perspiration was collecting in the legs of their wet suits, sloshing with every step. Nels had bought them loose on purpose, so they wouldn't have any problems with skin suffocation, but the loose fit was creating some very raw places in the soft skin between their thighs.

Lee was loath to break the rhythm of his breathing, but the combination of the pain and the sloshing was driving him crazy.

"Can we stop?"

Nels never broke stride. "Why?"

"Apply . . . bandages . . . dry out . . . suit . . ."

"Bandages . . . later . . . we may . . . have to . . . drink it . . ."

The thought of drinking his own perspiration made Lee feel a little ill, but he didn't have long to think about it. Nels grabbed him and pulled him facedown on the ground. Only as his breathing subsided did he hear the engines of the approaching aircraft. Nels must have seen the running lights.

Keeping his arms over his head as Nels had instructed, he breathed in and out slowly, hoping the heat from his breath would dissipate before it seeped out into the night air. The noise from the engines grew steadily louder, and then softer, as they receded into the distance. All was quiet for several minutes before Nels finally tapped his companion on the arm, and the two men resumed their march.

FORTY-SIX MILES NORTH OF LOS ANGELES, CALIFORNIA SEPTEMBER 23, 2:56 A.M.

Tyler had been sound asleep for forty minutes when she was awakened suddenly by the disjointed chatter of a printer at the rear of the van. Wally tore a sheet off and flipped on an overhead light.

"We've got a change in orders. Authorization code one-one-alpha-two-baker. 'Proceed to warehouse district, Belize City, Belize. Stake out Gulf Shipping Company, corner of Ciudad and Mataron Streets. Fugitives may try to contact Interpol Agent Ilya Stehn, proprietess.'"

Tyler exhaled in frustration. "Where's the nearest airport?"

"Bakersfield, I think," Nash replied.

"Turn it around."

There was no traffic in either direction for as far as the eye could see, so Nash made a U-turn across the median and started back north. Tyler peered at Nash, trying to assess his condition. Policy demanded a change of drivers every two hours, but they had never done this much driving, so she pretty much let people gauge themselves.

"You want me to take over for a while?"

Nash shook his head. "No, I'm fine."

But Nash was not fine. The caffeine and sugar high from his coffee and apple pie at the restaurant had worn off quite a while ago, and for the past twenty minutes, he had been really fighting to stay awake. He willed his eyes to stay open . . . told himself it was ridiculous . . . just mind over matter . . . only a few miles . . . his eyelids were not that heavy . . . but no matter how he tried, his eyes kept closing. He fought it off as long as he could, too proud to ask for help, and twelve miles south of Bakersfield, he dozed off.

The van swerved onto the shoulder. Tyler yelled, "Nash!" but it was too late. The van careened off the shoulder, teetered on two wheels for a moment, then rolled, once, twice, and came to rest in an upright position. As the dust settled around the battered vehicle, Tyler found her voice again.

"Is everyone okay? Nash?"

"Sore neck, but I think I'll be all right. Sorry about that."

"Wally?"

"I whacked my elbow, but I don't think anything's broken."

"Kyle?"

"All body parts present and accounted for. Ow. I think I jammed my wrist."

"Rick?"

No answer.

"Rick? Wally, can you see Rick?"

There was movement in the shadows in the back of the van, and Tyler held her breath waiting for an answer.

"He's on the floor. I don't think he was wearing a seat belt. Oh! He's bleeding."

They stabilized Rick as best they could using the first aid kit, but only the fact that the radio was still working saved his life. When the ambulance arrived, along with a highway patrol car, Tyler sent Kyle with their fallen comrade, then joined Nash and Wally in the patrol car. After a brief explanation to the officer that it was official business, they were under way.

"Where to?"

"The airport in Bakersfield."

"If you would tell me your destination, I could call ahead and make arrangements for you."

"We're going to Belize City."

NO-MAN'S-LAND,
CALIFORNIA/MEXICO BORDER
SEPTEMBER 23, 3:34 A.M.

Still placing one boot-covered foot in front of the other in seemingly endless succession, for the first time in quite a while, Lee wondered what was going on back on campus. He had been gone almost a week, but there was no doubt in his mind that life moved on without him. His mind drifted almost lazily through the lesson plans for each of his classes in minute detail, with several tangential diversions into related topics, then mentally reviewed the faces and performance records for each of his students. If he was away much longer, he could easily find that he had no students when he got back. At the fringes of his consciousness, however, he knew he was never going back, and the impression saddened him. Then he wondered if Sharon had found someone new, and he felt worse. Feeling sorry for himself made him think of Beth, and he hoped maybe she was thinking about him, too. Right. Not likely.

Looking up from the boots in front of him, Lee was saved from his maudlin frame of mind. The blackness of the sky along the horizon was tinged with a deep blue. Dawn was coming. Over the space of twenty minutes, the horizon changed from dark and foreboding to light and, well, something less than cheerful. The land was barren, but at least they could see it.

To Lee's great relief, Nels stopped, removed his backpack, began unzipping his wet suit, and motioned for Lee to do the same. Standing there, dripping in their underclothes, they drank a quart each, which finished the last of the water bottles, and rested for a few minutes. Reluctantly Lee reached for the top piece to his wet suit, but Nels stopped him.

"You can leave it. We're in Mexico."

With wounds bandaged and dry clothes on, they covered the wet suits with stones, shouldered the packs, and set off once more. The walk was almost pleasant for a few miles, but the weight of the packs, the growing heat of the morning sun, and the cumulative aches and pains from the trip thus far soon made it again feel like a death march. They pressed on through the day, stopping every three hours for rest, food, and water from a canteen, and more than once, Lee caught himself looking for vultures circling overhead. But other than a couple of lizards and something that looked like a kangaroo rat, they didn't see another living creature the entire day.

The sun was well on its way down when they stepped onto a dusty road headed east-west. Lee's hopes for finding civilization were quickened a bit, but Nels simply turned west and continued walking. At dusk, the sound of an engine and a cloud of dust signaled the approach of a vehicle of some sort. If it was the police or worse, there was nowhere to run, and at that point Lee didn't care. The way every part of his body ached, even a short sprint would probably kill him.

The vehicle turned out to be an old pickup truck with a lone man behind the wheel. Nels flagged him down and had a brief conversation with the man in Spanish, pointing southeast and patting the wad of bills stuffed in his shirt pocket. The man shook his head, and whatever he said, it had a profound effect on Nels. Tears welled up in his eyes, and he motioned for Lee to put his pack in the back and join him in the truck. The truck rolled on down the road, and after a polite interval, Lee asked Nels what had happened back there.

"I offered him $400 to take us to Puerto Peñasco. It's about 250 miles. He turned down the money, but said he would take us there on one condition: that we have dinner with his family."

Lee's mouth dropped open in disbelief. If ever there was proof they were in a different world, that was it. Forty minutes down the road, their host pulled into a small fenced lot, which appeared to be an old homestead. Lee and Nels left their gear in the truck and followed him into the house. The interior was rustic, but comfortable, and there was the sound of children playing out back. The most obvious decoration was a large crucifix on the wall with an inscription that said something about "Jesucristo" and "Salvador." He watched with fascination as their host explained the situation to his wife. Instead of the argument Lee anticipated, however, the woman turned to her unexpected guests with a warm smile.

"Welcome. Our home is your home."

The woman was big boned and strong, yet somehow delicate and feminine, and as Lee watched her patiently double the amount of food on the table, he remembered what Nels had said about Jesus being "a good idea" and couldn't help agreeing. Christian charity had become something of a cliché in the American media, but here was a living example of it, and it was humbling to see. In his entire life, Lee had never seen someone so at peace with herself, at peace with her life. *I don't think we're in Kansas anymore, Toto,* he thought.

Once everyone was at the table, including four children, all under the age of eight, with beautiful brown eyes, the father held out his hands, and everyone, Lee and Nels included, joined hands for the blessing. When the man spoke, it was in English.

"Father, we thank You for these and all Your blessings. Please bless this food to our bodies and help us bring glory to You by the way we live. Bless our new friends as they travel. Keep them safe, and let Your goodness and mercy follow them all the days of their lives. Thank You for giving us Your Son. We pray in His name. Amen."

The meal was eaten in silence, though the children spent considerable energy trying not to stare at the scruffy strangers seated across from them. When dinner was over, the plates were cleared, and the children poured out the back door like a flash flood. Their father watched them go with a look of unabashed affection, then turned to his guests.

"I am Joseph Garcia. This is my wife, Marina."

"Thank you for your gracious hospitality. I am Nels Thiessan, and this is my friend Lee Teller. You speak very good English."

"I lived in San Diego for five years before my father died and left me this farm."

Lee glanced out the window at the desolate waste stretching to the horizon. "This used to be a farm?"

"Up until 1953 there was a river that came out of the San Ysidro Mountains. Things were green. They diverted it for irrigation or something."

Nels nodded toward the crucifix on the wall. "How long have you been a believer?"

Lee cringed at the question. Nels was nothing if not direct, but Joseph showed no sign of being the least bit offended. "Since I was a boy. And you?"

"Since my wife pestered me into it."

Joseph laughed heartily and cast an admiring glance in his wife's direction. "We would be lost without them, no?" Joseph turned to Lee, "Are you married, Mr. Teller?"

"Divorced. I'm not seeing anyone at the moment, so if you happen to know a wealthy heiress interested in a physics tutor, I might be available."

"Sorry. All of the heiresses moved out when the river dried up."

That time, it was Lee's turn to laugh, and it surprised him. Humor and exhaustion rarely went hand in hand in his life, but there was something almost contagious about the good nature of the family. Marina heard the laughter, but she had also heard the hurt behind Lee's words. Dish and towel in hand, she leaned out of the kitchen and offered what comfort she could in stilted English.

"God's timing is perfect, Mr. Teller."

Joseph nodded agreement. "And ours leaves much to be desired. Which reminds me, we have a long drive ahead of us."

Following various expressions of heartfelt thanks and farewell, the three men prepared to climb aboard the truck amidst a whirlwind of scampering children, while Marina watched from the doorway. The children hugged their father, and one of the youngest wrapped himself around Nels's leg until the mother came and pulled him away.

"Vaya con Dios," Marina said warmly.

Nels smiled wearily out the passenger side window. "We will, I assure you."

The dusk was already fading into night, and Joseph had to turn on the headlights. The drive to Puerto Peñasco would take about six hours, and as the miles ticked by, Joseph found himself becoming increasingly curious about his two passengers. It wasn't polite for him to ask too many personal questions, although they had dined together and could arguably be considered members of the family. On the verge of inquiring about their business, a quick glance sideways saved him the trouble.

Lee and Nels were fast asleep.

Chapter Six

SCHIFFER BROS. GAS STATION, SAN DIEGO, CALIFORNIA SEPTEMBER 23, 9:34 P.M.

Sitting in the passenger seat of the Sunset Racquetball van, holding the new cellular phone, Gerard Dinaé was on hold again. Due to the risk of telephone logs at CIA headquarters, they had ditched the old phone immediately after Polly terminated the call. Dinaé had been on the phone all afternoon it seemed, trying to reach Polly at the safe house in Vienna, Virginia, and checking with the satellite office in New York to see if she had checked in, all to no avail. He felt as if his ear might fall off, but he had one more place to check. Finally, a woman's voice came on the line.

"Central Intelligence Agency. Thank you for holding."

"Yes! This is Jack Smith at Fidelity Mutual. Polly Sutton gave me this number as her work number. I need to speak with her on a matter of some urgency."

"I don't show anyone here by that name."

"Are you sure? She said she was in the steno pool."

"I show no Polly Sutton in the steno pool."

"Thank you."

Dinaé put the phone down, hoping that Polly wasn't dead. If she had escaped, she might have made her own plans, and if not, then the cyanide capsule would have taken her. He would know for certain only if she reported in somewhere, but he could not waste any more time trying to find out. The CIA and the DGSE had a historical, and unofficial, understanding that just because two countries sign a treaty does not mean either can be trusted implicitly. So, while the countries made a great show of being friends, each placed operatives in the other's government as high as they dared. If the agent were discovered and apprehended, suicide was the only option that would save face for the offending country. Dinaé rubbed his eyes and turned around to face Jerome, who was seated at the communications console, still sifting through the information transmitted by Polly before the sudden disconnection.

"Anything new?"

Jerome shook his head and swore. "They have as much paperwork as we do. Maybe more. I have nothing to add. Based on the information we have, they may be headed for Argentina or Belize."

"Tell me again about Argentina."

"Thiessan was there for four years. Former contacts include six agents, one dead, two inactive, so a total of five possible contacts."

"And Belize?"

"An Interpol agent named Ilya Stehn in Belize City. Apparently she helped Thiessan take down a narcotics operation. No other information."

Argentina or Belize. If he guessed wrong, they would be out of the game completely. Argentina had the most possible contacts, but any one of them might turn on Thiessan. An Interpol agent would have no direct allegiance to the CIA, and so might make the most logical choice. Thiessan had managed to elude his own government, and so clearly was no fool. Dinaé turned to the driver.

"Take us to the airport."

OFFICE OF THE DIRECTOR, CIA HEADQUARTERS, LANGLEY, VIRGINIA
SEPTEMBER 23, 11:48 P.M.

Carter Ellis was beginning to hate his office. As a home away from home, despite the plush furniture, the room left much to be desired. The phone sat in his limp hand, and he rested his head on it. His head hurt, his stomach hurt, and the report he was in the process of receiving wasn't helping matters at all.

"What do you mean, 'They may have left the country'? Maybe they're in hiding."

"Tyler doesn't think so, and her gut feelings are usually dead on.

Her team is already on the way to Belize, so I'd say we're already committed to this course of action."

"I hope you're right. Go ahead and mobilize some teams in South America. While you're at it, put a fixer team on Tyler's tail. Maximum of three. And whatever you do, don't tell her."

"Isn't that risky?"

"This whole infernal operation is risky! We've got to have backup. Remember, these are American citizens. If Tyler gets cold feet, we've got to have someone who can pull the trigger. You know Tyler's personality type. She'd think of backup as a sign that we don't trust her. I don't want her distracted from the primary objective."

"Suit yourself. I have one other item. We got the work-up on Polly Sutton. She's not one of ours."

Ellis felt his stomach muscles tighten. "Who was she working for?"

"We're not sure. Whoever did her background did a very professional job. Probably a friendly government, maybe even one of our allies."

Ellis closed his eyes, and the pounding in his head worsened. "Send two extra teams to Argentina, and be ready to pull the Panama office if we need it."

Ellis hung up the phone, and a wave of exhaustion overtook him. He groaned. Somehow, he was going to have to come up with something to say to the Joint Chiefs of Staff at 6:00 A.M. tomorrow.

CALLE CORDOBA,
PUERTO PEÑASCO, MEXICO
SEPTEMBER 24, 1:26 A.M.

Standing on the damp cobblestones of a foreign city late at night, Lee felt the scene had an almost surrealistic quality. He watched Nels embrace Joseph, and then the truck rolled down the street, disappearing into the night. Nels assured Lee that he knew how to find Cordoba Street, but the search took quite a while. In the end, Nels blamed the clouds overhead for blocking the light of the moon.

Reduced once more to overnight bag and satchel, Lee was not sorry to see the backpacks depart with the truck. Joseph would not accept money, so Nels insisted he take the packs, since they would only throw them away, and it was the least they could do, considering Joseph's gracious hospitality.

"We really should have paid him," Lee remarked woodenly.

"I put $400 in his glove box while he was helping you with your gear. He may not find it for a month, but so much the better."

Nels led Lee into a doorway that was discernible only because it was blacker than the surrounding darkness. After several seconds of persistent knocking, a light came on inside, and the door opened, revealing a man about Nels's age, but short, with a full head of coarse white hair, glasses, and a bristly silver-white beard. The man apparently slept in his clothes, and Lee's first impression was that he might be a tailor.

"Yes?"

Nels spoke precisely. "My mother sent me over for some chicken soup."

The man apparently had no patience for coded phrases and dismissed the statement with a wave of his hand. "Ja, ja. Come in, gentlemen. You'll have to excuse me. I wasn't told you were coming."

The accent was thick and Germanic, the voice quite robust and gravelly. They followed the little man up a flight of wooden stairs, and to Lee's surprise, the second floor was not an apartment, but some sort of bizarre workshop. An old printing press sat next to a modern image setter, then a camera mounted in front of a gray screen, and some chemical baths for film developing. Two large wooden workbenches hosted an assortment of tools and devices, some of which Lee had never seen before. The little man stopped and turned to face his guests.

"And what can I do for you this evening?"

"We need to pass for Argentine citizens," Nels replied as if ordering a ham sandwich.

The man walked over to Lee, grabbed his face, and turned it from side to side. "Argentina? Hmmph. This one will never do."

The man walked over to a bin, pulled out a bottle, and tossed it to Lee. "Go wash your hair with this."

Lee did as he was told, and when he finished, his hair was jet black. The man nodded approvingly. "Better. Now, the color of your skin. Perhaps some dark base . . ." He bustled over to the bin and produced a tin of base makeup. After he applied it to Lee's face, neck, and hands, Lee looked distinctly Hispanic. He applied a different shade to Nels, then stood back to admire his handiwork.

"Much better. You'll need soap to get it off."

He placed them one at a time in front of the camera, then set to work at one of the workbenches, making passports, driver's licenses, and other forms of identification. When he was finished, he handed Lee his official documents.

"You are Mario Esteban, from Santa Rosa in La Pampa province. You haul manure for your uncle. No other family."

Lee smirked at the thought of such an unlikely field promotion, and the man turned to Nels, handing him his documents.

"You are Herman Montenegro, also from Santa Rosa, La Pampa province. You are his uncle . . ." The man peered curiously at Nels before continuing. "You look familiar to me. Do I know you?"

Nels's eyes seemed to soften slightly for just a moment, but he shook his head and smiled apologetically. "I don't think so."

The man followed them downstairs, and Lee kept waiting for him to ask for money, but he didn't. He closed the door behind them, turning out the light. Apparently the man's services were covered by the agency. Lee didn't have long to wonder about it, for without hesitation, Nels turned to the left and started walking. Lee felt as if his heart were pounding in his throat, and when they passed the end of the street, he spoke in a husky whisper.

"Nels! He recognized you!"

"Jorge is a good man. He does excellent work."

Lee was starting to feel panicky. "He knows you, Nels. We've got to do something before he tells somebody."

"Perhaps one bullet behind the ear? Hardly a week, and already you're thinking like a field agent. Which is not a compliment."

"But . . ."

"Calm yourself, Lee. Sometime between now and tomorrow morning, he will remember who I am. The realization will inspire a call to his supervisor, who will be told we are going to Argentina, which we are not."

It was another ruse, and Lee felt both irritated and relieved. "Would it be too much to ask that you let me know what you're doing once in a while?"

Lee couldn't see Nels's face in the darkness, but his voice sounded distinctly sarcastic. "I don't always know in advance, but your complaint has been noted."

They walked on in near darkness, their passing lit occasionally by anemic lights in odd entryways, and a balmy mist began to fall. The cobblestones gradually gave way to dirt road, and Lee thought he could just make out fields and foothills in the near distance. The rain grew in intensity, and the dirt underfoot turned to mud. Lee tipped his head back as he walked, letting the water run off his face. The air was fresh and moist, the raindrops delightfully cool, and Lee opened his mouth so the droplets would hit his tongue. It was a definite improvement over hiking through the desert in a wet suit.

Lee was getting used to losing track of time and not really paying attention, so when Nels pulled up short suddenly, he nearly ran into him. A dark mass was discernible just ahead, and then Lee heard Nels knocking on a door. The knocking was answered before long by a gruff male voice, shouting something about "madrugada!" followed apparently by a string of expletives. For the moment, Lee was thankful he didn't understand Spanish.

A heated argument ensued, but Nels shouted something that caught the man's attention. The door opened slowly, and a sliver of pallid light fell upon the two drenched strangers standing out in the rain. Nels waved a wad of bills, and the man grunted.

"Uno momento."

The door closed again, and they waited as patiently as possible in the rain. The temperature was dropping, and Lee tried to comfort himself with the thought that they really couldn't get any wetter. The man emerged from the far end of the building, maybe forty feet away, holding a flashlight. Not knowing what else to do, they followed him. Something up ahead was catching the light strangely, but Lee couldn't see what it was. As they drew nearer, the dim reflections ahead resolved themselves into the shape of an airplane. The outside was bare metal with no identifiable markings, the inside austere almost to the point of being military. The chairs had no upholstery, and the walls were the same bare metal they had seen on the outside. Lee had seen pictures of these aircraft—circa 1940! However, once Nels paid the pilot, the engines came on with no trouble, and the plane taxied toward the end of the runway.

Nels sat near the back and strapped himself in, and Lee sat beside him.

"How much money do you have?" Nels asked over the growing roar of the engines.

"Maybe $150. You?"

"About $200. We're headed for Belize City, with a fuel stop in

Monterrey. I offered the pilot an extra $100 if he gets us to Belize before lunch."

Lee leaned his head back and closed his eyes. The seat felt clammy next to his dripping shirt, but he was beyond caring. "Where's Belize?"

"On the coast, off the southeast tip of Mexico, bordered by Mexico, Guatemala, and Honduras. I have an old acquaintance there who might be able to help us."

MONTERREY INTERNATIONAL AIRPORT, MONTERREY, MEXICO
SEPTEMBER 24, 11:17 A.M.

A club soda. His first chance to do something really important, and Dinaé was sitting at a table drinking a club soda. At the moment, he would have given a week's wages for some coffee and croissants. The connecting flight didn't leave for another forty minutes, and he was already extremely tired of waiting. Despite a two-hour layover, his companions seemed to be faring a little better, perhaps because it wasn't a make-or-break mission for them. Dinaé had a dozen years on Jerome, the oldest of the other three, and because he was commander for the operation, punishment for any failure would fall on Dinaé's head. Then he would be lucky to get a job as a janitor.

The conversation had varied widely from world politics to sports, but the men could make only idle conversation, partly because they weren't really Americans, and partly because they didn't know each other. Any personal anecdote would most likely be a fabrication, since their identities were made up anyway. Not really interested in the latest soccer scores, Dinaé found his mind wandering, and he began watching the people passing by.

Airports on the whole do not encourage distinctions, offering passage as they do to people from all walks of life as long as they have money to pay, and this airport was no different. The people crowding the stone walkways looked to be from every walk of life, some hurrying, some taking their time, all with that peculiar aloofness of the soul in transit. A businessman complete with three-piece suit and briefcase, then a peasant woman seemingly wrapped in rags with two children in tow, then two more peasants in . . . no, not two peasants, but clearly lower class, except for the luggage. The overnight bags and leather satchel were too expensive, while the clothes were at the bottom end of casual and had obviously not been changed in quite a while. Odd.

While Dinaé watched, the two men disappeared into a public rest room, and he stared at the doorway with a curious expression. It couldn't be. The idea was preposterous. He had tried to imagine what Teller and Thiessan might look like, and other than the skin color, these two were surprisingly close. But here! Now! No, it must be coincidence. Thiessan was a former agent, and neither man had a place to conceal a weapon. Surely he wasn't walking around unarmed! Unless . . . unless they had to travel light. A jacket and holster could become burdensome on a forced march through an arid climate.

Not wishing to appear foolish, Dinaé excused himself and walked over to the rest room. Inside, he took up an open position next to the younger man. A surreptitious glance sideways didn't tell him much. If the skin color was makeup, it was a professional job. The younger man glanced sideways, and Dinaé smiled and nodded.

"Buenos dias."

The younger man ignored him, finished what he was doing, and moved toward the door to wait for his companion. Dinaé took a long time washing his hands, cleaning under each fingernail, and at last his patience was rewarded. The older man came out of one of the stalls and stood beside him to wash, then hesitated, changed his mind, and headed for the door. Why not wash the hands? Perhaps because the skin color washes off?

Dinaé made a big point of ignoring them, and he moved over to dry his hands. In the next moment, two strong hands hit him from behind, driving his head into the towel dispenser, and he collapsed to the floor unconscious.

"Nels! Why did you do that?"

Nels dropped to one knee and opened the unconscious man's jacket. The shoulder holster held a .9 mm Beretta, standard issue for the DGSE. "I didn't like his accent."

With Lee's help, he dragged the man to a stall and sat him on the toilet with his head between his knees. Nels was furious with himself. "Probably French intelligence. He must have noticed the bags. Idiot! I must be getting senile. Come on."

Nels dragged Lee out of the rest room, smacked him upside the head, and started into a chiding torrent of Spanish invective. To the bystanders who turned to watch, it appeared to be a family spat. Once out of sight of the rest room area, Nels picked up the pace. "He probably wasn't alone. Hurry!"

Back at the table, René noticed the commander's absence and walked over to the rest room. He emerged a moment later, highly agitated, and dashed over to his comrades. "Alarm! C'est le . . . the commander is injured!" Jerome and Henry hurried over and they gathered around Dinaé, who was slowly regaining consciousness.

"We must get you to a doctor," Jerome said.

Dinaé's eyes opened, and he winced. "No, you idiot. It was them. Pursue . . ."

René helped his commander to stand. "What did they look like?"

"Like their descriptions . . ." Dinaé grabbed his head and steadied himself against his young companion. ". . . only made up Hispanic."

With René on his arm, Dinaé staggered out of the rest room. They looked in both directions, but the fugitives were nowhere in sight. Dinaé cursed in French, then remembered his cover. "Let's get to the plane. Maybe we'll get lucky."

Barely a hundred yards away, Nels and Lee scrambled aboard their airplane and nearly tumbled into the backseat, gasping for breath. Refueling was nearly complete. They would be in the air in ten minutes. Lee got his breathing under control, but his heart was still pounding.

"What does French intelligence have to do with any of this? And how did those guys find us?"

"They didn't find us, or we'd be dead already. My guess is, they were monitoring CIA communications when the file was stolen."

"But the French are on our side."

"I told you this goes beyond any national allegiance. They may not know what they're after, but we can't take that chance. If the French know about it, you can bet other countries aren't far behind. We have to get rid of the file."

Lee instinctively clutched the satchel tighter. "But this is our bargaining chip."

Nels seemed to be only half listening. "The only thing of value is the recipe for cold fusion. The rest of it is easily deniable by our government. I should have thought of this before. If we get caught by foreign agents while carrying the file, they can dispose of us immediately. Stashing it somewhere might buy us some time. Do you think you can remember how to assemble the device?"

"For the rest of my life."

"Good. That might give us some bargaining room."

"You act as if it's a foregone conclusion that they're going to catch us."

"The fact that foreign agents are involved doesn't improve our chances. The mere existence of the file may be enough to start a war." Nels paused and looked sympathetically at his friend. "I'll bet you never thought you'd be involved in anything like this. I'm so sorry, Lee."

Lee shrugged. "I suppose I brought it on myself. No one forced me to go meet Miles."

"True. But I'm still sorry. Maybe we can ditch the file somewhere outside Belize City."

A short time later, the plane was airborne once more, and Nels breathed a sigh of relief. His wrists were sore from the assault in the rest room, but all things considered, the situation could have been much worse. The effort of constantly trying to anticipate all possible variables was taking a toll on him physically and emotionally. Perhaps that was the reason he overlooked the luggage. It was a very unforgiving business. They were fortunate to be alive.

Nels closed his eyes and felt a little pang of guilt somewhere in his abdominal region. The attack on the man in the rest room had been a reflex, but he couldn't blame the old training entirely. There was time to think, time to ask himself if what he had in mind was right, but he ignored his conscience. No, he suppressed his conscience, beat it down, and told it not to bother him with any moralizing, thank you very much. That wasn't right, and he knew it. More than that, it wasn't smart. A conscience beaten down becomes calloused, and a person with such calluses might find himself with a problem at the end of his life when finally face-to-face with God.

After his conversion to Christianity, Nels had made a separate peace about his false history, mostly by simply not talking about his past. Occasionally, however, some bureaucrat or nosy parishioner would pry, and he would be forced to lie. The incidents were few and far between, but he regretted every one and wished there was a way out. Utta told him he was just doing his job, but the deception distressed him all the same. Fortunately there was something else Utta used to tell him. "'There is therefore now no condemnation to those who are in Christ Jesus,'" she would say, always on her way out the door, so there could be no argument. Up until recently, Nels had made sure that he spent

time on his knees every morning, but the unexpected arrival of Lee
Teller, and their subsequent dash for the border, had furnished a
significant disruption to what had once been a very stable schedule.

As the plane bounced its way over the lower eastern range of the
Sierra Madre, Nels thanked God for the miracle that they had made it
this far. Apparently the prayers of Joseph Garcia and his wife were
being answered, and Nels decided he was long overdue for a little
divine communication himself. Uncomfortable at first because of his
time away, he soon felt the familiar assurance that God was not angry
with him, and he relaxed, forgetting for the moment the seriousness
of their situation. Freed from the myriad concerns of his life for the
moment, his mind began to drift.

Shaken awake by an air pocket sometime later, he checked on Lee
and found that he was staring out the window. Nels poked him in the
shoulder, and Lee turned slowly. He looked shell shocked, and that
could mean slower reflexes and an inability to make critical decisions,
either of which could be fatal. He needed something to quicken his
thoughts.

"Take out your notepad."

Lee stared blankly but made no move.

"Take out your notepad, Lee."

Lee frowned, but had no will to argue. He leadenly pulled a notepad
out of his overnight bag.

"You'll need something to write with."

Too motion sick to sleep, Lee had been hoping for a diversion to
get his mind off the unpleasant sensations emanating from his stomach,
but taking notes from a retired sociology professor did not sound like
the solution. Grimacing with the effort, he fished a pen out of his bag
and sat poised to write, a look of gray-green resignation on his face.

"Make six long dashes."

Lee made six long dashes.

"Make a vertical line to the left."

Lee did so.

"Make a horizontal line at the top of the vertical line, heavy toward
the right."

As Lee was making the second line, he realized Nels had just set
them up for a game of hangman. "We're going to play hangman?"

"Pick a letter."

It had been a long time, but Lee remembered his old strategy of
starting with vowels. "Um . . . A."

Nels took the pen and drew a circle under the cross bar. "Nope."

"*E.*"

Nels drew a stick body under the circle head. "Nope."

Lee went through the rest of the vowels and was foiled at every turn. With *AEIOU* written at the bottom of the page, and a body with head, two arms, and a leg, he was still facing six empty spaces.

"What kind of a stupid word is this? It's gotta have . . . oh." Lee rolled his eyes. "*Y.*"

Nels put a *Y* in the third space and glanced at his companion. The mind was definitely working. Lee made seven more guesses, ending up with R _ Y T _ _ before he was hung. Nels filled in the rest of the letters.

"*Rhythm?* That's a great word. I was looking for something more scientific."

Nels peered intently at Lee. "When I was in field training, this was the first skill my instructor taught me."

"Hangman?" Lee quipped.

"Rhythm. We used to practice doing tasks in time with a metronome. Changing batteries in a flashlight, brushing our teeth, cleaning a pistol, all in time with the click. He told us that the idea of rhythm extended to life-and-death situations as well, that people who learned to read the rhythm of a situation usually survived longer in the field. Knowing when to draw your sidearm, and when to hold very still, like a musician knowing when to play and when to be silent. Only in life you don't have a score to follow, so you have to improvise." Nels handed the pen back, and his eyes hardened a bit. "You're going to have to learn to improvise, Lee. There's no other way. I was watching you a little while ago. You were withdrawing into yourself. If you withdraw, then you're already dead. You've got to focus here and now, or you could die here and now. Do you know why they fire live ammunition at troops in training?"

Lee nodded. "So when the real thing comes, they won't be shaken by it."

"Right. Only it doesn't always work once they hit the front lines. About one in two hundred soldiers looks instead of diving for cover and never gets off a shot. Your training is going to happen with live ammo, and frankly your only chance is to be focused. Your whole purpose in this is to stay alive."

Something had been bothering Lee, and when Nels mentioned staying alive, the question came clear suddenly. "Are you sure we're doing the right thing by staying alive? If cold fusion can have such a devastating effect on the human race, who are we to say our government is wrong?"

"They're not wrong in principle. They are wrong about thinking they can suppress it. The discovery would have happened sooner or later. Too many people are working on it. We just happened to be first. If other groups develop it, and they will, they could actually use it as a weapon to destroy our economy and others. If my plan is successful, there will be no economic collapse, no rioting, no war. Here, write this down." Nels rested his face in his hands for a moment before continuing. "We would have to start with the major energy-dependent nations—the U.S., Russia, China, Japan, and two or three of the European Commonwealth countries."

"Which ones?"

"I don't know. Maybe England, France, Germany for starters. The energy-related industries would be given an exclusive right to produce the device in all its numerous forms, and time to retool. The government could help phase in the transition. Power companies could redesign their generation plants, and keep the existing infrastructure of power lines for a time. Rates could be reduced to mirror reduced generation costs, and since the only place to get the device legally would be the power companies, most people wouldn't take the risk of getting caught or the trouble to convert their homes to cold fusion and get off the transmission grid. Over time the producers of the device would see the economic opportunity in mass distribution and sales of it and the efficiencies and benefits would be dispersed widely, but not in a way that would destabilize the economy. Are you getting all this, or am I talking too fast?"

"I'm getting it, but what about the auto industry?"

"I was coming to that. First, the auto manufacturers would have to have the same exclusive right to produce the device for cars that electric and gas utilities would have for the electric and gas systems. Cars could be fitted with the device, but in all probability the limited availability and cost of retrofitting existing cars would be more than your average citizen is going to be willing to pay for the savings involved. And in large parts of the country getting seawater, or its equivalent, wouldn't be easy. New cars would be made with the new engines, but it would be several years before the capacity to produce electric motors and all the components that go into an electric car would be available in large numbers. Even if they were, not everyone would switch over immediately, so to some extent, the phase-in for the auto industry would be self-regulating."

Lee shook his head. "Perhaps, but in a few years, about 80 percent of the cars would not be using gasoline. What happens to the oil companies and gasoline refineries?"

"They would have to diversify somehow. I'm picturing a phase-in that would give them between five and ten years of a declining oil and petroleum products market. They have large cash receipts and would, no doubt, reinvest in other things, maybe even the companies that would be manufacturing and marketing the new energy devices. You might see mergers between the big oil companies and the defense engineering firms. This could be a big break for the concept people designing space stations. A series of large orbital stations would require tremendous resources and man power. It would essentially be a mammoth 'make work' project, but whether it ultimately succeeded or not, the result would be a redirection of industry instead of its destruction. Even space projects might be made more economical . . ."

Nels went on, outlining plans for reassigning people in the oil industry from riggers to petroleum geologists, retraining of energy industry specialists, a new mission for the Strategic Petroleum Reserve, retooling of the transportation industries, transition plans for manufacturers, and creation of a public relations agency to disseminate information, undermine any attempts at a black market, and prevent panic. When he finished, Lee was again looking a little shell shocked, and the pen wasn't moving. Nels hastened to conclude before he lost his scribe completely, "Let me sum it up this way. The key to the whole plan is that the device must not be just dumped on the world market in some kind of free-for-all fashion, which would bring about the catastrophe everyone fears. If it is phased in so that vested interests can relocate their capital and retrain their workers, it is possible that the world would enter a whole new, and better, era, maybe even one of universal peace and prosperity like you envisioned at the beginning of all this."

The summary sparked Lee's interest and more discussion, and by the time the airplane began its descent to the airport outside Belize City, Nels noticed he was getting hoarse. He motioned for Lee to put his notepad away and watched the lush countryside rushing past the window. The touchdown was surprisingly smooth, and once the plane came to a stop, the pilot opened the door and held out his hand for the $100 bonus. With the money in hand, he ignored them completely.

The air outside was quite moist, and Lee had to endure a few seconds of discomfort before he got used to the humidity.

Nels led the way through a utilitarian terminal and bypassed the short row of taxis waiting for customers. Lee's legs were complaining all the way, still quite sore from all the hiking, and the complaint quickly reached his mouth.

"We're not going on foot!"

"We have to ditch the file, and there can't be any witnesses."

"Why not just burn it and toss the lockbox in a garbage can?"

Nels stopped and checked back the way they had come. No one was in earshot. "We may need to retrieve it later. If we burn it and then think of a use for it later, we're out of luck."

Lee groaned, but he knew there was no reasoning with the man. He trudged on, losing track of time again, resenting every step, feeling like a sour little brat on his first hiking trip. He could imagine a time not far in the future when he might have to kill Nels just to save himself. After all, the death marches had to stop. He could claim temporary insanity. What court would convict him? *Like I'm ever going to see the inside of a courtroom. Somewhere out there is a bullet with my name on it. Or a bomb. Or a garrote. And it's all Nels's fault.*

Lee knew he would never lift a finger to hurt Nels, and thinking about it wasn't making him feel any better, so he turned his thoughts toward ways to keep himself focused. Nels led them off the main road, and Lee made a mental note of his surroundings. But it wasn't enough just to be alert, he had to be thinking about what the next move would be, where the nearest cover was, what to do the moment he heard gunfire, whether that building up ahead posed any threat . . .

The building turned out to be an abandoned dwelling, and Nels went inside. It was long deserted and far from the road. Nels apparently thought it an excellent place to stash the satchel. He tore up two floor boards, placed the satchel underneath, and replaced the boards. The satchel would not be found without a deliberate search, and from the look of the place, no one had been inside the hovel for years.

Feeling decidedly lighter, but missing the familiar weight of the satchel, Lee followed Nels back to the main road. After a few moments jotting down landmarks in the notepad in a simple code using a three-letter shift in the alphabet, they walked back to the airport and took a cab to Belize City. Several miles farther east, they passed a dilapidated fueling station, and Lee added it to his list of coded landmarks. Thankful for a chance to rest his aching legs, Lee closed his eyes and thought about taking a nap, but Nels nudged him when they reached the Belize City limits and reminded him they weren't out of the woods yet.

Taken on appearance alone, the waterfront district could have been located in almost any major coastal town in the world. Huge boxy warehouses lined perpendicular rows of streets, and at a few minutes after 4:00 on a lazy fall afternoon, activity at the loading docks was minimal. The taxi came to a stop in front of a single-story office building next to one of the warehouses. Painted on the window in faded green, red, and yellow were the words GULF SHIPPING COMPANY in English. Nels wondered briefly at the logic behind having an American name for the front of an operation in Belize, but he had never learned much about the inner workings of Interpol, nor was he about to start now. He peeled some sweat-sodden bills from the wad in his pocket, paid the cabdriver, wrapped sore fingers around the handle on his overnight bag, and shuffled toward the door. Lee limped after him, his legs torturously stiff, almost as if rigor mortis was setting in.

Inside the office, the furniture was all wicker and canvas, the end tables made of some dark wood that was not mahogany, trimmed with stained bamboo, and oriental rugs. The air smelled of sea salt and creosote, and the walls appeared to be covered with some sort of blond cane thatch. Somewhere outside an open window, waves lapped at the supports beneath the building. Once more, Lee was struck by the sensation that the place in which he stood was utterly foreign, and the odd thought that under different circumstances, the room smelled like a vacation spot.

Out on the street, down four blocks, two workers in coveralls, frozen in the act of loading a crate onto the loading dock half a minute earlier, stood transfixed. Jerome put his binoculars away and spoke into his radio.

"They have arrived."

Chapter Seven

The charter plane from Potosí, Mexico, was not nearly as pleasant as the Mexican Airlines connection through Mexico City, but after reviewing the options, Tyler had decided that eliminating a two-hour layover was worth a little discomfort. According to the report from Puerto Peñasco, the fugitives left sometime after midnight, which meant they might already be in Belize City. Tyler knew in her gut that the Argentine identification was intended to throw them off the trail, but Nash wasn't so sure. He complained about their "wasted trip" to Belize, all the way from Tijuana to Potosí, until she threatened to send him back to the States—as freight.

While in Tijuana, she had taken a few minutes to check on Rick at County General Hospital in Los Angeles. He was in serious condition, but stable, and she was able to put him out of her mind only by convincing herself he was in good hands. The call to headquarters had taken longer and initiated the move to the charter plane. At least Nash had used the time to locate the Gulf Shipping Company on the map.

Tyler looked down and saw the coast of Campeche going by, and wondered for a moment what it would have been like to grow up in the backwaters of some Latin American country. It was probably just another oppressive male-dominated society where women were second-class citizens or worse. No doubt she would be scrubbing floors somewhere. Probably in prison, for killing some overly amorous pig-headed jerk.

GULF SHIPPING COMPANY, WAREHOUSE DISTRICT, BELIZE CITY, BELIZE
SEPTEMBER 24, 4:38 P.M.

The man who finally came to see who was waiting in the reception area looked as if he had been born on the wharf. He was wearing grimy canvas pants and a sleeveless gray T-shirt. His face looked like it had been chiseled out of barnacles, or maybe with barnacles, and he was missing a few teeth. The only things lacking were a bandanna and an eye patch to make him a fitting first mate on a pirate ship.

Nels ignored the machine gun slung over the man's shoulder and smiled. "Good afternoon. Would you please tell Ilya that Nels Thiessan is here to see her?"

Without a word, the man backed out of the room. A moment later, another man, taller and darker than the first, but no less swarthy, stepped in the room to keep an eye on the filthy strangers. They didn't have to wait long.

"Nels?"

The woman was tall, a few years younger than Nels, with a rough Slavic cast to her face and wearing glasses. The slacks and work shirt hung a little loosely, accentuating the broadness of her shoulders and hips. She was strong and sinewy, all bone and gristle, but the brown eyes danced much like her old friend's.

"Hello, Ilya. Or should I say, Buenos tardes?" Nels replied with a tired smile, which shined brightly from the midst of his dark makeup.

Ilya returned the smile, and her eyes lit up beautifully. When she spoke, the accent sounded Russian. "Nice tan. I should have known you'd turn up eventually. You look like . . ."

"I know. If you have a place where we could get cleaned up, we would be eternally grateful."

Ilya turned to face Lee, who was collapsed in a wicker chair near the front door. "Who's he?"

"Professor Lee Teller from Dartmouth College."

"This I've got to hear. But later."

Without further discussion, Nels and Lee were taken into the warehouse to the Interpol offices, through the offices, and into the living quarters. Warm, foamy baths were drawn, clothes were washed, and Ilya arranged for a masseuse to give both men a complete rubdown with oil. By the time they were dressed for dinner, Nels felt better than he had in years, and Lee felt almost human, although his legs were still a bit sore.

Ilya sat at the head of the table, with the visitors on her right and left, and introduced the barnacle-faced fellow as Marco and the taller one as Diego. Both nodded slightly, but neither said a word, and Ilya dismissed them with a wave of her hand.

"They work for me. Headquarters wouldn't send me another agent, so I had to make do with some local help. They've never given me any trouble."

"I'm not surprised," Lee said, but he was surprised that such a brazen remark would escape his lips. He must be more fatigued than he thought.

"I'll take that as a compliment, Mr. Teller," Ilya replied, eyes twinkling. "I've become something of a fixture around here. It's nice to be recognized as a human being. Marco and Diego aren't very good company."

Eager to move the conversation to less personal ground, Lee asked, "How long have you been here?"

Ilya frowned and looked at Nels for help. "You came out in . . . 1959, wasn't it?" Nels's mouth was full, and he could only nod. Ilya turned back to Lee and continued, "There was this group of Liberians smuggling opium, and Nels helped me stop them. That was two years after I was assigned, so it must have been 1957 when I first arrived. Back then this was still the capital, and Interpol wanted a presence in the capital city."

"Why change the capital?" Lee wanted to know.

"Hurricane Hattie blew through in October of 1961, along with a major tidal wave, and the city was devastated. It took nine years to . . . how do you say? . . . cut the red tape, but they finally moved the capital fifty miles inland to Belmopan. You can still see some hurricane damage on some of the older buildings." Taking another bite, she turned to face Nels. "Now, are you going to tell me why you're here or not?"

Nels hesitated. "I'm not ready yet."

"Fine. Then why don't you tell me what you've been doing for the last twenty years?"

Outside, in the narrow alley on the north side of the building, three figures stood motionless, so motionless that any average citizen would have had to conclude the shapes were a trick of the quickly fading light. Another figure slipped around the side of the building, just another shadow on shadow. The new arrival spoke in a barely perceptible whisper.

"They are in the dining area. There is an armed guard in the front hall. I could not locate the other man. We should wait until they come out."

Dinaé did not like to wait. Time was running out—for his mission, his career, even his life. "We cannot wait. They could be doing anything in there . . . buying weapons, destroying documents . . ."

". . . eating dinner, having polite conversation," René answered sarcastically.

At last it has happened, Dinaé thought. His team was losing confidence in him. They must have known his credentials, and now the youngest was ready to see the old bull put out to pasture. The naked presumption stabbed like a knife, and he slapped René hard across the face. In the silence of the alley, the slap rang out like a shot, and in the stunned silence that ensued, Dinaé whispered through gritted teeth, "Do that again and I'll kill you."

René put a hand to his face but said nothing.

———————

". . . after which I retired and took the emeritus position in the department."

"All right, Nels. Enough about your career. Are you going to tell me why you're here, or do I have to call Marco in to beat it out of you?"

"Ilya, if you get involved, it could mean trouble. Serious trouble."

"Better that you should tell me. I know you, Nels. You wouldn't have come here unless you were already in serious trouble."

Nels looked suddenly frustrated. "What bothers me the most is, we may be endangering your life just by being here. I suppose more than anything, that gives you a right to know."

Ilya arched an eyebrow. "You've certainly piqued my curiosity."

Nels proceeded to explain everything that had happened since Miles stole the file, up to and including the hiding place a few miles outside of town. Lee was taken aback by the frankness with which Nels acquitted himself, and he said as much. Ilya smiled kindly and explained that, while taking down that opium ring all those years ago, he had taken a bullet for her. In response, Lee could offer only a reserved nod.

Obviously the bond between the two old friends went far beyond company affiliations. As far as they were concerned, nothing more needed to be said.

"If you're headed for Israel, you're going to need a ship. The only ship headed out this evening is going to Morocco. If you want to leave tonight, she's the only game in town."

Nels nodded. "Morocco is well situated. We wouldn't have any trouble from there. But if there's any way the two of us can stay here for a day or two, we could sure use the rest."

"You'd be welcome."

"I know. But we ran into some agents in Monterrey. Someone could be hot on our trail."

"I'll call the shipyard and set it up. At least then you'll have the option."

Ilya was on her feet and out of the room, leaving Lee and Nels alone. She walked through the living quarters to the offices and stopped in the communications room. Ilya had long ago learned to be tough with the men at the shipyard. If they didn't particularly like her, at least they respected her, and that was all she needed from them. She confirmed the schedule time and asked to be put through to the captain of the ship. Last-minute passengers were never a problem, it seemed, because the ships always had extra space, and the captains always wanted the extra money. Captain Delo of the freighter *Saldanha* was no exception, and she finished the call in less than two minutes.

As she started back down the hall toward the living quarters, she saw something inexplicable. Shoes. Legs. Diego's from the look of them. Certainly he hadn't had too much to drink? Still adjusting to the semidarkness, her gaze traveled up the body, stopping abruptly at the neck. A hairline cut appeared to circumscribe the neck, marred intermittently by a faint trickle of blood, and there was a wire protruding from either side.

Ilya opened her mouth to scream, and a pair of strong arms grabbed her from behind, clamping her mouth shut. "Silencio!" a male voice demanded, and the point of a knife was pressed against her neck. Two shadowy figures strode down the hall toward the living quarters, while two others brought her along. Horrified and utterly helpless, she knew there was nothing she could do. If she made any attempt to break free, she would be dead long before she could cry out.

The two men in the lead burst into the dining area, brandishing machine pistols, and Lee and Nels recoiled in shock. The man in charge spoke calmly.

"Please do not move. We don't want to hurt anyone else. Just give us the file, and we'll be on our way."

Nels recognized him as the man from the rest room in Monterrey. "I'm afraid we don't have the file."

Dinaé's eyes narrowed. "No games, Mr. Thiessan. There are many who would kill for it."

"Why do you think we got rid of it? If you want the information, you'll have to take us with you."

"Give it to us now, or we will kill the woman."

René tightened his grip on Ilya and pressed the point of the knife a little deeper. Nels held up a hand. "The woman is not involved. Let her go, and we will come with you without a fight."

Dinaé laughed. "As if you could put up a fight. I don't think so. No. You will tell us what we want to know here and now, or she dies."

The old training kicked in, quelling the rising fear in his chest, and Nels spoke evenly. "What do you want to know?"

"Everything you know about the Prometheus operation and the Pandora Project."

"That could take quite a while."

"We're not going anywhere . . ."

The statement turned out to be prophetic, at least for Jerome—who was standing beside René, holding a machine pistol on Nels—for at that moment, Marco appeared in the kitchen doorway and opened fire with an Uzi submachine gun. A spray of bullets threw Jerome into the wall, and René instinctively let go of Ilya to return fire along with his comrades. As Ilya made a desperate lunge for the nearest window, a hail of lead sent Marco sprawling backward into the kitchen. Dinaé saw Ilya running, turned, and opened fire with his pistol. In the next instant, she crashed through the window and fell with a splash into the water below. René ran to the window and sprayed the surface of the water with bullets, but there was no sign of his prisoner.

Dinaé glared at Henry and René and motioned toward Lee and Nels. "Bring them."

René glanced toward the lifeless body of their fallen comrade. "What about Jerome?"

Dinaé walked over and pulled Jerome's pistol from his shoulder holster. "He should be clean. Besides, we don't have time to take him with us. Interpol won't investigate for at least a day, two if we're lucky. They will have questions and no answers."

Rough hands dragged Lee and Nels from their temporary haven and into the night. Haste actually made for slower going, for by the time they had gone a block, the three men were nearly dragging their captives. At last, in the dark behind a brick building, they tied their hands and threw them into the back of a van. The van rolled slowly onto the street, picking up speed as it went, its occupants oblivious to the black Peugeot following without lights far to the rear.

Tyler, Nash, and Wally were nearing the warehouse district in a rented van. Tyler hated being without a radio, but without a CIA office in town, getting the right equipment could easily take a day or two. Nash suggested they make the best use of their personal units and hope for the best, and she was forced to agree.

They rolled toward the intersection near the Gulf Shipping Company, and Wally killed the lights and pulled over to the curb. Nash was still a little shaken from the accident, and he had gladly relinquished the driving responsibilities. At a nod from Tyler, Nash slipped out the passenger door and disappeared into the shadows. He returned in the same manner barely five minutes later, his expression unpleasant.

"The place was hit less than an hour ago. Come on."

Wally and Tyler scrambled out of the van, grabbed some gear from the back, and hurried to follow Nash to the front door. They hurried through the offices, stopping briefly to examine Diego's body, then to the living quarters. In the dining area, Tyler got down on one knee next to Jerome's body, while Nash inspected the corpse just inside the kitchen. Wally went over the scene in general, trying to guess how the action unfolded.

Nash held up Marco's weapon. "Uzi."

Tyler nodded toward Jerome. "Looks like your man got one of theirs before the others took him out. Any sign of the woman or the fugitives?"

"No."

Wally proudly held up a slug dug from the wall near the broken window. "Nine millimeter, and it looks like someone left through the window."

Tyler took prints off Jerome's thumb and forefinger. "Bring the slug."

They went back to the offices and found the control room. Agents could go there to get information off the Interpol network. Tyler's team didn't have the access codes for the network, but most of the communications and analysis equipment was available. If the fingerprints turned up negative, their only chance was a ballistics test on the bullet, which was a million to one shot.

Using equipment in the room, they enlarged the fingerprints, called the lab at CIA headquarters, and telecommunicated the prints to the specialist working the swing shift. A complete search of the database with fingerprints as the only criterion took just under ten minutes, and when the specialist came back on, she sounded a little surprised.

"You're in luck. We have a positive match. The prints belong to Philippe LeMieux with French intelligence. Do you want his stats?"

"No, thanks. You can mark him deceased. Could you try to pull up the location of any DGSE safe houses in Belize City?"

"Just a sec . . . okay . . . here's the DGSE file. I'm showing two safe houses in Belize City."

"Which one is closest to the warehouse district?"

"There's one in the warehouse district. On Raton Street, halfway between Miguel and Rubio."

Nash pulled a crumpled, soiled map out of his hip pocket and unfolded it. "We're twelve blocks away."

Tyler said, "Thanks!" into the headset and terminated the connection, then all three ran for the van.

The DGSE safe house in the warehouse district of Belize City was just a sparsely furnished loft on the third floor of one of the warehouses. They kept it chiefly as a place where agents could hide out when necessary. A woman came once a week to clean and restock the shelves as needed, but the place didn't see much traffic during the year.

Upon arrival, Dinaé had placed a call to headquarters, explained that the American fugitives were in custody, and requested further orders. Due to the sensitivity of the situation, the orders were to extract the information using whatever means necessary, then dump the bodies in the bay. Despite his violent tendencies and years of training and experience, Dinaé felt a faint twinge of remorse over a death sentence for two civilians, but they were hardly innocent, and under the circumstances, it seemed the only reasonable course of action.

René dragged two heavy wooden chairs to the middle of what passed as a living room. There were no neighbors and, hence, no curtains, though there were blinds that could be closed if desired. That particular apartment had been chosen because the positions of the buildings across the street meant there was no direct line of sight into the room from any window. At the moment, no one seemed to care. Nels and Lee were tied to the chairs, and Dinaé stood facing them.

"Now, Mr. Thiessan, tell me everything you know about Prometheus."

Nels frowned, then raised his eyebrows. "He gave the secret of fire to man and was condemned to have his liver eaten by a bird every morning for all eternity."

Dinaé slapped his face. "Forgive me, but I am under orders, and I'm afraid I'm running out of patience. Once more, tell me about the Prometheus file."

———————————

Two blocks down from the DGSE safe house, a lone figure slipped out of the black Peugeot, opened the trunk, took something out, closed it, and looked both directions. The street was completely deserted, and it had been for more than an hour. Walking as if in pain, the figure had moved a block closer to the safe house when, several blocks away, a van pulled onto the street, headed the same direction. The figure darted quickly into the shadows of the nearest alley.

The van headlights turned off, and the vehicle slowly rolled to a stop a block away from the safe house, on the far side of the street, directly across from the alley where the figure stood, watching. A woman in a jumpsuit climbed out, joined quickly by two men. They spoke in English.

"Take the rifle and an infrared scope up to the top of that building. Wally and I will try to get in there undetected, but stay alert." The woman pointed to the warehouse opposite the safe house.

"Who's the target?"

"Anyone but the fugitives."

"The order was termination."

"We have to find out how much the DGSE knows."

The man shrugged, pulled a long briefcase from the van, and disappeared down the nearest alley. The woman and Wally crossed the street diagonally to the front door of the safe house, defeated the lock, and slipped inside. The dark figure watched until the door closed, then continued down the alley, away from the street.

"Stop it! You'll kill him!" Lee shouted.

René ceased his battering of Nels's face and took a step back. Nels looked much older, with one eye swollen shut, a trickle of blood from one nostril, and a large bruise on his cheek. When he spoke, his voice was thick.

"I won't tell you anything, so you might as well kill me and get it over with."

Since Nels was a CIA agent, their captors had more or less ignored Lee up to this point. What would a physics professor know about top secret documents? But they knew Nels wasn't exaggerating. He would die before he told them anything. Dinaé pulled René aside and spoke quietly in French. René answered hotly, and then both men were swearing at each other. For one hopeful moment, Lee thought they were going to come to blows, but the third man stepped in and separated the two men. When they came back, René took out his pistol, grabbed Lee's hair, jerked his head back, and pressed the barrel of the gun against his head.

Nels's good eye widened slightly. "Wait!"

Dinaé moved a little closer. "You have something you want to tell us?"

Nels's face was a mask of tortured grief for a moment, but he closed his eye in despair. "No. I'm sorry, Lee."

Lee nearly gagged on bile, but he managed to choke out, "I understand." He squeezed his eyes shut and breathed in sharply. There was a terrible rushing sound in his ears, and his body tensed, waiting for the gunshot. When the shot came, it sounded far away. Then he realized it came from outside. The hand holding his hair came loose, and Lee opened his eyes in shock. René lay dead on the floor, a gaping wound in his head. People were moving, and more bullets tore into the walls. Dinaé grabbed his gun and shot out the lights in the room. If the marksman on the roof opposite had an infrared scope, they would have a few seconds while he adjusted the device. Dinaé and Henry cut loose their prisoners and dragged them out of the room, down a hall, and down four flights of back stairs to the basement.

The tunnel had never been used, but the door came open easily enough, and the two DGSE agents hurried their captives into the dank, musty darkness.

From the ground floor inside the safe house, Tyler and Wally heard the gunshots and pounded up the main stairs to the third floor. On a three count, they burst into the room with guns drawn, but the room was dark. Tyler produced a small flashlight and discovered the room was empty except for a body on the floor.

"There's probably a tunnel in the basement. They could come out anywhere in a four-block radius. Let's go stake out the other safe house."

The group in the tunnel walked on for almost a minute, with Henry in the lead, arms outstretched. He grunted suddenly as his arms hit the door at the far end, then he opened it, they went up a short flight of stone steps, and they emerged onto a dim, deserted street. Not twenty feet away, a car was parked for precisely this kind of emergency. Henry started toward the car, followed by Nels, Lee, and Dinaé.

Suddenly, out of the shadows nearby, a string of muzzle flashes erupted, coupled with the sharp crackle of automatic weapon fire. Caught off guard, Henry was thrown back and rolled off the hood of the car, dead before he hit the pavement. Dinaé dropped to one knee and returned fire, but the deadly rain of bullets found him first, and he jerked wildly and twisted, falling back down the stairs to the tunnel's exit.

As Nels and Lee stood gaping in dumbfounded horror, a figure stepped out of the shadows. Ilya.

"Hurry! This way!"

"Those were gunshots!" Tyler stopped in the middle of the street, and Wally pulled up short beside her, then she ran to the van. Nash wasn't back yet. "Wait here for Nash. I'll check it out." Tyler climbed in the van and sped away. Not thirty seconds later, Nash walked out of the alley and immediately noticed the van missing.

In response to the look on his face, Wally answered, "We heard shots a few blocks away. Tyler took the van."

Nash did not look pleased. "Figures."

Clutching her side, Ilya crept down the alley toward her car, with Nels and Lee close behind. The street was clean, and they were able to pass almost soundlessly. As they neared the end of the alley, Ilya caught sight of two men standing across the street, engaged in quiet conversation. Slowly she swung her machine pistol around until it was pointing at the two men and hesitated. The distance was almost sixty feet, and she wasn't sure she could be very accurate from so far away. If the two men were CIA agents . . .

Tyler was beginning to give up hope. Street after street had turned up only an occasional car, and there was nothing resembling a shoot-out. Out of the corner of her eye, she caught sight of yet another car parked along the street, and she turned to have a look. There! Someone was lying in front of the car.

She parked and got out, instinctively trying to imagine what had taken place. A small powerful flashlight provided some illumination, and she could see that the fellow lying facedown on the street, with one foot still on the sidewalk, had rolled off the hood. She turned around and looked at the shadows toward the end of the building. That would put the gunman about there. But where did they come from? Maybe this set of steps leading down . . .

She followed the steps to the bottom. A tunnel. She shined the light on the steps. Bloodstains, but no body. *Apparently someone walked away from this little soiree,* she thought.

Nels put a hand on Ilya's arm and shook his head once, and she lowered her weapon. Reaching in his pocket, he pulled out a pocket-knife, handed it to Lee, and motioned for him to throw it down the street away from Ilya's car. Careful to roll up his sleeve so it wouldn't make any noise, Lee threw the knife, which sailed down the street, clattering into the gutter almost a block away.

With alarming speed, the two men produced pistols and aimed

them toward the sound. The shorter of the two whispered something, and they started down the street. Ilya stepped out of the shadows behind them to the right and kept her gun trained on them while Lee and Nels moved to the car, then backed up slowly to join them. Through a complex set of hand motions, barely visible in the dim light, she managed to communicate that they would open their doors together.

At the sound of the Peugeot's doors being opened, both men stopped in their tracks and turned. Nels barely had time to dive in the backseat before Lee and Ilya dropped into the front. One of the two men yelled, "Hey!" Ilya, in a remarkably smooth motion, turned the key, slammed the gear shift into reverse, and stomped on the accelerator. Lee had never seen a car burn rubber in reverse before, particularly from the inside, and he watched in fascination until the first bullet came through the windshield. Shards of glass went everywhere, and Ilya swerved wildly, nearly careening off the nearest wall, then arcing across the street again, before getting it under control.

Tyler stuck her head up out of the stairwell. The sound of gunshots rang out once more in the distance, this time pistols. She swore and ran for the van. Those were her men back there. If anything happened to them . . .

With the safe house far behind, Ilya let up on the accelerator, applied the brake, and got the car turned around so they were going forward. Her relationship with the Belize City police was not entirely cordial, and if she got stopped for a traffic infraction, they might haul her in for questioning. And the *Saldanha* would not wait for them.

Like a shadow on wheels, the black Peugeot rolled through the open gate of a shipyard, and Ilya maneuvered through mammoth stacks of shipping crates, stopping in an open space near an enormous rust-colored cargo ship. Two cranes mounted up on the deck were loading containers into the hull, while a skeleton crew sauntered to and fro carrying out the orders of the captain. On the hull, near the front in badly faded white paint, were the words *Saldanha, South Africa.*

Nels was not even out of the car when a dark man in khaki pants and maroon T-shirt walked up and spoke briefly with Ilya, and some money changed hands. While Lee and Nels looked on, the Peugeot was crated up and hoisted aboard the ship. Nels moved closer to Ilya.

"You're coming with us?" She nodded, and Nels continued, "I won't allow it. You've done enough already."

"You think your CIA friends back there aren't going to tell Interpol that I have been giving aid to fugitives? At the very least, I'll be out of a job."

She was right, though Nels didn't want to admit it. She would be sacked for her part in all this, and what was worse, if Lee and Nels were unsuccessful, the CIA might hunt her down because she knew too much. Not one to just give up, Ilya would be doomed to a half-life on the run. They both knew it, and from the set of her jaw, Nels could see she wasn't going to budge.

"Welcome aboard," Nels said without enthusiasm.

They boarded the ship, were shown to their quarters, and the ship was under way in less than half an hour. The room had no carpet, two beds, and a cot, which was much better than anyone had expected. Bathroom facilities were minimal but amazingly clean, and Lee thought he just might be able to get used to it. Ilya sat down and winced. Nels looked at her with concern and for the first time noticed the bloodstain on her shirt.

"When were you hit?"

Ilya repositioned herself hoping to ease the pain, but only made it worse. "When I went through the window. It's just a scratch."

Nels squinted, trying to see better with his good eye, but he knew it was no scratch. "Lie down on the bed."

Ilya was about to protest, but another wave of pain wracked her body, and she lay back on the bed. Nels unbuttoned her shirt carefully and pulled the two parts gingerly to either side. A bullet hole was visible just below her ribs. Tiny flecks of bone offered hope that the bullet had been deflected from the major organs. The wound itself was oozing a little, but she was not losing much blood.

"How long were you in the water?"

Ilya clenched her teeth, trying not to moan. "The adrenaline is wearing off. Three, maybe four minutes."

"We've got to get you to a doctor. I'll tell the captain to turn the ship around."

Ilya started to sit up and grimaced. "No! You can't go back . . . too dangerous." She lay back, panting to catch her breath, and closed her eyes. "Besides, the captain would never agree to it."

Nels looked angry. "It's nine days to Morocco! You'll never make it."

Ilya opened her eyes tiredly and grabbed his hand, a sort of thank-you for his concern. "There's a doctor on board. He can take care of me." The look in her eyes said it all. She was unwilling to endanger their lives to save her own. From the standpoint of the mission, she was right, and as much as he hated the idea, Nels had to agree with her. Ilya pulled him close and spoke into his ear.

"Don't let them bury me at sea."

Nels understood. The thought of his body at the bottom of the ocean had always terrified him, and he needed no explanation. He called for the ship's doctor, and Lee pitched in to rearrange the furniture so the doctor could operate. No one doubted he was doing the best he could, considering his moderate training and the lack of an operating room, but the facilities were primitive at best. Fortunately the one item in which he was well stocked was anesthetic. Ilya was unconscious during the operation, and the bullet was easy to find. With the incision closed, and the patient resting comfortably, the doctor told Lee and Nels to keep an eye on her. He quietly moved to stand by the door of their room.

The look on his face did not instill confidence. "She will live or die now. I saw no damage to her internal organs, but the infection is already spreading. I have given her antibiotics, but I don't know if it will be enough."

Nels set up vigil beside Ilya's bed, and Lee did the only thing he could under the circumstances. He collapsed on his bed and fell asleep.

Thanks to her unfamiliarity with the streets, Tyler took about five minutes to locate the safe house once more. To her tremendous relief, Nash and Wally were waiting, albeit impatiently, right where she left them. They climbed in the van, and she could see they were fit to be tied.

Nash bit his tongue for a moment, then spoke calmly, "Someone left here in a big hurry just after you took off on your little excursion. They were driving a black Peugeot. Ilya Stehn drives a black Peugeot. Did you know that?"

"No. I didn't. Did you happen to notice if she was alone?"

"At least one other person got in the car with her."

"Why didn't you pursue?"

Outraged, Nash spluttered, "We were on foot! They were in a sports car . . . ," then he noticed the smart-aleck grin on Tyler's face. Wally started laughing, and a sardonic smile gradually overtook Nash's mouth. "Okay. So what do we do now?"

"We have three different scenes to piece together. Maybe, when we're done, we'll have some idea what happened."

Chapter Eight

"Bill! Bill! Shut up for a minute! I can't understand a word you're saying."

Carter Ellis leaned forward and repositioned the phone so he could listen better, knocking over a cup of coffee. Watching helplessly as the liquid soaked into his felt blotter, he reflexively smacked the receiver with his palm, but the connection was still bad. Bill Sidwell had called him from a car phone in Annapolis, Maryland, and the signal kept breaking up. Only by shouting was Sidwell able to make himself heard.

"I'm on my way . . . airport . . . call from Chip down in San . . . the fixer team is airborne . . . Tyler's team made contact with the fugit . . . still at large . . . rently they ran into a team from French intelligence, but . . . casualties."

Ellis growled with frustration. "Bill! Call me back from the airport! Do you hear me? CALL ME FROM THE AIRPORT! I'm getting every third word!"

The line went dead. It was not a good start to the day. Ellis glanced at his calendar. At least the Joint Chiefs weren't meeting this morning. Maybe by the time they did, he would have some good news for them. Sure. And maybe the members of Congress would vote themselves a pay cut.

GULF SHIPPING COMPANY, WAREHOUSE DISTRICT, BELIZE CITY, BELIZE
SEPTEMBER 25, 9:48 A.M.

With the aid of some carefully worded calls from CIA headquarters, Tyler was able to get permission from Interpol to use the Gulf Shipping Company for a temporary base of operations, but not before she put out the equivalent of an APB through the local police, listing a description of Stehn's black Peugeot. That would more or less cover the roads and the airport. To get out of the area, they would have to swim for it. The APB had been out for two hours, and they hadn't received a single lead. Either people weren't talking, or Stehn was holed up somewhere. A trail like that gets cold fast, but Tyler was ready to go knocking door to door if necessary.

She sat down in the swivel chair in front of the computer console in the control room and buried her face in her hands. Lack of sleep was making it hard to keep a cogent thought in her head. Maybe she would be able to think more clearly after a nap. The adjacent room had a canvas cot, with a window wall that provided a breathtaking view of the ocean. Tyler lay down and closed her eyes. Sleep would have claimed her almost immediately, were it not for a blast from the horn of a large freighter chugging out to sea. Irritation gave way to revelation as she realized there was one avenue out of the city that they hadn't covered.

"Nash!"

From his ongoing excavation of bullets in the dining room, Nash heard the call and hurried out of the room, carefully stepping over the bloodstains on the carpet. He was glad the bodies had been taken to the morgue.

"What is it?"

"A boat! They may have taken a boat."

Nash leaned up against the doorjamb. "They were here barely four hours. I doubt they came planning to take a cruise."

Tyler's eyes were wide. "Don't you get it? The place was hit before they could make plans. The Stehn woman saved them from the DeeGees and they had to take the first boat out of town."

"A little convenient, isn't it? Finding a boat just when you need it?"

"This is a major port, you idiot. Ships leave all the time. Come on."

Tyler brushed past Nash, who reluctantly fell in step behind her. "Where are we going?"

"To the shipyards."

TWO HUNDRED MILES SOUTHWEST
OF THE DOMINICAN REPUBLIC, CARIBBEAN SEA
SEPTEMBER 25, 3:23 P.M.

The weather was cloudy overhead, but the forecast said nothing about storms, so the crew was expecting clear sailing. Though the furnishings aboard the freighter were meager, the food was palatable, but Lee couldn't be sure it wasn't because he was ravenous. Nels refused to eat at first, but with some prodding from Lee, he acquiesced, though he refused to leave Ilya's side.

Ilya slept soundly only because she was heavily sedated. When she approached consciousness, she moaned pitifully until the doctor came with more anesthetic. He forced some water down her throat before administering the injection. The sick bay had no equipment for intravenous feeding, so at some point, they knew they would have to wake her.

By late afternoon, bored out of his skull, Lee found a chair and sat down next to Nels, who was making notes in Lee's notepad. Nels looked a little better today, and the swelling around the eye was going down. He spoke without looking up, "We're running out of paper. We have to get another notepad."

"What are you writing?"

"Outplacement plans for the Gulf states." Nels closed his eyes and put a palm to his forehead. "When I started on this, I grossly underestimated the number of interdependencies. It's going to take a miracle to pull this off."

Lee placed a hand on his friend's shoulder. "Why don't you get some rest?"

"I am resting. Besides, I need to talk to you."

"What about?"

Nels opened his eyes and looked at Lee matter-of-factly. "Eternity."

"I'd rather talk about your outplacement plans."

"No. You don't seem to understand something, Lee." Nels gestured to Ilya's body. "That could be you. Or one of those bullet-riddled corpses lying in the morgue in Belize City. You've seen how quickly death can happen. Are you prepared to meet your Maker?"

"I don't think my 'Maker' would go to the trouble to meet me. I'm not even sure I believe in God, Nels. I'm sorry. I know it's important to you."

"Have you ever known me to take anything at face value?"

"No."

"Do I strike you as someone who has committed intellectual suicide?"

"Of course not."

"Then listen to me carefully. I have researched the Bible, Lee. It is the most historically accurate ancient text in the world. The Bible asserts there is a God, and the order of the universe suggests the existence of God. In fact, based on the overwhelming body of scientific evidence, it would take more faith to be an atheist. Are you an atheist?"

No one had ever put it to him in just that way. Lee frowned and thought about it for the longest time. There was an awful lot of order in the universe. An awful lot. To think it evolved by chance would indeed take a lot of faith. But God? Forced to make a decision, Lee decided that to be intellectually honest, he had to concede that there was at least a possibility that creation was a deliberate act, with an intelligence behind it. "I don't think so."

"Good. Then you believe in God."

"I don't know if I believe in God."

Nels waved his hand impatiently. "Okay, so you're an agnostic. If you accept at least the possibility of God, you must accept at least the possibility of Jesus."

"Why?"

"Are you prepared to deny the existence of Jesus of Nazareth as a historical figure?"

"No."

"Then you must accept the possibility that He lived. Who do you think Jesus was?"

"One of the great teachers. You said yourself He was a good idea."

"That's not an option, and I'll tell you why. Standing before the religious leaders of His day, Jesus claimed in no uncertain terms to be God in the flesh."

Lee looked skeptical. "I don't believe it."

"It's right there in the Bible, in black and white. They asked Him if His authority was from Abraham, and He answered, 'Before Abraham was, I am.' "

"What kind of nonsense is that?"

"None at all if you're a Jew. When Moses met God on the mountain, he asked God what His name was, and God said, 'Yahweh,' which translates literally as 'I am.' The ultimate expression of being. When Jesus said, 'I am,' the word He used was *Yahweh*, God's name spoken to Moses. For the Jewish leaders, there could be no other interpretation. Jesus said, 'I am God,' and they eventually killed Him for it."

"Why? Why not just lock Him up as a lunatic?"

"It's not the same thing as one of the great thinkers of our time standing up and saying, 'I am a bowl of pudding.' His arguments were sound, His teachings full of love and mercy and compassion. People loved Him, and the leaders were afraid of Him. So we have Jesus, one of the greatest teachers and philosophers of all time, claiming to be God. Are you prepared to believe He was insane?"

"No. Of course not. I don't know anyone who thinks He was insane."

Nels turned his chair, so he could face Lee without getting a cramp in his neck. "Good. Then you accept the possibility that He was in His right mind. Are you prepared to believe He was diabolically evil?"

Lee recoiled as if Nels had said the pope reads dirty books. "Certainly not. Why would you ask that?"

"Because Jesus told people to trust Him for eternal life. If He was lying, then countless millions have thrown away their lives for no reason. Martyrs and believers throughout the centuries have given their health, their wealth, their very lives, for the promise of the gospel. A man who knowingly lied on this scale could be described only as diabolically evil. Wouldn't you agree?"

Lee sighed with resignation. "I suppose I must, Nels. You speak very convincingly of possibilities. But Christianity stands or falls on the Resurrection. Can you show me one shred of proof that Jesus actually came back from the dead?"

"The empty tomb, for one."

"The disciples could have stolen the body."

Nels smiled. "Preposterous. The disciples were whipped, beaten. They were cowering in a room, terrified that the Romans were going to kill them, too. But something happened to change them from a grieving band of peasants to the most effective evangelistic force the world has ever known, with the possible exception of the Muslims or, if you prefer a more recent example; the Communist Party. After the Resurrection, every one of the remaining disciples, except John, was executed for preaching that Jesus was alive, remember? My pastor asked me, 'Who would die for a lie?' and I'm asking you the same question."

Lee didn't have an answer. The conversation continued like that for what seemed like hours, with Nels reading periodically from a pocket Bible he kept in his overnight bag, Lee trying to defend his position at every opportunity. The longer the discussion went on, the less sure Lee was that he really had a position. More and more, Nels's words began to make sense, but something inside Lee would not let him accept it as truth. Finally Nels stopped talking and put his Bible away. They ate a late dinner in silence, which suited Lee fine. He had a lot to think about.

When the lights were turned out, Lee rolled on his side, ready to sleep. Before he could drop off, however, Nels spoke.

"Lee?"

"Yeah."

"What if it's true?"

For just an instant, Lee saw the universe and himself in relation to it, indescribably small and insignificant. It was not a pleasant sensation. He knew the question was rhetorical, but the answer was inescapable. *If it's true, then I am very, very wrong.*

SITUATION ROOM, WHITE HOUSE, WASHINGTON, D.C. SEPTEMBER 26, 5:57 A.M.

The deep blue carpet in the foyer for the West Wing seemed unusually forbidding. Walking from the security desk down the hall toward the situation room, Ellis and Sidwell looked calm and purposeful despite the fact each felt he was going to his own execution. They stopped at the security station, showed their IDs, and passed through.

Much like his first meeting on the Prometheus DISASTER, as Ellis was in the habit of calling it, the Joint Chiefs were there along with White House Chief of Staff Hank Joram and top officials from the CIA and NSA. Joram called the meeting to order, and everyone quieted down.

"Mr. Ellis, I believe you have an update for us?"

"Yes, sir. As you know, yesterday evening, the fugitives were spotted in the warehouse district of Belize City. Our agents have verified they made contact with an Interpol agent named Ilya Stehn. The Interpol office was hit by a team from French intelligence."

Joram lifted his hand a few inches off the table. "French intelligence? What are they doing hitting an Interpol office?"

"Our analysis suggests they may be after the file. It's possible that Polly Sutton was working for them. Anyway, our agents located the fugitives at a DGSE safe house and had to intervene to prevent them from being executed."

"I thought the order was termination."

"It was. Our team leader decided since they were already in French custody, there was a need to find out how much information had changed hands. Two DGSE agents fled with the fugitives, but someone—probably the Stehn woman—got the drop on them coming out, shot both agents, and fled with the fugitives by car."

"Why weren't the French agents eliminated with the fugitives?" It was Harmon Kelsey, army chief of staff.

Ellis looked at Sidwell, who nodded and answered, "The attempt was made, sir. Our information is incomplete at this time, but every effort was made to . . ."

Kelsey waved a hand to stop the flow of information. "Forget it. It's a moot point now."

"Not necessarily, sir. One of the DGSE agents is unaccounted for. Our agents found bloodstains at the exit but no body."

Joram took off his glasses and started cleaning the left lens. "So where are the fugitives now?"

"We believe they might be on a South African freighter, headed for Morocco."

"Why Morocco?"

"I don't know, sir."

Joram replaced the glasses and looked at the faces around the table. "Gentlemen, we have the best-equipped army in the world, and up until last week, I would have said one of the finest intelligence networks anywhere. Wouldn't you all agree this embarrassment has gone on long enough? The president is ready to dismantle the entire lab program and bury half the CIA in pink slips. This morning he asked me if we could nuke Belize City. Now, we all know he was only kidding, but the man needs some answers, gentlemen."

The chief of staff for the navy spoke first. "We could nuke the freighter."

Joram actually smiled. "We can't just vaporize a South African freighter. The South African government might object."

Kelsey jumped in. "What about a SEAL team? They could sink the freighter, and no one would ever know about it."

The chief of staff for the air force picked up the thought. "Why even bother with the ship? Just have them locate and eliminate the fugitives."

Joram turned to Ellis. "If memory serves, with an operation like that, we have an 87 percent probability of civilian casualties and a 63 percent chance of living witnesses?" Ellis nodded. "I'd rather sink the ship. How sure are we that the fugitives are actually on board that ship?"

"Confidence is high, sir."

Joram removed his glasses once more, but he set them on the table and rubbed his eyes. His voice fairly dripped with sarcasm, made more pointed by his southern drawl. "We have to be sure, gentlemen. Sinking ships is often considered an act of war, and I don't think the president wants to go to war with South Africa."

Bill Sidwell raised a tentative hand. "I may have a solution, sir."

"Well, spit it out, Bill."

"You could search the ship. Say we got a tip that they were carrying drugs or weapons, I don't care. Anything. If we find the fugitives, we take them into custody and disappear. If we don't find the fugitives, we suffer a little embarrassment, write a nice apology to the South African government, and everyone's happy. No sunken ship, no dead bystanders, and a minimum risk to the president's image."

When Sidwell finished, the room was silent. All eyes were on Joram. The silence stretched on for thirty seconds, then a minute. Sidwell clenched his teeth and resisted the urge to fidget. When Joram finally spoke, his tone left no room for dissent.

"I like it."

SALDANHA FREIGHTER, ONE HUNDRED MILES SOUTHEAST OF PUERTO RICO, CARIBBEAN SEA
SEPTEMBER 27, 2:42 P.M.

As the South African freighter *Saldanha* left civilization behind and churned toward the open sea, the crew settled in for an uneventful trip. In the cabin assigned to the passengers, Ilya's condition was getting worse. The doctor had been in once that morning to give her the last of the antibiotics, then quietly explained to Nels that it was only a matter of hours until the infection took her.

Shortly after lunch, when the anesthetic was beginning to wear off again, the doctor returned to give her another injection, but Nels stopped him. The doctor looked at him in surprise.

"She is having much pain. One more injection might take her peacefully through the end."

Nels spoke softly, but firmly. "I know Ilya. She would want to face death with her eyes open."

The doctor shrugged and left the room. Watching Ilya come out of her drug-induced torpor was difficult, so much so that Lee asked if it wouldn't be better to keep her sedated. Nels set his jaw and shook his head. Her moans gradually grew louder, then subsided a bit and her eyes came open halfway, a hint of the old fire in them.

"You stopped the painkillers, didn't you?" Ilya winced as another wave of pain swept over her.

"Yes. The doctor says you don't have long to live."

Ilya weakly took hold of Nels's hand. "Thank you." She closed her eyes, apparently not suffering too much at the moment. "You know, just before I woke up, I was back at my house in Bratislava. I was eight years old, dancing on my mother's sitting room floor." Ilya took a long breath and let it out slowly, painfully, and closed her eyes. "My grandmother used to tell me Jesus had made me His dancer. I was so happy then."

Nels squeezed her hand. "You are His dancer, Ilya. And you can dance for Him again. Do you want to dance for Him again?"

The eyes came open again. "Oh . . . yes . . . yes . . . I want to dance again . . ." Her voice was weak, but for an instant, Nels thought he could see the little girl behind the eyes.

Pain wracked her again, and Nels waited for it to pass before speaking. "Thank Jesus, Ilya. Thank Jesus for saving you. Ask Him to take you by the hand . . ."

Ilya prayed. The outpouring of her heart was sincere and long overdue. Tears streamed down her face as she confessed long-forgotten sins, broken promises, a ruinous trail of broken relationships, anger, bitterness, jealousy—all came pouring forth unbidden until the torrent became a stream, and finally dwindled to nothing as she recalled the earliest transgression she could remember—stealing a loaf of bread from a baker's stand on the streets of Bratislava when she was seven years old. And as the miracle of divine forgiveness transformed her, the tears stopped, and the pain on her face was replaced by a peace that was beyond understanding. Her expression was so serene, it brought tears to Nels's eyes, and Lee looked away in humiliation. Such a thing seemed too wonderful to him, and he felt a profound unworthiness in the depths of his soul.

Nels held her hand for minutes or hours, no one really knew. The pain returned, but not as bad and seemed to be gradually becoming less and less. With it, the color drained from her cheeks and the life from her eyes. Her breathing was becoming erratic when suddenly, she gripped his hand so hard, it hurt.

"He's coming . . . can you see it, Nels? . . . oh, it's beautiful . . . you can't believe how beautiful . . ."

Her voice trailed away, and the grip relaxed. Ilya breathed her last, and Nels lay the hand gently on the bed. In his mind's eye, he saw a woman of nineteen, standing hand in hand with the Lord, in a resplendent, dazzling array of light. She turned for a moment, looking curiously at the shell of her body back on the bed, then danced off into an eternity of joyous luminance, still hand in hand with her glorious escort.

Nels smiled and wiped his eyes with a handkerchief, and Lee wondered at it. "What are you smiling about?"

"She's home. No more pain. No more sorrow."

Lee moved down to the end of his bed, so he was next to Nels. A struggle unlike any he had ever experienced was going on inside Lee's mind. In all the many years spent conditioning and feeding his mind, nothing he had studied had prepared him for what he had just witnessed. Isolated on a ship at sea, with nothing else to do but ponder his existence—always aware that the end of that existence could be right around the corner—his mind was beginning to ask some very difficult questions. His old reflex to brush the questions aside, with the promise to look at them later, filled him with an inexplicable dread. He felt as if his intellect were telling him to put a gun to his head and pull the trigger without first making sure the chambers were empty.

Something deep inside Lee, something almost smothered by a lifetime of digested knowledge, something primal in the depths of his being, wanted to live, and live not just now, but forever. He was absolutely confident in it as a little boy, but growing up eroded that confidence, as it must, and he chose to defer thinking about it until the time was right.

Lee looked over at Ilya's body, and he knew without a doubt that the time was right, and that the time might never come again. If he was lucky, maybe, just maybe, the little boy could live forever. "When I die, I want to go there, Nels . . . to the place that she saw. Tell me what I have to do."

"Talk to God. Tell Him what you're feeling." Nels put a hand on Lee's leg, bowed his head, and started to pray silently.

Lee closed his eyes. He felt foolish, and more than thirty years of secular indoctrination caused his intellect to complain loudly, but there was no denying that something important was happening inside him. For Lee, in the relative noise and activity of the city, the exercise would have been completely pointless, but the rolling silence of the ship made a soothing backdrop for his awakening, and he welcomed it. Lee spoke haltingly at first, not really sure where to begin, then with increasing conviction, and to his utter amazement, he began to feel released from years of emotional baggage, almost as if someone was physically lifting an actual burden from his back.

As he continued speaking softly, his mind slipped into sort of a waking dream, and images were slowly paraded before his mind, each one seemingly calculated to give Lee a picture of how he truly was beneath his civilized exterior. It was all there—the sins of his youth, his failures as a husband and a father, his selfishness in his relationship with Sharon—and he felt an intense self-loathing that brought tears to his eyes. But he forced himself to look, whether as punishment or penance, but then something was added to the image, something that made no sense. The self-portrait, with all its grotesque selfishness, vile perversions, and stubborn pride, stretching all the way back to his childhood, should have been too horrible to look at, but there was a blood red sash nailed across it, which read, "Paid in full," and without even understanding what he was seeing, he felt comforted by it.

Lee opened his eyes. "Nels? I just saw a picture of myself, kind of a Dorian Gray thing."

"You mean that fellow who pollutes the world and his photograph looks more and more like a pile of trash?"

"Right. Only across my picture was a red banner that said, 'Paid in full.'"

Nels pointed a finger. "That's it, Lee! I was praying for something like that to be shown to you. Everything I was trying to tell you the other day is all summed up right there. When Jesus was on the cross, at the moment He died, He yelled with a loud voice, 'Tetelesthai!'

which is often translated, 'It is finished!' But that's not the whole story. This phrase can also be translated from the Greek as 'paid in full.' People in Jesus' day used it in business to signify the closure of a transaction. If that was Christ's intended meaning, it would make perfect sense. Everything you ever did wrong, or ever will do wrong, is covered by His blood, shed on the cross at Calvary."

Lee looked unsure. He felt as if he had been stripped and left naked on the universe's front porch. "Does this kind of thing always happen to you?"

"First time. But I've never been in a situation like this, either."

"So, what do I do now?"

Nels picked up his Bible and tossed it to Lee. "Read this. Pray. Live. Do what you think is right. He'll take care of the rest."

"It's that simple?" Lee asked.

"It's that simple. And I think you'll find it one of the greatest challenges you've ever faced."

Nels summoned the captain and explained Ilya's wish not to be buried at sea, so her body was sealed in an airtight bag and kept in the cargo hold. Lee and Nels spent the rest of the day and most of the following morning working and reworking plans until Lee could recite most of the major points from memory. They were so engaged in the subject that when the captain burst into their quarters late in the afternoon, he received two blank stares.

"We have company. One of your warships is on an intercept course, and it is maintaining radio silence."

Nels was on his feet immediately. "You must hide us somewhere. If they don't find us, they will leave you alone."

"Come with me."

The captain led them out, pausing only long enough to bark some hurried orders to one of the crew, then down into the cargo hold. At the far end of the hold, they stopped in front of a massive bilge pump. With the aid of the biggest wrench Lee had ever seen, the maintenance hatch to the pump was removed by the crewman. The hole was just big enough to crawl through, but the captain held up his hand before they could move.

"There is a float attached to a sensor in the chamber. You will just have room to sit, but you must hold up the sensor so it will appear to be full of water. They will be less likely to suspect you are in there."

Lee raised a finger. "What happens if they turn it on?"

"You will be blown out into the sea."

"I was afraid of that."

Nels and Lee crawled into the hatch, and the crewman was about to bolt the plate back in place when Nels's voice came from inside. "Wait! The body! Get the body!"

The captain and the crewman ran to the bag holding Ilya's body and carried it to the bilge pump, sliding it in, then the hatch was bolted shut. Inside, Lee and Nels squeezed and grunted and pushed until each was roughly in a sitting position, with the body between them, then Nels lifted the float and water sensor as instructed. The purging chamber was just a pipe three and a half feet in diameter and six feet long, capable of pushing forty thousand gallons an hour out of the cargo hold. Both men sincerely hoped no one threw the "on" switch.

From inside the chamber, they could feel the vibration of the engines stop. The warship came alongside the freighter and two small craft bucked and humped across the waves, crossing the distance all too quickly for the captain's comfort. For their part, the freighter crew had their weapons trained on the navy contingent as they came on board, and the sailors knew it. The commander hastily addressed Captain Delo.

"By order of the Joint Chiefs of Staff for the United States Army, Navy, and Air Force, we request permission to search this vessel for illegal narcotics. If you fire upon us, we will return fire, and our orders are to sink this vessel."

The captain's face was impassive, but he spoke forcefully, "This is an outrage! We will protest to your government in the strongest possible terms!"

With the formalities completed, the crew of the freighter put down their weapons, and the two squads of sailors spread out to search the ship. The captain wandered around the ship trying to keep an eye on the sailors and appear helpful. Down in the cargo hold, they opened a few shipping containers but ignored the crate with the black Peugeot inside. Then one of them stopped by the bilge pump and called the captain over.

"What is this rated?"

"Forty thousand gallons per hour."

"Turn it on for me."

"I cannot do that. This is an old model. The engine will overheat and explode. That's why we keep water in the chamber when it is idle." The captain pointed at the indicator that said the purge chamber was full of water. The sailor nodded and moved on.

The entire search took forty-five minutes, and when it was complete, the commander apologized for the inconvenience and left quickly. Captain Delo hurried down to the cargo hold with the crewman from earlier, and the plate for the maintenance hatch was removed in a hurry. Nels and Lee came out gasping for air, but otherwise unharmed. The captain helped Nels to his feet.

Nels managed a halfhearted smile. "Thank you. I was so worried about being blasted out to sea, suffocating hadn't occurred to me."

GULF SHIPPING COMPANY, WAREHOUSE DISTRICT, BELIZE CITY, BELIZE
SEPTEMBER 27, 5:14 P.M.

The Interpol office had been crawling with agents for the past thirty hours, trying to figure out what had happened, despite Tyler's assertions that her team had already figured it out. When she offered them her evidence and analysis, including a copy of the manifest for a ship departing the same night the office was hit, they politely refused. Normally the response would have infuriated her, but she understood the bureaucratic need to reinvent the wheel if only to be absolutely certain it was the right wheel.

For her, awaiting new orders was the hardest part of a field assignment, and they had been cooling their heels for the better part of two days. Nash had holed up next to a bookcase and seemed quite content to read anything, from romance novels to repair manuals, while Wally nosed around in the computer room as much as he could without stepping on anyone's toes.

When a call finally came through for Tyler, she nearly pulled a muscle jumping to her feet and fairly threw people out of the way in her dash for the communications console.

"This is Tyler."

"Ty, it's Chip. They searched the freighter. No luck."

"No! They've got to be there!"

"Sorry. I'm told the navy did a very thorough job. You can come home."

A mixture of fury and despair churned her stomach, but Tyler kept her voice relatively calm. "We'll go to El Jadida. We can meet the freighter and make sure . . ."

"No. They could be anywhere on the planet by now. You did all you could."

"Chip, please. I know I'm right about this! You've got to give us a chance. If I'm right, we complete the operation successfully. If I'm wrong, we end up coming home a few days later. Please. Let us meet the freighter. If they aren't there, we'll come straight home."

Her request was met with static for a moment, but her plea did not fall on deaf ears, and Chip finally answered, "All right. You can meet the freighter. Call me when you're in El Jadida."

"I will."

Tyler terminated the connection and ran down the hall to the sitting room, startling Nash nearly out of his chair. "What?"

Tyler grinned. "We're out of here!"

Across town, in the critical care ward of the city's largest hospital, Gerard Dinaé was upgraded from serious to stable condition. The three bullets the doctors had taken from his upper torso had done only moderate damage, and the surgery had gone very well. Of greater concern was the concussion he had suffered falling down the stone steps, but now the swelling had gone down, and he looked as if he would pull through.

No sooner was Dinaé awake than he received a call from headquarters. He felt weak, and the utter failure of his first mission didn't help matters. When he explained what transpired to his superior, the man erupted into such a vehement torrent of profanity, Dinaé wondered if he would have a stroke.

"It was a simple intelligence-gathering mission. I should have known better than to send an . . . an amateur!"

Dinaé closed his eyes and could see all the years of hard work, the training, the long hours, all lying in ruins. "With all respect, sir. We were ambushed in a dark alley. Henry never even drew his weapon."

The superior's voice was thick with contempt. "You will return as soon as you are able! I see now I overestimated your abilities, Dinaé. You are barely qualified to file papers."

Like a dagger in his mind, the last statement knifed through to the very core of his insecurity. Subconsciously he knew his men were dead precisely because he was barely qualified to file papers. In an instant, every missed promotion and reprimand in his life was personified in the man on the other end of the phone. The veneer of self-control snapped, and Dinaé swore. "I'll kill you for that. I'm going to finish this mission, then I'm going to find you and put a bullet in your skull." The veins stood out on his throat, and his lips drew back in unbridled fury. "You're dead, do you hear me? Dead!"

"Dinaé! Don't be a fool!"

Dinaé slammed the receiver down and threw the phone across the room with all his strength, setting up a terrible pounding in his head. As the throbbing subsided, he looked at the shattered remains of the phone. "It's too late. If you want to stop me, you will have to kill me."

Chapter Nine

Tyler Stills stood, hands on hips, looking for all the world like a general surveying a battlefield. Next to unraveling the action at a crime scene, it was her favorite part of the job—planning the action herself. This was a long shot, and everyone knew it, so she felt unusually lighthearted. If they failed completely, then they could go home and chalk it up to experience. The area had three cranes and a few dedicated vehicles, but the smell of machine oil was very strong, probably from the junk heap near the cement pad where they were standing. Part of the docking facility was being renovated, so it looked a little like a lumberyard at the moment, but that only made it more of a challenge.

Tyler glanced toward the ragged particle board cubicle that served as the office for the yard. A long conversation with the yard master, along with a considerable wad of local currency, had gotten them through the front gate without a detour to the police station, but if they needed any real cooperation, their little operation was going to get very expensive.

Nash noticed the look of determination on Tyler's face. "Assume, just for the sake of argument, that they aren't expecting anyone to meet them. They could just walk off the ship."

"No. Not Thiessan. Teller, maybe, but not Thiessan. They could be disguised as crew members, or they might be carried out in one of the shipping containers."

Nash rolled his eyes. "If they're inside a shipping container, how will we know?"

"Wally will have to find a way to look inside each one." Yep, the operation was definitely going to be expensive.

Wally checked into the conversation for the first time. "Why me?"

"Because Nash will be up on the water tower with the rifle."

Nash looked at the water tower. "Uh-uh. No way. I've seen the movies. The guy in the water tower always gets picked off."

Tyler smiled sweetly. "Then be sure and scream convincingly when you fall."

SALDANHA FREIGHTER, SEVENTY MILES SOUTHWEST OF EL JADIDA, MOROCCO
OCTOBER 3, 8:42 A.M.

Thrum. Thrum. Thrum. The engines churned ever onward, providing a hypnotic backdrop to the white noise of the water rushing past the hull. Every night, the sound and vibration had helped Lee drop off to sleep, and every morning, they had awakened him. But not this morning.

When Lee yawned and rolled out of bed, he felt it immediately. They weren't moving. The rushing sound was still there, but they weren't moving. Curious about the odd sensation, he walked in a straight line—for the first time—over to the porthole and peered out only to find the ocean racing by as it had every morning for the past nine days. The sea was not particularly smooth, so the only explanation was the long anticipated arrival of his sea legs. And on their last day at sea. Perfect.

He sauntered over to the mirror to see what nightmare visage might be passing for his face this morning, and he was pleasantly surprised to find that, though his hair might have been borrowed from a mad scientist, his beard was coming in nicely. As he stood there trying to drag a comb through the stringy disaster on top of his head, he mused on the felicitousness of the term *mad scientist*, for so he was. Certainly a *sane scientist* never would have embarked on such foolishness. Instead, he would have come up with an entirely different set of options, such as, "bury myself in doughnuts and eat myself to death," or "take up skydiving and don't bother packing a chute," or even better, "become the projectionist at a movie theater in Chugwater, Wyoming," assuming they have a movie theater in Chugwater. Any one of these and more, a sane man might have come up with. But not Lee. No, Lee had to make a run for it. The funny thing was, he didn't care anymore. Out of all his reading in the past few days, one verse kept haunting him in a most encouraging fashion: "Take heart! I have overcome the world."

He finished shaving his neck without a single nick or cut, then headed toward the door for his morning walk above decks. From Nels's side of the room came a muffled voice.

"Where are you going?"

"For a walk."

"Stay below decks. We may be visible from land."

Lee shook his head, marveling at the consistency of his companion. Lee was what he was through a God-given gift of intellect and half a lifetime of scholastic achievement. Nels was what he was through exhaustive, meticulous training. Up until recently, Lee hadn't believed it was possible to change an individual's personality, but the mechanistic efficiency with which Nels went about his business seemed to subjugate every other human quality. Perhaps it was impossible to truly know Nels, the real Nels, buried somewhere under the conditioning. Perhaps that part eventually died from lack of attention. But who was to say the real Nels wasn't the one Lee saw every day? Perhaps the buried Nels was merely the "old" Nels, who had been replaced by a "new" Nels.

And taking the thought farther, when had Lee ever shown his true self? Never. Or, at least, not since he was a little boy. From the first perceived injury, he had started building walls around his heart, so no one could hurt him. But the little boy inside wanted someone to find a way in. The contained nature of the physical body enforced a certain level of isolation, so there was no hope for two souls to ever really know each other. If one can't even know oneself, then certainly there was no hope for union, only desolate loneliness. *Take heart! I have overcome the world*. From womb to tomb, the journey was predestined to be taken alone. *Take heart! I have overcome the world*. God must have known that, or He wouldn't have created us to live in pairs. *Take heart! I have overcome the world*. What was it he had been reading . . . "For now we see in a mirror, dimly, but then face to face . . ."? *Take heart! I have overcome the world*. Perhaps it would not be utterly hopeless to believe the journey would not always be a lonely one.

Lee realized his forehead was so furrowed he was giving himself a headache, and that was no way to stay focused, so he raised his eyebrows and concentrated on his surroundings. His walk had taken him through the cargo hold, past the engine room and the galley, and he was nearly back to the cabin. When he walked in, Nels was sitting on his bed, staring blankly at the opposite wall.

"Good morning, Nels."

"Mmm."

"Is something wrong?"

"Everything."

Lee sat down next to the suddenly grief-stricken old man, a concerned look on his face. "What's the matter?"

"It's useless. It's all useless. Even if we succeed beyond our wildest hopes, people will still be people. There will be wars. Bloodshed. Hunger. People will still die." He squeezed his eyes shut to stem the flow of tears and was mostly successful. "Forgive me. I dreamed about Utta again. Then I woke up, and I couldn't stop thinking about Ilya. I'm afraid it makes everything seem a little hopeless this morning."

Take heart! I have overcome the world. Lee couldn't say it. He wanted to. Nels needed to hear it, but coming from Lee, it would sound like a greeting card. Lee grabbed his notepad and started writing. When he was finished, he handed it to Nels. On the page was a game of hangman with thirty letter spaces. One corner of Nels's mouth turned up, and he started guessing. The game was won easily enough.

"'Take heart! I have overcome the world.' You're right, of course. And in my current frame of mind, I won't last two seconds out there." He jerked his thumb toward the porthole.

Lee smirked a little. "You didn't exactly hit the deck when the bullets started flying back in Belize."

Nels shrugged. "Nobody's perfect. I suppose I saw the muzzle flashes and just froze, like . . ."

"Like Bambi caught in my headlights. I have a corollary for your theorem about rhythm. If you focus on one thing too long, you can give yourself a headache."

Nels stretched, stood, and shook himself. "All right. If you're so smart, tell me why we're going to Israel."

"To convince them that the cold fusion technology will seriously weaken, if not destroy, the Arabs' domination of the world energy market."

"Who is our contact in Israel?"

"Any conservative member of the Knesset, and then, with a little luck, the prime minister."

Nels pressed the point. "Why a conservative member?"

"Because a liberal might be sympathetic to the Arabs."

"And what happens after Israel?"

"Passage to New York with the Israelis. Announce the technology at a General Assembly of the United Nations. Set up a commission to administer the disbursement of the technology. Pass out plans."

Nels nodded. "A minus, Mr. Teller."

"A minus? I was flawless!"

"In content, yes, but you didn't use complete sentences."

Lee's face broke into a broad grin, and he shook his head. "Someone should give you a good spanking."

Nels continued his questioning until somewhere overhead, the freighter's horn sounded, and the two men quickly gathered their things. So anxious was Lee to be off the ship, he nearly collided with the captain coming down the stairs.

"We will be docked in ten minutes. My men will see the woman's body delivered to the morgue. Forgive me, but we haven't discussed payment."

Nels had seen the money change hands back in Belize but merely patted the captain's shoulder and said, "You can keep the car." The captain thought for a moment, nodded, and left in a hurry to make certain the crate with the Peugeot was not unloaded. Lee started up the stairs, but Nels grabbed his belt. "Where do you think you're going?"

"Off this ship."

"Not that way. Follow me."

Nels led the way to the cargo hold, up a tall ladder, along a metal walkway, up another short ladder, and out a hatch. Cool, fresh salt air hit Lee in the face, and he drank it in for a moment before noticing where they were. The hatch opened out of the deck between two bulkheads on the side of the control tower, effectively hiding them from the view of anyone on shore. Nels pulled a pair of binoculars out of his overnight bag and peered carefully around the edge of the bulkhead. After a minute or two, he handed them to Lee.

"Look at the water tower north of the dock."

Lee did so. Standing almost out of sight on the walkway around the perimeter of the water tower was a man holding a high-powered rifle. Lee swallowed hard. "If they knew we were on board, why didn't they just sink the ship?"

"They don't know we're on board. The man in the tower is the only sniper I spotted. If they knew we were here, the place would be crawling with agents. My guess is, someone at the agency wasn't willing to settle for a search done by the navy."

Nels slipped around the bulkhead to the rear with Lee in tow, then watched the shore, always keeping the tower between them and the dock. When the ship was moored, he used the extra rope from one of the lifeboats to lower himself down into the water on the ocean side of the ship. Lee followed.

The water was warm and were it not for the thought of a high-powered rifle nearby, ready to turn them into fish bait, the swim would have been rather enjoyable. They rounded the front of the ship and moved along the pilings, trying to steer clear of the barnacle-encrusted poles, despite the insistent push of the tide. The dock gradually gave way to a rocky shoreline, but Nels paddled on for another quarter mile before they finally pulled themselves up on some large volcanic rocks. Tall grass came all the way down to the shore, and Nels was quick to crawl into it. Hurrying to catch up, Lee slipped and cut his hand, but not bad, then he was in the grass. They walked bent over for fifty feet, then were safely behind the cover of a large sandstone building at the south end of the dockyard.

Lee stood up. "Oh, my back."

Nels followed suit. "Mine, too. Come on. We need to find a place to stay. I still have a little money."

Now in the habit of following Nels without question, Lee fell in step behind him without the slightest hesitation.

"I can't believe we missed them!"

Tyler was fuming. The sun was going down, and none of them had seen any sign of the fugitives. With the help of the yard foreman, Wally inspected every shipping container that left the freighter, but he had no luck. Nash kept his eyes peeled all afternoon and saw nothing. The rifle was stowed in their rental car, and Nash was sitting on a fifty-gallon drum close by, ready to give up.

"Can we go home now?" Nash asked sourly. Wally stood nearby looking gloomy.

Tyler tried to adopt a conciliatory tone but didn't quite make it. "Come on, guys. We've got to see this thing through, or we'll hate ourselves when we get back."

Nash crossed his arms. "You mean you'll hate yourself when you get back. I've seen that look before. You're obsessed with this thing and won't let it go, like some little pit bull."

Tyler's eyes flashed at the insult, but she held her tongue. "Then don't fight me. Nash, you know I'm right on this one. As long as there's a legitimate course of action, we have to go after it. Do you really want to slink home humiliated with your tail between your legs?"

"Not really, no."

"Great. I have a job for you."

"Oh, goody," Nash said deadpan.

"I want you to go inside the freighter. See if you can find any sign of them."

For all that Nash was in a grumpy mood, it was the kind of assignment he loved. Tyler could have all the niggling, forensic nit-picking, the endless hours of analyzing fiber, running ballistics tests, taking partial fingerprints, and poring over phone logs. Nash would gladly trade it all for one nocturnal penetration into hostile territory. The objective wasn't exactly a heavily armed fortress, but it beat waiting or, worse, making the long trip home in defeat.

Forty minutes later, night had fallen, and while Tyler and Wally waited in the car, Nash—in black camouflage—ran from shadow to shadow across the docking yard, one moment invisible, one moment a flicker of motion, an extra shadow near two crewmen, part of a large crate, then over the edge and down one of the pilings to the water. He swam to the far side of the ship, hoping to find an anchor chain to climb, but the freighter had no anchor in the water. He would have to climb back up to the dock and try to get aboard on one of the mooring ropes.

Nash was about to head back when he saw a rope just dangling in the water. A trap? No, it couldn't be. But if the fugitives had been aboard, they might have used the rope to get off the ship. Climbing hand over hand, he pulled himself silently up the rope, dropping soundlessly into the lifeboat. A quick scan left and right showed no one on deck, and he quickly made his way to one of the hatches.

Down below he heard sounds from the galley and conversation from the crew's mess. He turned the other direction, down a short hall, then a ladder, and he was at one of the entrances to the cargo hold. He would have ignored it altogether, were it not for the single large crate off to one side. Unable to resist, he hurried across the open space and into the shadows behind the crate. Removing his knife from its leg sheath, he began working at one of the boards. One end came away cleanly, and he pulled a small waterproof flashlight off his belt, shining it through the opening.

Inside the crate was a black Peugeot.

PA H'DAR STREET, OLD DISTRICT, EL JADIDA, MOROCCO
OCTOBER 4, 7:14 A.M.

The apartment was on the second floor of the building, small and run-down with a rickety table, two chairs, a filthy mattress, and little else. The bathroom was barely big enough to walk into, and there was no shower, so any baths would be taken by washcloth in the sink or not at all. But the price was only a few dollars a day, and it was much better than sleeping on the street.

The old district of El Jadida was a peculiar hybrid of old sandstone and wood architecture, combined with more contemporary materials, and the walls of the apartment reflected the haphazard mixture. One wall was part sandstone, part plaster, two others appeared to be made of plywood, and the last out of plasterboard. Lee could have understood the scene in war-torn Beirut, but he couldn't recall any accounts of civil war in Morocco.

Wearing hat and sunglasses, Nels had left while it was still dark to try to make arrangements for the first leg of their journey to Israel. Thanks to the reception at the dock, he was unwilling to risk the more public means of transport, which probably meant they would be riding in the back of some merchant's manure truck.

Unwilling to think ill of the man who had kept him alive so far, Lee set his mind on developing a plan for how to occupy his time until Nels returned. The plan came quickly, and he saw that it was good. He would sleep until he woke up. Then he would sleep some more.

POLICE STATION,
EL JADIDA, MOROCCO
OCTOBER 4, 7:53 A.M.

Tyler awoke with a start because someone was shaking her shoulder. She looked up, both bewildered and angry. The police officer smiled and tried to offer an explanation in halting English. The man was different from the one she had spent the better part of an hour talking to regarding the urgency of their plight. All that begging, all that translating, all that money, could easily be flushed down the tube just because her benefactor forgot to mention it to the boss when they changed shifts. She'd seen it happen.

Not receiving any response to his explanation, the officer tried once more. "You . . . were . . . sno . . . snoring."

Tyler nodded, and the fellow returned to his desk. She had worked half the night on a stack of posters with pictures of Nels Thiessan on them and text stating that he was her father, an Alzheimer's patient who had escaped from his hospice. The poster in front of her was ruined because she had been drooling on it for three hours, but there was a sizable pile completed on her right, and only a few dozen left to paste together.

As she was finishing up, Nash and Wally walked in, looking entirely too perky. Nash smirked impishly. "Well, don't you look . . ."

Tyler cut him off with a glare. "Don't mess with me. I've had a very bad night."

"Well, this should brighten your day. We found Ilya Stehn's body at the morgue."

Tyler closed her eyes and sighed with relief. Up until that moment, she had wondered if the car had been shipped as a ruse, or perhaps, however unlikely, they had changed ships in the open sea. She had asked Nash and Wally to find some sign, any sign, that they weren't wasting their time, and a body at the morgue was more than she dared hope for.

"Nash, I could kiss you."

Nash picked up one of the posters, admiring her work. "If you really love me, you'll stop at the hotel long enough to shower before we start passing these out."

Tyler wadded up the ruined poster and flung it at him, but he ducked and the paper landed on the desk of an unfriendly looking police officer. Doing her best to look contrite, Tyler grabbed her things and scurried out the door, with Wally and Nash close behind.

When Nels returned to the apartment late in the afternoon, he found Lee sitting at the table, reading his Bible. Lee looked up.

"I was beginning to wonder."

Nels dropped his hat and glasses on the mattress and sat down at the table. "There's not as much independent commerce as you might expect."

"Were you successful?"

"Yes. I found a truck leaving tomorrow for Algiers. It's a long drive, maybe seven hundred fifty miles, but from there, we can fly to Israel."

Lee was almost afraid to ask. "What's the cargo?"

"Linen. We should be quite comfortable." Nels grabbed the Bible to see how far Lee had read. "Numbers?"

Lee nodded woefully. "It's pretty slow going."

Nels laughed. "Then skip it for now. Move on to Joshua. Or Judges. Don't kill yourself on the law of Moses in your first week. And there's nothing wrong with reading from the New Testament at the same time."

Lee closed the Bible and rubbed his eyes. "You know, this was kind of exciting at first, but I'm really beginning to hate all this cloak-and-dagger stuff. Just once, I'd like to walk through an airport, order a ticket under my own name, and get on an airplane without worrying about being shot."

"It could be worse. We could be staying in Casablanca, fifty miles up the coast."

Lee laughed. "Oh, that would be rich! We'd have to wear overcoats and fedoras."

Nels did a bad impression of Bogart. "Of all da houses near da university, you had to wander into mine."

"I'll bet you're sorry you were home."

"I didn't have anything better to do. Listen, this has been a real shot in the arm for me. If I survive the ordeal, I might live to be a hundred."

Lee's face darkened a little, and he spoke more seriously than he intended. "I'll be happy just to make it through the day."

Nels smiled ruefully. "Congratulations. Now you really are a field agent."

Tyler and company spent most of the day handing out posters all over town, then collapsed at the hotel to wait. They played cards, but there was no television, and no one had brought anything to read, other than the file on the fugitives, so Tyler spent much of the time rereading the file and lying on her bed, thinking. No matter how many times she pushed it aside, the same thought kept popping into her head: *What makes these men worth killing?* She could see a potential threat in a former agent like Thiessan, but the background on Lee Teller was squeaky clean. The man didn't even have any parking tickets. If he was some sort of double agent, that would be one thing, but a physics professor from a respected university? It didn't make sense. More than that, it was wrong.

Someone at headquarters, or maybe higher up, had to be trying to cover some tracks. Chip said Teller and Thiessan saw something they weren't supposed to see. Mistakes like that happen all the time, but people don't get killed as a result. If they were a threat to national security, that would explain a lot, but she had been around long enough to know that even a threat to someone's career might be sufficient to order someone's termination. Killing on somebody else's whim had driven her out of fieldwork before, and nothing had happened in the interim to change the revulsion she felt one bit. And she knew instinctively that it would be her only chance to "redeem" herself in the eyes of her superiors. If she couldn't pull the trigger, they could easily yank her back to a desk job. Kill or quit. Neither option was remotely tolerable, and it occurred to Tyler that maybe, just maybe, she was in the wrong line of work after all.

The evening passed slowly, which gave Tyler a chance to catch up on some much-needed sleep, but it was well into the following afternoon before she heard anything on the posters. The call came from an elderly woman, who claimed to have seen her "father" going into an apartment building with a younger man on Pa H'dar Street in the old district. Tyler thanked the woman profusely, and her team moved out.

Afternoon traffic was slow, and it was almost dusk by the time they reached Pa H'dar Street. Tyler was restless enough to chew her fingernails down to the bone, but she managed to keep it under wraps, so she was the very picture of calm efficiency when they finally parked the car. Nash was out without a word, ready for a standard recon mission. He spotted the building easily enough, thanks to the woman's description, but getting around the building was going to be a neat trick. Whoever erected the edifice apparently thought alleys were things to be avoided, and Nash had to walk all the way down to the end of the block just to look at the other side.

There were two exits, which should make containment easy, and the streets were straight confines, so there would be nowhere to run, even if they made it out of the apartment alive. The builders of the units across the street didn't share their neighbor's reluctance about alleys, and Nash was able to find a rickety fire escape, though the thought of climbing it made him nervous.

On the roof, he crawled along the wall, peering over every thirty feet or so, and discovered he could see into every apartment across the way. Some of the rooms had blinds that were open, but no one seemed to care much for curtains in this part of town, or couldn't afford them, so he saw more than he would have liked of the bottom crust of El Jadida society. When he spotted Nels and Lee sitting in their little rented apartment as if they owned it, instead of elation, Nash felt a twinge of disappointment. On a subconscious level, he had been hoping they would make it. Nash had been trained to kill when he had to, but not like this.

He hurried back to the car and climbed in. "I found 'em. They're on the second floor."

Tyler's face said it all. She felt like Nash did. But the sun was down, the light was almost gone, and they had a job to do. "Nash, you have the roof. Wally, watch the door in case they make a break for it."

Nash jerked his thumb over his shoulder. "What about the other door?"

Tyler's expression was hard. "They're not expecting anyone, or you wouldn't have spotted them so easily. Thiessan must be getting tired."

Quietly they climbed out of the car, and Tyler and Nash made their way in the gathering gloom to the fire escape in the alley. Wally drew his pistol and stood near the corner where he could get a clear shot at the front door. Up on the roof opposite, Nash scooted into position, with Tyler close behind, and carefully put his rifle together. Through a shoddy set of blinds partially covering the window, Nels and Lee could be clearly seen, sitting at a table and talking, making notes, and occasionally reading from a small book. Nash double-checked his rifle, loaded it, and looked through the scope. *Very careless, Mr. Thiessan. I can see you, but you can't see me.* Nash drew a bead on Nels's forehead and spoke softly to Tyler, who was crouched next to him.

"I'll take Thiessan first. Teller might be slower to react."

Tyler looked from the rifle to Thiessan, then back again. Unseen in the dark, her face bore an anguished expression, and her clenched fists trembled with the agony of the decision she was being forced to make. Nash's finger tightened slowly on the trigger. Tyler made up her mind suddenly, and the trembling stopped. Careful not to startle him, she gently brushed his arm. "Wait."

Nash looked sideways. "We may not get another chance."

"I know. It's my responsibility. Take Wally and go back to the hotel. I'm going to try to make contact."

Nash tried to keep his voice down. "Make contact! Are you crazy?"

"We don't know what they did with the file. For all we know Thiessan may have sent it to his lawyer marked, 'To Be Opened in Event of My Death.' We don't even know if they're guilty! Are you willing to blow away two innocent civilians?"

"I don't like it any more than you do, but if that's what my orders say, the answer has to be yes."

"You would have made a good Nazi. I'm your commander, and I say there's more going on here than meets the eye. Take Wally and go back to the hotel. If I don't call in twelve hours, take the first plane out of here back to the States."

Nash set the rifle down. "You're taking a big chance. You know if you blow this, HQ might send me back. And this time you might be the target."

Tyler understood. But the choice was made, and one way or the other she was going to see it through. For the first time since they left the United States, she really felt she was doing the right thing. "No regrets. I'll see you around."

As she disappeared into the shadows, Nash shook his head and disassembled his rifle. He joined Wally down on the street and turned the corner, angrily criticizing Tyler's decision as both men walked toward the rental car. Wally was worried about Tyler, but he was never really comfortable questioning authority, and he rationalized that it wasn't really any of his business anyway. When they reached the car, Nash paused for a moment.

"You go back to the hotel. I'm staying. If I don't call you in twelve hours, get out of town as fast as you can."

"You're both idiots," Wally stated matter-of-factly.

"Yeah."

Wally looked at his friend for a long moment but knew better than to debate him when his mind was made up. With a shrug and a wave, Wally climbed in the car and drove away, leaving Nash to disappear into the night. Back on Pa H'dar Street, a man stood in the shadow of a doorway, watching the place where the sniper had been on the roof. He had seen the team split up and the departure of the car. When no shot came after several minutes, the fixer walked several blocks down to a squalid little restaurant with a public phone. He dialed a long string of numbers and waited. Finally a man's voice answered.

"Bill Sidwell."

"Mr. Sidwell, this is the repair shop. Your primary unit has malfunctioned. The target unit is still active. It is possible the primary unit may contact the target unit. Please advise."

Sidwell was quiet for some time before answering. "If the primary unit contacts the target unit, remove them both."

PA H'DAR STREET, OLD DISTRICT, EL JADIDA, MOROCCO
OCTOBER 5, 9:17 A.M.

Most of the shops in the old district opened with the rising of the sun, as soon as the muezzin finished his morning call to prayer, a centuries-old custom perpetuated by Muslim merchants who believed Allah blessed the efforts of the man who used every moment of daylight for the purpose of selling. Tyler had no trouble finding an inexpensive modest brown dress and perfume, but the search for a convincing wig took her many blocks out of the old district on foot.

The transformation from jumpsuit to shoulder-length hair and dress was remarkable. The woman Tyler saw in the mirror was all softness and curves, and she hated the image. Softness was the same as weakness, and the curves did nothing but attract the enemy, but she could think of no other way to get close to the fugitives. Walking all the way back to Pa H'dar Street in nice leather shoes was hard on her feet, after so long in tennis shoes, but the masquerade had to be believable, and it had been a while since she had worn nice shoes, so she needed a little time to get used to them.

She decided on a modest dress because it was a Muslim country, and anything seductive or revealing was liable to get her thrown in jail. Thiessan spoke several languages that she didn't, so she chose an identity that hailed from Istanbul, a city with which she had some familiarity, and which was metropolitan enough to produce an intelligent, headstrong girl. Tyler didn't speak the language, but neither did Thiessan, so the playing field should be equal.

Going through the plan once more in her head, she started up the stairs to the second floor of the fugitives' apartment building.

Inside the apartment, Lee sat at the table eating rolls and cheese that had also served as dinner the night before. He had slept well for the first time since leaving Hanover. No one knew where they were, which meant the trip to Israel should be smooth sailing, and he wondered whether he and Nels might not finally be out of the woods.

Nels was still sleeping peacefully on the mattress when there was a commotion out in the hallway, followed by a woman's bloodcurdling scream. Nels sat bolt upright, and Lee ran for the door.

"Lee! Don't!"

It was too late. The door was already open. But instead of the dreaded onslaught of bullets and well-armed bodies, the hallway outside was empty. Lee stuck his head out and saw a woman's form lying at the end of the hall. *She has to be dead,* Lee thought. *No one could scream like that and still be alive.* Cautiously he stepped out into the hall and moved toward the body. Whoever she was, she was beautiful. Lee checked for a wedding ring, found none, and then mentally kicked himself for looking in the first place. *Get a life, Lee! The woman's just been assaulted. You shouldn't be sizing her up like a side of beef in a meat locker.*

Lee gingerly took her hand in his. "Miss? Are you all right? Miss! Can you hear me?"

The woman slowly came to, and Lee's heart skipped a beat. He had never seen such big brown eyes. "Miss? Are you okay?" The woman looked at him for the first time and pulled back in fear, but said nothing.

Nels walked up then and spoke. "Hola, señorita. ¿Habla español?"

As Lee watched in fascination, those perfect lips moved, and she spoke. "I don't speak Spanish. Who are you?"

Her accent sounded East European, and Lee found it utterly captivating. Nels responded cautiously. "We live here. We heard you scream."

"I should go."

The woman tried to stand and promptly fell into Lee's arms. Her perfume was intoxicating, and he nearly dropped her. With Nels's help, Lee walked her back to the apartment and closed the door. They seated her in one of the chairs at the table, and then Nels sat opposite, fixing her with a penetrating stare.

"Who are you, and what are you doing here?"

The woman hesitated a moment, then spoke softly. "I am Aydan Fayad. I came here looking for my brother."

"Your brother lives in this building?"

"No. My brother moved to El Jadida from our home in Istanbul two years ago. We never heard from him again. Our father is sick, so I came looking for him." Tears came to her eyes, but she continued, "I found out this morning he is dead. And now they have taken my money."

"Who has taken your money?"

"The men who attacked me." The woman dissolved into tears, and Lee's heart went out to her without reservation.

Nels was not convinced. "That still doesn't explain what you were doing in this building."

Lee shot Nels an irritated look. "Lighten up, Nels."

Nels ignored him. "What were you doing in the building?"

The woman was beginning to look frightened again. "I needed a place to sleep. I was up all night at the police station. I told the cabdriver I need a place that is not much money. He bring me here."

Nels searched her face for any sign that she was lying. The circles under the eyes were real enough. She certainly looked like she had been up all night. If she was an agent, he had no clue what her orders might be. Everything in his training and his logic told him not to help stranded women, but he had served a higher law the past three years, one written in blood on a cross two thousand years ago. Nels would err on the side of compassion, and God help them if he was wrong.

"We're taking a truck to Algiers this afternoon. It's about seven hundred fifty miles up the coast. You'd be welcome to join us, but I must warn you, there are people trying to kill us."

The woman's eyes widened. "Are you criminals?"

"Our government thinks we are. We're just a couple of college professors. We saw something we weren't supposed to see."

The woman looked as if her curiosity got the better of her. "Can you tell me what it is?"

Her lips were slightly parted, the eyes enchanting, awash with anticipation, and before Nels could stop him, Lee blurted, "Cold fusion."

"Lee!" Nels nearly shouted. Lee came out of his trance and clamped a hand over his mouth, looking for a moment like a little boy who just swore in front of his mother.

The woman started to smile. "You must be joking." The looks she received in reply told her it was no joke. With her background in economics, Tyler knew instinctively at least some of the catastrophic ramifications of such a discovery, but a headstrong girl from Istanbul would certainly not have a clue what Lee was talking about. "What is this 'cold fusion,' and why does it frighten you so?"

"Never mind!" Nels gritted his teeth. He wanted to scream. He wanted to hit Lee. He wanted to scream and hit Lee. Didn't Lee understand this woman might turn them in just on the chance there was a reward? Well, it was out now, and her presence was no longer an option. "I'm afraid you're going to have to come with us."

The woman looked a little confused. "You . . . you are kidnapping me?"

"No. We offered you the chance to come with us. I am merely insisting that you accept."

"But you said it will be dangerous."

Nels nodded. "It will."

The woman looked around the room and sighed with resignation. "That's okay. I'd rather be killed than stranded in this God-forsaken place."

Nels felt agitated, as he always did when it seemed that a situation was getting out of control. At his suggestion, they packed up what few things they were still carrying and left the apartment immediately, first Nels, then the woman, then Lee. They walked out on the street, and in an instant Nels knew something was wrong. A man in a jacket and cap was walking toward them, clearly in no hurry, barely twenty feet away, but the clothes were all wrong for Morocco. As Nels watched in horror, the man reached into his jacket and pulled out a pistol. Nels yelled, "Trap!" Then he stood with his arms and legs apart, a human shield. Before the man could fire, however, his head jerked sideways, shot from above, and the impact threw him down on the sidewalk. He hadn't hit the ground yet when the report from the gunshot finally sounded from the rooftop across the street.

Up the block, a car door burst open, and a second man opened fire with his pistol. Nels went down, and Lee was about to dive on the woman to protect her when she hiked up her skirt, drew a pistol from a thigh holster with incredible speed, dropped to one knee, and returned fire. Their assailant lurched back against the door frame and then pitched forward. Lee flinched and looked skyward. There were more shots from above—a second sniper was shooting at the first.

As the first sniper fell from his perch, Tyler sighted in on the man responsible and squeezed off three shots. The second sniper twisted backward into a sandstone buttress, failed to steady himself, and plunged screaming to the street. Fearing the worst, Tyler hurried toward the sniper who had come to their rescue. *It's Nash. Oh, no. Please, no. Of all the stupid* . . . Apparently she wasn't the only one who couldn't follow orders.

For the first time since she was eight years old, Tyler sank to her knees and wept. Free at last, the torrent of repressed emotions roared up from deep within the desolation of her barren heart, breaking up the fallow ground as it came, and the anguished tide of loss nearly carried her away. Great, heaving sobs wracked her frame, for her mother, her father, her life, her friend. It was too much all at once, and she feared she might go mad with grief. The sound of sirens in the distance pulled her back from the brink, and she arose weakly to her feet once more, staggering back up the street.

She passed the spot where Lee sat beside Nels, but for the moment she was consumed with the thought of finding out who had tried to kill them. A quick glance told her the first man would not be recognizable, so she ran down the block to the car. Tyler had seen a lot of bizarre scenes in her day, but nothing quite like the one before her. The man at the car had fallen forward, wedging his neck in the V between the door and the frame, as if his face were on public display. And it was a face she knew.

"Mike Riley. I killed Mike Riley."

It was her worst nightmare, and up until now, it had been only a fear in the back of her mind. She had killed someone from her own agency, and now her mind was grappling with a nightmare become reality. The fact that he had tried to kill her was no comfort. Tyler turned around and started numbly back toward the apartment building. Something had gone terribly wrong. She hadn't followed orders, and now men were dead.

Her instructor's words came rushing back with painful clarity: "There is no room for conscience in the field. When you follow anything but orders, the wrong people start dying." But she had to find out about the stolen file, didn't she? No. She knew the orders, but deep down, she wanted to see if there wasn't some way to save the two men—no, not two men. Two fugitives. Condemned to die because they got their hands on a process for cold fusion. The end of the rainbow. Or the end of the world. It was not inconceivable that a discovery like that could start World War Three. At least three men had died trying to stop it—trying to do their duty. What had she done?

Tyler stopped a few feet from Lee and raised her pistol until it was pointing at his head. Lee didn't look up. He was too concerned for his dying friend to notice.

"This is all my fault. I never should have helped that woman," Lee said in anguish.

Nels was short of breath. "No . . . don't you see? She saved us . . . we would both be dead right now if it weren't for her." Nels looked at Lee's face, and his eyes softened. "Don't grieve, Lee. I'm going to see my Utta."

"You can't die, Nels. I don't know what to do . . ."

"Pray . . . live . . . God . . ." Nels gasped for breath, unable to continue.

The sirens were getting closer. Lee finished for him. "God will take care of the rest." Nels nodded and closed his eyes, and Lee grabbed his hand hard, blinking back tears. "I don't think I can go on without you."

Nels opened his eyes, and the old fire returned for an instant. "Oh, yes, you will." He reached into his pocket and pressed a wad of bills into Lee's hand. "Here. Take this. You're . . . you're going to need it." Nels looked at his friend and smiled, tears in his eyes. "I envy you, Lee. This will be the adventure of a lifetime . . ." The light in the eyes faded, Nels's head lolled to one side, and he stopped breathing. Lee wept.

Tyler knew in that moment that she could never shoot him. She holstered her weapon and grabbed Lee by the arm, pulling him to his feet. When she spoke, the accent was gone. "Come on. I think we can do better than a linen truck."

As Tyler and Lee ran down the street, Nels gasped once more and opened his eyes to watch them go, the barest hint of a smile tugging at the corner of his mouth. Once they were away, he laid his head back down and closed his eyes. Good. Now there would be no foolishness about trying to take him along. He knew he was dying, he would never see the vehicles racing to the scene, but at least Lee would not be waiting around when the police arrived. Though the sirens were drawing nearer, they seemed to be getting farther away with each passing second. Nels realized he couldn't feel his arms and legs or anything else for that matter, then he was dimly fascinated by the sound of his last breath escaping his lungs. As the steady rise and fall of his chest ceased, and all the muscles relaxed, his last earthly thought blazed a phantom trail behind a spirit set free from the bonds of flesh. *I mustn't keep my Utta waiting.*

Chapter Ten

Fresh on the heels of his first decent night's sleep in two weeks, Carter Ellis felt quite cheerful this morning. At last report, the fugitives had been located in Morocco, and two hit teams were virtually in place. The only dark spot in his mood was caused by the fact that Bill Sidwell had not given him an update in more than twelve hours. Ellis shook off his feelings of apprehension. They were after an old man and a college professor, for Pete's sake. Forget that they had managed to remain at large for two weeks. Six agents ought to be able to pull off a simple assassination.

That issue resolved—for the hundredth time—Ellis's cheerful mood returned, enough so that he didn't even mind the traffic on Pennsylvania Avenue. He stopped at the White House entrance next to the Old Executive Office Building, and after checking his ID against a list of expected visitors, the guard passed him through.

Ellis parked the car and strode across the narrow parking lot with renewed confidence. For too long he had felt like a condemned man going to his own execution, but at the sight of the massive mahogany security desk and blue carpet, he felt the old "seat of power" thrill once more. During the short walk to the hallway, he mentally put the finishing touches on his presentation, wanting to put the best possible spin on the facts. The ground floor of the West Wing didn't seem nearly as threatening this morning. People were going about their business and completely ignoring him, which was just fine. In the situation room, the same group was seated, looking as unfriendly as always, but Ellis didn't take it personally.

He walked purposefully up to the front of the room, set his notes on the podium, and turned on the little light. "Good morning, gentlemen. Let me begin by saying I am expecting a call from Bill Sidwell back at headquarters at any time, confirming the elimination of the two fugitives in question and the recovery of the missing file. Last night, the fugitives were located in an apartment in El Jadida, Morocco. We have two hit teams in place, either of which could complete the operation. Four more teams are en route or already on location. As I have no further information at this time, I would like to open it up for questions."

Hank Joram spoke first. "I take it there will be no press release."

Ellis hesitated a moment. "No, sir. It's old news. A few people may wonder what happened to them, but it's already a dead issue in the press."

"That was a joke, Mr. Ellis. I know there won't be any press release. The CIA doesn't do press releases, does it?" Ellis shook his head. "Fine. Do we need to worry about French intelligence?"

"We have no evidence that suggests the French agents were told anything, but if you'd like, we can . . ."

Ellis was cut off by the ringing of the phone. Joram picked it up. "Joram. Yes, Mr. Sidwell. Mr. Ellis has been expecting your call." He held up the phone, clearly unconvinced by the rosy picture painted by the CIA director. "Shall I put it on the speaker, Mr. Ellis?"

Ellis swallowed hard and nodded. "Bill, it's Carter. What's your report?"

Bill Sidwell's voice came over the speaker phone. "There was a shoot-out this morning outside the apartment building."

"A shoot-out?" Ellis asked incredulously. "Thiessan actually returned fire?"

"No, sir. We just received photographs from the police department in El Jadida. Thiessan is confirmed dead."

"Then the operation was successful?"

Sidwell cleared his throat. "Not entirely. We think Tyler Stills may have made contact with the fugitives. As you ordered, sir, she was not told there was a backup team at her location. When Mike Riley's team attempted to complete the operation, we think she may have returned fire."

"Tyler is dead?"

"Tyler Stills and Professor Teller are unaccounted for. Mike Riley's team has been wiped out. Nash Dewitt was also dead at the scene. He had his rifle, so we can only assume he helped Stills eliminate Riley's team."

Ellis's world was crumbling. "What about Wally Beason?"

"He returned to the States a short time ago. According to his report, Beason and Dewitt were ordered home by Stills. Dewitt chose to stay behind."

Ellis closed his eyes against the news he was hearing. "Any idea where they're going?"

"No leads at this time, sir."

There was silence for some time, broken finally by Hank Joram, who spoke with quiet menace. "It would appear, Mr. Ellis, that once again you have left the president's cheese out in the wind. What do you intend to do about it?"

Ellis's shoulders slumped, and he looked down at the table. "I offer you my resignation, effective immediately."

Joram sat back in his chair. "Your resignation is accepted, sir. Mr. Sidwell, are you still there?"

"Yes, sir."

"Due to the untimely resignation of Mr. Ellis and the critical nature of our current situation, you are hereby promoted to the position of acting director until such time as a suitable replacement can be sworn in. Your first official act will be to send out a press release about his resignation, saying it was 'for personal reasons, accepted with great regrets by the president' and so forth." Joram smiled at the Joint Chiefs as if sharing a private joke. "Well, what do you know? I guess the CIA does do press releases. Do you understand the orders, Mr. Sidwell?"

"Clearly, sir."

"Then this meeting is adjourned."

GULF SHIPPING COMPANY, WAREHOUSE DISTRICT, BELIZE CITY, BELIZE
OCTOBER 5, 8:23 A.M.

Gerard Dinaé stood a little uneasily in the same spot from which he first viewed the Interpol office. The mission had been an unmitigated disaster, and now Jerome, René, and Henry were all dead. Eleven days in the hospital had made him well enough to travel, though the physician strongly cautioned him to take it easy. Unfortunately every day spent in bed, the trail grew colder, and Dinaé knew if he wanted even a slim chance of completing the original mission, he had to get moving.

The mission, as he saw it, remained the same—find out about the secret projects so carefully guarded by the CIA—with one significant modification. In his mind, Dinaé was now a free agent. His old employer would no doubt send hit men looking for him. In fact, he had spent the latter half of his hospital stay in the basement under an assumed name, just in case the DGSE turned out to be unusually efficient in dispatching its assassins. So, his purpose was to locate Thiessan and Teller, find out as much information as possible, then sell it for as much money as possible before disappearing forever to some warm, subtropical locale as far away from Greenland as possible. A worthy cause, to be sure.

Dinaé squared his shoulders and walked across the street, then through the glass doors into the reception area. A male secretary looked up from his desk behind the counter. "Can I help you?"

Dinaé flashed his false identification. "Andre Dupond, with the DGSE. I was told to meet a team of CIA agents here. We are trying to locate two fugitives."

"Hold it. Let me see that."

The secretary took the identification and scrutinized it closely. "I don't know anything about it. Sorry."

"Look. I know you're busy, but I'm in serious trouble here. My supervisor said I could lose my job over this. The orders were to meet a CIA team here as part of a joint operation, but as you can see, I'm running behind schedule."

"You're about nine days behind schedule. Agent Stills's team left for Morocco more than a week ago."

"I was recuperating in the hospital. Do you know if they caught the fugitives? Maybe I can just go home."

The man thought about it for a moment, then stood up. "Let's find out."

They walked back to the computer room, and the operator searched available information on the Interpol network. "Here we go. El Jadida, Morocco. Gunshots in the old district. Several CIA agents were killed. One fugitive and a renegade agent still at large."

"Do you have information on the renegade agent?"

"Let me see . . . oh, no. It's Agent Stills. Tyler Stills. She's armed and very dangerous. Wanted for murder, espionage, and treason."

Dinaé read the report again. A renegade agent would need new papers. "What are the nearest cities where the CIA has offices?"

The operator performed another search. "The nearest are in Athens, Cairo, and Istanbul."

"Show me a map."

Dinaé examined the map closely. Cairo was the closest by land, and time would be critical. If he were in her shoes, that's where he would go.

"Thank you for your help."

FORTY MILES SOUTHWEST OF TBESSA, ALGERIA, NEAR THE TUNISIAN BORDER
OCTOBER 6, 3:44 P.M.

All things considered, the airplane was entirely adequate. The seating was cramped and the ride bumpy, but at least they were out of Morocco. During a fuel stop three hours out, Lee asked the woman where they were going, but apparently she wasn't speaking to him. So, he sat in the back with his eyes closed, trying to think about anything but his uneasy stomach.

Shortly after leaving Pa H'dar Street, running as fast as the woman's shoes would allow, Lee had clutched his side and slowed to a fast walk, to the evident disgust of the woman. Fortunately a main thoroughfare and then a cab were quickly located, and soon Lee found himself at a small airstrip, waiting while the woman haggled with a pilot over money. Were it not for the pall cast over Lee's mood by the death of Nels, it might have begun to feel like a normal day.

They were airborne quickly enough, but thanks to the pilot's thriving delivery business—which he had carefully failed to mention during negotiations with the woman—a series of short hops got them only as far as the border with Algeria before nightfall. The woman had been furious, but the pilot assured her they would be under way first thing in the morning. There was nothing to do but set out with Lee to find a place to pass the night. When Lee asked where they were going, she wouldn't answer, whether because she didn't know or she just didn't want to talk, he couldn't tell. They slept out under the stars in a brown field of stubble, near the airport, but when they returned to the runway at dawn, the plane was gone, and it was almost noon before they were able to find another plane for hire.

Lee hazarded a look out the window and saw only desert in all directions. Then he remembered that the Sahara stretched most of the way across the northern part of the African continent. Lee's mouth was suddenly dry. *Oh, Lord, please don't make me walk across the desert.*

The plane remained aloft, and as the afternoon sun made its casual way toward the horizon, the plane descended toward a modest landing strip not far from a city that looked as if it had been carved from the desert hills. As they rolled to a stop, the pilot threw open the door, and a blast of hot air hit Lee in the face. The woman was already out the door, and Lee had to hurry to catch up.

As they walked toward the squat cube that passed for a terminal, Lee's curiosity found a voice once more. "Where are we?"

This time, the woman answered, speaking again without an accent. "Tbessa, Algeria."

"I thought we were going to Cairo."

"We are, but we can't use Libyan air space to get there."

No nonsense, this one. Lee knew she was different from the moment her pistol broke leather, but he couldn't get his first impression of her out of his mind. There was a colossal discontinuity between the "little girl lost" act and the lethal outburst he had seen with his own eyes. She was an agent obviously, but the performance in the apartment had been so convincing, Lee couldn't shake the strong sense of being her protector when it was really the other way around. But who was she? What did she hope to gain by saving his life? And more important, what would Nels do? Nels would try to gather information.

"Who are you?"

The woman never broke stride. "A fool."

"I said 'who,' not 'what.' And saving my life hardly qualifies you as a fool in my book."

The woman turned on him savagely. "You have no idea what happened back there, do you?"

Lee's eyes hardened. "Yes. I watched a dear friend die."

The woman's anger seemed to ebb slightly. "Well, so did I."

She faced forward and didn't speak again until addressing a taxi driver in front of the terminal. The cab took them into town, and Lee followed her as she went from shop to shop, picking up a few essential items like clothes and toiletries. Lee still had his bag, but she bought him one complete change of clothes as well, without asking his opinion, and Lee was in no mood to complain.

Then began a search for he knew not what. She went into shop after shop, asking each merchant the same question, too quietly for him to hear. Finally she found what she was looking for, and the merchant scribbled something on a piece of paper, then they were out the door again. A walk of maybe two miles brought them to an older residential section of town, consisting mostly of beige sandstone buildings, none taller than three stories. Only after the woman accosted one of the residents and began dickering with him over the price of a vehicle did Lee understand what she had in mind.

The car was old and foreign made, and Lee wasn't sure it would run, much less take them anywhere. The owner was the epitome of a salesman, one minute complaining that the woman was stealing food from the mouths of his children, the next telling her what a splendid piece of merchandise she was considering. In the end, he started to walk away, and she gave up, paying quite a lot in Lee's estimation. But the engine turned over, and in moments they were rolling down the street.

"This is a piece of junk," Lee observed rhetorically.

"It only has to take us a hundred fifty miles."

"To Cairo?"

The woman looked at him incredulously. "To Tunis. Cairo's about twelve hundred miles from here as the crow flies. What kind of professor are you?"

"One who was never very good at geography."

They drove on in silence, leaving the city far behind, and the surroundings took on a rather hostile, arid quality without much variation. Lee finally succumbed to the boredom, and he asked the question he had been dying to ask since they fled Morocco.

"Who are you really?"

Tyler thought about answering for a long time. She hadn't intended to become a fugitive, only to prevent an unnecessary murder. Now she would be hunted down by her own people. In her mind, she heard Chip saying, *Then I'd have to kill you,* and she knew beyond a shadow of a doubt that he was dead serious. There was never any question which she would choose when faced with a choice of quitting or fighting. Which meant she was likely to be spending quite a bit of time with Professor Teller over the next few days. They would have to learn to get along with each other.

"My name is Tyler Stills. I'm a field investigator for the CIA. We tracked Miles Orsen to Hanover and followed you and Professor Thiessan all the way from Seattle to Morocco."

"What happened back in Morocco? Who were those people?"

"A CIA fixer team. They were sent to back me up, only no one bothered to tell me about it."

"You shot your own people?"

Tyler chose to keep her agony private and merely shrugged. "It happens. I just never thought it would happen to me."

"What were your orders?"

"Eliminate you and Thiessan, and retrieve the file."

"Eliminate us? Just like that?" Lee snapped his fingers.

Tyler gritted her teeth. "Obviously not. You're still breathing, aren't you?"

"Why? Why am I still breathing?"

"Because I couldn't follow orders! All right? I couldn't pull the trigger. Nash tried to, but I stopped him . . ." Tyler's face contorted with rage and grief, and she began slamming her clenched fist into the back of the bench seat between them. Tears streamed down her cheeks, and she cried out wretchedly with each blow, "I didn't . . . sign up . . . to kill . . . civilians!"

The car started off the road, and Lee yelled, "Look out!"

Tyler got both hands on the wheel and steered back onto the road. There was no traffic, and no obstacles off road, but if they got stuck in the sand, there would be no tow truck, either. She got her emotions under control with the help of embarrassment and adrenaline, and she had a memory of rolling the van when they were in California. It seemed like so long ago. Having lost Nash, she had a strong impulse to check on Rick, Kyle, and Wally, but they would have to report it or face a felony conviction, and it would only make matters worse. She was feeling alone and friendless. A black cloud of depression began to wrap its oily tendrils around her heart and mind, but she pushed the feelings aside, angrily reminding herself that she had to keep alert if she wanted to survive.

"Tell me something, Professor."

"Please. Call me Lee."

"All right. Lee. What could you possibly hope to accomplish by running with that file?"

"Just staying alive, at first. Then Nels came up with a plan to release the process safely."

"How can you possibly release a process like that safely?"

"Mostly by going slowly and making sure you have enough work for everybody."

"Why didn't you just turn in the file?"

"Nels told me the CIA would kill me if I turned it in. After reading what was inside, I believe it. The government decided to kill the scientists who discovered the cold fusion process, and the president knew about it. Miles Orsen was on the list. I don't know how he saw the file in the first place, but I guess he wasn't ready to die."

Tyler didn't want to believe it. "The CIA wouldn't kill you for giving back a missing file."

"Apparently you've never heard of S clearance. Nels said there's an agency within the agency. People who see these files without the proper clearance are killed. No exceptions."

Tyler took a long breath and blew it out. "I've heard rumors. I always thought they were just stories made up by some desk-bound paper pusher. Where's the file now?"

"We stashed it under an abandoned house outside Belize City."

"You idiot! How do you know that piece of information wasn't the only reason I've been keeping you alive? Didn't Thiessan teach you anything?"

"He taught me to duck."

"Well, obviously it didn't take."

"Nobody's perfect. Besides, the way I see it, we're in the same boat. If you had S clearance, I'd be dead, and you'd be on a plane to Washington about now."

Tyler looked out the side window and chewed her lip for a moment before continuing. "Fair enough." Then her tone turned sarcastic. "So what's the plan, Lee?"

"You're the one taking us to Cairo."

"That's just so we can get new papers. What was your original destination?"

"Israel. Nels thought the Israelis wouldn't mind seeing a few oil-producing Arab states destabilized by a new source of energy."

"I might be able to help when we get there. I have friends in the Mossad."

CIA OFFICE, RAHOUF DISTRICT, CAIRO, EGYPT OCTOBER 6, 6:22 P.M.

Former DGSE Commander Gerard Dinaé didn't remember when he had been so hot. The sun was down, but the ambient heat from the sandstone walls kept the air over the sidewalks in the low nineties, and his jacket wasn't helping at all. According to his map, this was the street that housed the CIA office, but in the fading light, most of the buildings looked the same. Directly to his left, light was coming through venetian blinds, and he could make out the CIA insignia on the glass door, which turned out to be locked. His knock was answered by a man in a short-sleeved white shirt.

"Can I help you?"

Dinaé handed over his false ID and spoke with his French accent. "Yes. Please forgive the intrusion. I am Andre Dupond of the DGSE. I am on the trail of a rogue agent named Gerard Dinaé. This is most embarrassing for us, but we are suspecting he may be masquerading as one of your agents."

"Dinaé? I've heard of him. He's wanted on both sides of the Atlantic. Come in." Dinaé followed the man to his desk. The man sat down and went through an extensive password screen. "We'll take a look at his file. What did this guy do?"

"He shot up an Interpol office in Belize City."

"That's right. Now I remember. The report said he may have gunned down his own team."

Dinaé clenched his teeth, but said nothing. He should have expected the DGSE to pin the deaths of his team members on him, but somehow hearing it from an American made the sting more unpleasant.

The man went through a number of screens, trying to verify the story. "Here it is. Interpol office in Belize City. Two dead, one missing, presumed dead. Let's check the alert list . . . here's your boy. Commander Gerard Dinaé. Commander? There's something you don't see every day. Fancy an officer blowing a gasket like that."

"You see why we want him apprehended."

"Oh, absolutely. Interpol would like a piece of him, too. Let's see what this guy looks like."

Dinaé reached into his jacket, wrapping his fingers around his pistol. The man keyed in the request for a photograph but received a message that the photo was unavailable. Dinaé removed his hand from his jacket. "That's okay. I think I know what he looks like."

"So how can I help?"

"All I need is the location of your document shop. He's going to need a new passport, and I'd like to be there if he makes an appearance."

The man opened a drawer, pulled out a small notebook, wrote on a scrap of paper, and handed the paper to Dinaé. "Here's the address. I hope you find him."

"Thank you. He's close by. I can feel it."

TUNIS INTERNATIONAL AIRPORT, TUNIS, TUNISIA
OCTOBER 6, 7:43 P.M.

In the passenger seat of the rattletrap jalopy Tyler had purchased in Tbessa, Lee sat with his eyes closed, listening to the sounds all around. Plane and car engines provided much of the background noise, but he could hear snatches of conversations in Arabic and other languages, and the occasional bray of a mule pulling one of the two-person carriages interspersed with the more modern taxis. The smells were pungent and varied, first jet fuel, then a mixture of animal smells and something sickly sweet, like a decaying carcass not quite far enough away.

Lee thought back over the road trip from Tbessa. A few miles after Tyler nearly left the road, they arrived at the border. Tunisia and Algeria were on good terms, so the border crossing had been simple, then more desert. Embarrassed by her emotional display, Tyler didn't feel much like talking, and Lee was inclined to respect her privacy. The remainder of the trip passed without incident, with one notable exception. Once, and only once, Lee caught Tyler looking at him with an odd, appraising expression.

Though she would never admit it, Tyler had been spending a lot of time searching her feelings over the past day or two, and the sensation was foreign to her. With the death of her mother all those years ago, she had started erecting walls around her heart to protect against the pain. When her father left, the walls grew higher until they were a fortress that no one could get through. The memory of a long string of broken relationships—dashed to pieces on the stone around her heart—bothered her when she thought about it, so she had made a conscious effort to ignore it. Until yesterday.

The death of Nash had hurt her more than she thought possible, and she was beginning to realize that over the years, she had let her defenses slip. The odd thing was, she felt better for it. No one ever told her that by walling off her heart, she was dooming herself to a half-life without feeling. Having denied emotion for so long, however, she had always been fearful that at even the slightest crack in the wall, the dam would break and she would be swept away, her mind would snap, and she would become psychotic or, worse, catatonic. So, she chose to feel nothing, and the absence of joy seemed like a fair trade for the absence of pain.

She discovered living was easier when one was only half-alive, but now she realized that half-alive is also half-dead, and the thought that she had taken the easy path made her feel loathsome. So, she faced her feelings head-on. To her great surprise and relief, the pain did not drive her mad or send her into a violent frenzy, but actually made her feel more aware. For the first time, she admitted that there were people she cared about, people she missed when she was separated from them, and it hurt, and she saw that the hurt was good. Pride would not allow her to express her newfound feelings with tears, but she made no effort to close them off.

And there was something else. Awash with guilt over her part in the deaths of Mike Riley and his team, torn from the only life she had known for the past ten years, and on the run from her own people, she desperately needed someone else for support. The sensation was also foreign and contemptible, but as with the emotions, she chose to let this new wind blow where it wished. If it made her uncomfortable, so be it. But even worse, as long as she was being honest with herself, she was beginning to have feelings for Lee Teller, which was impossible. Teller was a man and, therefore, the enemy, or at least she used to believe that.

Her difficulty stemmed from the realization that even in the short time she had spent with him, he seemed . . . nice. *Nice* and *man* were two words that had never belonged together in her vocabulary, so on some level she was naturally suspicious that Teller was just putting on a good front, but on that same level, she had to acknowledge that if she was wrong, and he really was one of the good guys, her unfavorable assessment of men in general might be in trouble. And Teller could turn out to be—was it possible?—someone she would enjoy spending time with. *Love* was not paired with anything in her vocabulary, with the possible exception of milk chocolate, but the concept of enjoying a man's company was nothing short of revolutionary.

All of this was a bit much to handle all at once, so Tyler set the most complicated issues aside and decided to adopt a wait-and-see attitude. If Teller was a jerk, she would know soon enough.

Still waiting in the car, Lee settled into his seat and thought about dozing off. For all that the car was a wreck, the seat was comfortable enough that he wouldn't mind spending the night on it. The noise was soothing in its own way, but suddenly his ears picked up a dip in the sounds as if someone had walked close by, then he noticed more smells. Musky, feminine, like sweat and perfume. Tyler's perfume. Lee opened his eyes and found hers looking right back at him.

"Bang. You're dead," she said, her face deadpan.

"Do you always greet people that way?"

"You wouldn't last ten seconds in the jungle. Good news. There's an evening flight to Cairo leaving in twenty minutes."

"I thought you wanted to go by boat."

"Too slow. There are probably half a dozen teams on the continent right now. We'll have to go straight to the document shop and make the passports ourselves. With a little luck, by the time they know we were in Cairo, we'll be in Israel."

Great, Lee thought. *And then the dogs will be on our heels again.* "What do we do with the car?"

"Leave it here as a present for some enterprising thief."

They wandered inside and found a wooden bench near the departure gate. There was no one nearby, and Lee felt it was safe to talk. He turned to Tyler and caught her looking at him again. She averted her eyes, and Lee felt his tongue cleave to the roof of his mouth. This was turning into a schoolboy crush, and he felt like an idiot. "Idngya sungthig ung?"

Tyler looked at him with a quizzical expression. "Excuse me?"

Lee closed his mouth and prayed for a divine dispensation of saliva. "I said, 'Is there something wrong?'"

"Why do you ask?"

"The way you were looking at me."

Tyler blushed slightly, looked away for a moment, then looked back, trying to be cool and offhanded. "I was just noticing, you have nice eyes. Your mug shot wasn't very flattering."

Lee's cheeks flushed hotly, and he stammered, "Th . . . thank you." He forced his mouth closed, but his mind was shouting at him: *You moron! You already had your midlife crisis, and now is not the time to go through puberty again. Once was more than enough.*

A painful silence ensued, and mercifully Tyler broke it. "So, what do we do after we get to Israel?"

"Join the delegation to the United Nations. We present the cold fusion process to the General Assembly, then move to set up a special council to disseminate plans for introduction of the technology into each society."

"Sounds ambitious."

"It is, ridiculously so. But Nels died believing it had a chance of working . . ."

Thankful for a subject he could sink his teeth into, Lee began explaining the plans he and Nels had spent so many hours crafting. Tyler nodded and closed her eyes, trying to picture the events as Lee described them, but the words started to run together, and she found them replaced by a single thought, which wouldn't go away, no matter how hard she tried to ignore it. *He has a nice voice, too.*

The flight to Cairo was noisy and completely uneventful, so Lee and Tyler both used the time to catch up on some sleep. Hot air rising from the desert floor made the descent a little bumpy, but the landing was smooth, and soon they were walking toward the main terminal It was the first really major metropolitan center Lee had seen in a while, and if it didn't feel like home, at least it felt more civilized. A thriving tourist trade had spawned a host of Western amenities, including a hot dog stand, and it took most of his self-discipline not to beg Tyler to buy him a chili dog.

A wad of bills greased their way through customs, and soon they were on board a taxi, headed for the Rahouf District.

BALBASA STREET, RAHOUF DISTRICT, CAIRO, EGYPT
OCTOBER 6, 10:13 P.M.

After only a few days on his own, Dinaé had started to feel that was the only way to work. His money wouldn't last long, to be sure, but there were fewer arrangements to be made, travel and lodging were less expensive, and best of all, there were no reports back to headquarters.

Everything was less complicated. Except surveillance. With no partner to talk to, minutes stretched interminably into hours, and he had to stand to keep from falling asleep. On his feet for more than two hours, bored nearly to tears, Dinaé decided to sit down and rest his legs for a few minutes. Then he decided to close his eyes, only for a few seconds.

Dinaé quickly nodded off to sleep, so he did not notice a short while later when two shadowy figures slipped silently through the front door of the print shop down the street.

Chapter Eleven

Filo Morris was one of the best in the business. Apparently born with an innate ability to forge documents—a talent that did not endear him to his parents, teachers, or the Federal Bureau of Investigation—ten days after his nineteenth birthday, Filo found himself locked up in his own private cell at the Leavenworth correctional facility. After he spent only three months behind bars, the CIA got wind of his unique abilities and offered him a "community service job" for the remainder of his twenty-year prison term. He accepted. Then he learned the job was in Cairo, and the community to be served was the CIA.

Planted near the middle of the only land route to or from the African continent, and more or less centrally located between the European and Asian continents, Cairo was a major hub for the intelligence community. Filo's soon-to-be legendary skill quickly earned him the code name "Wizard," and agents sometimes went out of their way to use his services. Filo was quick. Filo was good. Filo was also smart, which is why when he sensed someone in his room, turned on the bedside light, and found himself staring down the muzzle of a pistol, he didn't move a muscle.

"Hi, Wiz."

"Hello, Tyler. When I heard you were in Morocco, I had a feeling you might drop by, which is why you won't find a gun anywhere near me. I'm going to bring my hands up so you can see. See? Nothing in this hand, and nothing in this hand. Now I'm going to stand up. You aren't going to shoot me, are you?"

"I'd rather not."

"Good. I was hoping you'd say that." Filo looked at the rugged, bearded fellow behind Tyler. "You must be Professor Teller. Welcome to my shop. Please make yourselves at home while I grab the duct tape."

Tyler kept her gun trained on him as he walked over to a work table and picked up a fresh roll of duct tape. He handed the roll to Lee, and then stood with his back against one of the support posts for the ceiling. "You can use the whole roll. Please start at the shoulders, and don't make it too tight."

Lee looked at Tyler, and Tyler nodded. She kept her gun on Filo until his arms were immobilized, then went to work at the printing press. Each plate she used, she carefully cleaned and mixed in with the others, and each new file created on the computer was deleted as soon as she was finished with it. Filo made a big show of looking elsewhere, and when she was finished, Tyler came and stood in front of him.

"Sorry about this, Wiz. Where are your car keys?"

Filo nodded toward the bed. "On the little table next to the bed. Please keep the car. I can get another one."

Tyler collected the keys, then picked up the phone receiver, dialed a number, and held the receiver to Filo's ear. "This is your branch office here in town. By now, everyone's gone for the day, so you should be able to leave a message. If no one comes to help you, you'll be dead from dehydration in four days, so make it convincing."

Filo nodded and waited for the beep. "This is Filo at the print shop! Tyler Stills was here! I can't move! Somebody send help!"

Tyler hung up the phone and started toward the door with Lee in tow.

Filo spoke. "Tyler?"

Tyler turned. "Yeah?"

"If you think of it, could you call the branch office again in three days, just to make sure they got my message?"

Tyler smiled apologetically. "I'll try."

Dinaé awoke with a start. Where was he? He had been sleeping! He lurched to his feet, cursing under his breath. Idiot! The light in the print shop was on, and he ran down the street to a better vantage point. As he watched the door, two figures came out, silhouetted enough that he could see a man and a woman. They walked down the covered sidewalk toward a car parked nearby, and Dinaé realized with sudden consternation that they were going to take the car. As the two figures climbed into the car, Dinaé dashed from his hiding place, keeping to the shadows, and ran for the back of the car. The rear window was small and made of cloudy plastic, so he at least had a chance of not being seen. Driver and passenger were busy trying to locate the ignition, and Dinaé stopped behind a sandstone pillar, then crept into the shadows behind the car. The bumper was attached to, rather than molded with, the body, and he lay down on his back with his head and shoulders under the rear of the car. When the engine started, he reached up and gripped the bumper with both hands, gritted his teeth, lifted his knees, and curled his body up off the dusty street.

The car started moving. Dinaé knew he couldn't hold on for long. The strain on his biceps and stomach muscles was enormous, and he could already feel his fingers beginning to slip. Just when he felt he couldn't hold it any longer, the car stopped at an intersection. He rested for a few seconds and noticed the occasional passerby staring at him from the sidewalk, then the car started up, and he nearly lost his grip. His body dragged on the street for twenty feet before he was able to lift it up once more. The speed couldn't have been more than thirty miles per hour, but that would be quite sufficient to grind off his clothes and skin if he couldn't keep it up. But whatever happened, he was determined not to let go.

The car didn't stop again. Dinaé put all his heart, mind, soul, and strength into keeping his body off the street, his face twisted in agony, sweat pouring off his brow, muscles screaming, until at last it was too much. Despite his will to the contrary, his stomach muscles relaxed, and his body hit the street. His grip on the bumper never faltered as he made his back as flat as possible and kept his knees bent, so only his back and the soles of his shoes would touch the street.

For several minutes, the waterproof synthetic outer shell of the jacket resisted the persistent onslaught of dust and tiny rocks, but the fabric finally gave way, tearing into shreds, and the shirt underneath lasted barely fifty feet. Dinaé clenched his teeth against the searing pain until he couldn't stand it. Against his will, his hands let go, his legs came sideways, and he rolled to a stop in the middle of the street. Slowly, painfully, he got to his feet and limped off to the side, watching in disgust as the car continued without him.

To his great surprise, however, near the end of the street, the car pulled into the parking area for the bus depot. He hadn't lost them! Dinaé loped down the street as fast as his injuries would allow, hoping against hope that they would be detained by something, anything, until he could discover where they were going.

The depot was newer than most of the surrounding buildings, but the exterior was built in the same style, in accordance with city codes, to look like its component parts had been hewn from sandstone. Inside, the floors were marble tile, and the signs and counters gave it a much more contemporary appearance. Dinaé slipped through the front doors and immediately began circling the large open area inside, trying to stay out of sight. There was the man, sitting on a bench, but where was the woman? He checked the lines in front of the ticket counters and spotted her almost immediately.

Dinaé had some experience with lipreading, and he maneuvered as close as he dared to the bench where Lee Teller sat. The woman would have no doubt been trained to minimize her lip movements when speaking, but Teller was a professor. His training should have included good diction and careful pronunciation.

The woman returned to the bench with tickets, and Teller spoke to her, but his lips hardly moved at all! Stupid American professor! How did your students learn anything? The man spoke once more, and Dinaé tried again, this time in earnest: . . . seems a little . . . rus . . . risky . . . after you have . . . uh . . . contract . . . contact . . . muss odd. Muss odd? More sod? Mossad! They were trying to contact the Mossad. Dinaé backed away and watched them until they boarded a bus, then went back to the ticket counter and asked the agent where the bus was going.

"Jerusalem."

"Thank you."

Dinaé walked over to a bank of phones near the front entrance, pulled out a little black book, deposited a fistful of coins, and dialed a long string of numbers. After two rings, a businesslike female voice answered.

"Central Intelligence Agency."

"I need to talk to Bill Sidwell. I believe he is chief of special projects."

"I'm sorry, but Mr. Sidwell is now the acting director, and he can't be disturbed."

"This is an emergency. Tell him I have information on the whereabouts of Lee Teller and Tyler Stills."

The line went dead for only a few seconds, and then a male voice came on. "Sidwell."

"Mr. Sidwell, this is Gerard Dinaé, formerly with French intelligence. I want to know what the reward is for information leading to the capture of Lee Teller and Tyler Stills."

"It's $50,000. Each."

"That is acceptable, but I have one other requirement. As you may or may not be aware, I am currently out of a job. I am not ready to retire, and I was wondering if there might be a place for me in your agency."

"I'm sure we can come up with something."

"Good. I am in Cairo, Egypt. Have your men meet me at the airport at midnight. I will be standing at the first gate, wearing a torn, filthy jacket."

FIFTEEN MILES EAST OF THE SUEZ CANAL, NEAR PORT SAID, EGYPT
OCTOBER 7, 2:23 A.M.

An unusually large pothole shook Lee out of an already restless sleep. A bleary look out the window told him little, besides the fact that the sky was cloudless and the half moon was already low in the sky. Tyler's eyes were open, glistening as if with fairy dust in the pale moonlight. The line of her jaw was exquisite, her nose and chin perfect. Lee felt that giddy, love-struck schoolboy feeling again, as if at any moment he might ask her to go steady or ask her out to the sock hop on Friday night after the football game. Beyond his straight A average, Lee's experience in high school, or more accurately with the people in high school, had not been pleasant, and the feelings he was having were churning up some very painful memories—memories forgotten up to the moment he first looked into this woman's eyes. Tyler caught him staring at her, and he looked away.

"How did you sleep?" she asked.

"Rough. You?"

"Not at all. It's the price I pay for napping."

Something in her voice betrayed her true feelings, and Lee decided it was concern. "What are you worried about?"

Tyler swore. "It's that obvious? I must be getting soft. I guess I'm worried we're not going to make it. The odds don't seem so good at the moment."

Lee wanted to touch her, to hold her in his arms and say, "There, there," but figured, not unreasonably, that she might blow off his kneecaps. "Why do you say that? No one knows where we are or where we're going."

One side of Tyler's mouth pulled up in a wry smile. "You are so naive. Jerusalem is going to be crawling with agents. The first station of the Via Dolorosa is a very public place."

"What is it?"

"I think it means 'Street of Sorrow.' It's the traditional route Christ took when He carried His cross to Calvary. There are quite a few tourists this time of year. Maybe Uri thought we would be less noticeable. I did as you suggested and told him what we were bringing with us. I hope he doesn't sell us out."

"If he does, we're going to need to get out of there fast."

"If he does, we'll be dead before we can even start looking for a way out."

She was right, of course, but the thought of making it so far only to fail was depressing, so he changed the subject. "Have you been to the Holy Land before?"

"Yes, though it might be more accurate to say through. When you're carrying an important package, constantly watching your back, you don't have much time to say, 'Oh, wow, this is where Jesus walked.'"

At the mention of Jesus' name, Lee bent over, fished around in his bag for a moment, and came up with Nels's Bible. "I know you may not want to hear this now, but the most extraordinary thing has happened to me. Over the past few days I have been reading Nels's Bible, and I'm starting to believe it's all true."

"You and a billion other people. What's so extraordinary about that?"

"Most of them did not start out as aging, agnostic professors."

"Point taken. But if you're thinking of pushing it on me, don't bother. A person in my position can't afford to believe in God. I've got too much to answer for."

"We all do. That's why Christ had to die. We can't make it on our own."

"I've been doing just fine, up 'til now."

Lee shook his head. "I mean, no one can make it into heaven on his or her own. God is perfect, and we're imperfect so we can't be in His presence unless Jesus stands for us."

"Save your breath, Professor. I'll never make it in, anyway. You could count my good deeds on one hand. I haven't said the Rosary for more than twenty years."

Lee leaned a little closer to make himself heard over the noise of the bus. "But that's just it! So many people have got it all wrong. You can't earn God's forgiveness. Everything you've ever done wrong," Lee paused, remembering the dead agents in Morocco, "everything, is covered—paid in full—by the blood of Jesus," he pointed out the window for emphasis, "on the cross. It's a free . . . I know it sounds trite, but it's a free gift. All you have to do is receive it."

Tyler frowned. "Sounds like blasphemy to me."

Aided by references he had written on the inside back cover and a penlight supplied by Tyler, Lee began walking her through the Scriptures, trying to explain God's love and how Jesus was both the fulfillment of the Old Testament law and the promised Messiah. Lee found it refreshing to be teaching again, even if only to one student. Suddenly Tyler put a finger to her lips.

"We're stopping."

Lee looked out the window. "I think we're at the border. Do you have our passports?"

Tyler reached into her bag and pulled out their documents, and at the front of the bus, the doors opened and two armed soldiers started down the aisle. The overhead lights came on, momentarily blinding everyone, and the soldiers continued in their task of checking each passenger's identification. When the soldiers reached their seat, Tyler handed him their passports.

Dressed in khaki fatigues, the soldier looked tough, but the face was not unfriendly. "Mr. and Mrs. Miller, from Pittsburgh, Pennsylvania. Where is your wedding ring, Mrs. Miller?"

Tyler answered evenly. "I don't wear it when we travel."

"Ah. That is probably wise. There was a time when you would not have had to worry. Are you bringing anything into the country you would like to tell us about?"

"Only clothes and toiletries."

The soldier smiled and handed the passports back to Tyler. "Enjoy your stay."

The remainder of the inspection passed quickly, but it wasn't until the last soldier was off the bus that Lee started breathing normally. "How long until we're in Jerusalem?"

"Several hours at least."

As the bus pulled away from the checkpoint, Lee tried to pick up the discussion where they left off, but he was still nervous from the border crossing, and it was difficult to get back into the rhythm of the conversation. Tyler helped by appearing interested, whether she was or not he couldn't tell, and before long, the crossing was forgotten. Isolated, as it seemed, in their own universe of sheet metal, vinyl, and darkness, they read and talked until the first hint of morning light came over the horizon. At last, Tyler fell silent, and Lee turned the light off and put the book away to give her some space.

After several miles, Lee was already lost in his own thoughts so that when she spoke, he had to ask her to repeat herself.

"I said, 'It sounds too good to be true.'"

Lee nodded. "I know. I had the same reaction." Suddenly Lee remembered Nels's question to him, and he asked it with some sadness: "But what if it is true?"

The bus rolled on toward Jerusalem. By the time the sun had risen fully in the sky, they could see the City on the Hill, the City of David, Jerusalem, shining almost like gold in the rays of the morning sun. All too soon, the bus was in the modern part of the city, and the passengers were looking out the window. Lee had seen pictures of Jerusalem, and so he was not surprised by its metropolitan appearance. The bus made a stop at a hotel tower called the Plaza, and Tyler indicated it was their stop.

Inside the plush lobby, she found a pay phone and called her friend. "Uri, it's me. I'm at the Plaza Hotel."

"Take a cab and meet me in one hour."

At Mossad headquarters, Uri Narov slowly hung up the phone and looked up at the men crowding his office, including his supervisor, two CIA agents, and a man from French intelligence. "I hope you're right about this."

His supervisor put a comforting hand on Uri's shoulder. "This is a political matter. There is nothing else we can do."

One of the CIA agents, a man named Macaulay, nodded agreement. "We appreciate your assistance in this matter. If we all keep our heads, maybe we can bring in Agent Stills without anyone else getting killed."

FIRST STATION, VIA DOLOROSA, OLD DISTRICT, JERUSALEM, ISRAEL OCTOBER 7, 9:23 A.M.

Barring a few minor modifications over the millennia, the street had remained largely unchanged since the city was built. Broad, worn stone steps climbed gradually upward between narrow alleyways confined by cut-stone walls. It was no stretch of the imagination to picture the tortured figure of Christ carrying His wooden cross through this part of town. Oblivious to the ominous implications of that final journey for the human race, clutches of tourists wandered about, looking at maps, pointing, and taking pictures.

Having recently read about the suffering of Christ, on some level, Lee was disgusted by their ignorance and a little offended that Tyler's friend thought they would fit in with these people. Then he saw a young man of maybe fifteen with his family. The boy's expression was one of awe, and Lee knew in an instant that the boy was a believer, thrilled to be anywhere that Jesus had been. Lee felt a little ashamed for his blanket judgment of the tourists, and he realized he probably deserved to be lumped in with them after all.

Exactly one hour from Tyler's telephone call, a man in shirt sleeves and slacks walked up. He was about Lee's height and age, but the skin of his face was smooth and a deep, rich olive hue, with a bushy black mustache under a magnificent nose. Tyler said nothing, but threw her arms around him. The man's response seemed cool, if indeed they were such good friends, and Lee could only assume he was concerned about being out in the open.

Tyler pulled back to make introductions. "Professor Lee Teller, this is Uri Narov."

"What kind of name is Narov?" Lee asked, offering his hand.

Uri shook the hand. "Ukrainian. Please come with me."

They walked back down the alley that took them to the first station, turned down two other streets, and arrived finally at a small plaza. Various tables were set up around the perimeter, and local citizens, including some Arabs in robes, stood haggling with the merchants over the merchandise. For no good reason, Lee felt the hair stand up on the back of his neck, and he started looking for some sign of danger. They were only a short distance through the square when as one, the people around them turned, and Lee and Tyler found themselves face to muzzle with more than twenty machine pistols and hand guns.

Uri looked at Tyler. "I'm sorry. They arrived just before you did."

Tyler spit in his face. While the Mossad agents looked on, Lee and Tyler were handcuffed and led out of the plaza by the contingent of CIA agents. Uri stayed behind with his fellow agents.

Uri turned angrily on his supervisor. "This is very bad, Jacob. I understand the politics, but she trusted me."

"Peace, Uri. The day is still young."

CIA FIELD OFFICE, JERUSALEM, ISRAEL OCTOBER 7, 11:17 A.M.

The CIA office on Independence Avenue, not far from the Arab District, was standard issue right down to the Schlage Corporation door stops, which meant contemporary office furniture, vinyl tile on the floor, and fluorescent lights overhead. While Lee and Tyler were held, each by two agents, the commander picked up the phone and dialed.

"Agent Macaulay calling for Mr. Sidwell . . . hello, sir. The fugitives are in custody . . . no, no casualties . . . yes, sir . . . yes, sir . . . I'll see to it, sir."

Macaulay hung up the phone, and a man emerged from one of the offices. He was dressed differently from the others, and Lee recognized him immediately. "You! I thought you were dead."

Gerard Dinaé smiled mirthlessly. "Not yet, Mr. Teller. Your friend from Interpol did a very professional job on my team, but as you can see, I have recovered from my injuries. My comrades were not so lucky."

"Why are you doing this?"

"I need the money. You see, after my men were killed by that . . . woman, my reputation with La Piscine was—how do you say—in the toilet." Dinaé turned to Macaulay. "What are the orders?"

"There is an army transport waiting for us at the airport." Macaulay looked grimly at the two captives. "Our passengers will be getting off somewhere over the Atlantic."

"Very well." Dinaé felt some remorse over the loss of a beautiful woman, but he blamed Teller and his friends for the death of his men, and he hoped that with a little luck, Macaulay would permit him to pull the trigger.

The group moved out to the street and piled into the two cars parked out front, with Lee in the back of one, Tyler in the back of the other, both flanked by agents. A leisurely drive to the airport would normally take about fifteen minutes through downtown, but there were construction delays, and the lead driver was accustomed to taking a shortcut through the Arab District.

As they passed the broken-down stone wall separating the two sections of town, Lee saw bullet marks around some of the second-floor windows above the small shops lining the street. "What are the bullet holes from?"

The agent on his right looked out the window. "Those are about ten years old. I think they had some trouble with snipers."

At the next intersection, the light was green, and the first car continued into the intersection. From the left, a moving truck ignored the red light and plowed into the side of the lead car, and the second car skidded sideways, smashing into the side of the truck. As the conglomeration of twisted metal came to a shuddering halt, agents burst out of both vehicles, guns at the ready. Nothing happened. The driver of the truck put his hands in the air, and people on the sidewalks screamed and ran for cover. Agent Macaulay walked around the truck, surveying the damage, then yelled at the driver.

"Get that thing out of here!" Macaulay turned and saw his men still brandishing their weapons and the citizens cowering on the sidewalk. "Put away your weapons. We'll be moving again in a minute. Darrell, can you still drive it?"

The driver of the first car started the engine. "As long as the fender isn't bent against . . ." He never finished his sentence for at that moment, gunfire erupted from both sides of the street. A small army of men dressed in black, with black headdress, swarmed out of their hiding places, guns blazing. Somebody yelled, "Hamas!" and the bystanders dove for cover in earnest. Macaulay died reaching for his pistol, and the agents standing around the two vehicles were cut down over the space of a few seconds. One agent was shot in the back trying to flee for cover, and Dinaé got off two shots from behind a car door before a storm of machine-gun fire found his position. He did not walk away this time. The terrorists were wearing body armor, and when the shooting stopped, the only casualties were around the target vehicles.

Covered with blood and cowering in the backseat, Lee was dragged from his vehicle by two of the terrorists, and he could see the same thing happening to Tyler. Fearing execution in the street, Lee prayed that God would spare them. Their terrorist escort didn't stop, however, and instead hustled them to a van parked with the engine running in a nearby alley. With their hands still cuffed behind their backs, Lee and Tyler were thrown unceremoniously in the back. Lee took a moment to recover from the impact, then caught a glimpse of one of the terrorists back at the intersection, shooting the wounded. Then the door closed, and the van sped away.

Tyler rolled on her side so she could see Lee. He was bleeding from a cut under his eye where his face had hit the cleat attaching the rear seat to the floor of the van, and his shirt was covered with blood. He looked as if he might pass out at any moment. Tyler looked concerned. "Are you shot?"

"I don't think so." He looked down, and gradually the realization that he was covered with someone else's blood came to his mind. Lee rolled away from Tyler and was violently ill. The van ride was mercifully short, and when the rear doors opened again, the surroundings appeared to be the inside of an automotive garage. The terrorists helped them out of the van, ushered them into a small unfurnished office, and closed the door on their way out.

Lee looked nervously at Tyler. "What happens now?"

"We give them what they want, or they kill us."

"What do they want?"

"Your cold fusion process, of course. And anything I can give them on the CIA."

"If we give them what they want, won't they just kill us anyway?"

"Yes."

Tyler's face was impassive, and for a moment, Lee envied her training. Nels had said Lee would have to learn as he went, but Lee kept finding himself in new situations, and the old situations were doing a lousy job of preparing him for the new ones. Thoughts of torture flooded his mind, and he threw Scripture verses at each one until he ran out of verses. Failing that, he started to pray, and almost immediately the fear started to subside. In that moment, Lee understood the sovereignty of God—that God could do whatever He wanted, and it would be all right in the end—and Lee felt a peace unlike anything he had ever experienced. In his mind, he saw Ilya's face, and he finally understood the mystery of serenity he had seen there. *My peace I give* to you, not as the world gives. Nels had it. At the end, Ilya had it. And now Lee had it. No wonder these people didn't fear death.

The door opened, and one of the terrorists came in, peeling his gloves off as he came. With his hands free, he pulled off his headdress.

"Uri!" Tyler gasped.

Uri grinned. "Want to spit in my face again?"

"That depends. Are you going to take off these cuffs?"

Uri held her wrists and examined the handcuffs closely. "We have some hydraulic bolt cutters that ought to do the trick." He turned to face Lee. "Sorry about the eye, Professor. We were in a hurry."

Lee nodded, but something was clearly troubling him. "I appreciate the rescue, but why shoot the wounded?"

Uri's smile faded. "Because that's what Hamas do. We had to be completely convincing, or our relations with your government would be over. Then the Arab nations would make good on their promise and push us into the sea. This is war, Professor Teller."

Their host led them out into the garage and, after flagging down one of the workers, located the bolt cutters. In moments, both sets of handcuffs dropped to the floor. Tyler rubbed her wrists. "Thank you. Whose garage is this, anyway?"

"It belongs to the Mossad. This is where we service our vehicles."

"Aren't you going to get in a lot of trouble?"

"Unlike you, I was following orders," Uri replied, his smile returning.

Tyler ignored the jab. "Whose orders?"

Uri leaned forward conspiratorially. "The prime minister's."

"You're joking. This operation was approved by the prime minister?"

Uri peeled off his tunic and wrapped it around his neck like a towel. "Your president has been making overtures to Syria and Jordan for months now. Iraq has a trade agreement drafted and awaiting delivery by your ambassador. One by one, the United States is making friends with our enemies, and with the 'peace at all costs' movement in our country, since the establishment of the Palestinians in Gaza, we can do nothing to stop it. The idea of weakening a few neighboring economies was very appealing to the prime minister. You have the device with you?"

Tyler turned to Lee, who answered, "In my overnight bag. Unfortunately I have no idea where my bag is at the moment."

"We have it. Come to think of it," Uri said as he looked down at the handcuffs on the floor, "we probably have the keys to the cuffs, too. Ah, well, c'est la guerre. There's food in the back room and showers. Meeting in the big conference room at 1300 hours."

Uri walked out then, and Lee and Tyler just stood there looking at each other. Lee was desperate for a shower, but he hadn't completely forgotten his manners. "Ladies first."

Tyler wrinkled up her nose. "No. Please. You go first. I insist."

OFFICE OF THE DIRECTOR, CIA HEADQUARTERS, LANGLEY, VIRGINIA
OCTOBER 7, 10:06 A.M.

Bill Sidwell knew better than to trust in his circumstances. True, he was acting director of the CIA, a promotion he might not have seen for ten years, maybe never, were it not for a streak of luck; and true, if he did an exemplary job and the president took his time appointing a successor, the promotion might become permanent. Add to that the fact that two extremely dangerous fugitives were as good as dead—something his predecessor was unable to accomplish—and one could think he had reason to rejoice or even throw a party. But Sidwell's years in the field had taught him two things: a clear path is not always clear, and the red spot on your tie could be lunch or a laser sight from a high-powered rifle. He would allow himself to relax slightly only when he was looking at photographs of the fugitives' dead bodies.

When his emergency phone rang a few minutes later, he knew even before he picked it up that it was bad news. "Sidwell."

"Bill, it's Chip. I'm down in ops. The team carrying the fugitives has been hit by terrorists. No one has claimed credit for it yet, but one eyewitness said they were Hamas. None of our agents made it, including the Frenchman, but a man and a woman matching Teller's and Stills's descriptions were seen being dragged from the scene."

Sidwell closed his eyes and put a hand to his forehead. "Oh, this just keeps getting better and better. You're not gunning for my job, are you, Chip?"

"Nope. Not even a little bit. After hearing what Ellis went through, I don't think you could pay me to take it."

"Smart boy." Sidwell took a deep breath and let it out. "Get me the head of the Mossad. What's his name?"

"Shiloh Gilboah."

"Right. Get Gilboah on the line immediately."

MOSSAD AUTO MAINTENANCE FACILITY, JERUSALEM, ISRAEL
OCTOBER 7, 1:04 P.M.

Well fed and really clean for the first time in a long time, Lee was sitting at the conference table with two agents when Tyler walked in. His first impression was that she had cut her hair, but the color was slightly different, and he realized she must have been wearing a wig. In place of the brown dress was a beige jumpsuit, and the feet were shod with high-top tennis shoes, all of which made her look more like a garage mechanic than a field agent. She was still pretty, but she also looked hard and unapproachable. Lee felt the unpleasantly familiar pang of adolescent rejection, as if he had been jilted the morning after a first date, which was ridiculous, since nothing had happened between them. Nothing at all.

Tyler looked at him and smiled, and he returned it, trying to hide his relief. She was the same woman he had gotten to know on the bus. She sat down at his end of the table, facing him, and Mossad agents began to file into the room. Uri joined them a few minutes later, and he sat at the end of the table to address the group.

"Sorry I'm late. I was receiving last-minute instructions from Gilboah. He says the CIA director called him personally. We have no evidence that anyone suspects anything. For those of you who have not been informed, this is a meeting of utmost importance and secrecy. Our guests are Professor Lee Teller of Dartmouth College and Agent Tyler Stills, formerly of the CIA. Professor Teller, would you please explain why we are all here?"

Lee cleared his throat and stood up. He started with the cold fusion process, receiving some appropriate looks of astonishment, and proceeded directly to the potential destabilization or, at the very least, weakening of oil-producing nations. Finishing with a high-level overview of the dissemination plans, he sat down. After a long pause, Uri spoke softly.

"So you see why it is important that our new friends here succeed in their mission. Professor Teller, we will offer you whatever assistance we can."

Tyler raised a hand. "The first thing we need is a plan for getting into the United Nations building . . ."

The meeting went long into the afternoon, and by the end, the tabletop and walls were strewn with large flip chart sheets detailing different parts of the plan, from airplane tickets to diplomatic papers to a hand-drawn map of the first floor of the UN building, by memory from one of the agents who had served with the Israeli delegation. Uri had been able to find out that there was a general session on October 13, which didn't give them much time. Computers and various peripheral devices were brought in just before dinner, at Tyler's request, so they could begin formalizing the presentation Lee would give to the General Assembly.

One persistent problem Uri kept having was interruptions by well-meaning employees who weren't supposed to know anything about what was going on. Fed up with the disruptions, he pulled aside a young agent named Matan. "Make arrangements for our departure."

"But wouldn't it be better to stay here several days?"

"No, there is too much foot traffic. We leave tomorrow."

Matan appeared a little flustered, as if searching for the right words. "I think you should reconsider. There is safety here. We have weapons and men to use them."

"Yes, but I am not comfortable here. Now complete your orders."

After dinner, the Mossad agents cleared out, leaving Lee and Tyler alone in the conference room. Page by page, they built handouts for the delegates from Nels's notes and Lee's memory, gradually falling into a rhythm and finding a common format for all the documents. At the back of Lee's mind, he knew the handouts by themselves would never be enough. Someone would have to spearhead the effort. Someone like Nels.

About halfway through the night, trying for a second "second wind" with the aid of a pot of coffee, Lee really hit his stride. They were trying to come up with a plan for a small nation, which Nels had overlooked. As the pieces to the solution fell into place, Lee became more excited and began to feel he really might be up to the task for the first time. Then he saw Tyler looking at him with that same appraising expression.

Lee blushed. "What? Too far-fetched? What?"

Tyler looked at him for the longest time. She couldn't deny it, the attraction was getting stronger. It was both frightening and wonderful, and she decided it was time to find out what kind of man Lee Teller really was. She leaned forward and kissed him. The touch of her lips was gentle at first, then stronger, more urgent.

The capacity for conscious thought left Lee, and he felt set adrift, suspended in time and space over a roiling sea of passion. All he had to do was let himself fall in, and the sea would engulf him. Holding on by mere fingertips, his mind reasserted itself, and he became aware that he was clutching Tyler's back almost hard enough to tear the fabric. She didn't seem to mind. The sea beckoned, but on some level he was resisting. Why? She was the woman of his dreams. If she wanted him, who was he to say no? Then he heard a still, small voice. *Stop while you still can.* At first, his mind rejected the thought out of hand. Tomorrow could be the last time either of them saw the light of day. *Stop while you still can.* But she's beautiful! I think I may be in love with her. *What you're doing is wrong. Stop it while you still can.*

Lee pulled away from the embrace, his breath coming haltingly. Looking into her eyes, his heart aching at the separation, he knew then that he loved her. He loved her enough to stop. "We should get back to work."

Tyler was shocked by his reaction and her own. She didn't want him to stop, and it occurred to her that she failed her own test. She was incredibly attracted to a man who a few days ago she would have dismissed as a weakling. But he wasn't weak at all. It took strength to keep going on when everything looked hopeless, to get up each morning knowing it could be your last, to deny the desires of your own flesh and press on toward an elusive goal, and Lee had managed to do it all without losing his sense of humor or becoming cynical. Incredible, really, if one took the time to think about it. By all appearances, he seemed to be holding up pretty well in her world, and she couldn't help wondering how she might hold up in his. The silence stretched on until she realized she was staring at him, and still reeling a bit from the passion of his embrace, she struggled to regain her composure. "You're right. We don't have much time."

They worked side by side, each trying to pretend nothing had happened, both painfully aware that a line had been crossed. And there could be no going back.

Chapter Twelve

News that the CIA entourage carrying the fugitives had been hit traveled quickly, but ironically the agents manning the Jerusalem office were among the last to hear. When the call came through, Agent Peter Mason was reviewing the latest report off the Teletype and looking forward to a leisurely lunch.

"This is Mason . . . no . . . aw, no . . . Macaulay? Joe! They got Macaulay."

Agent Joseph Gould was already listening to Mason's end of the conversation. "Who got Macaulay?"

Mason was ashen as he repeated the question to the voice on the other end of the phone. "Who got Macaulay? Are you sure it was the Hamas? . . . They can't all be dead . . . Harris . . . Mitchell . . . Darrell . . . what? Who?" Numb with shock, Mason spoke out of the side of his mouth to Gould. "They didn't get everyone. Teller and Stills were taken hostage."

Gould was out of his seat and across the room, leaning against Mason's desk, hanging on every word. Mason kept trying to relay the conversation as it happened. "You think they're after the fusion process? What would the Hamas want with a cold fusion process? . . . Yeah, sure, but who would want to buy it? Once it's used anywhere, people can copy . . . Hostages? Teller and Stills? Not even the Hamas are that stupid. Anyone with any connections at all has to know they're fugitives . . . yeah . . . yeah . . . you got it."

Mason hung up the phone, lost in thought. The silence stretched on until Gould couldn't stand it anymore. "Well?"

"The Israeli police are cleaning up what's left of the convoy in the Arab District. The State Department is sending representatives to take care of the paperwork. We're supposed to cool our heels and wait for further orders."

"Isn't anyone looking for the terrorists?"

"They're long gone by now."

Gould looked beseechingly at his partner. "They killed Macaulay and the others. Someone's gotta pay for that."

Mason's eyes narrowed. "Someone will. I promise you."

The two agents spent the next hour calling every contact they could think of in the intelligence community in town and some out of town. Nobody knew anything, or at least no one was talking. Mason slammed the receiver down after yet another dead end and looked at Gould, who was sitting back, staring at him with his arms crossed. "What are you lookin' at?"

"Hey, take it easy. I was just thinking."

"Yeah, I thought I smelled something burning." Mason made a thick black mark on his list, crossing off his latest failure.

"Funny. No, really. I was thinking we should look up the rodent."

"Drahkari? He's a third-rate drug runner with a few flimsy contacts in Syrian intelligence."

Gould started picking his teeth with a fingernail. "Fine. We'll go with your list. Who's next?"

Mason looked down at his list in disgust. "Mine all have lines through 'em. Where's the rodent holing up these days?"

"Somewhere in old town."

SHIMEI'S CURIO SHOP, STRAIGHT STREET, JERUSALEM, ISRAEL
OCTOBER 7, 2:17 P.M.

Designed as it was for tourists, the curio shop was adorned with a plenitude of trinkets both regal and common, but most of the prices tended toward the regal end of the scale. A gilt-edged sign behind the counter insisted the shop was in business at the time of Christ, and was actually frequented by the apostle Paul before he embarked on all those long, ill-advised, and ultimately fatal journeys up north. When asked by tourists what a rigid Pharisee would want with gold and brass baubles, the proprietor always had the same answer—we are people of flesh and spirit, you and I, and even the most religious men have physical needs.

Mason hated these little shops, but he had to admit being there was better than sitting behind his desk. Just. "We should get out more."

Gould looked up from a set of brass bookends. "Until headquarters sends some replacements, we'll be getting out a lot more."

Through a doorway strung with hanging beads, an older Arab man emerged, wearing a soiled oriental robe and carrying a small porcelain dish. "Can I help you, gentlemen?"

"We're here to see Drahkari."

Before the owner could answer, there was a sound from the back, like a bench being overturned, and both agents bolted for the beaded doorway. A small figure in a brown tunic was almost to the back door. Mason vaulted a workbench, clearing off a section with his trailing leg, and landed amidst a small storm of clattering merchandise. The door was open, but Mason collided with it full force, and the door slammed shut. The figure pulled out a dagger and backed quickly away from the door.

"What do you want?" the figure asked fearfully.

"Hey, Drak. Long time no see."

"Peter! Oh, don't scare me like that." The nervous little man put his dagger away.

"Sorry. But if you'd made it out that door, you'd be halfway to Haifa by now. I need a little favor. Seven of my associates were just gunned down in the Arab District."

"I know."

Mason exchanged a look with Gould. "What else do you know?"

"I know that it was not the Hamas. For the right price, I might be able to help you find out who the real killers are."

"How does $2,000 sound?"

"Ach! I could barely feed my family with that kind of money. I want $10,000."

Mason snorted. "Ten grand? You don't have any family that I ever saw. Three."

Drahkari shook his head. "Peter, Peter. These are violent men. I could be killed. Make it $9,500."

"I don't have time for this, Drak." Mason gestured toward the proprietor. "Shimei here is my witness. I'll give you $5,000 if we find the men responsible."

"Deal."

Drahkari opened the door and indicated with a toss of his head that Mason and Gould should follow. The streets in that part of town were narrow and somewhat homogeneous, and before long, the two Americans were hopelessly lost. Their guide kept up the pace, however, and after some distance they noticed the quality of the buildings deteriorating, seemingly with every step. The Israeli authorities knew the area well, mostly because of the level of unrest maintained by the Arabs who dominated the neighborhoods. Mason had never seen the poorest section of the city that close before, and he hoped he never would again. Overcrowded with unwashed, impoverished people, who didn't think kindly of most foreigners, the streets suddenly felt quite forbidding, but Drahkari had a reputation of sorts, and most people left him alone.

Drahkari rounded a corner and started down a blind alley, and Mason and Gould suddenly found themselves held from behind and neck to muzzle with two submachine guns. Despite the threat of sudden death, Mason managed to keep his voice steady.

"Uh, Drak? What kind of company are you keeping these days?"

Drahkari smiled nervously. "Forgive me, Peter. They are a little suspicious."

Out of the shadows behind a stack of old crates, from a hidden doorway, a figure in turban and khaki fatigues stepped out into the open. The face sported a bushy black mustache, and the eyes were hard and piercing. When he spoke, it was with a thick Arabic accent. "Who are these men, Drahkari?"

"CIA agents. They are looking for the men responsible for the slaughter this morning."

The man in fatigues walked up to Mason, then Gould, giving each a long, penetrating look before turning and walking away. "Then we share a common purpose. We cannot talk here. Come inside."

The dwelling was badly in need of some remodeling. The timbers supporting the roof were rotting away, and the walls seemed nearly worn through in some places. Judging from the smell, some serious cleaning and plumbing were also long overdue. Their host led the two frightened agents into a central area that was clear of refuse and sat down opposite them at a rickety wooden table. Mason eyed the armed guards nervously.

"Please, calm yourselves. We will not harm you." The man spoke as one educated, and Mason found his fear being replaced by fascination as the man continued. "My name is Abi Nassar. I am in the employ of several nationalist organizations with headquarters in Damascus and Amman. We exist to oppose the exploitation and mistreatment of our Arab brothers in Israel. While we would normally applaud the extermination of Western agents, the timing of this incident was very bad. It is no secret that we have been trying to demonstrate our willingness to seek peaceful resolution of our differences. A violent attack like the one this morning merely reinforces the notion that we are unwilling, or unable, to change."

"So the Hamas had nothing to do with it?" Mason asked.

"I guarantee it. If the Hamas had dared to hit something that big, Professor Teller and the renegade agent, Stills, would have been killed as well. You see, we have learned about your cold fusion process. We think it is very dangerous, and we are already making plans to put a stop to it."

Our network leaks like a sieve, Mason thought. "Then, like you said, we share a common purpose. But who took them hostage?"

"Who has the most to gain by the release of the technology in this region?"

Mason blanched. "The Israelis? No . . . they wouldn't. They couldn't. If word got out that they wiped out a CIA convoy, the U.S. would ditch 'em in a heartbeat. For the first time in four decades, they'd be standing all alone. I think the stakes are way too high."

"Nevertheless, we have an informant in Israeli intelligence who says we will find Teller and Stills at a garage run by the Mossad."

Mason pressed his lips together, thinking. "What do you suggest?"

"I think the CIA should pay a little visit to this particular garage."

MOSSAD AUTO MAINTENANCE FACILITY, JERUSALEM, ISRAEL
OCTOBER 8, 4:53 P.M.

With the approach of sunset, Uri and several of his men were preparing to move out. The day had been largely spent finalizing plans and making arrangements by phone. Most of the day personnel had gone home, but the garage was becoming something of a liability as a hideout—too many nonsecured personnel frequented the building. Lee and Tyler were still living out of overnight bags, and they ended up

waiting in the conference room for the others to finish their prepara-
tions. The walls and floor were spotless, and there was no sign that it
had been a war room the previous day. All of the information on the
flip chart sheets had been condensed to a few notebook pages, which
Uri kept on his person at all times.

Surrounded by armed men devoted to his protection, Lee felt really
safe for the first time in weeks. "Do we really have to leave?"

Tyler looked a little impatient. "You heard what Uri said. If we're
discovered here, it could be very hard to explain. We'll be safe in
Joppa."

"I know. It's just nice to be able to relax. I'm tired of looking over
my shoulder."

"Once we're on the move again, you'll be fine."

Tyler seemed a little distant, and for the moment, Lee didn't mind.
After their encounter the previous evening, he needed time to sort out
his feelings, and from the way things were shaping up, time was
likely to be in short supply. Uri had planned a circuitous route from
Jerusalem, through Joppa, to Cyprus, Crete, Athens, Naples, then
Rome, Paris, and finally New York. Using a combination of ground,
sea, and air transportation, he was reasonably sure they would be able
to negate any possibility of being followed.

When Uri stuck his head in the room to announce their departure,
Lee was quite relieved, then he noticed Tyler checking her pistol. He
couldn't get used to the sight of her holding a gun. "What are you
doing?"

Tyler checked the magazine, then put the pistol back in the holster
strapped around her waist. Not really thinking about what she was
saying, she answered with the same sarcastic tone she had so often
used with Nash. "Well, as Uncle Ron used to say, 'The world is full
of well-armed idiots.' I intend to go prepared."

"Uncle Ron?"

In her mind, her words seemed to echo for a moment, and Tyler
flashed back to the last time she and her team had been together at
the office, and she felt a pang of sorrow. "Sorry. I must have skipped
a groove. When Wally first joined the team, he was always quoting
his Uncle Ron. Nash hated it, so I used to get quotes from Wally and
pass them along, just to rattle his cage."

Lee could see she was in pain and wanted to help, but he knew she
had to work through it herself. He could think of nothing comforting
to say, so he put a hand on her shoulder and then led the way out of the

conference room. Two cars stood ready to receive the seven passengers, which included Lee and Tyler and four men handpicked by Uri to carry out the mission.

"Where's Matan?" one of the Mossad agents asked Uri.

"Isn't he still on duty?"

Uri had little time to worry about his missing man, for no sooner were Lee and Tyler in the car he planned to drive than there came a pounding at the side door. Uri produced a pistol and leaned in the car. "Stay down."

He walked over to the side door and opened it a few inches. Outside were two men in suits. The one nearest flashed his identification. "Agent Mason of the CIA. We have reason to believe two American citizens are being held hostage on these premises. We respectfully request permission to search the building."

"Request denied!" Uri slammed the door and locked it. He made a run for the cars, but a thunderous blast knocked him to the floor. At the far end of the maintenance bay, a plume of smoke and jagged metal were the only things left of one of the large garage doors. Armed figures came through the opening, and Uri's men opened fire. The men leading the assault were cut down in midstride, but after a moment, they got back up and continued advancing.

"Flak jackets!" Uri yelled over the gunfire. One of his comrades went down, while another dug a grenade out of his bag, pulled the pin, and rolled it across the floor. The explosion rocked the floor, sending enemy bodies in several directions, and giving Uri the cover he needed to get behind one of the cars. He opened the trunk and pulled out a submachine gun loaded with Teflon-coated shells. As more figures poured through the opening, Uri took aim and opened fire. The armor-piercing rounds tore through the flak jackets, sending the surviving enemy combatants diving for cover.

Uri grabbed Tyler by the arm, dragged her out of the backseat, and pushed her toward another vehicle. Hands over his ears against the cacophony, Lee saw Tyler go, then grabbed his overnight bag and followed her. Uri sent another volley toward the opening, then joined them in the new vehicle.

Tyler pulled out her pistol. "Why the new car?"

Uri started the engine and put the car in gear. "The windows are bullet proof!" He stomped on the accelerator, swerving around the crater in the floor, then raced toward the opening. Frantic attackers abandoned their positions and dived sideways, narrowly escaping the hurtling vehicle, and Uri took the car through the blasted-out doorway. Out in the parking lot, the first thing he noticed was the driveway blocked by a truck. Then a steady stream of bullets started ricocheting off the windshield.

In the fading light, not more than thirty yards away, Tyler caught sight of a man standing beside the truck, raising a rocket launcher to shoulder level. As Uri gunned it toward the fence, Tyler yelled, "Roll down your window! Lean back! Lean back!" Swearing in his native tongue, Uri put his window down and pushed himself back against the seat. Tyler sighted past her friend's chest, just under the rocket launcher, and squeezed off three shots. The man holding the launcher lurched backward, and the weapon discharged. The rocket arced over the garage, and the explosion briefly lit up the early evening sky, but they couldn't hear the blast over the whine of the engine and Uri cursing at Tyler. The car crashed through the fence at an angle and roared up the street amidst a salvo of bullets, disappearing into the gathering dusk.

Nassar gave the order to fall back, and the men who could retreated from the garage, piled into the vans waiting in the street, and fled the scene with the truck close behind. The sirens of the Israeli police were already fast approaching, and no doubt the army would not be far behind.

Barely two miles from the garage, the vans and truck pulled into a vacant lot and through a large doorway into a warehouse. By choosing a hideout so close to the target, Nassar got the vehicles off the street quickly, and unless the police did a door-to-door search, they would never find them, even with eyewitness descriptions.

When the wooden double doors were closed and lights turned on, Nassar took a head count and found he had lost seven men. He would know in a minute whether they were acceptable losses. Nassar walked to the truck and accosted a man climbing down from the rear holding an armload of equipment.

"Did you get it, Farouk?"

"I think so. I won't know until I develop the film."

Just then, Mason and Gould walked up, looking none too pleased. Mason crossed his arms in frustration. "Well, that was a colossal waste of time and manpower."

"Not necessarily, Mr. Mason. We may have the fugitives on film, racing away from a Mossad installation. I suspect the prime minister will have no explanation, and when the facts are known, the United

States will be forced to withdraw its support from Israel. Then it is a simple matter of declaring jihad."

"Even if the U.S. withdraws its support, I don't think the Americans will stand idly by while the Arabs wage a holy war against Israel. There are too many powerful Jews in our country."

"Perhaps. Even so, the prime minister will be embarrassed, and the Palestinians in Gaza will have more bargaining power with the Knesset. At any rate, I want to thank you for your assistance. We couldn't have done it without you."

Without so much as changing his expression, Nassar clutched the machine gun hanging from a strap around his neck. Gould threw up his hands and Mason went for his gun, but Nassar moved too quickly. The machine gun bucked and jerked in his hand, catching both agents in a lethal volley of steel-jacketed death, and as the echo faded away, Nassar looked dispassionately at the bodies on the floor.

"Make sure they're never found."

TEL AVIV HIGHWAY, TWELVE MILES WEST OF JERUSALEM, ISRAEL OCTOBER 8, 5:21 P.M.

As soon as the garage was behind them and Uri was certain they were not being followed, he asked for silence from his companions to give him a chance to think. In shock, and nursing a sore neck from the jolt when they broke through the fence, Lee sat back in his seat and watched the arid landscape go by in the near darkness. In the passenger seat, Tyler was lost in her own thoughts. At last, Uri turned to her.

"Why would the CIA be involved with a gang of Arab terrorists?"

Tyler had been wondering the same thing. "They both want us dead, I suppose. How did they know where to find us?"

Uri's voice was matter-of-fact. "That's easy. Matan betrayed us."

"Who's Matan?"

"One of our newest agents. I was foolish to trust him."

Lee leaned forward, sending shooting pains through his neck. "Ow! Would it be too much to ask where we're going?"

"Tel Aviv."

"I thought we were going to Joppa."

"Not anymore. If I am right and Matan betrayed us, then our enemies know where we are going and how we planned to get there. We must choose a different route."

The drive to Tel Aviv was uneventful—Lee might have said blissfully uneventful—and they arrived at a small marina on the southwestern edge of the city shortly after 6:30 P.M. The end of daylight had shut down the marina, though the city boasted a thriving night life, and Uri had no trouble finding a parking place. After a brief search and some squinted reading of registry numbers, he led Lee and Tyler to one of the slips and onto a thirty-foot sailboat.

At the question on Tyler's face, Uri responded, "It belongs to my sister and her husband. I don't think they would mind us staying here for a day or two. It would appear, however, that Professor Teller is the only one who had the forethought to bring his luggage. If I am not mistaken, there is a market not far from here, but it won't be open until morning. I need to find a telephone. Why don't you both come with me? Under the circumstances, I think it wouldn't hurt to stick together."

Together, they walked up the dock to the deserted manager's office and found a pay phone on the side of the building nearest the street. Uri dropped in two coins and dialed a number from memory. After three rings a familiar voice answered.

"Shalom, Jacob. Forgive me for calling you at home."

"Uri! You're alive!"

"For the moment. What news from the garage?"

"The dogs withdrew right after you left. Japheth was the only casualty. Timon was wounded, but he's expected to make a full recovery. Do you know how they located our guests?"

"I think Matan may have betrayed us. You might want to put a man on him."

"Matan? Are you sure?"

"He tried to convince me to keep them at the garage, then didn't show up for duty."

"I hope you're wrong, my friend. But I will have him watched. Don't tell me where you are. I don't want to know. Call me first thing in the morning and we will come up with an alternate plan."

"Thank you, Jacob."

"Shalom, Uri."

OFFICE OF THE DIRECTOR, CIA HEADQUARTERS, LANGLEY, VIRGINIA
OCTOBER 8, 4:10 P.M.

Perhaps the most irritating aspect of Bill Sidwell's job was having to deal with people who refused to tell the whole truth, which meant—though he never showed it—he was irritated much of the time. In three calls and as many hours on the phone with the head of the Mossad, Mr. Gilboah handed him such a mountainous pile of manure, he could fertilize the entire fruited plain. Six agents were dead, Mason and Gould were missing, and the Mossad didn't have a single lead. Sidwell remembered his global strategy sessions in training. These kinds of events were sometimes a prelude to war.

But Israel against the United States? The idea was preposterous. The only force keeping the Arab nations from obliterating the Israelis was the threat of the U.S. military. Would the prime minister really risk losing that support, just to get an economic edge over his neighbors? Maybe.

Sidwell picked up the phone and called Chip Nicholson. "Chip, I'm not 100 percent sure the Israelis didn't set up the attack on Macaulay's team. Until I am sure, I want every person entering the country from the Middle East triple-checked to verify his or her identity."

"We'd have to put about twenty people on it full time. I don't have the budget."

"Then take it out of surveillance or forensics. No, wait. I've got a better idea. Redirect the remainder of the annual salaries for the dead agents. The widows will be taken care of out of the pension fund. If we find out who really pulled the trigger, maybe we can make their deaths count for something."

Sidwell terminated the connection and called White House Chief of Staff Hank Joram. Joram was already in a bad mood, and Sidwell found his effete southern drawl particularly grating. "Hello, Bill. More bad news from the Holy Land?"

"Not exactly. I'm working on a theory that the Mossad may have been behind the hit on our people in Jerusalem."

"Now, that would be something to chew on. The president will want to hear it. Can you be at the Oval Office at 9:00 tomorrow morning?"

"Yes, sir."

GIBRAEL-BAR-GIBRAEL MARINA, TEL AVIV, ISRAEL
OCTOBER 9, 6:48 A.M.

Moist wood. There was something delicious about the smell of moist wood. Not the mildewy kind, rotten and ripe with decay, but that special sea salt and varnish smell common to well-kept sailboats. Add to that the throaty, intermittent lap, lap, lap of tiny waves against the wooden hull and the delicate omnipresence of the damp sea air, and the ambience aboard ship could be quite hypnotic.

Lee lay absolutely still in his berth, more or less comfortable on a terry cloth–covered foam rubber cushion, breathing slowly in and out through his nose. He had slept on a friend's boat once as a boy, and the sensation of being adrift somewhere on Lake Michigan was uncanny. To his semiconscious mind, it seemed an unreasonable stretch to believe they were actually moored on the coast of Israel in the Mediterranean Sea. Such a silly idea, really, being on a boat in a distant land. The stuff of nonsense and fairy tales. Merely a little boy's daydream of adventure.

He lay like that, not moving, floating lazily about the wind-rippled surface of Lake Michigan for the longest time, until Uri sat up from his berth opposite. Tyler was still asleep. Uri put a finger to his lips, then an imaginary phone to his ear, and walked up the short flight of steps to the deck. Lee decided he would busy himself with a search for breakfast.

Uri returned to the manager's office and the pay phone beyond, inserted two coins, and called the office. As soon as he had Jacob on the line, he could tell something was desperately wrong.

"Jacob, what is it?"

"You must leave the country at once! I am not supposed to even be talking to you."

"At least tell me what's going on."

"The Arabs have a videotape of you leaving the garage with Professor Teller and Tyler Stills. His identity is somewhat in doubt, but when she fired out the window, they got a clear shot of her face and yours. They are trumpeting it in the press and sending copies to our allies. The prime minister is already distancing himself from you, calling you a traitor and a terrorist collaborator. We have been ordered to shoot you on sight."

"Does the prime minister want the mission aborted?"

"The prime minister's desires are unchanged. But any action you take will be on your own, and we will try and stop you."

"I understand. Shalom, Jacob."

"Go with God, my friend."

Uri slowly returned the receiver to its perch and stood for a moment, gazing out over the sublime azure plain that was the Mediterranean. His life had just become very complicated, and he would have to choose his steps carefully. He dropped his last two coins in the coin slot and dialed his sister. At least they would not have put a tap on her phone yet.

"Daria, it's Uri."

The voice on the other end sounded groggy. "Uri? Why are you calling so early?"

"Daria, please listen to me, and don't interrupt. I have run into some trouble. For political reasons, the government has declared me an outlaw. If they catch me, they will kill me, so I must leave the country at once. Now, listen carefully. I am taking your boat. I'm not sure where. Maybe Larnaca on the island of Cyprus. I will send word to you when I arrive, so you know its exact location. I am sorry to have to tell you this, but I couldn't take the chance you would report it stolen. Some men may come around asking questions. Tell them you haven't heard from me."

"But . . ."

"Don't speak. Now, I am going to hang up. Please, don't breathe a word of this to your husband unless he asks about the boat. Good-bye, Daria. I love you."

Uri hung up the phone and ran down the dock to the boat. Tyler was sitting up on the edge of her berth, and Lee was still poking around in the cupboards, looking for something to eat. "We have to set sail immediately."

Lee nearly hit his head turning to face Uri. "Why?"

"The Arabs filmed our departure last night. Apparently they got a clear shot of Tyler and me. The prime minister had to deny any prior knowledge. I have been branded a traitor and terrorist collaborator. The standing order is shoot to kill."

Tyler ran a hand through her hair. "I'm not even out of bed, and this is already a bad day. Where are we going?"

"It's about two hundred miles to Larnaca on the island of Cyprus. If the wind is with us and the engine holds out, we should arrive an hour or so after sunset."

While Tyler looked over the engine and inventoried supplies, Lee followed Uri off the boat to the car. Uri started pawing through the glove compartment.

"What are you looking for?" Lee asked.

"This," Uri replied, holding up the operator's manual. "I want to be sure there are no surprises on this car before we sink it."

"Sink it?"

"If the police find it, the Mossad will know we left by boat. A fighter jet would be able to catch us very quickly."

Lee looked over Uri's shoulder at the manual, which was written in Hebrew, and laughed. "This was translated from English, wasn't it?"

"I think so. Why?"

Lee pointed to the page. "Look at the back axle. It's labeled 'bekexle.' And the front axle is labeled 'front bekexle.'"

Uri smiled. "At least our syntax is mostly correct. Here, you drive." He handed Lee the keys and got out of the car. Lee started the engine and followed Uri's directions as he led the car across the grass and down a broad ramp to the dock. The timbers creaked under the weight of the car, but held. At the end of the dock, Uri drew his finger across his neck, and Lee cut the engine.

"Put it in neutral, and make sure the parking brake is off."

Lee did so and got out, standing behind the car with Uri. Both men looked around for observers and, finding none, put their hands on the bumper and pushed for all they were worth. The car was heavy, but they were able to give it sufficient momentum to carry it off the end of the dock. A terrible cracking sound was followed by a muffled splash, and the car quickly sank from sight. Bits and pieces of the end of the dock were left floating, scraped off by the underside of the doomed vehicle. Uri fished around in the water, collected as many scraps of wood as possible, and positioned them so that from any distance, the dock would appear undamaged. He surveyed his work, none too proudly, and shrugged.

"Well, we have burned the bridge behind us. Let's get going."

Chapter Thirteen

The tape was remarkable, not because of its clarity, brevity, or cinematography, but because it was real. The action on the screen lasted only a matter of seconds, but it was like a scene out of a Hollywood movie. A car shot out of a gaping hole in a nondescript wall, along with a seemingly endless chattering of machine-gun fire, then the driver's side window came down and someone in the passenger seat fired three shots. As the car disappeared off the left side of the screen, a rocket trail started into the sky, then the image went to static. With a little magnification and almost no enhancement, the face of the shooter was immediately recognizable. Tyler Stills.

"And you say the driver is a Mossad agent?" the president asked incredulously.

Sidwell turned away from the monitor. "Uri Narov. Emigrated with his family from the Ukraine in 1964, at the age of eleven. The prime minister has admitted it. He says Uri Narov is in league with the Hamas."

"Do you believe it?"

"No, sir, I don't. The Israelis hate the Hamas. For reasons we have already discussed, I think the prime minister wants to see the fusion process go public."

The president frowned. "Enough to gun down friendly agents in cold blood?"

"He probably told Gilboah to rescue Teller and Stills and let the Mossad work out the details. They didn't have much time, and Macaulay's team was well armed. Under the same circumstances, we might have done something similar."

"It seems awfully desperate, doesn't it?"

Hank Joram chipped in. "You have been making overtures to the Arabs over the last year or so. Perhaps the Israelis are getting a little skittish."

"Aw, Hank. You know how intractable they can be. I'm trying to encourage peace in the region, and the Israelis won't even discuss the Golan Heights. Damascus refuses any accord that doesn't include the return of the Golan Heights. It's just a scraggly patch of desert, covered with about three million land mines. Why do they even want it, anyway?"

Joram leaned back in his chair. "You've heard of the old Arab farmer who lost his goat to robbers? His sons came the next day and told him, 'They've taken your sheep,' and the farmer says, 'Go get my goat.' The day after that, his sons tell him, 'They've taken your horses,' and the old man says, 'Go get my goat.' The following day, his wife comes to him and says, 'They have taken your sons and daughters!' and the old man says . . ."

"'. . . go get my goat,'" the president finished.

Joram nodded. "In 1967, during the Six-Day War, the Israelis took the Syrians' goat. And the Syrians want it back."

The president looked out the window, thinking about the events of the past year as they concerned Israel. "I guess I thought if the prime minister weren't so cocky about being our ally, he might listen to reason."

"Let me tell you another little story, Mr. President," Hank Joram intoned. "A fox and a scorpion were standing beside a river, and the scorpion asked the fox for a ride. 'No, sir, Mr. Scorpion,' the fox replied, 'for you would sting me and I would drown,' but the scorpion explained, 'If I sting you, we will both drown.' Now, that seemed reasonable to the fox, and he told the scorpion to climb aboard. However, as you may have already guessed, they were halfway across the river when the scorpion stung the fox. As the poison took effect, and the fox began slipping beneath the surface of the water, he gasped, 'Why? Why did you sting me?' And the scorpion replied, 'Because this is the Middle East.'"

The president was quiet for a long time before speaking. "Mr. Sidwell, I want proof—concrete, irrefutable proof—that the Mossad was behind the hit on Macaulay."

MEDITERRANEAN SEA, TWENTY MILES SOUTHEAST OF LARNACA, CYPRUS
OCTOBER 9, 7:34 P.M.

When they set sail, Lee said a prayer for their safety, and for the most part, the trip had been smooth, not counting a few large swells from a passing ocean liner. The engine could make twelve nautical miles per hour with no trouble, but there was a fine, strong northerly wind, and the current seemed to be with them. In fact, the trip had gone so well, Uri considered bypassing Cyprus and heading up the Aegean Sea to the Bosporus—effectively making the whole trip to Istanbul by boat—but Lee and Tyler threatened to feed him to the fish, so he stayed on course for Larnaca.

In the rush to leave, there had been no breakfast. The larder was mostly empty to begin with, so they had pretty much finished the meager emergency rations at lunch, except for several gallons of distilled water, and were feeling quite ravenous by sunset. Tyler was the first to spot the lights of Larnaca.

"There! About ten degrees to starboard."

Uri was fighting the wind, so he stowed the sail and ran with the engine. As they drew nearer, he could see the channel markers and steered toward them. The southern coast of Cyprus was rocky, and from the configuration of the lights on shore, Larnaca appeared to be built at least partially on cliffs, though in the dark it was difficult to be sure. Uri headed for the largest cluster of lights, which turned out to be the harbor. There were numerous places for boats of all sizes to tie off on the waterfront, and Uri found one right away.

Lee looked in wonder at the throngs of people walking the cobbled streets, a mixture of tourists and locals, but the buildings were partially decorated as if heralding some sort of festival. "It looks like we're just in time for the party."

"They keep it decorated like this for the tourists," Uri explained. As he finished with the mooring ropes, a customs official in uniform stepped onto the boat without being invited.

"May I see your passports, please?"

Lee and Tyler complied immediately, and Uri chose one of several he had stashed in his bag. The official looked them over carefully. "Purpose and length of your visit?"

Uri smiled easily. "We are on vacation for three days."

The official handed the passports back, said, "Enjoy your stay," and after a cursory examination of the boat, walked back the way he had come.

Uri watched him go. "Not much of a welcoming committee."

Tyler snorted. "We don't exactly look like the upper crust of society, you know."

"I noticed. Follow me, please."

Uri wasted no time finding a small cafe and ordering a hefty meal for the three of them. Lee had never much cared for Greek food, but he had never had it when he was so hungry. They shoveled through a meal of lamb, rice, and assorted greens, all mixed with olive oil, not saying a word, and ignoring the offended expressions on the faces of a few of the other patrons.

With dinner a contented memory, Uri paid for the meal, then walked outside holding his bulging stomach with both hands. "Perhaps I ate too fast. Oh, but it was worth it. Now, I have to make arrangements for my sister's boat. You two see if you can find a place for us to sleep. We'll meet right here in one hour."

Lee and Tyler found a street leading away from the waterfront and walked until they found an apartment house with rooms to rent. The prices were aimed at tourists, and they decided to move on. That section of town seemed alive with cheerful activity, as Lee always imagined a place like Rio de Janeiro to be, with people wandering here and there in search of entertainment or just enjoying the balmy sea air. As they walked along, Tyler snaked her hand into his, and his heart started racing. She didn't say anything, which was for the best, since Lee didn't think he could make his tongue move. They walked on like that for some time, and Lee had a minor revelation. He didn't need time to sort out his feelings where she was concerned. He was just afraid of being rejected.

Lost as he was in his reverie, only aware of the cool smoothness of the skin of her hand, Tyler had to drag him off the sidewalk when she saw a small hotel sign hanging in a shallow cul-de-sac. The cottage was brightly lit inside, and in answer to her knock, a portly woman opened the door.

Tyler smiled. "We need a room for the night. There will be three of us."

The woman returned the smile and spoke with a thick accent. "Yes! Yes! Come inside."

The room she led them to was cozy and rustic, all pillows and oak, and the price surprisingly reasonable. The bed was a four-poster, with just enough room for two, but the woman rolled a cot into the room, waited patiently for Lee to count out some money, and then disappeared. Lee looked from the bed to the cot to Tyler.

"You get the cot."

"Why me?"

"Because I'm sleeping with Uri in the bed."

"Chivalry is dead." Tyler sulked.

Lee smiled. "It's not dead, just mortally wounded."

Tyler pushed her hands into the soft mattress on the bed, then sat down on the cot. "I'll sleep better on the cot, anyway."

She offered her hand to Lee, and he helped her to her feet, but as she stood, she put her arms around him and kissed him. Lee had never been with an aggressive woman, and he was discovering that he liked it. A lot. Maybe too much. Nearly overcome by the intensity of the emotion, his knees almost gave way, and he had to grab one of the bedposts to steady himself. Tyler pulled away first. In a most endearing way, she traced the line of his lower lip with her finger.

"We should go. We're going to be late."

Lee swallowed hard. *And I might do something I'll regret later.* He held out his hand toward the door. "Ladies first."

With mischief in her eyes, Tyler grabbed his beard just hard enough to hurt a little and then held the door open for him. "I'm no lady, Professor. And don't you ever forget it."

The stroll back to the waterfront was leisurely and entirely pleasant. The tranquillity of the place cast a spell over the visitors, and the cares of the day seemed to melt away. Like a couple on vacation, they pointed out little bits of the local culture to each other and talked about frivolous things, like the weather and the taste of certain exotic foods. After all the horror and tension of the past few days, it was not unlike dying on the battlefield and suddenly finding oneself in heaven.

They took a little longer than intended getting back, but Uri did not seem to mind. They found him sitting on a bench, watching the stars overhead, a look of complete serenity on his face. Tyler leaned over his face and smiled.

"Bang. You're dead."

Uri stretched and stood up. "I might as well be. I'm not sure I want to leave this place."

"We found a place to stay not far from here, but it's still early. Why don't we find a place to sit?"

A modicum of detective work turned up a sidewalk cafe right next to the water, and they ordered drinks for sipping and watched the boats in the harbor. Myriad small vessels and a few large ones were floating out under the stars, and the sounds of celebration seemed to be everywhere. At last, Lee tore himself from the view and looked at Uri.

"I take it you have been here before."

Uri nodded. "Several times with my sister. I'd forgotten how beautiful it is."

"How old is your sister?"

"She won't tell me. Somewhere in the neighborhood of thirty-six. She is married and has three beautiful children, who think their crazy uncle Uri races around the world in fast cars, shooting bad guys. I've tried to explain about desks and paperwork, but they always change the subject. My sister and I are from the Ukraine originally. My mother told me we lost some relatives during Stalin's purges in the late '30s, but back then there was nowhere to go. When Israel was formed, my parents wanted to emigrate but didn't have the means. Then Stalin died and Khrushchev came to power, but he didn't bother us much, or so my mother says. When Brezhnev took over in the early '60s, my father feared he might be another Stalin, and since they had the money, my parents decided to immigrate to Israel."

"Are your parents still alive?"

"My mother is, but she won't speak to me. My father died in the Six-Day War, during the assault on the Golan Heights. The Syrians had mounted an attack with one thousand tanks and pushed the border troops back all the way to the valley beyond the heights. They stopped for the night, planning to wait for daylight to launch their offensive into the heart of Israel. The commander dispatched teams with missile launchers to take out the tanks one by one under cover of darkness. The plan worked beautifully, except for one thing. The Syrians were able to use the muzzle flashes from the launchers to pinpoint our positions. Casualties were high—my father was only one of many—but by morning, the tank force was nearly wiped out, and we chased them all the way back to Damascus. We lobbed a few shells into the city as a warning before going home."

"Why won't your mother speak to you?" Tyler asked.

"She says I'm a fool to work for the Mossad. She thinks they are nothing but a band of paid cutthroats and killers."

Tyler smiled. "Aren't they?"

Uri was amused, but thoughtful. "I suppose so, from a certain point of view. But perhaps we can be forgiven for being a little over-zealous after living so long among our enemies."

Just then, a large flat-topped boat drifted into view, close enough they could hear the music playing and see numerous bodies dancing on the deck. With the stars overhead and the multicolored lights in the foreground, the impression was of a group of party goers, "con-demned" forever to frolic about the harbor without a care in the world. Lee laughed and asked, "Is it always like this?"

"Only during the tourist season."

"How long does the tourist season last?"

Uri grinned. "About twelve months." He finished his drink and let out a long, contented sigh. "We have a busy day tomorrow. We should get some sleep."

"What are we doing tomorrow?" Lee wanted to know.

"Trying to get to Istanbul."

JERUSALEM INTERNATIONAL AIRPORT, JERUSALEM, ISRAEL
OCTOBER 10, 7:53 A.M.

Matan Weisberg had never been so terrified in his life. For nearly half a year he had carefully infiltrated a Muslim extremist group until one misstep blew his cover. The only reason he wasn't killed was that Abi Nassar saw an opportunity. Since he knew Matan's true identity, he offered an exchange. For the lives of Matan's family members, he would permit the young agent to return to the Mossad with false information. Matan continued as a double agent for some time because he knew the Mossad would not be able to protect his family and Nassar would eventually make good on his threat.

All those months he thought being a double agent was frightening, but his present situation was infinitely worse. He had given Nassar critical information, and one of his own people had been killed. Matan stood self-condemned as a traitor, and all he could do was flee like a dog. He knew the Mossad was spread thin at the moment, trying to keep too many people under surveillance, so he took the opportunity to make a run for the airport.

Wearing sunglasses and average clothing, he walked toward his gate, carrying a small travel bag. The flight to Switzerland would not be crowded, and since he was traveling under an assumed name, there was little chance of being followed. As he neared the metal detectors, the people in line suddenly turned on him, there was a flurry of motion, and he found himself immobilized by a dozen hands.

One of the agents, a hirsute brute named Levi, gave him a murderous look. "Leaving so soon, Matan? Next time, don't call your girlfriend."

GIBRAEL-BAR-GIBRAEL MARINA, TEL AVIV, ISRAEL
OCTOBER 10, 8:17 A.M.

The manager for the marina arrived early and in a foul mood. One of his customers had nearly killed himself stepping on a loose board and had burned up the phone line for almost five minutes telling the manager just what kind of wretched dog he was. The manager had taken the job for the express purpose of not getting up before 8:30 in the morning, and being awakened two hours early sometimes ruined his entire day.

Muttering to himself about the unfairness of life and the universe in general, he walked out to the end of the dock where the mishap occurred. There was a loose board, all right, several, in fact. Probably the kids from the park. No, the park was too far away. And those scrape marks . . . like something very heavy went into the water. He leaned over, careful not to put his weight on any of the broken boards.

The rays of the morning sun streamed through the placid water, and he could just make out a patch of color—roughly in the shape of an automobile.

MEDITERRANEAN SEA, LARNACA, CYPRUS
OCTOBER 10, 9:06 A.M.

"Your name, please?"

"Gabriel Stein. These are my business associates, Mr. and Mrs. Miller." Uri handed his false identification over the counter, along with

Tyler's and Lee's. The travel agent keyed in the relevant information from the passports and handed the documents back.

"You are confirmed on flight 714, departing at 2:05 P.M., to Ankara, Turkey. From Ankara, the shuttle for Istanbul takes off at 4:30 P.M. Your seats are confirmed. You will be staying at the Ataya Hotel for three nights."

"Thank you."

Uri handed the passports back to Lee and Tyler. They walked out of the little storefront travel agency, heading back toward the harbor. Lee was enjoying the scenery, but Tyler seemed distracted.

"Why are we going to Istanbul?"

"I was wondering when you would ask me that. I have a friend there. He is Mossad, so I have to be very careful how I approach him since I am a wanted man."

"You have a plan?"

"I am hatching one, yes."

Tyler did not look convinced. "Do you think your friend will help us?"

"That will depend on which side of the fence his loyalty falls."

Lee noticed some brightly colored shawls on a thatch table and considered pointing them out to Tyler, but suddenly his heart wasn't in it. "What if his loyalty falls with the Mossad?"

Uri didn't answer. They walked on in silence, and to each, it seemed that the city had lost some of its magic or, perhaps more accurately, that they had. Larnaca was a place for people without cares, people in no hurry to go anywhere. Uri, Lee, and Tyler didn't fit that category anymore. So they walked, halfheartedly perusing the wares of the local merchants, watching the seagulls circle the harbor, the tourists parasailing, all the while feeling like outsiders. Lunch was a joyless exercise, passed largely in silence, and by the time they boarded a cab for the airport, Lee was feeling thoroughly sullen.

Upon arrival at the airport, Uri was on full alert, and his nervousness spilled over onto his companions. Lee preferred being edgy to being gloomy, and he experienced a kind of grim satisfaction to find his mind slipping back into "field mode," as he called it. If anyone tried to stop them, they were defenseless, since the guns had to be packed—unloaded—in their bags, and the bags had to be checked. Their worries were needless, however, for no one so much as looked at them as they made their way to the gate.

The flight to Ankara took about one and a half hours, then one more hour to Istanbul, and the sun was nearing the horizon as they landed. In front of the terminal, Uri flagged down a cab. As the driver maneuvered through the busy streets, Lee noted that Istanbul was a booming metropolis, indistinguishable from any other major city, not counting the lettering on the signs and the occasional swollen spire of a mosque.

The Ataya Hotel could be reached only on foot. It was located at the end of a narrow alley, which stank of raw sewage, but the stench did not carry into the lobby. Although the accommodations were somewhat antiquated, everything appeared to be clean, and the staff was polite. Even better, their room had a balcony with a view of the city.

Tyler leaned on the railing and sighed. "Why does everything look gray?"

Because it isn't Larnaca, Lee thought. "Because it is gray, the buildings, I mean. That, and the sun is going down."

They walked back into the room and found Uri sitting at the table, writing. He looked up just long enough to indicate the chairs around the table. "Sit down, please. We have to talk. Tomorrow morning, I am going to the Mossad office very early. I will wait outside until Joshua shows up, then I will follow him when he leaves for lunch and look for an opportunity to approach him. If I am successful and he can convince some others, we will take whatever help we can get. If something goes wrong, you will have to get out of Istanbul quickly. I do not want to know your plans in case I am captured and they are effective in their interrogation. I will call at 9:00, 12:00, and 3:00. If I am more than ten minutes late reporting in, get out of here."

In his mind's eye, Lee saw Ilya's body and once again heard Nels's assertion that it could be him, and he knew death could be just around the corner for any of them. With no thought to the consequences, Lee blurted, "Can I pray for you?" Uri looked at him as if he had just offered him a pork sandwich, and Lee hastened to continue, "You said it yourself. We'll take whatever help we can get."

Uri thought for a moment before answering. "Go ahead. Just don't tell my mother. If she finds out I let a Christian pray for me, she'll kill me with her bare hands."

"Your mother must be some woman."

Uri's face was grave. "Believe it."

Without any fancy words, Lee asked the Lord to protect them and especially to watch out for Uri tomorrow, to help him succeed in his efforts, and to prepare Joshua for their meeting. It was simple and heartfelt, and Tyler was touched by it. When Lee was finished, Uri looked up in surprise. "That's all? I thought you would say something in Latin, or 'hail, Mary,' or something like that."

Tyler smiled. "That would be my department. I'm the fallen Catholic."

"Nels told me praying is just talking to God," Lee said, smiling. "I don't think you have to memorize anything to get Him to listen."

Uri looked from Lee to Tyler. "Try telling that to any little Jewish boy about to have his bar mitzvah. He'll club you over the head with the Torah." Uri stood up. "Let's get some dinner."

MOSSAD HEADQUARTERS, JERUSALEM, ISRAEL
OCTOBER 10, 5:46 P.M.

In the field operations department, Jacob Iveson sat at his desk, trying to focus on the latest report from an informant in Amman, Jordan. The information was important, but Jacob had not been sleeping well since that business at the garage. Of all the agents under his command, Uri was the most like a son, and the thought of him on the run from his own people was very troubling. Suddenly a large hairy figure filled his doorway, and he looked up.

"Come in, Levi."

The big man handed him a folder, his face downcast. "Matan is dead. He committed suicide as soon as we returned him to his cell. I don't know. Considering the charges, maybe it's for the best. At least he gave us a name before he did it. Abi Nassar."

"Nassar! Do you know where he is?"

"In the old district. I have the address."

The phone rang then, and Jacob picked it up. "Yes . . . where? . . . No, not now . . . I said not now! Bring them in tomorrow morning. I want them in my office by 9:00 sharp." Jacob hung up the phone. "They found the car Uri took from the garage in the water near a marina in Tel Aviv. Apparently his brother-in-law owns a boat there, which is now missing."

"And you don't want to bring them in for questioning?"

"Not tonight. Tonight, we have to arrange a little reception for Abi Nassar."

MOSSAD FIELD OFFICE,
ISTANBUL, TURKEY
OCTOBER 11, 6:34 A.M.

Bolstered by a stiff cup of Iranian "goat-eating" coffee—the kind that was half grounds, half water—Uri watched the front door to the Mossad field office. Several agents had arrived since he started his surveillance, but none of them was the one he was looking for. Joshua could be on assignment. That could make this a very long stakeout. Uri needed to find out if Joshua was even in town, but his options were limited. Calls to his old office were being monitored by now, and the receptionist in Joshua's office was not likely to give such information over the phone.

Moments later, Uri was saved from further meditation on the subject as Joshua walked up the sidewalk and let himself into the office. Uri let out a sigh of relief and settled in for a long wait. At 9:00, he found a public phone nearby and called the hotel. At 12:00, he repeated the process. At 12:20, Joshua emerged from the front door of the field office and started down the sidewalk. He was a large burly man with a bushy beard, and following him would present no problem. Uri followed.

Joshua walked four blocks to a small plaza with some round tables out in the open air. He sat down, apparently in his usual spot, as a waiter recognized him and came to take his order. When the waiter walked away, Uri came up on Joshua's blind side and sat down.

"Uri!"

"Keep your voice down."

"What are you doing here?" Joshua slowly moved his hand toward the pistol tucked in his belt, beneath his jacket.

"Put your hands where I can see them, or I'll kill you," Uri said quietly.

Joshua slowly put his hands, palms down, on the table. He leaned forward and spoke in a hoarse whisper. "Have you gone mad, Uri? They say you shot up the garage in Jerusalem and took two American fugitives. Are you working for the Hamas?"

"Bite your tongue! You know I would rather die than work for the Hamas. It's a bit more complicated than that, I'm afraid." Uri looked around to be certain no one was within earshot. "These Americans are carrying a working process for cold fusion. We were about to move them to a safer place when a group of Arab terrorists attacked. Someone took pictures of the fugitives in my car, and the prime minister had to say I was an outlaw."

"Why, Uri? You were obviously trying to save them."

Uri leaned forward. "We had to kill some CIA agents to rescue them in the first place."

Joshua pursed his lips. "Ooh. If the media find out, America pulls out, and the Arabs turn our homeland into a parking lot."

"Something like that. The Mossad is looking for us, as you know, but unofficially the prime minister still wants the mission to succeed."

"What is the mission exactly?"

"To get the Americans to the United Nations building in New York City for a meeting of the General Assembly on October 13. Once the process is no longer a secret, the oil-producing nations will have their hands full trying to adjust."

Joshua nodded. "And perhaps Israel will be forgotten, at least for a while. Why have you come to me?"

"I need your help."

Joshua's face broke into a smile, and he started laughing. "Of course. Of course, my friend. It all makes perfect sense now. I dreamed about you last night. You came to me in chains, and I unlocked them. When your hands were free, you clasped them around my neck, but whether in anger or in friendship, I could not tell. When you sat down just now, I thought you might kill me. But now, you have thrown the millstone of friendship around my neck and offered to cast it into the sea."

"Will you help me, Joshua?"

Joshua smiled until his eyes seemed to brim with tears. "If we must be drowned, then let us be drowned together."

Chapter Fourteen

**OVAL OFFICE, WHITE HOUSE,
WASHINGTON, D.C.
OCTOBER 11, 6:47 A.M.**

"It's confirmed, sir. The armies of Jordan and Syria are massing along Israel's borders. We have unconfirmed reports of Iraqi divisions rolling through Jordan, on maneuvers supposedly."

The president looked hard at Harmon Kelsey, chief of staff for the army. "I can't take action without confirmation, Mr. Kelsey. What are our options?"

"We can put the *Missouri* in the Mediterranean on some maneuvers of our own. Two destroyers and an aircraft carrier should be sufficient to keep them on their side of the border."

"And if we do nothing?"

"The Israelis will probably shoot first. Since any action by them will precipitate all-out war, my guess is, they'll start with nuclear warheads."

"You really think they'll use their nukes?"

Kelsey leaned forward, rested his arms on his knees, and clasped his hands. "Let me put it this way. What have they got to lose?"

The president turned to his chief of staff. "Hank, do we have anything on the Mossad yet?"

"Nothing. The prime minister is sticking by his story, and our operatives have not been able to uncover anything."

"What if we wait?"

Kelsey shook his head. "I don't think waiting is an option. The tension over there is growing exponentially."

The president mulled over his options, then stood up. "We will wait for two hours. Let the prime minister sweat a little. Then send the destroyers and the aircraft carrier. Until we have proof, we have to treat Israel as an ally. But I want the prime minister to wonder whether next time we'll come at all."

"With all respect, sir, you're taking a terrible risk."

The president's face hardened. "So is the prime minister."

MERCA SID-AL-RYAD MARKET, ARAB DISTRICT, JERUSALEM, ISRAEL
OCTOBER 11, 2:11 P.M.

Abi Nassar stood, as he saw it, godlike in the center of the room, surrounded by his servants. The table before him was covered with battle plans worthy of a World War II invasion. Troops were massing on the Jordanian border, a similar buildup was occurring on the border with Syria, and the Iraqis would join them within two days. So far, there had been no word from the United States. If the Israelis behaved according to type, they would launch a preemptive strike, and the war would commence. For his part, Nassar would do his best to secure Jerusalem from within before his Arab brothers ever breached the city limits.

Nassar circled every major outpost for the army and the police stations just to be sure. The number of armed Israeli forces within the city limits was considerable, but terrorist units were gathering in several parts of the city, some professional and some amateur. What his ranks lacked in numbers, they more than made up for in ferocity. It was the battle many of them had long been waiting for, and if Allah smiled on them, they would finally own the land.

"The first unit will take out the barracks on the base in this quadrant. At the same time, unit two will destroy the road here . . . and here, blocking any support from the garrison and police stations in this part of the city . . ."

Nassar's voice trailed off as his man nearest the door slumped to the floor. For just an instant, every man in the room was frozen as if posing for a photograph, then through the doorway came five heavily armed men, three with M-79 grenade launchers—shooting smoke and .22-caliber rounds—and two with flamethrowers blazing. Nassar's plans lay forgotten as hell came to visit, his men running, screaming, trying to return fire. In moments the room was transformed into an inferno of carnage and death, and then the shooting stopped. The assault team pulled back to the doorway, flamethrowers covering the room with a final blanket of fire, and the last man called out as he disappeared through the door.

"Matan sends his regards!"

ATAYA HOTEL, ISTANBUL, TURKEY OCTOBER 11, 4:15 P.M.

When Uri came through the door with several men in tow, Lee was glad Uri had phoned ahead to warn them they were coming. Tyler kept one hand near her pistol, just in case. Introductions were made, and once Tyler saw Joshua smile, she relaxed a little. There were two men besides Joshua, who sat down in the comfortable chairs, while Joshua stretched out on the bed. Uri sat down at the table and kicked his shoes off.

"This calls for a celebration! Joshua, break out some drinks. In the little cabinet by the sink."

Joshua put on a humble face. "I only live to serve, master."

Tyler held up a hand. "Wait a minute. Shouldn't we be talking strategy?"

"We have spent all day talking strategy! The UN meeting is in two days. Between now and then, we need to make one secure communication to the prime minister so that he can make arrangements on his end. Then all we have to do is change places with the security team when they land in London."

"Piece of cake," Tyler muttered as she turned and walked out to the balcony.

Lee followed her outside. "What's the matter?"

"He talks as if we're planning a party."

Lee put his arm around her shoulder. "Cut him some slack. He's glad to be alive. He didn't have to kill a friend. We have more help than we counted on. This has been a good day."

Tyler smiled a little and put her head on his shoulder. "You make it hard for a girl to stay mad."

"Good."

Tyler lifted her chin and kissed him on the neck, then turned her face so she could watch the boats on the water in the distance. For Lee's part, he didn't care if the sun ever set. Inside, amidst much good-natured back pounding and bravado, Uri proposed a toast, "To the millstone of friendship!" More back slapping and general good spirits followed.

All too soon the sun dropped below the horizon, casting shadows across the water, as the homogeneous gray of the buildings faded to black, and a host of tiny lights came on along the waterfront and here and there along the city streets. If the overall effect was not entirely festive, it made up for it by being almost cheerful.

Lee glanced sideways, without moving his head. In the fading light, Tyler's face quite literally took his breath away. He wanted to lean over and kiss her with all his heart, but the curtains to the balcony were wide open, and he couldn't escape the sensation that her father might come through the door at just the wrong moment and catch them in a passionate embrace. The moment was gone then, for she patted him platonically on the back and said, "We should get back inside."

Inside, the mood was noticeably subdued as the celebration had given way to the business of making sleeping arrangements among the available beds and furniture in the hotel room. They were men who knew how to use a stone as a pillow, so even a blanket on the floor would not come close to what they would consider roughing it.

As the bustle of activity slowed down, after each person enacted his or her own preparatory ritual—brushing teeth, shaving, showering— Tyler took Uri aside and looked at him with a serious expression.

"All kidding aside, what are our plans?"

"Not to worry. We take the first flight out tomorrow to Heathrow. We switch places with the UN delegation from Israel and board the Concorde. Before you know it, poof! We're in New York."

Tyler eyed him skeptically. "Just like that?"

Uri nodded. "Just like that. It's all arranged. You can trust me."

Tyler smiled halfheartedly and patted him on the shoulder but didn't say what she was thinking. *It's not you I'm worried about.*

SITUATION ROOM, WHITE HOUSE, WASHINGTON, D.C.
OCTOBER 12, 8:02 A.M.

Hank Joram was really getting tired of the whole affair. It was one thing to plan global strategy around multiple, multifaceted, interconnected moving targets, but it was quite another to wake up each morning not knowing if the current presidency might be blown out of the water by some exclusive report on one of the cable news shows. As long as the Prometheus file was out there somewhere, the president would not be able to relax.

As if that wasn't enough, now there was the ridiculous confrontation with Israel. The U.S. show of strength in the Mediterranean seemed to have stopped the buildup along Israel's borders, and at last report, the Iraqi troops were withdrawing from Jordan. But the situation should never have developed in the first place. The president seemed to think he was finally going to bring peace to the Middle East, but on that score, Joram knew history was against him. The president's belief that the Israelis were the only thing standing in the way of harmony in the region seemed extremely naive and dangerous. Had he so quickly forgotten the war between Iran and Iraq? Or the Iraqi invasion of Kuwait? Without Israel, the region would simply feed on itself until one nation reigned supreme or there was nothing left. Joram had tried to explain these facts on numerous occasions, but the president stubbornly refused to believe it. And now, for the first time, Joram began to wonder if he hadn't hitched his wagon to the wrong star.

Bill Sidwell walked into the room, carrying a satchel, accompanied by two assistants. "Sorry I'm late, gentlemen. There has been quite a bit of intelligence gathered in the past forty-eight hours. Our operatives have been working overtime gathering information about troop movements and strengths. The reports of Iraq's withdrawal from Jordan are confirmed. Our estimates are that border troops will be back to normal levels within seventy-two hours."

"What news of the fugitives?" Hank Joram drawled.

"We lost their trail in Jerusalem. I doubt they're still in Israel. They may be lying low."

"For what? Until when?"

"Maybe they're waiting until we can't sustain the manhunt anymore. Then they can move about freely."

Joram took off his glasses and set them on the table. "If they go to a foreign news organization, what are the consequences?"

"If the organization is reputable, the Associated Press would pick it up and make it global in about fourteen hours. It would be news for a while, but without events to sustain the story, something would displace it before long. There would be a lot of behind-the-scenes diplomatic posturing, but I think it would create only a ripple on the national scene."

"Then tell me, Mr. Sidwell, what are they planning to do?"

Sidwell looked down at the material laid out before him, willing some answer to appear out of the chaos, but nothing came. "I wish I knew, sir."

SUPERSONIC TRANSPORT,
SOMEWHERE OVER THE ATLANTIC
OCTOBER 12, 10:51 A.M.

Lee had never been on the Concorde. In fact, he had only seen still photos of it until this morning. When the El Al plane from Istanbul had descended into London's Heathrow Airport, he caught a glimpse of the Concorde, the only one of its kind, sitting next to the terminal, waiting for passengers to whisk away on its two-hour-and-fifty-one-minute trip to New York City. But there had been an important operation in progress, and Lee had a lot on his mind.

It had turned out to be a beautiful piece of work, really. When the UN delegation from Israel arrived in London, they began a brisk walk through the airport toward the Concorde gate. When one of the delegates expressed a need to visit a rest room, the entire entourage veered right into the nearest men's room, leaving one man outside to keep other travelers out. After three minutes, the entourage emerged to continue the journey to the gate, only Lee, Uri, and his men had replaced the security contingent. As they passed the ladies' room, Tyler slipped into their ranks as if she had been there all along. When the entourage was out of sight, the original security men came out of the rest room one by one, in civilian clothes, and went their separate ways, each with his own route back to Israel.

Lee was dressed semiformally, and he sat beside Tyler, who was in a discreet executive dress. She sat beside Uri, who was dressed like Lee. The rows immediately in front and behind were occupied by Mossad agents also in suits—not counting the two genuine Israeli delegates—and all in all they looked just like a genuine UN delegation. Uri checked his watch and started rummaging around in his bag, eventually producing an odd assortment of documents.

"Here are your UN ID badges. Keep them with you at all times. You already have your passports and driver's licenses. Here is an official work order for three full sheets of baklava, on UN stationery. Joshua will be your driver."

Uri nodded toward the burly figure seated across the aisle, uncharacteristically formal in a suit, then turned his attention back to Lee and Tyler. "Turn on your televisions. It's almost time."

Tyler started to ask, "Time for what?" But Uri waved her silent, and she put on her headphones and turned on the armrest television. Uri punched up the appropriate channel for all three sets, then waited, nervously rubbing his knuckles together. A phone company commercial dragged on too long, then the network logo and header music came on and an attractive, businesslike woman started on the headlines.

"In our top story today, two Americans who were taken hostage in Jerusalem almost a week ago are being held for ransom. On October 7, Professor Lee Teller of Dartmouth College and his wife, Tyler, were abducted from their car by a Hamas splinter group calling itself the 'Arsenal of Freedom' . . ."

Tyler's eyebrows shot up. "Wife?"

Uri grinned. "One of my men saw you kissing. I thought it added a certain pathos to the story."

Tyler grunted and returned to the newscast. ". . . claim to have a process for cold fusion, a claim denied as outrageous by the scientific community. To prove its claim, the Arsenal of Freedom has promised a demonstration somewhere in the nation's capital. Police and emergency services are on full alert at this hour . . ."

Uri laughed out loud and slapped his knee. "This is good. You can bet Jamal Assid and the rest of the Hamas leaders are plucking their beards out about now, trying to figure out what's going on. I wish I could see their faces."

OFFICE OF THE DIRECTOR, CIA HEADQUARTERS, LANGLEY, VIRGINIA
OCTOBER 12, 11:22 A.M.

"What channel?"

Bill Sidwell nearly tripped over his desk reaching for the television as the voice on the other end of the phone told him what to watch. The image came to life, and he caught the tail end of an interview with the chief of police, then the scene dissolved to a reporter on the sidewalk outside the grounds of the White House.

". . . If you're just joining us, there has been a ransom demand for two Americans kidnapped in Jerusalem nearly one week ago. Dartmouth Professor Lee Teller and his wife, Tyler, were abducted on

October 7 from their car by a Hamas splinter group calling itself the Arsenal. The terrorists claim to have stolen a process for cold fusion, which has been flatly denied as ridiculous by the scientific community, but the Hamas have planned a live demonstration somewhere inside the beltway. The army and police are on full alert, but with such an expansive area to cover, we have noted some frustration on the faces of law enforcement officials. There have been no other communications from the kidnappers, but we can only assume that will come after government officials are convinced that their claims are valid . . ."

Sidwell stopped listening. His ever-present facade of control began to slip. He had been foolish to hope for a quiet resolution to the problem. The Hamas terrorists wanted a no-holds-barred media circus with lots of free publicity. Well, two could play that game. He picked up the phone and called Chip Nicholson.

"Chip, it's Bill . . . yes, I'm watching it right now. I want a list of every person in the city who has any connection with, or suspected sympathy for, any of the Muslim extremist groups with a presence in the area. I want them all brought in for questioning . . . I don't care if it's a thousand people, I want them arrested. We don't have to keep them overnight, but bring them in. We'll show these gutless wonders how to play hardball. And one other thing. Call a press conference." A smile slowly tugged at the corners of his mouth. "Tell the media there is no splinter group. The call was a hoax by an Arab hairdresser who is now in protective custody."

Sidwell terminated the connection and began making notes to himself. The cold fusion process was of little use to them for the time being, and if they went public with the Prometheus file, the CIA could simply deny it. For now, his best bet was to try and get them so infuriated they would do something rash. If the terrorists went ballistic and killed Teller and Stills, so much the better.

TENTH FLOOR, IMPERIAL HOTEL, NEW YORK CITY, NEW YORK OCTOBER 12, 7:43 P.M.

Lee sat back against a clump of bolster pillows, luxuriating in the opulence of the hotel room. With Tyler's help, he had been putting the finishing touches on the presentation for the General Assembly. The prospect of addressing a host of foreign delegates made his stomach feel uneasy, but it was a subject he was finally comfortable with, and from a certain perspective, they could be viewed as a group of older students.

"Lose the last bullet. Put a subbullet after 'graduated phase-in for local utilities' that says 'coordinate with rate schedules.'"

Tyler made the changes with a felt-tip pen and looked up. "We may be reaching a point of diminishing marginal returns."

"You're right. It's all starting to mush together in my head. Okay, no more changes. Whatever else happens, one way or another, by this time tomorrow it will all be over."

Tyler set the pen and presentation down, stood up, and stretched. "Do you think the Israeli delegates are in any danger?"

Lee shook his head. "Not unless somebody starts shooting. They have diplomatic immunity."

"I wouldn't mind having a little of that myself. Wouldn't it be great to just flash an embassy card and go home?"

"Unfortunately this isn't a foreign country. And we're not ambassadors."

"Always the practical professor. I'm going to bed."

Lee got up and walked her to the door. When she turned to say good night, he kissed her. Coming at the end of a strategy session, the kiss was both less passionate and more intimate, as if they had been together for much longer than a couple of weeks. Tyler pulled away, ran her hands up his arms, and gave him a look that gave his willpower a run for its money. "Do you want to come with me?"

"More than you can possibly imagine, but I can't. It's not right."

All in a rush, Tyler understood. Lee was trying to do what was right, for her sake and his, even if it meant ignoring his feelings and being separated from a woman he obviously cared about. Until that moment, she hadn't thought a man existed who would do such a thing, and tears came to her eyes, then she brushed his lips with hers. "Thank you."

Tyler let herself out, and Lee leaned his head against the door. Nels never told him how hard it could be to do the right thing. Or how good it felt. Lee walked into the bathroom and turned on the cold water. Looking at his face in the mirror, he marveled at the changes there. The gash under the eye, not yet healed; the beard covering a face made lean by long days and not enough food; the weathered skin, exposed to the elements more over the past month than in the past five years; the coarse sandy brown hair, brushed back and not very stylish. Lee had never been terribly style conscious, and it was a good thing. An ordeal like this could have murdered his self-image.

Lee splashed cold water on his face, then did it again, and toweled off, did an internal assessment, and found that the raging portion of his desire had quieted to much less than a dull roar, enough so that he could entertain the idea of going to bed and actually falling asleep. The bed was queen-sized, and rather than consider his options for filling the space beside him, he turned off the light and faced the wall, determined to think about blank chalkboards until he dozed off. And such a parade of chalkboards the world had never seen.

The next morning, Lee was up—bleary eyed, but up—and dressed by 6:30. Breakfast was brought to the room, and he found he was ravenous. He was only halfway through when there was a knock at the door. It was Uri, beard trimmed neatly and wearing a suit and tie.

"You look like a diplomat," Lee said by way of greeting.

"Please. It is too early for insults." Uri walked across the room and switched on the television. Once again, the backdrop was the White House, but this morning, the scene in the foreground was very different. Parked in front of the White House was a van clearly marked "Faud's Bakery" blocked at both ends by Lincoln Town Cars. The driver stood spread-eagle with his hands against the side of the vehicle, while a platoon of Secret Service agents and plainclothes police officers read him his rights and searched the back of the van.

"What's going on?" Lee wanted to know.

"I sent the Secret Service some doughnuts. I guess they're not hungry." Uri reached out and turned off the set. "In ten minutes, one of my men will call the CIA with a list of demands. We must be checked out and on the road by then."

"You sent an Arab delivery boy to the White House? Today?" Despite the cruelty of the act, Lee couldn't help laughing.

"We must keep the focus in Washington if we can. If they are looking for you there, they will be less likely to find you here."

OFFICE OF THE DIRECTOR, CIA HEADQUARTERS, LANGLEY, VIRGINIA
OCTOBER 13, 7:23 A.M.

"What do you mean 'doughnuts'?"

Bill Sidwell sat transfixed, staring at his television, his anger mounting, as the media continued reveling in the ritualistically barbaric practice of broadcasting stupid events as they happened. Chip Nicholson's voice came quick and nervous over the phone.

"He had a work order. The doughnuts were for the Secret Service."

"Did you find guns, explosives, anything?"

"We did a complete sweep of the van and didn't find anything that didn't belong there."

Sidwell ran a hand through his hair. "This is very bad, Chip. We just spent all last night harassing the Muslim community, and now we have arrested an Arab baker for delivering doughnuts ON NATIONAL TELEVISION!" He took a second to get his voice under control before continuing, "We'll be lucky to make it through the day without starting a holy war."

"But why doughnuts? And why an Arab baker?" Chip asked in frustration.

"It must be some sort of sick joke. Someone in the agency must have . . . wait a minute. What if it wasn't someone in the agency?"

"Then who? It doesn't fit any terrorist MO I've ever seen."

Sidwell's face darkened. "Precisely." He had more or less dismissed the notion that the Mossad had anything to do with the abduction of Teller and Stills, but now suspicion reared its ugly head once more. If his suspicions were justified, the implications were almost unthinkable. "Chip, I want a list of every party of two or more, originating in Israel, arriving in the U.S. within the last forty-eight hours. Restrict your search to parties with at least one woman."

"That could take a couple of hours."

"I want it in five minutes."

IMPERIAL HOTEL, NEW YORK CITY, NEW YORK OCTOBER 13, 7:31 A.M.

In the semicircular driveway in front of the hotel, two vehicles sat waiting to receive their occupants. The first—the car Uri would be driving—was a black luxury sedan, a diplomatic vehicle with small Israeli flags flying over each front fender. The second vehicle was a subcompact with barely enough room for four people. Standing on the walk with Uri, Lee, and Tyler were the two Israeli delegates and three Mossad agents. Uri gestured at the smaller car.

"Mr. and Mrs. Teller, this is your car. We will be going to the UN building via separate routes. Joshua knows the route I want you to take. I should arrive a few minutes before you and be waiting at the service entrance. If I am not there, go on without me." He turned so he could address the whole group. "Leave your guns in the car. All the entrances are equipped with metal detectors."

Impulsively Tyler threw her arms around Uri. "Thanks for all your help."

"Please, Mrs. Teller. Not in front of your husband."

Tyler pushed him away. "Dog. Don't think I haven't seen all the news reports calling me his wife." She pointed her finger, a mock threat. "When this is over, I'm going to hunt you down."

Uri grinned expansively. "I hope you do, for that would certainly be something worth celebrating."

Tyler caught his meaning. Now that the moment was here, she realized it could be the last time any of them saw each other, and her smile slowly turned poignant. "Good luck."

"May Jehovah be merciful."

Uri helped the two Israeli delegates into the backseat, along with one of his men, and another man climbed in the passenger seat. Uri got behind the wheel and checked his watch. It was time to move out.

OFFICE OF THE DIRECTOR, CIA HEADQUARTERS, LANGLEY, VIRGINIA
OCTOBER 13, 7:37 A.M.

To his credit, twelve minutes after Sidwell's request, Chip Nicholson was walking into the acting director's office, holding a two-page report. Never mind that several schedules and work spaces in his department lay in shambles. His people got the job done. Sidwell snatched the report out of his hands and scanned it.

"What's this group from the Energy Ministry?"

"They're attending a symposium at Georgetown University. It's been scheduled for months."

"What about this tour group?"

"No late additions to the roster. Everyone on the passenger list has been paid up for at least three weeks."

"I see there's a UN delegation."

"The General Assembly is meeting today in New York."

"What's the normal head count for the delegation?"

"Uh . . . six, I think."

As if on cue, the receptionist's voice came over the intercom. "Mr. Sidwell, there's an urgent call for Mr. Nicholson."

Chip picked up the phone. "Nicholson . . . okay, I'll be right down." Chip hung up the phone and started toward the door. "That terrorist splinter group just called with a new list of demands."

"Belay that."

"Sir?"

Sidwell looked up from the report in his hands. "There were two extra people in that Israeli delegation."

UNITED NATIONS BUILDING, NEW YORK CITY, NEW YORK OCTOBER 13, 7:42 A.M.

Owen Lucas hated pulling UN duty, especially when the producer used it as a club. An ex-marine with an attitude, Lucas was one of the top reporters for World Cable News. He had a reputation for getting the tough interviews, but when someone irritated him, he had the bad habit of saying the first thing that came to mind. His most recent gaffe, the one that landed him the UN beat, happened during an interview with the foreign minister of Singapore. Goaded by an unnecessarily smug response to one of his questions, Lucas responded, "So tell me, as a ranking official in one of the most repressive regimes on the face of the planet, did you sell your soul all at once or piece by piece?" The ratings were good; the vitriolic letters from the State Department were not. Add to that two threats to pull advertising, both from major accounts, and he was lucky not to be grounded at a desk somewhere in the research department.

The worst part about shooting the General Assembly meeting was taking three hours of footage, only to have two seconds of it used at the tail end of some dry international piece. His cameraman, a slightly overweight, pasty-faced greaseball with bad skin and a God-given gift for camera angles, lugged his gear into the press gallery and asked Lucas where to set up.

"Anywhere you want, Mac. This is a milk run."

Cameramen on the whole were not very outspoken, and Kevin Macadam was no exception. He preferred to be called "Kevin," but everyone called him "Mac" anyway. After seven years he was used to it. Mac didn't mind milk runs. They fit nicely with his placid disposition, which meant most of his assignments with Owen Lucas had been a real stretch. If he was really honest with himself, Mac didn't mind stretching, either. As long as he didn't snap.

Chewing thoughtfully on his lip, he went about the business of setting up his tripod, looking forward to a quiet and altogether uneventful day.

BROADWAY BOULEVARD, NEW YORK CITY, NEW YORK
OCTOBER 13, 7:44 A.M.

Behind the wheel of the diplomatic car, with each passing minute, Uri began to believe they might have clear sailing. He had seen no police officers, and morning rush-hour traffic was moving, so the chance of gridlock was minimal. When a siren came suddenly from behind a moment later, he resisted the urge to stomp on the accelerator. In the rearview mirror, he saw a patrol car swerve out of an alley and maneuver into the spot behind them. Uri addressed his important passengers in the backseat.

"It's your call, gentlemen."

"What happens if we pull over?" one of the delegates asked.

"They will probably start looking for a second car."

The delegate took a deep breath. "Then I think they may be terrorists and we should get out of here."

Uri smiled and put the accelerator to the floor.

Chapter Fifteen

Standing in front of the entryway to the headquarters building, Bill Sidwell watched with a sense of awe as a Harrier came to a stall over the front lawn and slowly dropped down until it rested on its landing struts. On loan from the marine contingent at the naval base in Annapolis, Maryland, the Harrier was the only jet-powered craft capable of landing on the headquarters lawn and available on such short notice.

Sidwell ran across the lawn, feeling a little out of place in his business suit, and climbed on board. With his helmet on, the pilot was able to speak to him over the roar of the idling jet engines.

"You don't have a G suit, so no power climbs."

Sidwell struggled to fasten the seat belt. "No power anything will suit me just fine. Just make best possible speed to the UN building in New York City."

With the canopy closed, the jet lifted slowly off the grass into the morning sky. Once clear of the treetops, the pilot tilted the engines for forward flight, and the Harrier took off on a vector for New York City. Unaccustomed to anything faster than a Boeing 747, Sidwell tried to relax in his seat and let the G force have its way with him. By the time the Harrier reached cruising speed, he was feeling pretty green about the gills.

"What happens if I puke in my helmet?" Sidwell asked miserably.

The pilot didn't miss a beat. "You have to wear it all the way to New York. And I'll have to tell all the guys back at the base."

"I was afraid of that."

With a twist of a knob, the pilot thickened the mixture to his queasy copilot, and the extra oxygen helped Sidwell get his stomach under control. "Whatever you did, it's working. Thanks."

"Sure . . . hang on, incoming message for you. I'll patch it through."

Heavy with static, Chip Nicholson's voice came over the comm system. "Bill? Bill, are you there?"

"Go ahead, Chip."

"The police in New York are chasing an Israeli diplomatic car. The car ignored the order to stop and pulled away at high speed. The officers are giving chase."

"Tell them not to fire unless fired upon! Do you read? Tell them NOT to fire unless fired upon!"

"Roger. Responding fire only. If they ask me why we're trying to stop the Israeli delegation, what do I tell them?"

Sidwell had to think for a moment. "Tell them we have reason to suspect a terrorist group is trying to infiltrate the UN in the guise of an Israeli delegation."

"Roger that. I'm off."

Sidwell looked out the window, half hoping to see some sign of the New York skyline, but saw only the lush, verdant hillocks of northern Virginia. He looked at his watch.

"What's our ETA?"

"Our current trajectory should put us into La Guardia at 0830."

"We're not going to the airport. I need to go directly to the UN building."

"I'm not cleared to land at the . . . hold it . . . another message." The pilot was quiet for a moment, and when he spoke, his voice was subdued. "It's the president. I'll put you on a secure channel."

Sidwell cleared his throat. "Yes, Mr. President?"

"Hello, Bill. Hank Joram is here. He tells me you think the fugitives may be in New York City."

Sidwell's stomach was queasy again. How did he find out? "I . . . I didn't want to alarm you, sir. We have reason to believe they might be trying to reach the UN building."

"Is the place cordoned off?"

"Working on it, sir. By the time they get there, the building should be secure."

"I want them dead, Bill. If they find some network news camera or make it into the General Assembly, damage control could be impossible."

"We'll handle it, sir."

The line went dead, and Sidwell poked the pilot until he came back on line. At his request, Sidwell was patched through to Chip Nicholson on another secure channel. "Chip, it's Bill. I need five men for a suicide mission."

NEAR CEDARHURST, NEW YORK CITY, NEW YORK OCTOBER 13, 7:58 A.M.

Uri had never driven on the sidewalk in his life, and at the moment, he was thankful for the surprising agility of the New Yorkers in front of him, diving for their lives. Seeing an opening in traffic, he swerved off the sidewalk, across four lanes, and turned into an alley. For the moment, there were no police cars in sight, but he knew they couldn't stay there for long. Miraculously the only casualties were a newspaper box, a hot dog stand, and one delegate's breakfast. Diplomatic immunity or no, Uri had no desire to injure innocent bystanders.

After a moment to collect himself, he put the car in gear and rolled slowly down the alley. Expecting patrol cars at either end at any moment, he was looking for alternatives and finding very few. Even fleeing on foot would be hopeless. There were no fire escapes, and the only exits were forward and back. To everyone's great relief, they reached the far end of the alley without being boxed in, and the cross street didn't look as busy. He merged with traffic, but they had gone only a block when more sirens began wailing. There was nowhere to go until the drivers in front of him began pulling over to make way for the police cars. Slowly, agonizingly, one car at a time, the diplomatic car moved forward, but the police cars were gaining.

Uri waved at his man in the passenger seat. "The map! The map!"

The man fumbled in the glove compartment for a moment, finally producing a map of New York City. "Where do you want to go?"

"Some place with more maneuvering room. Try the waterfront. We are at . . . Broadway and Washington. I need to get off soon."

The man searched the map for a moment. "Go left at the next light."

"The next light is one way, the wrong way."

"You said you needed to get off soon."

Uri conceded the point. He would have preferred a high-speed chase through the Negev Desert to all this risky stop-and-go business, but at least they hadn't been stopped yet. He checked his watch. Joshua and the two Americans should be there by now, but he would try to keep this up for five more minutes, just to be sure. If they survived that long, he suspected his passengers would be quite glad to be taken into custody.

UNITED NATIONS BUILDING, NEW YORK CITY, NEW YORK OCTOBER 13, 8:02 A.M.

The United Nations building turned out to be an impressive sight up close, not so much because of its size, but because of the national flags of member nations flown around part of its perimeter. Lee was struck by the heroic efforts of conciliation represented in those flags, efforts by countries scattered around a world that seemed ever on the verge of tearing itself apart. And now, all of those efforts might very well stand or fall depending on what happened in the next few hours. *I wish Nels was here,* he thought.

As they approached the service entrance, Joshua saw the police barricade first. "Quickly . . . get your coats on."

Joshua slowed almost to a stop. All three grabbed the white coats labeled "Imperial Hotel Catering Services" in modest burgundy script, which Uri had "borrowed" from the hotel, and put them on over their street clothes. They could see other vehicles parking and various groups walking through the checkpoint after some simple questioning. Joshua found a parking place, pulled something out of his pocket, and bit off a piece.

"What's that?" Lee asked.

"Garlic beef stick. When we get up there, let me do the talking."

Tyler picked up the stack of boxed, spiral-bound presentations off the floor of the backseat and wedged her way out of the car, and Lee offered to take half of them. As they drew near the only officer not busy with some other group, Joshua started talking with a flawless Brooklyn accent.

"I can't believe it! The one time I let Murray take an order, he messes it up completely." He pretended to notice the officer for the first time and turned to Lee impatiently. "Yo, Lenny, you got that work order?" Lee handed Joshua the UN work order for three sheets of baklava, and Joshua thrust it into the officer's face. "See what I have to live with? Ma warned me not to go into business with Murray, but oh, no! I had to find out for myself. So now I got to go tell the chef he'll be serving lunch without rolls." Joshua leaned forward and, with a mighty exhalation of garlic, said, "Will you tell me what I'm supposed to do with three sheets of baklava rotting in my trunk?"

The officer wrinkled up his nose and backed away, waving them on. "You can take it up with the chef."

Joshua stormed through the gate, with Lee and Tyler close behind. They were through.

WATERFRONT, NEW YORK CITY, NEW YORK OCTOBER 13, 8:05 A.M.

On the waterfront, the diplomatic car raced between the warehouses, while four blocks back a posse of three police cars narrowed the gap. Pushing sixty miles per hour, Uri half expected an obligatory moving van to suddenly block the roadway, but the street ahead remained clear. Then the buildings were behind, and the diplomatic car went roaring across a loading yard, the last barrier between the city and the Hudson River.

Uri considered his options. Fishing them from the river would certainly take more time, but the risk of losing someone, or everyone, in the car was much higher. He stomped on the brake with both feet, and the car went into a skid, finally coming to a shuddering halt only a few feet from the river.

The police cars stopped on three sides, disgorging officers with guns drawn. Uri drew his pistol, and his men did likewise. The officers halted their advance and took firing stances with their weapons pointed at the occupants of the vehicle.

"Put down your weapons!"

Uri rolled down his window. "Please show us some identification."

"Put down your weapons, or we will open fire!"

"I am afraid we cannot comply without first seeing some identification."

The patrolman's face flushed with rage, but he fished out his ID badge and held it so Uri could see it. "I'm Sergeant D'Agostino of the ninth precinct. Now, will you please put down your weapons, or should we all start shooting?"

Uri and his men put down their weapons.

UNITED NATIONS BUILDING, NEW YORK CITY, NEW YORK OCTOBER 13, 8:14 A.M.

With fifteen minutes to go before the start of the General Assembly meeting, the security forces for the building were on full alert. The call came through from the CIA barely ten minutes ago, warning of a counterfeit Israeli delegation bent on terrorism, and the news traveled quickly. Guards were pulled from other floors to help secure the entrances and exits and the auditorium where the General Assembly would be meeting.

Joshua, Lee, and Tyler had taken a wrong turn somewhere, and they had to ask someone for directions before they found some signs leading to the auditorium. They couldn't help noticing the number of uniforms passing by, and as they walked through yet another hall, Joshua flagged down a passing security guard, using the Brooklyn accent again, and asked him what was happening.

The guard looked both ways to be certain no delegates were around. "We don't want to scare anybody, so keep this to yourselves. There may be a terrorist group here disguised as an Israeli delegation."

Joshua nodded. The guard continued on his way, and Joshua spoke to his American comrades. "Apparently Uri has been caught, so we will not be able to join the delegates. We must come up with an alternative plan." They rounded the end of the crowded hallway leading to the auditorium. Joshua held up a hand. "There is more security than I expected. Take off your jackets."

Lee and Tyler removed their catering jackets and left them on the floor. Joshua turned his inside out and put it back on. "As soon as the security guards move away from the doors, you try to get past the security desk. Professor Teller, you can be yourself. Ask them what is happening and tell them you have an important delivery for the American delegate."

Without waiting for a reply, Joshua started toward the doors. While he was still fifty feet away, he screamed, "For the glory of Allah!" and charged with convincing fury toward the entrance. The guards came away from the door and, with considerable effort, wrestled the crazed zealot to the ground, as he screamed threats and invective, finally frothing at the mouth. Lee and Tyler, dressed once more in street clothes, slipped past the melee and moved quickly to the security desk.

The security guard focused on the two civilians standing in front of him. "Can I help you?"

"What's all the excitement?"

"I don't know. Some kook. Where are your name badges?"

Lee realized in horror that in all the excitement, they had forgotten to put on their name badges in the car. His mind seized up in panic, but Tyler was already speaking. "Our group coordinator picked them up, but didn't hand them out. Show him some identification, Professor Teller."

Lee pulled out his wallet and handed it to the guard. "I'm Professor Lee Teller from Dartmouth College. I have an important delivery for the American delegate."

The guard reached out and snatched one of the presentations, glanced at it, then handed it back, along with the wallet. "Okay, Professor. Make your delivery and then please find your coordinator immediately and get your badge, or one of the guards will have you ejected."

Lee managed a satisfactory smile. "Thank you."

They slipped through the large wooden door, still holding their stacks of presentations, hardly daring to believe they were inside. Most of the delegates appeared to be present, though many were at other tables talking with colleagues about everything from national security matters to the location of the best Italian restaurant or, in some cases where diplomacy demanded restraint, the weather. The feeling of power in the room was almost palpable, as if somehow the weighty decisions made since the organization was formed in 1945 had left an emotional residue. Lee led the way as nonchalantly as possible toward a row of unclaimed seats along the wall near the platform up front. Trying to breathe normally, they waited for the meeting to start.

CIA TASK FORCE, INVERNESS ARMORY, NEW YORK CITY, NEW YORK OCTOBER 13, 8:17 A.M.

"I'm sorry, sir. You'll have to repeat the order. I'm not sure I heard you correctly."

As commander of a CIA special operations task force stationed in New York, Terry Ballard was no stranger to difficult instructions. He had been given many over the years, but none quite so disturbing as the order he thought he just heard. Whatever means necessary usually resulted in a lot of dead people.

Chip Nicholson held the phone closer to his mouth and tried to speak more clearly. "Take five men to the UN building. Use whatever means necessary to eliminate the fugitives Teller and Stills. As far as the director is concerned, the mission never happened."

"Understood. Where are the fugitives?"

"We believe they are trying to deliver sensitive information to the General Assembly."

Ballard was taking notes, trying to keep up. "How soon?"

"The operation will commence immediately."

"With all respect, sir, we need time to study floor plans."

"You can study floor plans on the way. This order comes from the president."

Ballard put the phone down. Having followed the progress of the manhunt, he knew what Teller and Stills looked like. He had known Mike Riley, and though he suspected there was an explanation for his death other than the "rogue agent" story, he knew the fugitives had to be stopped. But the United Nations was not a very private place for a mop-up operation. A hit on the UN building would probably be a suicide mission, which was not unheard of, but the chance of VIP casualties was way up there. The order better come from the president.

UNITED NATIONS BUILDING, NEW YORK CITY, NEW YORK OCTOBER 13, 8:30 A.M.

At 8:30 sharp, the secretary-general of the United Nations ascended the platform and prepared to make some opening remarks to the General Assembly. Before he could address the delegates, however, a man in street clothes joined him on the podium and took him to one side. Guards at the rear of the auditorium started toward the front.

"What is the meaning of this?"

Lee spoke quickly. "I'm Professor Lee Teller from Dartmouth College. Forgive me, sir, but I have a message of the utmost urgency to deliver to the delegates." Lee looked at the guards, who were getting quite close to the platform. "It's cold fusion, sir. We've discovered a process for cold fusion."

The secretary-general's eyebrows went up, and he motioned for the guards to stay where they were. "You've actually done it?"

"In one of the national labs. I have a working model out in the car, but it isn't much to look at. Just a box with an electrical outlet. May I make a presentation to the delegates?"

"This is very irregular. Why wasn't I notified? I would have gladly put you on the agenda."

"We've had some difficulties . . ." Lee looked at Tyler. She nodded her support, and he continued, speaking quickly, "It was quite a challenge to get here at all. There are some who feel this should be buried and forgotten, and understandably so. I'm sure you realize some of the potentially catastrophic implications of uncontrolled access to a cheap, inexhaustible alternative energy source. But if we stop it now, we would just be postponing the inevitable. Now that we know it can be done, someone else will discover it eventually, or some other process, and we will still have to face it. We have a chance, right here, right now, to set up distribution of the technology in a safe, graduated fashion that would benefit all and keep the downside risks to a minimum."

It was a good speech. The secretary-general thought about it for the longest time, and Lee began to feel panicky inside. At last, the secretary-general nodded, and he stood to one side so that Lee could take the podium. The delegates had witnessed the whole conversation, though none had heard it, and all were expectantly waiting to hear what all the commotion was about. Lee took some notes out of his pocket, placed them on the podium, and cleared his throat.

"Good morning. Before we begin, I'm going to have to ask that the press gallery be cleared. We will be discussing a topic of extreme sensitivity."

Up in the press gallery, Owen Lucas swore under his breath. He'd been cleared from the gallery before during a normal session, but never like this. In his gut, he knew something incredibly important was about to happen. A guard politely ushered the members of the press out into the hallway and locked the door. Some reporters left immediately, thankful for the reprieve from a boring assignment. Some chose to hang around the door on the chance they changed their minds about excluding the press. Owen and Mac walked down the hallway, around the corner, and right past the elevators.

"Where are you going?" Mac asked.

Owen had that determined look on his face. Mac hated that look. "We have to find a way in there."

So much for the milk run, Mac thought.

As soon as the press gallery was cleared, Lee began. "I am Professor Lee Teller from Dartmouth College in Hanover, New Hampshire, in the northeast corner of the United States of America. Please pardon the unscheduled presentation, but when you hear the topic, I'm sure you will understand why it was necessary. As you know, for decades, many of us have been working toward discovering a process for cold fusion . . ."

Halfway across town, a black van—loaded with five heavily armed members of the special operations task force—rolled out of a private parking garage and headed toward the United Nations building.

On the fourth floor of the building, Owen and Mac emerged from a stairway and found the hallway deserted. Whatever was going on, all the security seemed to be concentrated on the first floor. Owen led the way down the hall and stopped in front of a door labeled "Auditorium Maintenance." The door was locked. Owen turned to Mac.

"You don't have a lock pick, do you?"

Mac made no effort to keep the sarcasm out of his voice. "Not on me."

Owen ignored him and started searching down the walls for something. The building was old enough, they just might have one. There! Owen opened the glass door to a cabinet containing a fire hose and a bright red ax, and he grabbed the ax. Mac saw him coming and took a cautious step back.

"What are you doing?"

"I should think it was obvious." Owen stood beside the maintenance door and reared back with the ax.

"You can't just chop a hole in the wall!"

Owen paused. "Why not?"

"It's not your wall. Didn't your mom ever tell you not to break other people's stuff?"

"Nope."

Owen swung hard with the ax, and the ax head went clear through the wall. The particle board was old and easily broken out by hand, and as luck would have it, the supporting beams were just wide enough to squeeze through. As they stepped through, they found themselves in a storage closet, and they had to let themselves out the door into the maintenance hallway. A short walk brought them to an access hatch. Beyond the hatch was the false ceiling for the auditorium. A simple network of walkways, anchored to the true ceiling overhead, crossed the area at several points, so maintenance personnel could repair any portion of the infrastructure, including lights, air-conditioning, and fire control. Owen climbed up onto the nearest walkway and started to make his way in the general direction of the speaker platform in the auditorium below.

Mac was complaining in a low whisper. "It's not just the cost of the wall. You got to figure it's some kind of federal offense to bust in here."

Owen was only half listening. "Last time I checked, the First Amendment was still part of the Constitution."

"You think wrapping yourself in the flag will make any difference? I could name a dozen congressmen and at least one entire federal agency that would love to see you hang . . ."

Owen put a finger to his lips. "Shhh. Here's your spot."

Owen stepped aside, and Mac stood in his place. Over the railing, between two diagonally mounted acoustic baffles, Mac had a clear isometric shot of the speaker platform. He disconnected the microphone from the body of the camera, so it would hang closer to the opening, and started filming.

". . . which is what has brought me here today. More than fifty years ago, this organization was formed for the purpose of saving future generations from the scourge of war, to develop friendly relations among nations and foster cooperation in solving international economic, social, cultural, and humanitarian issues. Whether our societies can survive the transition into the cold fusion era together will be decided to a great extent by what we do here today . . ."

Owen leaned over the railing, trying to hear. "Did he say 'cold fusion'?" Mac nodded and Owen plucked his portable phone from his jacket pocket, calling the technician down in the WCN truck out in front of the building.

"Marty, it's Owen. I'm going live in ten seconds."

He jammed the phone into his pocket and helped Mac attach the VHF transmitter, which would send the camera's signal to the truck, along with a headset microphone. "Marty, I'm ready. Are you there?"

Marty's voice came over the headset. "The signal is good. They're cuing the S.B. placard . . . and you're live in five . . . four . . . three . . ."

It was a nice job while it lasted, Mac thought as he pointed the camera at the speaker platform once more. Owen could barely contain his excitement, but he was no amateur, and his voice was strong and steady.

"This is Owen Lucas with World Cable News, reporting to you live from the United Nations building in New York. The man you see on the speaker platform is in the process of explaining a process for cold fusion. We will bring him to you now . . ."

Owen threw a switch on the side of the camera, and the voice below came on line. ". . . prepared presentations for each of you, detailing a possible approach for distribution of the technology in your society. You may use it in whole, in part, or not at all, but you will need something like it to minimize any destabilizing effects of cold fusion technology on your society. The cold fusion process itself is deceptively simple . . ."

In the semidarkness above the auditorium, Owen stood in stunned silence, listening to the world, as he knew it, changing forever. As he closed his eyes, he felt an odd combination of elation and terror. It was the kind of story a reporter dreams about, but he had broken a few rules to get it, which left him with two probable outcomes that were not necessarily mutually exclusive: a Pulitzer prize or a firing squad.

SOMEWHERE OVER
NEW YORK CITY, NEW YORK
OCTOBER 13, 8:37 A.M.

As the Harrier cruised over the city of New York, Bill Sidwell was in the middle of a heated argument with an air traffic controller at La Guardia Airport. "I don't care about your regulations! This is a matter of national security, by order of the president!"

Infuriatingly patient, the controller's voice came back. "I appreciate the fact that this is an emergency, but VTOL aircraft are not cleared for the UN building. And if I may respectfully reply to your earlier statement, this is not an 'arbitrary rule penned by some pencil-necked bureaucrat.' Professional engineers have performed stress analyses of the landing area, and nothing heavier than a two-man helicopter can land there safely."

Sidwell growled with frustration. "Then where is the nearest landing site?"

"There is a helipad on top of the Durham Building, about ten blocks south of the UN building."

Never in his life had Sidwell wished so much for a phone receiver to slam down. His muted request that the pilot close the channel did nothing to ease the aggravation knotted in his chest. He heard the now-familiar tone in his ear, followed by the pilot's voice.

"Did you want to put down at the Durham Building, sir?"

"Yes. Best possible speed."

The pilot changed directions and a few seconds later was back on the headset. "I've never had so much comm traffic in my life. Incoming for you again, sir."

"This is Bill Sidwell."

"Bill, it's Chip. Can you patch into the WCN feed from up there?"

The pilot cut in. "They'll have to patch it into the comm channel back at base. It should take me about twenty seconds."

Half a minute later, a voice came over the headset, not very clear but adequate, and Sidwell listened intently. ". . . to a DC to AC converter, which converts the electricity to the specifications of a normal house current. A unit with a ceramic plate the size of a slice of bread in a container about the size of a lunch box could run for six months on a single filling."

There was a sound of applause in the background, then another voice came over, quiet, like an announcer at a golf match. "This is Owen Lucas for World Cable News, bringing you live coverage of a man presenting a working process for cold fusion to the General Assembly of the United Nations . . ."

In shock and horror, Sidwell stopped listening. They made it through! Somehow they made it through. And now the whole world would know. Pandora's box had been opened, and the unimaginable, evil hosts within would be with humankind for all eternity. They had tried to keep the box closed, tried to protect humanity from itself, but they had failed. Now the entire world would have to live—or die— with the consequences. Sidwell slumped sideways in his seat, overcome by the appalling scope of his failure. *So, now it begins.*

"Chip, are you still there?"

"I'm here."

"Tell the task force to stand down. There will be no action taken against the fugitives until further notice."

UNITED NATIONS BUILDING, NEW YORK CITY, NEW YORK
OCTOBER 13, 8:52 A.M.

"So, in conclusion, I have been asked by the president of the United States to suggest that the General Assembly create a special council on cold fusion to help supply the necessary guidance to member nations as they grapple with the implications of this new era, that it might be an era of peace and prosperity. And may God help us all."

As Lee finished his presentation, the delegates of the General Assembly applauded, slowly coming to their feet. The standing ovation went on for well over a minute, before the secretary-general finally moved to reestablish order in the auditorium. With everyone seated, he addressed the group.

"I know I speak for all of us when I say I am awestruck and not a little terrified of what the future might hold. I therefore make a motion to the General Assembly that effective immediately, there be created the Special Council on Cold Fusion, with members of the Security Council as charter members of the new council and Professor Lee Teller as the chairman. All in favor say aye . . . all opposed . . . the motion carries."

It was Lee's turn to be awestruck. The secretary-general led the stunned professor back to the podium. "Professor Teller, do you accept this nomination?"

Lee was having trouble making his mouth move. "I . . . I do, sir."

Applause erupted once more, and Lee looked out at the small sea of hopeful, amazed, concerned faces. The die was cast, and only time would tell whether or not Nels had chosen the right path. Involuntarily Lee's mind retraced his steps from Hanover, lingering each time as a face he recognized appeared: Miles, lying on a sodden bench in a grove of birch trees; the look on Nels's face when he first saw the file; Ilya lying motionless on a hard bed on board a freighter; Tyler with long brown hair, lying in a second-floor hallway in an apartment building in Morocco; Nels dying in the street outside that same apartment building; Uri on the Via Dolorosa; the screams of dying agents in the Arab District of Jerusalem; the battle in the Mossad auto maintenance facility. So much suffering, so much fighting, so much dying, and still he didn't know if it had all been in vain.

And yet, seeing a cross section of so many nations, truly united in spirit and purpose, even if only for a moment, he knew there was at least a chance it would work. Whatever else happened, Lee knew beyond any doubt that Nels had been right about one thing.

It would be the adventure of a lifetime.

About the Author

David Ward is the author of the Perimeter One Adventures series for young adults. He is also a published poet, a scriptwriter, and a contributor to several Christian newsletters in the Rocky Mountain region.